a
season
unknown

a novel

Keith
Cohen

Brookline, Massachusetts

ISBN: 978-1-7359346-0-0

k+p press
Brookline, Massachusetts

For Roberta

spring

1

The red fox appeared out of nowhere. Judith went cold with terror, her heart shuddered, and her head swelled with a sharp throbbing pain. She had not taken her eyes off of her little boy for more than a moment and he had wandered across the yard. Judith felt numb and woozy, sounds suddenly grew muffled and distant, her vision narrowed and became distorted. Malach was just at her side, and now he stood alone, so far from her warmth and safety. Everything became a blur of agonizingly slow movement.

The animal sniffed at Malach's ankle and then raised its head, the white fur on its chest and neck exposed. Malach lifted his arms and took two steps back. The fox pressed forward, looming over him, licking at his throat.

From deep in her lungs sputtered a guttural sound that erupted in a thunderous shriek. The long tunnel of vision that separated her from her child collapsed and the animal came into sharp relief. She raced to her son, arms waving wildly, screams echoing in every direction. Startled, the fox, with its sleek body, thick and bushy tail, fixed its penetrating gaze on her, its eyes cold and unyielding. The animal bared its teeth, then abruptly turned and retreated, looking back several times before disappearing into the thicket.

Judith scooped up her child and held him tightly in her arms, her body trembling, her heart beating out of her chest. "I'm here. I'm here," Judith said, repeating her words reassuringly. "Everything is okay."

Malach cried out for the animal. "Fox, fox! Mommy, the fox." Her two-year-old son already knew the name for the beast and said it over and over as he reached one hand out toward the vanquished creature in a plea for its return, unaware of the danger he had just faced.

Thank God he was safe. Judith felt lightheaded, a wrenching churning in the pit of her stomach. She tried to clear her head, then slowly surveyed the yard. With Malach pressed close to her chest, she breathlessly returned to the house.

She was afraid to let herself contemplate what could have been. She swore to herself that she would never let him out of her sight again. For many days Judith did not dare permit him to venture outside. He sat himself down near the sliding glass doors of the kitchen and looked out at the woods that surrounded the house. He ignored the toys she put before him, pushed away books, glazed in front of the television or computer. He whined and cried until she finally relented. With Judith holding his hand firmly, watching his every movement and vigilant to the surroundings, Malach stepped again outdoors, and a smile spread across his face.

It was some time after resuming outdoor activity with Malach that she told Mark about the incident. The version of the story was carefully amended, as she was too ashamed to admit to her husband the ugly lapse in her caretaking. With his head in his planner, he buttered his toast and carefully salted his usual breakfast of three poached eggs. Barely registering her concern, he told her not to worry, that the Lord was looking over Malach. Even with the threat of harm to their son, Mark was distracted and distant, more consumed with his new job and the needs of everyone else in the community than his own family.

Now with Malach recently turned five, Judith looked out from the sliding glass doors of the kitchen to check on her son. Memories of those events were still vivid in her mind. Malach was playing by the stream that ran near the back of the house and was a bit further off than she liked, but she took a deep breath and went to make a pot of coffee.

Malach approached the edge of the creek, jumped up, and splattered the wet, saturated soil. He did it again, and then again, each time watching the mud squish between his toes and then slip around and over his bare feet. It was smooth and slick from the icy cold water of early spring. He stepped back and looked at his imprints, waiting as they slowly dissolved, the moisture leeching up through the ground, softening and then filling the hollows left by the soles of his feet. He squatted and traced with his finger the marks left by his heels or toes, his forehead scrunched and eyes riveted as he worked. When he was done, he walked away without so much as a glance back.

Heading toward the yard, he stepped over loose branches and soggy areas of flattened grasses, located a dry spot, and flopped down. The sun was strong and warm air pockets floated above the ground. He looked around, first up at a small flock of red-winged blackbirds in a tree, and then glanced toward the sound of a screeching hawk high in the sky.

With a cup of hot coffee in her hand, Judith looked out at her son again. He was so handsome, she thought, his dark brown hair always tangled and awry, big brown eyes wide and curious, an easy smile that melted her heart. She spent countless hours sitting at her kitchen table, carefully following Malach's activities. He was always busy, whether it was climbing on a cluster of old tree stumps, crawling under bushes and through gnarled undergrowth, digging holes in the ground, gathering and piling rocks, or watching ants swarm in and out of small openings in the soil. Other times, he was quiet and still, absorbed by the sounds around him. He listened with rapt intensity to the gusts of wind, the rustling of leaves, the chirps of crickets, the high-pitched calls of cicadas, or the humming strains of working bees. The rich smells of the early emerging spring growth, the fragrance of fully blossomed wildflowers of summer, or the pungent odor of decaying plants in the fall, all captured his attention.

Despite the warming weather, it was still too cool for the short-sleeved shirt he wore. Judith had long acquiesced to his choices. He hated wearing his shoes, balked at efforts to put gloves on him, and was always too hot for a coat, or a hat, or any outer garment for that matter. On bitterly cold days she had to force him to wear extra layers and keep his boots on his feet. Countless times she re-bundled him and as many times the clothes would come off. It took a long time for her worries to subside and to accept that he was suited to the climate, regardless of the time of year, and never got sick. His cheeks were rosy, his hands warm, and his feet already toughened to the terrain.

Judith took a sip of the hot coffee and remembered back to a time shortly after the encounter with the fox, to the beginning of events that would reshape her life.

Filled with excitement, Malach had popped out from of a huge pile of autumn leaves in the yard. "Surprise, Mommy! Here I am." Then tunneling back under he went. "You can't find me," he said as he burst out again, laughing with delight. Judith found his enthusiasm joyous. "More leaves, Mommy, more." As she slowly gathered another stack and then turned to place it on top of him, she was stunned to see a small bird perched on his finger. It was a beautiful little creature with a yellow breast and some white markings on its face. It fluttered repeatedly in the air, each time settling on his hand as he giggled, and it whistled and cawed in response. She struggled to catch her breath and stood frozen watching the exchange.

What was transpiring between Malach and the tiny winged creature sent a shiver through her. She was used to his talking to the birds, squirrels, raccoons, deer, or anything else that was alive on the land, flying through the air, or swimming in the water. She loved his imagination, brimming with the pleasure of discovery of every new part of his world. But what became evident that day, and in the weeks, months, and years to follow was the interest, or rather, the outright preoccupation of all of these creatures with him. He was the focus of *their* imaginations.

Judith let out a deep sigh remembering those early encounters as she watched him now at play in the yard. He sprang up from where he was sitting, and headed toward a pile of sticks, ones he had gathered in the fall. After a short time, she went to prepare him lunch.

With a curious look on his face, and a sudden widening of his eyes, Malach bent down on his hands and knees, then pressed his face close to the ground. "It's you. Where were you?" *Sleeping.* "I missed you. I didn't think you were ever coming back. Why didn't you come out and play?" *I sleep a lot when it's cold.* Malach reached out and the small chipmunk darted into his hand and he cradled it close to his chest. "I was thinking about you so much. Were you sleeping the whole winter?" *Most of the time.* "Where? Where do you sleep?" *In the ground.* "Oh. What made you come back?" *There's lots of work to do. Not much food left, barely made it through the cold.*

Malach rose to his feet holding the chipmunk in one hand and marched off. He reached into his pocket and found part of a chocolate chip cookie. "I took it from the cabinet. I didn't like the oatmeal this morning. It was too thick." He gave it to the chipmunk, who held it in its front paws and nibbled on it. The small creature dropped the uneaten piece and followed it to the ground, not in search of the cookie, but rather scurrying toward the stone wall on the far side of the field.

Malach trotted behind with his eyes following its movement. "Are you okay? You're going slow." *My bones hurt.* The chipmunk found a crevice between the rocks and entered the wall. Malach kneeled looking for him between the stones and then crawled slowly along the edge of the loosely stacked fieldstones. The small animal seemed to come out of nowhere and stood on top of the low wall. Before Malach even noticed the chipmunk, it ducked back into a crack in the stones. While Malach waited, he inspected the lichen on one of the rocks, scraping it with his finger, then smelling the tiny piece he had dislodged before flicking it away. The chipmunk appeared again. *I think this is the spot.*

Malach picked up the chipmunk and together they walked further away from the house. Checking on him, Judith opened the sliding glass door and hollered for him to stay close and not wander off. She called again until he acknowledged her and began to move back toward the house. This was the parenting to which she had become resigned, inadequately supervising from the window her little boy at play with a wild rodent. She often anguished over her own judgment and mothering, sometimes questioned whether she was losing her mind in this desolate place. The winters were dark and endless, springs seemed never to arrive, summers passed before they began, and fiery autumns faded as quickly as they ignited.

Malach sat on the grass with the chipmunk, each facing the other as he leaned back and supported himself with his arms while the small animal perched on his bent knee. *There were not as many acorns this past season. Food's scarce. It was better the last cold stretch.* "I'll bring you something to eat. My mom's making a cake today. She'll give me a piece for you." Malach lifted his head to the stirring wind for some time and then looked back at the chipmunk. "I can feel the cold coming." *I noticed it, too.* "Make sure you stay in the ground tonight."

No matter how many times Judith witnessed these occurrences, each one astonished her as if it were the first. It was as though the world held its breath, a still silence permeated the air, the forces of the earth spotlighted on her son. Mark had yet to experience any of it. She knew she had to talk with him. It was bothering her more that she withheld this part of her life and this part of Malach's life from him. Was it some sort of retaliation for being taken to this remote and isolated place, self-preservation in a life of loneliness? Or was it disbelief in her own senses, a fear that Malach might not reveal his world to anyone else and she would surely be seen as unfit.

There was something in Malach's behavior when his father was present that made her believe that he did not want him to know. He never told Mark about the animals, not about his favorite places to play and explore, not about the changes he could sense in the weather, not about the arrival of migrating birds or the emergence of hibernating animals, not about shoots of spring growth that were starting to emerge, not about the pair of red-tailed hawks that were preparing to build their nest. This was part of his rambling chatter throughout the day, talking to her as though all that he experienced was obvious and that she knew all these things, too. She sometimes imagined, for a moment, her husband standing next to her, watching the magic their little boy spun, spellbound by the seamless exchanges between him and the world all around. But like Malach, she too had no desire to include Mark.

2

Over time, Malach's exploration across the land had begun to appear less random to Judith. When he maneuvered through thick undergrowth, climbed across a large downed tree, or scaled a rocky incline, there was remarkable agility in his movements. He would quickly regain his footing or right his balance when necessary. He did not aimlessly roam or wander, but rather there was purpose and direction to his actions. Judith watched as he unearthed unusual fungi, removed leaves covering the opening to a burrow of field voles, or separated a cluster of ferns to reveal a beautiful lady's slipper. His effortlessly exposing the secrets that the earth kept hidden remained another unexplainable puzzle to her.

When Malach first began to venture further and further from the house, she would shadow him, close enough to keep him in sight, while not hovering or restricting him. She felt physically challenged in places that he easily navigated. She was the one at the end of the day covered with bruises and scratches, not him. Soon her fear of him being injured in the woods began to recede, much like the fears she once harbored of the dangers posed by the animals he encountered. Only the creek made her nervous, especially now with the rapids swift and the levels deep from the winter runoff.

This spring Malach had spent more time on the long descending slope behind the house that was covered with hardwood trees and dense undergrowth of mixed low growing bushes, ferns, and flowering spring plants that had broken through the ground. She permitted him greater freedom, rationalizing it as her way of helping him become more independent, though she knew it was also due to the sheer exhaustion of following him about. As always, she held her breath as he slipped out of view. She would check on him later.

Malach took notice of the tiny white flowers sprouting on the forest floor as he made a path down the hill. He squatted and touched one, then pulled it free of the stem and held it to its nose. He carried the delicate flower until he stopped to gather some twigs, thin branches, and dried grasses. He moved on in the direction of a pair of wild turkeys as they turned to approach him. It was the female who trotted towards him, the larger male more distant. It was courtship season, and the male puffed and spread its dark and iridescent feathers in display, its red head and wattle pronounced as he spit and gobbled and strutted about. Malach followed the birds to the nesting site that they had established.

"I brought these," he said, and then arranged the twigs and grasses along the edge of the nest. With his small hands he weaved the material into the structure while the birds hovered close by. Hearing movements before she appeared, Malach turned and saw a woman approaching. She was startled by the sight of the large birds so close to him, the male now craning its outstretched neck, ruffling its feathers and spreading its wings over the small child.

"Be careful," she blurted out. "Don't get so close to those birds. It's not safe." The stranger quickly raced up the steep incline toward Malach, shooing the turkeys and gesturing for him to come toward her.

"They're my friends," he said.

She was uneasy with his bold confidence so near the turkeys and quickly stepped between Malach and the birds and waited until they retreated. "Are you by yourself?"

"No," Malach answered.

"Who are you with?"

He pointed toward the turkeys. With the birds now at a distance, she smiled.

"Where's your mom?" she asked. She imagined his mother would be frantic once she learned that he wandered off.

"In the house." He pointed in the direction up the hill.

"Does she know you're here?"

"Yeah… Who are you?" Malach asked.

"I'm Sky."

"What?

"Sky, that's my name."

Malach looked at the woman, looked up above and then at her again, trying to reconcile the incongruity in his mind. "I like your name."

"Thanks, and what's your name, if I may ask?

"Malach. It's just a regular name. You spell it M-a-l-a-c-h, but it sounds like a K at the end."

"Malach," she said, emphasizing the hard K sound at the end of his name. "That's a very nice name, not just regular but quite distinguished. It's a pleasure to meet you, Malach." With the large birds safely away, she found herself enchanted by the entire encounter.

"Do you think you could show me the way to your house?" Sky asked.

"Sure," he said, as he waved goodbye to the wild turkeys, and then led her to the top of the hill to his house. Sky remained between the boy and the birds while glancing back to assure herself again that they were safely distant.

"Mom! Mom!" he yelled across the large yard once the house was in sight. "There's a lady who wants to talk to you. Her name is Sky." Malach looked at a chipmunk on the rock wall as he passed. "That's her name," he said to the little creature before he turned toward the house. Sky noticed the chipmunk slowly raise its head and follow Malach with its gaze as they passed. "He likes your name, too." He made her laugh.

"Malach, where were you?" Judith said as she leapt up from her chair, looking startled by Sky's presence.

"At the bottom of the hill," he answered. "This is Sky."

Judith looked to the woman. "Is everything alright?"

"Yes, I was just hiking the woods and came upon your little boy. I just wanted to be sure he got back safely."

"Thank you. Thank you so much. That's so kind of you. He can sometimes wander. I always have to keep my eye on him. Please come sit down. May I offer you something, a cup of coffee?" Judith nervously tried to direct her unexpected visitor to the small table and chairs on the patio.

"No, that's not necessary," said Sky. She felt this woman seemed more surprised and concerned to see her than her son.

"Please let me bring you a cup, it's fresh."

"Why not? Just milk or cream, whatever you have." Sky looked around as she waited for Judith. She found the small two-story pale blue clapboard house quaint but weathered and a little neglected. It seemed lonely, situated among the surrounding woods, not a neighbor in sight.

Judith was in and out in seconds with two steaming mugs of coffee. She introduced herself and then turned to Malach. "Stay near the house, now." Sky felt she issued her remark with no urgency in her voice.

"How fortunate you were out in the woods today," Judith said. "Thank you again."

"Please, you've thanked me enough," Sky said as she took her coffee and sat down at the table with Judith.

"Tell me, what brings you out here?" Judith asked. "Do you live nearby?"

"A few towns over. I haven't been down this way in some time. I used to hike these woods as a kid. I didn't know there was a house here. Is it just the two of you?"

"Oh, no, my husband, also," said Judith. "We moved in five years ago. From the south, a small town in the Florida panhandle."

"Have you gotten used to our winters yet?" Sky asked with a grin.

"Don't know that I ever will," Judith said, returning the smile. "You can freeze to death in this place. Lots of layers, lots and lots of layers, I've learned that's the secret. I had no idea what twenty below plus a wind chill is like. It's nice to have spring again. It took a while, but it's finally blossomed."

"Way up here in the northeast, it always feels like it'll never come but once it does, it helps you forget the winter. We all get used to it. In time, you will, too. I think this one of the most beautiful parts of our country."

"Yes, it's beautiful alright," said Judith, "in the spring and summer and even into the fall. Winter is another story. That's when I miss the Gulf waters, the beaches, the warmth of the sun. It's hard to beat in January and February, and around here even in April and May. Have you ever been?"

"No," said Sky. "I've traveled the country a bit but for some reason never ventured into Florida. I'm not really a hot weather person. What about you, what brought you up north?"

"Mark, my husband, is a minister. God's work can take you pretty much anywhere and everywhere, though I suppose I'd never expected it to bring me here. I fantasized about missionary work in Tanzania or Kenya or some place exotic. A little town in these mountains never crossed my mind. But it is what it is. A preacher's work is needed everywhere and a preacher's wife shares that life. It's important work. God knows this world needs more of what faith can offer."

"Was the church your calling as well?" Sky asked, still trying to size up this woman.

"I didn't grow up with my husband's devotion and commitment," Judith said. "He's third generation in his family. His grandfather founded a church back home and his father was his successor. Mark's father wants him to do the same, but he's still young and healthy and not ready to step down. It's not a church that can support two clergy.

Regardless, I think Mark wanted to venture out on his own for now, though I'm certain when the time comes it will be hard for him to resist returning. They're all good people. My family, on the other hand, three generations of problems, but that's for another day."

"Where does your husband work?" Sky asked.

"At the church right here in town," Judith answered.

"So, your husband took over after Reverend Perkins passed away," said Sky.

"You knew him?"

"A soldier of Christ, my mother would say. Right there in the trenches with those most in need. My mother used to work at the church food pantry, collected used-everything for the thrift shop, taught Sunday school, joined him many times on an annual mission to Mexico. Whatever the Reverend thought up, my mother was there in body and spirit."

"How wonderful," Judith said. "Then you, too, had a strong Christian upbringing."

"Oh, we were church-goers. My mother had me in tow, the whole family for that matter. That was when I was little. I drifted later on."

"It's never too late to find your way back."

"It's been some time and, anyway, that was long ago, also a story for another day." Sky found herself bothered by Judith's awkward religiosity. There seemed something forced about it. "More importantly, tell me about that little one of yours. Is he your only child?"

"Yes, yes, though we pray for more children, if we are so blessed. But Malach, he's blessing enough."

"I want you to know that he did venture far from the house, at the very bottom of the hill. I was alarmed finding him very close to a pair of wild turkeys. They're big and can be aggressive, especially now, during mating season."

"I don't know what I was thinking," Judith said with a sigh. "Sometimes, being here, all alone, I just get distracted. It has always been so quiet out here. I just forget that there are wild animals so close. It was no accident that you were here today."

"Judith, I'm the last person to tell anyone about how to look after a child. I don't even have one of my own and I'm not sure I would even be very good at parenting if I did, but I do know the woods. I don't want to scare you but it's wild around these parts. We have bears, bobcats, moose, coyotes, big old raccoons. You should just be aware. I wouldn't want anything to happen."

"I appreciate your honesty," Judith said.

"One other thing," said Sky. "You must know he's fearless. He went right up to those birds – they're taller than him – treated them like they were big stuffed animals and told me they were his friends."

"*Friends*," Judith said slowly, her eyes widening. "He said that to you?"

"Wonderful imagination," Sky continued, "but it can be very dangerous, especially for someone his age, alone in the woods."

"I'll remember that," Judith said.

Sky felt something missing in Judith's words. It was as though Judith was merely telling her what she believed Sky wanted to hear, and not fully appreciating that in the vast wilderness of these old mountains it can be harsh and punishing. Something about Judith's reaction made her want to shake her, just a little, to get affirmation that she would do better.

Sky sat and talked with Judith for a good part of the afternoon as they watched Malach in the yard, dragging a big stick, talking to himself, lost in his play. To Sky, he seemed to glow with the energy of the spring changes, the blooms on the trees, the greening of the earth. She found Judith, on the other hand, to look tired and pale, her gray-blue eyes distant, her red hair carelessly pulled back and tied loosely in a braid. She reminded her of what a preacher's wife from generations past might have looked like, clothes simple with little attention to fashion. An oversized wool sweater for the lingering coolness in the spring air, jeans rolled at the ankles with mismatched socks coming out of her hiking boots. Even the red plaid laces of her boots were tied through the eyelets to uneven heights. The both of them were probably close in age, she thought, not yet out of their twenties. Judith had a delicate face with a straight thin nose and soft lips, her figure thin and willowy. Even with the strain in her face, she was very beautiful.

"What was it like growing up here?" Judith asked.

"Well, it's home for me, born and raised here," Sky answered, as she refocused her attention. "Small town life where everyone knows everyone else's business. You get used to that. It's the mountains that I always found special. From the time I was very young I loved it, or maybe I didn't know anything different. For me, there was something mysterious to these mountains and I took to it. I needed to learn about the wildlife and plants, everything that was part of this place. I read so many books, and then I would venture out and identify what I had studied. Eventually I grew more comfortable being in wilderness areas, learned to use a compass and how to read a topographical map, started to hike on some of the trails and later even off-trail."

"Weren't you afraid, being out there by yourself?" Judith asked.

"Scared to death at first. But it was a growing-up experience. I didn't mind the aloneness of hiking and exploring. It suited me in an odd way. So did the learning and studying, making the mysteries of the mountains familiar, it was part of the lure, it was a connection I felt with something bigger and more important than me. I grew to find that it began to feel where I belonged."

"I don't think I could have done that when I was young," Judith said. "I was always looking to be with someone. I didn't like being alone. Honestly, I think that's why it was hard being here at first. It's so isolated. If it wasn't for Malach, I'm not sure I could do this even now."

Sky didn't know what to make of Judith. The religious talk was off-putting, but once they moved beyond that, she felt a connection.

They finished a second cup of coffee when Malach approached in tears, barely able to catch his breath.

"Mom, he's dead. He just stopped breathing right in my hand." Malach held out the limp body of the small animal. "He said he was too tired, just too, too tired." Sky had the urge to grab the chipmunk, hoping it was not diseased, but before she could move, Judith held out her hand for Malach to place the small creature into, lifted him up with her other arm, and calmly consoled him.

"He's with God now, in heaven," she told him.

"Will he be okay?"

"Yes, he'll be more than that. Your friend will have a special place in God's heart."

Malach looked into his mother's eyes, a peaceful reassurance spread across his face, then she held him close, tears flowing as she rocked and comforted him. She was the picture of serenity and was completely unflustered by the dead rodent. She wrapped both arms around her son and held him tightly, the chipmunk still in her hand. Sky watched this tender moment and felt a wave of guilt, judging Judith as harshly as she had. It was hard to reconcile so much of the few hours she had spent with Judith.

3

The following day, Mark presided over the funeral. Judith insisted it be a serious and meaningful service, no different than if it were for a member of his congregation. Sky attended, finding Malach's heartfelt request moving. "He knew you and would want you to come."

Judith, Mark, and Malach were dressed as though they were preparing for church. Sky found herself self-conscious in her hiking clothes, not having considered her attire and, oddly, felt that she had not shown enough respect. Expecting something akin to the pet funerals of her childhood, Sky thought about the one for her dog, Ronnie, her brother's turtle, Mo, and the family cat, Newt. After each animal died, an old shoebox or carton was retrieved from a closet for the purpose, dad grabbed a shovel, and someone said a few words.

Earlier in the morning Judith had hammered together a tiny wooden box with her son, and placed a small crucifix on the lid, holding it in place with two large metal tacks. A small grave was dug, into which Malach placed the coffin. Mark read the twenty-third Psalm as Judith and Malach listened carefully. Judith eyed her husband and he added some comments. She did this twice more until she felt that there was sufficient reflection and acknowledgment of Malach's loss. After Mark finished, Malach covered the box with the pile of soil mounded on one side of the grave and patted the loose dirt firmly down. He stood and added his own eulogy. "He sleeps in the ground, but God took his soul to heaven." Judith nodded affirmatively.

Mark checked his watch at the end of the service to Judith's displeasure. He then knelt next to Malach. "He's with God now." He pulled his son to him and gave him a hug. Malach was solemn but broken-hearted. There were no more tears, just contemplation and aching loss. Mark stood and rubbed the back of Malach's head, looking at his watch once more. "Go to your mother." He nudged his son toward her. "I have a real, ah, another funeral this afternoon. Ned Smithson's father had been failing for weeks. I meant to tell you."

Judith glared at him. "I made lunch," she said to Mark. The tension bounced between them before she turned her attention to Sky. "I hope you'll stay."

"Please have lunch with us," Malach said, tears filling his eyes again.

"Of course, I would be honored," Sky said.

A half dozen chipmunks were perched on a cluster of rocks just a few yards from the burial site. Sky noticed Malach's attention shift to them, and then Judith turned to look as well. At that moment, they all stood up on their hind legs almost simultaneously. Malach mumbled something, after which they turned and scattered. Mark took no notice. It was an unusual sight, Sky thought. There was an uncanny synchronization to their movements, and then some response to Malach's unintelligible words. She shrugged off the thought that they came to pay their respects or maybe offer condolences to Malach.

While outwardly welcoming, Sky found Mark's strained glances toward her uncomfortable. They walked together into the kitchen through the back door. The kitchen was simple and had not been updated in some time. The counters were cluttered, a small table for four off to the side near the sliding glass doors. On the adjacent wall hung two small prints of biblical scenes – one of the Annunciation, the other of the Crucifixion. The table had been set with a tablecloth and what looked to Sky like their best dishes and flatware, maybe wedding gifts.

"Sky and her family were long-time members of the church," Judith said to Mark. "We met yesterday. She was hiking near our property."

"Is that right?" he said to Judith and then turned to Sky, a warm tone now in his voice. "Who are your folks?"

"Jerry and Lenore Ryder," Sky answered. "My mother passed some time ago. Dad lives in Arizona now. My brother Wynn does, too."

"Lenore Ryder, my, oh, my. I have heard that name around the church. How long has your beloved mother been gone?" Malach looked up from his plate to listen.

"Sixteen years now. After I finished high school my father decided to sell the house and moved with my younger brother to Flagstaff. I headed off to college in Oregon. My brother was only six when our mother died. It was hard for him and for my father. There was not much keeping them here, and most of the family lives in Arizona so they decided it was time to make a fresh start."

"What about you?" Judith asked. "You were just a girl yourself. In your teens?"

"Just before my thirteenth birthday."

"That's a very hard age to lose a mother," Judith added.

"It's hard at any age, but I suppose that's true," Sky said.

Mark launched into a short sermon on honoring parents and the pain of losing those who brought us into the world. Judith got up and placed the food on the table. Malach reached for Sky's hand on the left and his mother's on the right. Mark said grace and then Judith served the meal. She had prepared a casserole of macaroni and cheese with carrots and a thick layer of encrusted orange cheddar on top, Malach's favorite.

"What brought you back after college?" Judith asked.

"My father still had a piece of land here with a small cottage on it that he had been renting. It came available a few months before I graduated and I decided to give it a try. I took a job at the Conservation Center. I've always loved it here. These woods and mountains anchored me after my mother passed away. I believe the land, the earth itself, talks to me. All of it talks to me."

"They talk to me, too," Malach said, his face lighting up. "I know them."

Mark looked at his son. "All of the Earth's plants and creatures are God's creation like we read in the Bible. Jesus fulfills us and gives us our strength. It's the Lord who speaks to us, not the plants and the animals." Malach quieted from his ebullient expression and nodded.

"I'm sorry," said Sky.

"Don't be silly, that's fine," Judith interjected.

Mark gave a disapproving look. "It's never too early to instill an understanding of God's plan in our children's minds."

"I wasn't trying to imply that the land literally speaks to me. I think you'll find that in living here it's hard to remove yourself from these surroundings. It imposes itself, reminds one of how insignificant we are."

"Insignificant in the presence of the Lord," said Mark. "I'll give you that. Certainly, we can't know God's plan, but scripture teaches us that the creation was intended for man."

Sky decided to let it go, already bothered by Mark's company. She barely knew these people and today was for Malach, no need to make it any more than that. Judith noted the tension and shifted the conversation. Her irritation with her husband remained on her face.

During lunch Malach sat quietly and picked at his food. Mark inquired as to whether Malach said his prayers today. Malach nodded. Mark prompted him to speak up and affirm his devotion. "Yes, sir."

"Good boy, now eat your lunch. We must not waste." He put his hand behind Malach's back to remind him to sit straight at the table. Judith remained silent. Malach had little appetite but placed one bite after another into his mouth until his plate was clean. Mark reminded Judith to take his suit to the cleaners, then excused himself from the table. He thanked Sky for joining them, then signaled Malach to do the same. Shortly after, Mark left.

"I made dessert," Judith said. She and Sky sat together quietly for a short time before Malach went outdoors.

"Stay close to the house," she reminded him. "I love you."

"I love you, too," he chimed back as he went out the door.

"I'm sorry if all this was uncomfortable for you," Judith said.

"Oh, not at all," Sky said. Judith raised an eyebrow. "Well, maybe a little, but don't feel any need to apologize. This was for your family, for Malach."

"Malach asked you and I wanted you as well. It was important to him, and to me. It was a pleasure having you here yesterday. I miss having someone to talk to, adult conversation. I've been here over five years and you're the first person not part of the church that I've had to the house. It's a bit pathetic that you literally dropped in rather than me having invited you or anyone else for that matter. Mark issues the invitations and plans our social get-togethers. It's always church business, church members, committee meetings, planning sessions. I'm usually busy with the refreshments and small talk. I know it's wrong of me to say, but I hate small talk, always have. I don't like talking about the weather. I don't like asking a checklist of questions about someone's children. I don't like sharing recipes. I don't like listening to someone's ailments." Judith stopped and sighed and pushed some loose hair off her face and behind her ear. "I'm sorry to burden you, I just needed to say that."

Judith got up from the table and poured herself more coffee, then glanced out the window to check on Malach before sitting down. Sky found the conversation today a refreshing departure from the visit yesterday. It was heartfelt and honest.

"You don't really worry about him out there, do you?" Sky asked.

"No, I don't, not any more. I used to be in a constant state of panic when he was out of my sight."

"Yesterday, you knew he was in the woods. He didn't just wander off."

"That's right. Nothing will happen to him."

"I don't think you appreciate what it's like here," Sky said, finding herself getting irritated, her heart beating in her chest. "It's not some idyllic nature park with animals to watch. It's remote and isolated and the land belongs to the wildlife more than it does to us. How can you be so sure he'll be safe?"

"I understand what you're saying, but I just know."

"Do you believe God is looking over him, watching him?" Sky asked with not well-concealed annoyance now, unconcerned with overstepping her welcome, wondering why Judith was so naïve and reckless when it came to her little boy's wellbeing.

"I don't know if God is looking over him," Judith answered. "But it's not what you think. It's not out of some blind religious faith. That's not the reason I don't worry. Malach is just different. I'm sure of it, but I don't expect you to understand. I'm not going to let anything happen to him."

Exasperated, Sky shook her head. "I hope you're right. There's something very special about him that I felt from the first moment we met. Please, please be careful. You can never be too certain with the wilderness. It doesn't follow our rules. It has a mind of its own."

Judith nodded acknowledgement, but Sky was no more convinced that anything she said had sunk in. Judith changed the subject in a way that surprised Sky again.

"Yesterday you asked me something that I'm not so sure about."

"What's that?" asked Sky.

"About being a minister's wife and all that it entails. I thought about that a lot since we spoke. It just stayed with me. But quite honestly, this life is not at all what I expected, though I'm not sure what I did expect. It all happened so fast. Mark had the calling since he was a child. It was in his blood."

"Did you have a religious upbringing?" Sky asked.

Judith rolled her eyes and dismissively waved her hand. "Hardly. This is a world apart from my life."

"Does your husband know you feel this way?" Sky asked.

"I don't know what he thinks anymore. This is his life, what he believes," said Judith. "I envy that, to be so sure of yourself, of your choices, of facing what life throws at you. I lay in bed in the middle of the night, unable to sleep. I just think for hours. I try to pray, but I feel lost. I tell myself I need to calm down, to believe, but there is nothing there. He sleeps soundly, like a baby. I want to wake him, to shout that I can't do this."

"I'm very sorry," Sky said.

"I shouldn't burden you," said Judith. "You hardly know me."

"We've all been there one time or another," Sky said, feeling for Judith. She knew the pain of feeling lost, having her dreams shattered, not knowing where her life was headed. Since returning here, she had found some distance from it. She, too, spent nights staring at the ceiling in her bedroom, one long evening running into the next, first after the loss of her mother and then, years later, following the breakup with Alex, her first love and the man she was certain she would marry.

After the day of the funeral, Sky began to visit Judith regularly, each of them looking forward to their time together. Sky learned about Malach just weeks later. On a warm spring morning, Sky watched spellbound as Malach was running back and forth across the large yard, one arm raised, his body and head turned as he looked back over his shoulder as though he was desperately trying to catch a gust of wind to launch a kite in the breeze. Judith held firmly to Sky's arm, ensuring her friend witnessed every moment of what was transpiring before her. This child, a little boy filled with joy and pleasure, appearing absorbed and lost in his imagination and play, was, in fact, not holding the string to a diamond kite, but rather pointing toward a large red-tailed hawk, its wings spread in a majestic display tilting to one side and then the other, holding the draft of air as long as possible before beating its wings and gliding once again. The bird floated only a dozen or so feet above Malach as he ran and howled with pleasure. Finally, Malach collapsed on the ground, the air depleted from his lungs, as the hawk landed beside him. Malach talked to the hawk. It seemed to listen and made some screeching sounds in response. Sky turned to Judith who had tears in her eyes and a radiant glow on her face. Sky was dumbfounded, unable to speak, and tears came to her eyes, too, not knowing how to take in what she was seeing.

"I don't understand either," Judith said as she hugged her new friend. "It was something I wanted to tell you from the day we met, but you would have thought I was out of my mind. There's no way to explain it. You're the only other one who has seen this. He let you in. Thank you."

"Thank you? I don't know that I did anything," said Sky.

"You've done everything."

"How long – how long has he been able to do this?"

"I believe all his life." Judith sighed.

Sky looked to her friend and felt a swell of so many emotions, her mind unable to make sense out of anything she had just experienced.

4

I t was Sunday morning and Mark had taken Malach to church with him. It was the first time Judith had not accompanied them. She had decided to stay behind believing it important that Malach have a day alone with his father. Mark looked at her with poorly concealed annoyance for creating an unnecessary impediment to his day. She avoided his eyes and told herself that the two of them needed to find a way to get to know each other. On the way out the door Mark's impatience with Malach was already evident.

Judith watched from the doorway as they drove away. She took a deep breath and then walked across the field near the house. As she crossed the meadow already filled with spring grasses and early blooming wild flowers, she looked at the plants, insects, and birds from an entirely different perspective. Every scent, every color, every movement of life registered as though she were seeing it for the first time. Her son had changed the world for her. All of it was alive and breathing, no longer background noise or visual filler.

As she made her way along the edge of the woods, her mind turned over and over with memories from her childhood and the time spent with her grandmother.

"Judith Jane Hadley," Grandma Janie would say, always using her full name when she was being emphatic in making a point. "You can be whatever you dream when you grow up. You just have to want it." She knew even as a little girl that it was her grandmother's way of telling her that she did not have to turn out like her mother.

The wonderful aromas of food cooking in her grandmother's

kitchen always created a warm sense of comfort. Judith spent so many hours with her grandmother while she slowly and lovingly prepared her meals. Sometimes Judith helped and many times she just sat at the table and ate, read a book, or listened to her grandmother talk. There were so many stories, ones about growing up in East Texas and the awful treatment her grandmother and family endured at the hands of her alcoholic father, stories of her inadequate education, many about the neighbors – those people who gossiped about you and could never be trusted. Yet, what Grandma Janie wanted most for Judith was to keep away from trouble, stay in school and learn, and grow up to be someone.

She remembered those days so clearly, but it was her connection with Red that she could not get out of her thoughts today. Oh, did she love that horse. He bolstered her during the long anguished days when there was not a word from her mother. It had started with an impulse to sneak a carrot for him. With one slipped into her back pocket, she had skipped down the long dirt path across the property to the small corral near the barn. She climbed the fence, pulling herself to the top rail where she perched with one arm wrapped around the post for balance. With her legs dangling, she watched Red eat hay, drink water, snort and shake his head, and sometimes she got to see him sleep while standing up. It amazed her to learn that horses do that, wondering why they didn't fall over.

Red was twenty-seven years old, which her grandmother told her was very old for a horse, though Red didn't seem that old to her. There was a picture of Red in the house with Judith Jane's father, Mervin, sitting on the horse's back when he was just a little boy. Grandma Janie would tell her she looked so much like him.

"Red…Red, I have something for you," Judith Jane had yelled out. "I want to give you this." She held up the carrot and smiled when Red picked up his head and looked at her. He moved slowly in her direction walking across the corral. "I love you, Red. Grandma Janie said you're old, but you don't look old to me. Grandma Janie said that Mommy was sick, but she's going to get better. Mommy never told me she was sick." She remembered that her mother slept a lot during the day on the couch. "She doesn't stand like you do when you sleep," She looked at him and pleaded for reassurance. "Mommy will be okay, won't she?"

Judith Jane held out the carrot as Red slowly worked his way toward her and, when close, snatched it and gobbled it up in two bites. She didn't flinch, her hand steady and flat even after he ate it. He sniffed and wanted another but she only had the one. Red was so big when he came near and this was the closest she'd ever got to him. His eyes were dark and he looked right at her, lowering his head. She rubbed his forehead. It felt so good being close to him, giving her a funny feeling inside that made her happy.

He sidled closer and she held his mane with one hand. Then without even thinking, she leapt off the fence, flew through the air and right onto his neck. It happened so fast, like a flash. With her heart pounding in her chest, she slid down along his neck and held Red's mane with both hands. Once on Red's back, things began to change. Judith felt her body next to the horse, a sensation of warmth seeped through her. Everything began to move more slowly, sounds were muffled, and her eyes opened so wide that she could see everything extra sharp. The thumping of her heart slowed, the air felt soft and all her worried thoughts, all the ideas that made her afraid went away. Never before had she felt the wave of exhilaration that went right through her. It started in her fingers when she touched Red, feeling his coat, smooth in one direction, bristly in the opposite. His long mane of hair that she held between her fingers caused a tingling sensation that ran right up her arms. The musky scent of the horse filled her lungs, and the movement of the air as she rode filled her head with joy. When she rode on the back of Red, time stood still, the pulsing energy of the horse vibrated through her whole body, and she became part of another world, a world where all the parts worked, a perfect place.

She was just a little girl, slightly older than Malach, just six, when she found herself on the back of the horse. Those moments were seared into her mind and into her heart. The depth of her feeling still registered with unchanged intensity. Judith had come to believe that it was in that brief moment in time, on the back of an animal that appeared so large, so mysterious, so powerful, that she came closest to understanding the world Malach inhabited. Like her first awakenings to Malach's abilities – so uncertain of the veracity of what she witnessed and what she had experienced – the dream world she had entered when riding Red, touched the same chord in her consciousness.

Only days after she rode Red, Judith returned home, her mother informing her with unconvincing confidence that she was "clean." She did not know what that meant at the time but tried to feel reassured. Red died just weeks later, before she saw him again. No further occasions to watch him, feed him, or ride him. She had been devastated, utterly and totally devastated. It was as though the foundation of her life was pulled out from under her. All she could think about was Red. She would retrace in her mind every moment of that day. At night all she dreamed about was her horse. It was always the same; hands tightly adhered to Red's mane, trotting, then galloping, wind in her face, air filling her lungs, accelerating speed, the bumpy undulating movement steadying to a smooth and effortless flow, quiet, serenity, then gliding into the air, soaring high, flying through the sky.

Judith walked back toward the house, following the stone fence. She stopped and found a smooth rock to sit on and stared out at the land around her. She wondered, if they had not moved here, into this wilderness, whether Malach would have discovered the secrets and gifts he possessed. Her little boy was more anchored and connected, more confident and self-assured, more certain and determined when prowling these fields, woods, and streams, than she had ever felt in her life.

A chipmunk scurried along the wall and stopped a dozen feet from her. She watched him quietly, his movements short and staccato, a nervous energy pulsing through his body. She thought of the funeral for the chipmunk just a few months ago, the pain that she had seen in her son's face, the tears of anguish that ran from his eyes, the completeness of his grief, and the wholehearted goodbye he bestowed upon his friend. He was an amazing child. Tears came to her eyes, and she cried and cried. She cried for her little boy, his suffering the pain of loss at such a tender age, but she also cried for herself, for the little girl who grieved alone, whose world was shattered by the death of her horse and never having had the chance to say goodbye, for the loss of the haven and the hope he provided. She mourned a childhood pocked by the absence and indifference of a mother too possessed by her own tragic failings to notice her child or her child's needs. She mourned for all that she wished she had, but never found.

5

When Malach and Reverend Walker arrived for church, Roger noticed Judith's absence. Malach always had his mom by the hand, a skip in his step and a smile on his face. Today, he walked behind his father, his head down. The preacher took no notice. In his black suit, crisp white shirt, his tie straight and aligned with a tight knot at his throat, Roger thought he paid more attention to his appearance than to his son. With his head of perfectly combed dark hair, angular features and upright stature, he found the preacher a vain man, an attribute that he did not admire.

Roger sounded the church bell each Sunday morning at ten sharp – that's how the new preacher wanted it. Roger had tended the bell for many years, and found Mark Walker's strict punctuality irritating, something else he put up with. The church had long ago become Roger's second home and he had to admit that he was oddly attached to many of the folks in the congregation and even to the old building. There was something about its humble, white, weathered clapboard, tall, narrow steeple, and the simple cross at the top of the belfry that whispered the real McCoy. The idea that the preacher was taking donations and raising money for a fresh coat of paint bothered him, too. The man was too damned concerned with appearances.

Roger tried not to judge; he was no example for anything. He was already long past his good years. This morning, like every Sunday morning, he faced himself in the mirror to shave and was forced to see what time had done to him. His body stooped and crooked, thin white hair barely covering the top of his head, deep lines in his face, wizened skin.

Getting old was not what he had expected it to be. For Roger climbing up to the bell tower, with his bad heart and bum leg was a labor of love that became more difficult each year, every step unsteady, breathless the last few, until finally reaching the platform above. The preacher's boy came with him to tend the bell from the time he had been old enough to safely navigate the narrow spiral stairs. Having the boy along made the serpentine climb worth the tightness in his chest and the pain running through his knee and leg.

Coming to church was a reminder of the path his life had taken. More than twelve years ago he had lost his wife to cancer, and then three weeks later, to the day, the second wave of devastation had struck when his son was killed after having swerved off the road with too much alcohol in his blood. That double blow had nearly finished Roger. Nothing much mattered after that. Sometimes he forgot how bogged down with despair he was, a black weight on his chest. It was a wonder the old heart didn't just stop cold right then. Roger thought he could handle anything, but when he lost Edie and then Lee, he found he wasn't worth a piss. Holed up in the house, smoking again after quitting decades before, eating cold food from a can like a dog, if he ate at all, and drinking too much. The liquor was good, numbed him fine, but life was crap.

Reverend Perkins had visited, good man that he was, out of respect for Edie. She was the churchgoer, not him. Maybe she would get him there on Easter Sunday or Christmas Eve. The Reverend didn't give up. It took a while to realize the visits were not for Edie, but for him. That man didn't try to be anything but a good neighbor. He knew Roger was nothing without Edie. Might as well have been unanchored at sea, and when Lee drove off the road, he understood that Roger's own end could be near. There was no talk about Jesus, no preaching, and no promises of redemption or crazy notions that the Lord works in mysterious ways. Just one human being caring for another and somehow the Reverend brought Roger back from the abyss. Slowly, Roger began to look forward to the visits, sometimes two or three times each week. Reverend Perkins might stop by for just a cup of coffee, even a whiskey now and then. Other times, he settled in for a few hours as if he had all the time in the world. It shook him to the core when Reverend Perkins passed away. It happened fast; his heart just gave out. He never had a friend like him before. Three years the Reverend had kept at it until one day, he, Roger Stine, the doubter, the skeptic, the nonbeliever, had his own revelation. He had found Jesus. Reverend Perkins baptized him. He took Jesus as his Savior and went to church every Sunday since. It became his new life.

When that young preacher had arrived, Roger wasn't sure what to make of the man, so different from the one who saved him. Too preachy, but he tried hard to give him a chance, at first more for Reverend Perkins. During one of those early Sundays after his arrival, the preacher took him aside after service, leading him by the elbow, talking to him too loud and slow as if he were some feeble old uncle at the nursing home. Made him think more than once of leaving the church those first few years; that is, until the day the preacher's boy, then only three years old, took his hand, just the way he took his own mother's, and with an imploring look in his eyes asked if he could go with Roger up to the bell tower. After Judith's nod of approval, off they went. Later, he realized it wasn't the tug at his hand but the one at his heart that had pulled him back to the church.

Roger knew they were an odd sight, the little boy and the old man, hand in hand, at ease when they were together, an understanding from the beginning that there was something important about the other for each of them. It was a different kind of relationship. It started with the youngster talking about his yard, and woods, and the animals that were all around. Yet, right from the beginning Roger listened carefully, never losing interest, respectful of the boy's wholly fantastic outpourings. His imagination was so rich, his connection with the world around him so complete, and his understanding of the land and the animals unlike anything Roger had ever heard. There was a spirit in him that touched Roger's soul. It was not unlike the moment in the woods when he found his own salvation. A cold blast of air, a beam of sunlight striking his face, a feeling of well-being, a calling in his heart, all leading to an emotional moment of unexplained connection with God. When the boy spoke, he touched something similar in Roger. It was odd and unexplainable, but the child was special and Roger didn't know why he was the only one who could see it. Having grown up in these mountains, he knew the land like the back of his hand, listened to and understood its sounds, its moods and temperament. The boy understood it more.

Never one for big towns or cities, and especially for all the people, Edie used to say he was a hermit at heart. He liked to think that that was true, but after her death, even the mountains couldn't save him. He never talked much about the wilderness to anyone, even to Edie, knowing she'd have preferred to live in the village, closer to friends and the church. No matter the season, Roger found time to walk, and wonder, and listen, and smell, and breathe it all in. Malach, he spoke this same language and then some. It was still little-boyish, with his animal friends, but he had it in him. Roger grew possessive of the boy and covetous of the little time they had together. Their talks flew by but the child stayed in his thoughts in the intervening days between services. He'd been empty so long, deadened by losses, that the boy was like a sip of cold mountain spring water, awakening and nourishing something inside of him that he thought had dried up and shriveled away.

Week after week, month after month, he never stopped listening to Malach. At some point, they began to exchange stories. Roger liked to stretch the best ones over two or three or even four weeks. It was gratifying when the boy wanted more, and he was comforted by the thought that Malach would be thinking about him during the week. He never had that with his own son. Lee didn't like the outdoors; he was all TV and those damned video games, even as a grown man. Roger could never figure that out.

He had a special story for Malach today. He had been saving it for the right time. He hoped the boy would like it.

"Many, many years ago, I was in the Army."

"You were a soldier, Roger?"

"I sure was. I was just a young man, eighteen years old, and it was the first time I left home. I'd never been anywhere but around these mountains. I was excited, a new adventure and all, but I have to admit I was scared, too. That's the way it is when you do something you've never done before."

"Did you like the Army?"

"Actually, I didn't much like it. Everyone says its good for you, helps you grow up. For me, there were too many rules, too many people telling me what to do, but I managed. Sometimes, though, I'd miss these mountains, so when I'd get a few days off, I'd figure out a way to get away from everything, to get out to the country."

"I like that, too," Malach said.

"I know you do," said Roger. He admired the boy's clear focus and the enthusiasm he displayed when something resonated with him. "I took a bus to this little town. There was a big lake nearby and I rented a canoe for the day. It was far from here. In England, I don't know if you know where that is?"

Malach shrugged, as he was more interested in the story than the geography.

"It was getting on into the fall," Roger continued. "A nice day, real nice one. Calm, not even a whisper of a breeze, the water smooth like glass, the leaves turned, already losing their color, many off the trees. The air was cold and crisp, but so still and quiet. Do you know that feeling?" Roger always spoke direct to him, not in little-kid talk.

Malach nodded his head. "I like it when it starts to get cold. I can feel it before it comes."

"I can too," said Roger. "The cold gets me in my bones now, but I still like it. The air smelled so fresh, particular to that time of the year, different than the smells of spring or summer. I paddled across the lake. Each stroke left a ripple that glided gently away from the canoe. It was a beautiful day. Every day is a gift, but this was a special one. I knew there wouldn't be another like it until the next spring. I always treasure a day like that, still do. But what I saw on that day was not like anything I'd ever seen before, nothing. It came out of nowhere. It had nothing to do with the blue sky or perfect crispness of the afternoon. I heard it first, like a deep humming sound, and it started to get louder. Not sure where it was coming from, but when I looked behind me, it was a like a giant dark cloud over the trees, moving out over the water."

The boy raised his neck, his eyes wide. "What kind of cloud?"

"It moved and it shimmered, bending and folding over itself, moving one direction and then another, twisting and turning. Couldn't understand what it was. I had never seen anything like it before or since. I never even heard about something like it."

The boy giggled and smiled, almost couldn't contain himself, but listened raptly.

"It was the most amazing thing I'd ever seen. More so than the time I came face to face with that big black bear, or the time the bull moose charged me near the creek. You remember those stories?"

Malach nodded and laughed. "That moose was pretty mad."

"He sure was, lucky to get out alive that day. But here's the thing, it wasn't a cloud at all. Not some big thunderhead creeping over the horizon, not lightening or sudden downpour, no balls of hail. What I saw was alive, a living thing."

The boy gasped with anticipation and excitement.

"It was a tidal wave of birds. It was so many birds that you couldn't count them in a day, or even a week. Thousands and thousands, maybe it was millions, I don't know. All starlings, starlings. They were everywhere. But that day, it was like they all decided to get together in one giant flock."

"The gathering, you saw the gathering!" Malach shouted.

"The gathering, what do you mean?" Roger asked.

"It's when they do that, they join together." The boy was just giddy with excitement. "You saw it, Roger, you saw it!"

"How'd you know about it?"

He laughed some more. "I just know."

"Have you ever seen it?"

"No, no, I just know."

"You know why it happens?" Roger asked.

"Yes, it's in them. It's just in them."

Roger couldn't figure out for the life of him how this youngster even heard of a murmuration. Like he had some kind of extra sense. That was the thing about the boy that he found so hard to fathom. Malach knew things, just like he said; but how, where did he learn all this?

Roger told the boy every single last detail of the story that week. Malach seemed to know more about it than he did. Roger felt like he was listening to his own story.

Roger took out his watch to check the time. When he nodded that it was ten, the boy leaped to grab the bell rope, and today it was finally within his grasp. "Roger, look. I did it, I finally did it!" he shouted. For weeks that spring he had jumped and jumped, the rope just beyond his reach for a firm grip. "You said it would be any day and you were right."

"Congratulations, you get to ring it every week now all by yourself." The boy pulled the bell cord long and hard that morning, a deep sense of accomplishment on his face.

When all were assembled, more than a hundred members on any given weekend, the boy took his place in the front pew. His mother usually sat beside him, but this week Malach sat between Patricia Jamison and her husband Nathaniel who shared the bench with the pastor's family. Roger took a seat off to the side as the Jamisons snatched Malach up. They were good people, had been part of the church since they got married. Both were regulars, long-time friends of Reverend Perkins, had known him for the forty-eight years he had guided the church. They were on the committee that had selected the new preacher. In the beginning Roger blamed them, but now he felt that he owed them thanks – for the boy. They never had children of their own, had loved Malach from the time he was a baby, and were quick to seek him out each week for some hugs and attention. He took to the Jamisons like surrogate grandparents, and they were proud to know that they were special to him. It made Roger jealous at first, but once he discovered that the boy shared his stories only with him, he lost all envy.

There had been very few occasions since the preacher's arrival here when his wife was unable to accompany him to the service. It took a bad flu or high fever to keep her home. Seemed like it happened most the first year as she acclimated to the winters. The preacher's son was only a baby then so he had stayed home with her. Roger believed that today was the first time Malach showed up with just his father. Many were concerned about Judith; all assuming she was not feeling well. The preacher offered no reason for anyone to think otherwise. The boy looked perplexed with his father's answers and it made Roger suspicious. A few of the other young children had waved to Malach when he came into the sanctuary. He smiled and waved back, especially to the little dark-haired girl, Ginny Lucette. Roger liked her parents, no-nonsense people. She was the oldest of three girls, five years old like Malach.

The preacher began with what was now a well-established church tradition of having all the children included in the service for the first half hour or so. Then they would go out for some activities arranged by the mothers, usually a Bible story and play time. No one minded a crying baby or restless whining. The preacher was different with his son. He wanted him to set the example for the others. Roger noticed the little looks signaling Malach to sit still, listen, sing when it was time, and be polite and respectful for all. The boy was always a little impatient but easy going and tolerant of his father's requests. It was his nature.

"Welcome to all, and upon all let rain down the blessings of Christ." It was how the preacher began every week. He had said many times it was how his own father began the service and his grandfather before him. It was in him as deep as the Lord's Prayer. It was his connection with his roots and his upbringing, and now a part of his mission, making sure the next link in the chain was secured. The passing of the Word of God from one generation to the next was at the heart of his ministry. He believed it was where faith resided, where it was nurtured and where it grew. It was why he always wanted even the littlest ones to be present, absorbing the faith from all those around, from a mother and a father, a brother and a sister, a neighbor and a friend. It was why he talked to the children each week, trying to help them experience the church as their spiritual home, a place of comfort and joy. Roger found all of that okay. It was just that he felt the preacher was too full of himself.

"I want to take a few minutes to welcome all of our blessed children as we do every week before they run off." The young ones never fully connected with his formality, Roger thought, but he was not a good judge of those things. Parents liked the service and occasionally the preacher hit a few right notes, might even spark some laughter and a few smiles.

"I love the spring, especially late spring with the warmth settling in. I love the smell of the earth, and I love the sweet aroma of the flowers. Is it not wonderful to get outside and play and to know summer is almost here?" The preacher spoke in a low voice, his words trying to build with each sentence as if he were announcing the moment of creation itself. "When you go outdoors to play, be sure to look carefully all around to see what the Lord has made. God created this world in six days and rested on the seventh. He created a perfect masterpiece. He created the Heavens and the Earth, all the animals and plants we see and, of course, God created man, Adam, from the dust of the earth, blowing the spirit of life into him, and Eve from one of Adam's ribs. Look around, all around, when you are in the yard, everything God created is for us. God told Adam and he told Eve that they would rule over every living creature. All of this was there for them and now here for us, and for that we must be grateful. Yet, we do not worship the animals on the land or the fish of the seas or the birds in the air. We worship the Lord, the creator." The preacher loved to tell the children about God's creation, it was the story that he thought they most enjoyed. It gave him great pleasure to overhear one of the children tell another that God made that animal.

"What are your favorite animals, tell me, which of God's creatures do you love the most?" He invited the young members of the congregation to shout out and share during his little sermons to them.

"I love sharks," Robbie Killian quickly announced. "Great white sharks." He was a funny little boy, the first every week to answer. Maybe six years old, sandy brown hair, and a face full of freckles, he made everyone laugh. If he wasn't talking, he was restless and needling his older sister, Marion. "I love snakes, too, anacondas. I bet no one here ever saw one, but when we went to Georgia this winter to visit grandma and grandpa, we went to Jake's Snake and Reptile Farm and we got to see one and I touched it." That little one loved an audience. "Do you think God made anacondas, and what about copperheads and green mambas?" Robbie's parents were used to this and the preacher assured them that he was never a bother. They knew the preacher would move on when he felt it was enough.

"Robbie, thank you for letting us know what your favorites are. I can tell you for certain that God made every last one of the snakes you mentioned and sharks, too. Snakes have a long history in the Bible.

There was even one in the Garden of Eden itself. Who else has a favorite animal?"

Tammy Olsen stood up, nervous as she was every week, but determined to always participate. "My favorite animals are chimps. I learned in school that there are not as many as there used to be and I'm worried. Will God look after them?

"Don't worry about the chimpanzees, Tammy. God made that special creature for all of us to enjoy. They are in God's hands, and I'm sure He would never let anything bad happen to them."

Patricia Jamison nudged Malach. Roger eyed them and could hear her. "What's your favorite, honey?"

"Oh, I don't know, I like them all."

"Of course you do, but do you have a favorite? I'm sure one stands out."

Malach was thoughtful for a few moments. "There was a chipmunk that was, but he died a little while ago. I miss him." Roger remembered the boy telling him about the chipmunk a couple months ago.

Patricia looked at him and Malach teared up. He wiped his eyes quickly. "There are plenty of chipmunks where you live, dear," she said.

"I know, but he was my friend."

"Well, he was certainly lucky to have a friend like you," Patricia said softly to Malach.

"I was lucky, too."

"He must have been a special chipmunk," she added. The boy nodded his appreciation of her words. "What happened to him?"

"He was getting old, and it was cold this winter. It was hard for him. Mom said that chipmunks don't live that long."

"I imagine not. I'm certain you will make a new friend."

"I don't think there can ever be anyone like him. I miss talking to him. After he died, we made him a coffin and had a service for him. Mom said he needed a proper burial. I'm glad we did that."

"That was a very kind thing to do." Patricia put her arm around Malach to comfort him and then looked up to listen further to the preacher's dialogue with the other children.

"Anyone else want to share?" the preacher asked.

Malach sat quietly, two other children added their remarks and then they scattered out the door. Malach saw Ginny Lucette ahead of him and waved. Roger watched them go. He knew she was the boy's favorite, cute little thing, smart and sassy. They ran out together into the yard.

Roger looked about the church, a simple round stained glass window at the front. He liked the simplicity of the place, uncluttered, airy. There was an atmosphere of peace and serenity. He said a prayer for Edie as he did every week. He missed her terribly. Then he said a prayer for his son, his life cut short. Time helped with the losses, but some days it was still raw.

Today was altogether unsettling with the boy. He could not make sense of it, could not shake it out of his head. That youngster had surprised him before, but today was different. Roger got up and walked out before the conclusion of the service.

Out front he looked for Malach. He wasn't with the group but at the edge of the yard along the side of the building, looking into the woods. The church was tucked away on a wooded lot, not much open land, no other buildings around, maybe two miles or more from town. It was another thing that Roger liked about church. It was part of the wilderness. The boy was waiting for the Tomkins girl, Stacy, to retrieve a ball that had strayed down a gentle slope. He was watching her chase it. Roger could see her through the scattered brush. Suddenly, she stood frozen, her head down, the ball at her feet. He quickly glanced back at Malach and saw alarm in the boy's face. Then, Roger saw it, too. A few dozen feet from the girl a large bobcat was crouched, one paw eerily raised in a stalking position. It looked ready to pounce. Roger's heart pounded, his mind raced, his blood ran cold. My Lord, what was it doing so close to the building and to a yard full of children? Run. Run. He started to move, his legs hardly propelling him. Then he saw Malach hop over some rocks, racing right for the animal, his hand raised.

"No, not so close, no boy, not so close!" Roger shouted. Malach ran in front of Stacy, who stood with her hands covering her face, her body trembling. Roger hurried as quickly as his old, wobbly legs would take him toward them both. No one else in the yard had yet noticed their momentary absence but they were now startled and alarmed by Roger's scream as they headed toward the two children. What was happening? God no, please no! Roger had seen a bobcat only a handful of times in all his years. One had been dismembering a rabbit, blood on its face, fire in its eyes. No child should be so close. The boy was in danger, grave danger. A chill ran up his spine. Not the boy, not the boy. In that split second, the cat rose and leapt toward him. "No!" he screamed. But somehow, miraculously, the bobcat stopped at Malach's feet. It dropped to the ground, on its belly, and then inexplicably, stood and rubbed its head against his leg. How could this be? It glided across his leg like a house cat while Malach stroked its head and neck and then shooed it away. A piercing scream came from the girl as the adults came running. Everything happened so quickly. One of the mothers in the yard saw the cat now a distance away and grabbed Malach; another adult scooped up the girl and held her. Roger saw Ginny and realized by the shocked look in her face that she, too, had witnessed exactly what he had.

Within moments came the rush of parents streaming from the church, alarm in their faces. The preacher followed his flock and listened as Margie Peterson recounted what she saw, about the children in the yard playing, and how Stacy and Malach went to fetch a ball in the woods. Fortunately, Roger was there, through the grace of God he was there. He yelled out and came running as fast as he could. Roger scared the wild cat off. No one was hurt, thank the Lord, no one was hurt.

The preacher for the first time looked about for his son, gestured for him to come over, and put his arm around him. He shook Roger's hand. "Thank you, Roger, may God bless you." All the parents held their children close, then each in turn, like the preacher, thanked Roger and blessed him. Stacy's mother, April, hugged him with tears in her eyes, unable to speak. Her father, Billy, held back his own emotions and embraced Roger and thanked him.

Roger turned to see the boy. They looked at each other, the boy aware that Roger had witnessed what happened. The Lucettes held Ginny close, waiting for Stacy's parents to have the time they needed and then thanked Roger, too. He could see in Ginny's eyes the same disbelief that he had felt and realized that she knew. He saw her look at Malach and he back at her.

6

Mark's car pulled down the drive just minutes after Sky had arrived to visit Judith. He stepped out of the vehicle and helped Malach out of his seat, lifting him up and carrying him toward the house. Judith looked out the window when she heard them and became concerned watching the interaction between her son and husband. Mark was not inclined to coddle Malach and was always demanding grown up behavior. She hurried out of the house. Mark put Malach down and held his hand.

"Is everything alright?" Judith asked, looking Malach over for some injury or problem. She turned to Mark for final reassurance.

"I'm okay," Malach answered.

"Everything is fine," Mark added with a strained smile on his face. He was visibly shaken.

"Are you sure?" Judith asked.

"Why don't you go along," Mark said to Malach gesturing for him to head toward the house. Judith was relieved to see that he looked and acted healthy and well. "It was a difficult morning," Mark started to explain haltingly. "But everyone is going to be fine. There was an unexpected situation involving the children near the woods. There was an animal nearby. It could have been more serious but fortunately wasn't."

"A situation. What are you trying to say?" Judith interrupted impatiently.

"I don't think I've really understood what it's like around here. Where we come from, you just don't think about wild animals in the same way, well, with the exception of alligators or snakes. It could have been very serious, but fortunately, Roger was close by. Bless his soul. There was another child involved, too, little Stacy. We were also fortunate with her. She had a big scare, but wasn't hurt either." Mark looked for a reaction, expecting panic in her eyes, but she remained calm.

"Please tell me what you are getting at?" Judith said, now firm with her remark. "Tell me what happened. Everything, I want to know everything."

Mark proceeded to relate the details of the morning. Judith listened, as did Sky who stood awkwardly at Judith's side. Judith's expression was serious, her attention unwavering. Mark stumbled a few times when he told her that the animal was a wild cat.

"A wild cat. What kind of cat?" Alarm rose in Judith's voice.

"A bobcat," Mark muttered.

"A bobcat," Judith repeated. "A bobcat."

"Yes, I know what you're thinking."

"Did anyone see what happened?" she asked.

"What do you mean? I'm sure someone did. There were adults outside with the children. Roger was there."

"I know, but did anyone actually see how close the animal came to the children?"

"I don't know exactly, but Roger scared it away. He was fortunately in the right place at the right time."

"Was the bobcat near Malach or Stacy?"

"Stacy was further in the woods, down the slope on the side of the church. I think Malach was following her. It must have been closer to her, but I don't know. There was so much commotion after."

Judith stared silently at Mark as she let him fill in the details. "And Stacy is okay?"

"I believe she is, frightened, but not a scratch on her or Malach for that matter. Thank the Lord. It could have been..."

"Yes, we can thank Jesus for that," Judith said sarcastically.

Mark flashed her a look but did not respond, then glared warily at Sky.

"Maybe I should let the two of you have some time alone together," Sky said.

"No, there's no need for you to go," Judith said. "Did you talk with Stacy's parents?" Judith redirected her remarks to her husband.

After a long pause Mark answered. "They were a mess. April cried inconsolably afterwards, could barely catch her breath. Billy was numb. We spoke for some time. They were counting their blessings."

"And Roger, how is he? Was he shaken by what happened? He's not a well man."

"I think he'll be fine, but I could tell he wasn't himself. Poor fellow, running toward the kids, his legs barely working, arms waving and shouting. It must have taken a lot out of him. He barely uttered a word when we all came out. He had this look on his face, like he was in shock. Patricia and Nathaniel stayed with him after and offered to drive him home. Of course, he wouldn't let them. They know him best. I think I'll check on him later this afternoon."

"I'll go. I want to see him," Judith said.

"Good, you can come with me."

"I'd like to go alone," Judith stated firmly.

Mark winced but withheld comment again. "Are you going with her?" he snapped, gesturing with his head toward Sky.

"I said I'd like to see Roger alone. I want to talk to him."

"We can do that together."

"I'd rather have the opportunity to talk with him alone, that's all." Judith was clear. It was the first time Sky had seen her like this with Mark, not acquiescing. Mark nodded his acceptance.

Sky looked back at the house. Malach was digging with a stick and poking around in the ground. Judith and Mark turned toward him.

"He seems good," Mark said. Judith nodded and then walked back to be near her son. Mark went inside the house.

Judith crouched near her son, smiled at him and ran her hand through his hair gently pushing it off his face. "I'm sorry it was a bad day today. I think all the folks at the church were very scared." Malach nodded.

"What happened?" Judith gently asked.

"Everyone's mad at me." Malach's head was hanging down, tears beginning to fill his eyes.

"What do you mean? Why would anyone be upset with you?"

"Because of the cat."

"It wasn't your fault," Judith said. Malach only shrugged at her reassuring words. "Was the cat going to hurt you?"

"No, not me. But it was because of me," he said.

Judith looked at Sky and both were perplexed. He began to cry and she held him close as he sobbed. She stroked his head again and comforted him. He cried for several minutes before settling. She brushed away his tears and took a tissue to wipe his nose.

"She was looking for food. She has two babies who are hungry," Malach said.

"Did you see them?"

"No, they're still hidden. They're very little and are hungry."

"How did you know they were hungry?" Judith asked.

"I know," Malach said. Judith nodded accepting this.

"But I don't understand. Why was it your fault?"

"The cat came to me, but Stacy was there."

Judith did not know what to say.

"That's what cats do. That's what they do, Mommy."

Judith was silent, taken aback by Malach's words. "I know, I know, sweetheart." Again, she tried to comfort him.

"If I wasn't there…" Malach began to cry again. Judith held and rocked him, his pain now hers.

The screen door of the house snapped closed after Mark came out. "I'm going back to the church to look around. I need to see some things. I'll be back later this afternoon." Judith and he exchanged looks, but neither of them said anything. He turned, walked across the yard, got back into his car and drove away. Judith was quiet for some time, then took her son into the house and prepared something for him to eat. With his cheese sandwich and a glass of chocolate milk in front of him he seemed calmer. Sky and Judith sat at the table while he ate. Judith suggested a nap and Malach did not resist even though he rarely slept during the day any longer. She took him to his room and rubbed his back until he nodded off and then joined Sky in the kitchen.

"I never imagined something like this," Judith said, "but from the first moment that I understood, I feared for him. At first, it terrified me that my little boy could be in danger, but soon that stopped. But I'd never considered the danger for others. It just never occurred to me. Did you hear him? He brought the wild too close, far too close. I don't know what this means."

"I'm sure there's an explanation for this," Sky said.

"An explanation?" Judith snapped. "Like the same one we have for everything else he does. Is that the explanation you had in mind?" Sky could see the fiery look in her friend's eyes, part fear but also part readiness to strike with everything in her being to protect her son. Judith paced as they talked.

"Let's think this through," Sky said. Yet none of it made any sense. "He's just different." Sky recognized the utter ridiculousness of her remarks, pathetically trying to help, but could see in Judith's eyes that she was steps ahead of her.

"I know he's different, he's more than different. I know Malach is here for a reason. I don't know what that is. No one can know that. I don't expect you to. But I believe with all my heart and with all my soul, with every fiber of my being, that Malach is here to teach us something,

something we have forgotten, something about our place on this earth, something about our humanity. But he's not ready. He's still learning himself. He's too young now, too vulnerable, and I have to protect him until his time comes."

Sky nodded and felt for her new friend. Judith turned and looked out the sliding glass doors at the land around them and was silent.

7

Roger was not surprised when Judith came to the door. He was pleased to see her and relieved that she came alone. He was always fond of her, even while he had doubts about her husband. She was strong in a quiet way and knew she was cautious with whom she let close to the boy. She made him feel welcomed into the inner circle she created. The preacher gave the impression that Malach was his ambassador to the entire congregation, but Roger knew that was not the case.

"Thank you for coming," he said. "I needed to talk to you."

She smiled, took his hand and then embraced him. "I was worried about you."

"No need to concern yourself with me," Roger said, appreciating her words. She was like that, genuine and caring. "I'm well enough, I think. Please, come in. May I offer you something?"

"Of course, just something to drink."

Judith followed Roger into the kitchen and saw the clutter on the counter and she started clearing scattered newspapers, dirty dishes piled in the sink, and took a dishtowel and wiped down the surface. She ignored his apologies for poor housekeeping, not even bothering to respond when he begged her to let him do it. Roger knew the place was a mess, so different than when Edie was alive. She took pride in keeping the house, everything neat as a pin. Judith used two mugs she cleaned from the sink after finding none in the cabinet and took an opened carton of fresh cream from the refrigerator while he made a pot of coffee. She saw a small cake wrapped in plastic and cut two pieces.

Roger just came out and told her. "I don't have words for what happened today." She nodded and listened.

"I've spent my life in these parts. I'm an old mountain man. You know that, a cynical old mountain man. It's in my bones. I've hunted these mountains, fished the streams, chopped my own wood, even made my own booze. I'm a different breed than most folks around here. My family goes back generations on this land. Most of what you can see all around is mine, nearly this whole side of the mountain. Lots of folks have been trying to wrestle it from me for years, but I don't need the money and I don't want to see it spoiled. I've seen just about everything there is to see, I know just about everything there is to know about these parts, at least that's what I thought."

"Tell me what happened today, Roger."

He was still unsure what she knew. She was hard to read, and he liked that, too. He decided that he wouldn't play any games. He looked into Judith's blue eyes, but they gave nothing away. She looked right back into his, not even a flinch, a grimace, or a moment's hesitation. Nothing he was going to say would shake her. "I don't know how to make sense of what I saw today. Your boy has something in him that I can't even begin to name."

"You mean a great deal to Malach," Judith said. "I know we've never spoken about this before, but we should have a long time ago. I know he talks to you about what he does. You're one of the very few. When we come home on Sundays, he always tells me about it. Most important to me was that he believes you understand. He knows it intuitively. He loves to tell me your stories. He's always so excited when you had an adventure that you shared with him or if something unexpected happened to you when you were in the woods or on the mountain. He'd giggle about it. He loved that you told him everything, and didn't leave anything out."

"There's something that I felt about him from the time he reached out and put his little hand in mine," Roger said. "Damned most delightful youngster I've ever known. Each week that's gone by with him, he's been in my mind. Yeah, we shared our stories about everything that lives and grows in these hills. We might even talk about the wind, the smell of the ground, moisture in the air, the feelings in our bones when the weather is changing. It was silly and fun at first, that little boy had the most fanciful imagination I ever knew. But then it began to sink in. He knew things that little boys don't know, can't possibly know, that most old folks don't have a clear notion about. He knew stuff that made my mind dizzy." Judith listened and affirmed with a nod of her head all that he said.

"What did you see today, Roger?" she asked, needing to hear it for herself.

"By chance I walked out before the end of the service. I was just a bit restless this morning. The little ones were in the yard as they are on a nice day. I could see your boy off to the north side of the church looking into the woods and I didn't make much of it at first. Then I made out the girl and then the bobcat. She was so close to it, the cat on its haunches, its eyes set on her, creeping, ready to strike. I just kept thinking, I'm going to be too late, I'm going to be too late. Then your boy did something I couldn't even grasp. He ran toward the cat, right at it. I panicked. I had to stop it. I had to get there, all the time fearing I'd be too late." Roger watched Judith listen with no expression on her face. She gently pushed a loose lock of her lovely red hair off her face. There was no surprise, no shock, no fear, only a calm acknowledgement of another knowing her son.

"And then," she said. She had to hear it to the final detail.

"I couldn't breathe," Roger continued. "But then everything went in slow motion and I saw what I couldn't even imagine. This wild animal leapt right at him and landed at his feet. It dropped down to the ground and then rose and gently rubbed its head on his leg. It sounds downright crazy but your boy stroked the bobcat's head."

Judith nodded, satisfied now that Roger knew.

The two looked at each other, and sat silently for a moment and then Judith asked, "Are you sure you are well, Roger? It must have been a shock to your system."

"I'm fine. It's not my heart or my old bones that got rattled, just my mind."

She was silent for some time, poured him another cup of coffee, and then asked, "Did anyone else see?" It was at that moment that Roger realized that her agenda was not just to check on him, though she was truly concerned about his well-being. She was here to do damage control.

"Does your husband know?" he asked.

"No." Her voice was soft but firm and she said no more. He couldn't explain it, but he somehow knew before she answered that she would say that. He didn't know why, but it did not surprise him. "Only my friend, Sky. You probably remember her family, the Ryders."

"I do. Edie talked about her mother often. Good woman. May she rest in peace."

"What about Stacy?" Judith asked.

"The little girl, I don't believe she took in what happened. She was paralyzed with fear. That cat couldn't have been more than fifteen feet from her. She covered her face with her hands. She was just frozen."

Judith shook her head with sadness, trying to imagine the terror of the child. "Poor thing. How awful it must have been for her. I need to talk to her parents. What about the others in the yard?"

"They came rushing but the cat had moved away from them already. I'm certain of that. No one even mentioned anything that seemed unusual, other than the cat being so close to begin with."

"That's good," Judith said.

"But the other little girl. The one that the boy plays with, that little spitfire, Ginny."

"What about her?" Judith asked, her voice rising. "I hadn't heard that she was with them."

"She was right there, watching, I know she saw."

"Are you certain?"

"I could see it in her face," Roger answered.

"Did she say anything? Did she say anything to the others, to her parents?"

"I don't believe so, but I don't know," Roger said. He could see Judith's mind working overtime and he understood.

8

After meeting with Roger, Judith returned to the house where Sky had remained to watch Malach. She hurried inside and found Sky sitting at the kitchen table. Malach was still napping, making Judith realize how much the events of the morning had taken out of him.

"Everything is going too quickly," Judith said. "I'm not ready. Malach's not ready."

"What happened with Roger?" Sky asked calmly, trying to slow Judith down and help her think all of this through.

"Roger knows, he saw the entire thing, but I'm not worried about him. In my heart, I know that he can be completely trusted. He believes that one of Malach's friends also saw what happened, though. He was almost certain that it was only her." Judith paused for a long moment and added, "but what if there were others?"

"Right now, it was just a freak thing and likely just one child saw," Sky said. "Unless you actually see it for yourself, no one's going believe a story like that."

Judith slowly nodded her head, her mind already racing ahead.

"Do you know who it was?" Sky asked.

"A little girl named Ginny Lucette. She and Malach are wonderful friends. Sweet thing. Roger said he could see it in her eyes."

"Virginia Lucette's daughter?"

"Yes. Do you know her?"

"Once very well," said Sky. "Maybe I can help with that. We were very close friends when we were young. It's been a long time, but I'd be happy to talk with her. I can just try to feel it out, nothing direct."

"Maybe," Judith replied. "I don't want to do anything just yet."

Sky raised an eyebrow, wondering if Judith didn't trust her to handle this delicately, but she let it go.

"I keep blaming myself for not going with them to church," said Judith.

"You can't beat yourself up for that. You couldn't have controlled what happened."

"I don't know, maybe not, but the morning might have played out differently." Judith stared ahead, then turned to face Sky. "And what about Mark? He still doesn't know. Instead, he's running around like a madman today, thinking he'll work this all out when he has no idea about what even happened."

"Is it time to tell him?" Sky asked.

"It was time years ago. It's so complicated, you have no idea."

"Make it simple, then."

"If that were only possible. Everything about my life with Mark has been complicated." Judith paused, her lips tightened and eyes narrowed.

"I'm listening," Sky said, her words nudging Judith.

"It's a long story, but I suppose you need to hear this. Someone has to." Judith cleared her throat, her discomfort visible in her face.

"When Mark and I met, things couldn't have been worse in my life. I'd just left home for the last time, though I didn't know it then. Once again, I was on my grandmother's doorstep where I always wound up. I was so beaten down, broken, shamed beyond measure. My life was nothing but failure."

Sky nodded for her to continue. Judith looked into her friend's eyes, trying to draw upon whatever inner strength she could find.

"I had just spent the night sleeping on a bench in an all-night laundromat, waiting for the sun to come up before knocking on my grandmother's door. She could see I was a wreck, I was barely put together, my eyes were swollen and bloodshot, the smell of alcohol on me. She didn't ask any questions, just did what she always would do, put me in a hot tub, aware that I needed my own corner to tend to my wounds. I soaked in that bath for an hour, maybe two, thankful for the privacy, thankful to have a safe place to cry, and then cry some more. Clean, fresh clothes would be at the door, and a hot meal would await me whenever I was ready to join her.

"It took an entire week to get up the courage, but I had to get it out; it was like an abscess that needed to be lanced. My grandmother taught me that, too. You can't keep bad stuff inside or it will fester and eat you alive. That was true enough, though most of my bad stuff was still buried away. But this one was not going to be hidden in that pile."

Judith looked at Sky before continuing. "I was startled awake late the night before by a naked man crawling into my bed. He grabbed at my body, pulled at my underwear, poked his fingers between my legs, tried to force himself on me. I could smell booze on his breath. I screamed and screamed. I bit him as hard as I could, jammed my thumb into his eye, and threw him off of me onto the floor. I don't know where I found the strength. I leapt out of the bed, my heart pounding out of my chest, grabbed my clothes and bag, all the while still screaming, and bolted out of the room."

"I'm sorry," Sky said. "I had no idea that you'd been through something like that."

Judith released a deep sigh. "There's no need for sympathy. It is what it is. Though when my grandmother heard that it was my mother who brought this stranger into the house, no doubt the one who provided the drugs and alcohol, she was enraged, and if she could have, she would have taken the large kitchen knife she was holding and skinned him alive.

"I can say it all now, but at the time I was so ashamed. As I ran from the house, I saw my mother passed out in her room on the bed. That was my mother, that's how she looked out for me when I was six, when I was sixteen, and even that night at twenty-three.

"Yes, I have spent the past five years determined to be a different kind of mother, though motherhood was not something I aspired to. But that night, the recognition of my mother's utter failure to parent proved to be the start of my new life."

Judith got up from the table, took another deep breath and ran her hand through her hair. She filled her cup of coffee, offered Sky some more, and sat down again. With a deep sigh she continued.

"A week passed before my grandmother and I said another word to each other about that night. Then, at breakfast, she told me it was time to start over. She said I needed to march myself down to one of the churches nearby. Never mind which one, take the pick of the lot. It didn't have to be her church, even the Catholic one would do. There were meetings at pretty much all of them, some during the day, some at night. It was how I could get help with my drinking and everything else that was broken, how I could heal and take control of my life. It was the one thing she asked of me, so I agreed.

"At that time, even though I hated my mother with such intensity that I feared I'd do something crazy, the idea of these meetings scared me more. I always swore after some horror at home that I'd never go back. But I returned, always returned. Each time I was lured back with my mother's promise of change and pleading words of how much I was needed, how much I was loved. I hated myself for believing her, even more than I hated her. But that life in that awful home was familiar. It was a place I understood and, even with all the chaos, knew what to expect."

Judith wiped away some tears, but did not interrupt her story.

"Pacing back and forth in front of that church, I puffed away, one cigarette after another, trying to calm my nerves. Quitting was the least of what I knew I needed to do, but that was what stuck in my head. If I could only throw away the cigarettes, if I could only do that, then maybe I could take the next step. Even that felt like too much. That's how lost I was. I had nothing left in me. I swore I'd never be like my mother, yet there I was, just as aimless and lost. There was no pride in knowing that I never used drugs like she did. The drinking was shame enough. It was social at first and the alcohol made me feel good. It took over so fast it scared me to death. Every day I promised myself that today would be different, and every night I repeated the same failure. I felt worthless, simply pathetic and worthless."

Judith looked down into her lap and sat silently for some time. When she raised her head, she found patience and understanding in Sky's face and continued.

"The idea of going into that meeting made me feel even weaker and more beaten down than I already was. I didn't know if I could do it. But that's when I met Mark. He was carrying some boxes into the church from the back of a pickup. He walked by three or four times, always nodding with a big smile. After he unloaded, he parked the truck, and came over to see if I needed any help. Not very convincingly I shook my head no, but he insisted on walking me inside, knowing why I was there, and he just sat down next to me and stayed. We listened to the speaker. Afterwards, I thanked him and introduced myself. It was the first time I dropped my middle name. I was no longer Judith Jane, just Judith. I think it was a feeble effort to make a new start, to reinvent myself. The next day I was back and we saw each other again. He waved and came right up and started a conversation. It happened like that nearly every day for the next month, like he was waiting each day for me. I didn't know then that his father was the minister of the church or that he had just finished seminary. I wasn't looking for a boyfriend but he seemed to care and he made me feel better. I also didn't have a drink during that time and was more hopeful."

"He was very kind," Sky said.

"Yes, I suppose, but that's not what this is about."

Sky nodded, uncertain where Judith was heading.

"Whenever we spoke, he wanted to hear everything about me. That was the last thing I wanted to do, explain my life. He looked so intently at me, his eyes always locked on mine. Eventually, he asked me out on a date. I was panicked, but agreed. He picked me up at the house, came to the door and introduced himself to my grandmother. No guy I ever saw did that. My grandmother always warned me about guys who only want one thing, and to stay away from trash, but those were the guys I usually found. Mark was different. At the restaurant when the waiter asked if I wanted to see the wine menu, Mark told him that we didn't drink. I thought that was considerate and I thanked him. He said he never drank alcohol, that it was not moral behavior. I felt so humiliated, only imagining what he thought of me. At the end of the evening he dropped me off and told me if I let God into my heart, that beauty would also radiate through me from the inside out and not just from the outside. He gave me a kiss on the cheek and walked me to the door."

"He was very different then," Sky said.

"I don't know that he was different or that I was in no shape to judge anything about him."

"He tried hard to win you over."

"I was not in a position to make decisions like that."

"I suppose so," Sky said.

Judith continued. "We went out many times after that, for coffee, lunch. I liked him. He asked me to church a few weeks later. He was going to deliver his first sermon. Mark had already committed himself to this path, but I couldn't fathom that life. He was attentive and kind, but the whole church thing was foreign to me. He spoke that day about the bond of marriage and the unbreakable covenant of a man and a woman committing their lives to each other, starting out in the world as one. He looked at me several times. That night he asked me to marry him. He had the ring, got down on one knee, the whole thing. It was all so fast and so confusing. The two months I knew him, my life began to take shape from the chaos of the past. I met his parents and they welcomed me so warmly. His life was so ordered, proper – everything that my life never was. I was a stranger to all that but I convinced myself that it was what I needed and accepted his proposal. He was so excited. He'd been talking with the church here and was prepared to visit. Having me with him he believed was God's plan. I was so scared and so uncertain. My grandmother saw it as a path to a better life. These were good people, she told me, whatever that means."

"So, why haven't you tried to talk to Mark about Malach?" Sky asked. "I've been deeply moved by everything you've said."

"You know that we live a very controlled life," Judith said. "It has to be a certain way. He rationalizes that as being God's way, everything he deems necessary is what the Lord wants." Judith stopped and faced Sky, took a deep breath, reaching out to hold her friend's hand, making certain neither her thoughts nor her presence strayed.

"But he accepted everything about you," Sky said. "He didn't judge you. He fell in love with you."

"Yes, yes, but there's something else." Judith paused silently before continuing. "I had an on and off again boyfriend, Daniel. I never told Mark about him, but I saw him for the last time about three or four weeks before the wedding. Somehow, I never believed the wedding would happen. Nothing good ever happened in my life, and I was certain this, too, would end in failure. Daniel worked at the supermarket with me before I quit several months earlier. We had been sleeping with each other. He told me he enlisted in the Army and was heading to boot camp the next day. It would be his last night before leaving and he asked if we could spend some time together. He didn't know anything about Mark. I agreed and before I knew it we were in bed. A few weeks later I missed my period and knew I was pregnant. I never missed. It was the only reliable occurrence in my life. Mark and I married as planned."

Sky looked at Judith quizzically. "I had no idea."

"No one does," said Judith.

"Is that it, Mark doesn't want anyone to know?" Sky asked.

"No, that would be acceptable. He doesn't know either."

Sky did not know what to say.

"I couldn't tell him," Judith said. "Then time passed and it seemed he wasn't going to know. No one knew, not Mark, not Daniel. Then it was too late. I didn't know how I could explain, how could I rationalize what I had done, how I deceived him. It became my secret, the first of many. Later, when I learned about Malach's abilities, I didn't know what to do, how to make sense of it. I hoped that Malach would reveal himself to Mark, but he never did. Time went by, and I kept that from him, too."

Sky stared at Judith and realized her friend was not looking for or expecting judgment or approval. For her, it was merely the reality of her life, the facts of her existence, and as much as it created unsolvable problems, none of that mattered anymore. She would endure whatever befell her. What was becoming increasingly clear was that the vulnerable preacher's wife she met many months ago was not the same woman whom she knew today. Malach was Judith's only concern. Sky had come to grasp that Judith was oddly very much in control of her life. She was a survivor, and Malach would be protected at all costs.

summer

1

The high temperatures and humidity arrived early in summer, weather that rarely found its way into the mountains. Spring had been no different, with unusual warmth following a truncated winter. The water levels in the streams and lakes had overflowed their banks from drenching rainstorms the past several weeks. While the water had partially subsided, it was not before local flooding left some roads washed out and low-lying homes pumping basements. When the skies finally cleared, the start of the long heat wave began.

Malach surfaced from the bottom of the pond and took a slow deep breath before descending again. The cold water was revitalizing on days with sweltering heat. The pond was situated downstream from the house, about a fifteen-minute walk. Mountain springs fed the stream and pond with fresh crystal-clear water. Malach skimmed along the bottom of the pond as a scattering of rainbow trout emerged from hidden pockets in a pile of large stones and submerged branches and debris. The fish circled together as he extended his hand, then approached and nibbled at the tips of his fingers in a playful exchange. He propelled himself forward, his arms out with his legs gently kicking in unison as his body undulated through the water. The fish scattered and disappeared almost as mysteriously as they arrived. Small air bubbles expelled from Malach's nose as he scanned the underwater surroundings. He reached for a rock, partially lifting it and releasing a cloud of soil obscuring the freshwater crayfish burrowed into the sand.

Judith sat along the edge of the pond, her feet dangling in the water. It was just past midday, the temperature and humidity more reminiscent of Florida summers than the mountains. She admired Malach's graceful movements in the water and could easily have spent the entire day watching him in the deep still pool formed on the downside of a small rushing waterfall. She marveled at the two or three-minute intervals that he remained submerged. His comfort in the water allowed her to relax, no longer having to hold her own breath while waiting for his next one.

Malach again came to the surface, shaking the water free from his hair then pushing it back with his hands, squeezing out the excess moisture. He leaned back and floated effortlessly as his trunk and legs bobbed on the surface. He swam toward the edge of the pond where three lovely painted turtles rested on the rocky soil. All popped their heads out, instead of retracting into their shells as he reached for one and picked it up briefly before resettling it. Lifting the second and the third, he inspected each carefully before placing it down on the moist gravel. After he turned to plunge back into the water, the turtles plodded forward and Judith watched as they followed him into the pond. It was magic that he spun as he glided through the water, an aquatic menagerie of suspended shell creatures hovering nearby. Malach turned as the turtles, buoyant and surprisingly graceful, did their own dance.

Judith still had a hard time reconciling the time that had passed. Malach was now twelve years old and had almost transformed before her eyes in the last six months. He was much taller and leaner, his limbs gangly. Hair sprouted under his armpits, soft stubble on his chin, his voice beginning to crack and deepen. She could accept this, but it also saddened her – losing her little boy and the connection that was the focus of her life.

Malach no longer shared everything with her and often preferred to be on his own. And then there was the strain in his face that concerned her. Each time she tried to speak to him about it he was quick to dismiss her. He was pensive, distracted, and moody. It worried her at first, his behavior so different from the way he had always been. Adolescence, she reminded herself. She'd hated being twelve. Everything was awful, her moods dark, the awareness of her family's failings now evident – her understanding of the deceits, lies, selfishness exposed, everyone repulsive to her and every insincere overture another disappointment. That had been her life, so wretched and so vile. She attributed her misery of that time solely to her family never considering the hormones and changes in her body.

Malach swam for some time mostly in the deepest part of the pond, touching, probing, exploring. After his swim he walked downstream, the water well above his knees even along the river's edge. He bent to scoop up all sorts of little bugs and creatures from the surface. It was the small invertebrates that captured his attention – tiny freshwater clams, larvae of winged insects, aquatic worms, each requiring a moment of reflection. He saw them everywhere, where she noticed none. These creatures would ordinarily repel her but she pressed herself to look and then look again, each time more carefully, asking her son about these tiny animals. Surprisingly, she began to find herself mesmerized by their variety, intricacies, and uniqueness. He stared so intently at them, often for long periods, almost as if in scientific inquiry, but she knew it was more than that. She desperately wanted to be included, to understand what he discovered, what he knew, but she respected his needs and abided by the limits he created. Even joining him today pushed the boundaries, though the heat provided an excuse to be close.

This summer would be Malach's last before starting at a new school in the fall. It felt like it was arriving faster than she expected. He was leaving the small local school, and would be entering a larger regional one that in her mind had too many unknowns. She felt a warm sense of satisfaction having navigated the past half dozen years so smoothly. None of what she feared had come to pass. She was able to preserve the shield of protection. Malach's life remained safe with just Sky and Roger knowing, even as Mark remained unaware. It was this very confidence that began to produce new apprehensions. She knew being too certain, too assured, and too content was dangerous, and that weighed on her despite the seclusion and idyllic surroundings.

Judith thought back on how hard she had been on her little boy after the unsettling encounter with the bobcat at the church. She remembered those days and weeks that followed like they were yesterday. He was vulnerable, shaken, still trying to manage his own pain. She helped him prepare for bed the night after the incident. He had brushed his teeth and kneeled to say his prayers. He was silent for some time, Judith uncertain what he was contemplating. He rubbed his eyes and asked God to forgive him for scaring Stacy and to look over her. As Judith listened to his words, her heart ached. Her impulse was to just hold him and tell him that everything was going to be fine, but she knew that would only be a way to make herself feel better. She recognized that there were no good options to do what had to be done, and no good time to say what needed to be said.

Malach hopped up onto the bed and she snuggled him close, telling him that she was proud that he said a prayer for Stacy. She tried to gather her thoughts, struggling with how to have this talk, first telling him how much she loved him and that no matter what happened she would always love him. She explained that sometimes things happen that we don't expect and that is part of life. We do our best to find our way. Yesterday, at church, was one of those days, a day that surprised us all. Malach looked at her with his big eyes, listening carefully to her words, and then told her that he wasn't surprised. Once again, she was forced to adjust her thinking, to try to understand her son. She did not question him, but rather searched for words to let him know that even if she did not fully understand, she would be at his side and would do everything in her power to keep him and others safe.

She told him that he had a special gift and that he may be the only one in the whole world to have it, but that not everyone was ready to see what he could do. In time they will, but not now, not yet. She proceeded to explain that there were times when he would have to make the animals stay away, especially when he was playing with other kids. He could not tell the other kids about the animals, that some kids are afraid of animals and they were not like him. It was as if she were telling him that he was not permitted to be himself. He wanted to do the right thing, to please her, and while it broke her heart to do so, she made it abundantly clear that this was not a choice. Never had she tried to restrict or control him, but she emphasized that he had to do this, never considering whether it was even possible.

"Is it bad?" Malach asked her with a look of consternation in his face, trying to find his own words to respond. "I know the animals aren't in the other kids, but they're in me. Not just the animals here. I know them everywhere." She looked at him and felt a chill ripple down her spine.

Judith reassured him as best she could that nothing he had done was bad, ever. She told him she understood, though she did not, and reminded him it was not for the other kids, not yet.

After the talks she had with him, she noticed that there was a change with the animals. He never uttered a word about it, but there was a difference. They did not stop coming, but it felt less unpredictable, another level of exchange that she could not explain. When he was with the other children at church or school, he often told her later about animals that were not far away in the woods, be it a coyote, fox, ermine, falcon, or marten. He created an ebb and flow of connections.

Malach's words were still etched in Judith's mind. It was good to have that period behind them. She looked down the stream and saw that Malach was working his way back. He looked preoccupied but came close and sat beside her. Together they listened to the rush of water over the falls, sonorous and unrelenting, the power of a primordial force. Judith thought about this very spot, how long it had been like this, the regeneration of life, the hundreds, maybe thousands of years that it has existed in this form. Old trees and plants replaced by new growth, countless generations of insects, pond life, birds, and other animals that drew their sustenance from the land and water. There was comfort in the cycle of life, the connection of all these interrelated parts. She felt the heavy air, welcomed the occasional puffs of coolness from a gentle breeze as it brushed across the pool of water toward them, and savored the rays of dappled light fluttering through the leaves on this clear day.

Judith knew Malach was responsible for her love of the mountains. When she was younger she had been disconnected from her surroundings, from the outside world around her. The beach for her was suntan lotion, music, snack food, a large towel to minimize contact with the sand, and intermittent wading in the surf to splash water on her neck and body to cool herself off. Besides an alligator or pelican, the rest of the animals of the land, air, and water were unnamed bugs, birds, pests. Tropical storms and hurricane season were inconvenient and unwanted intrusions, never a source of curiosity or wonder. Fans, air conditioning, and screened porches were once necessities for her, to remove herself from the discomforts of the weather. Television was more interesting than a sunset, blossoming flowers, the smell of the salt air, or a late summer afternoon thunderstorm.

Much like when he was young, Malach was silent before sharing something that was on his mind. He sat with his knees up, his arms wrapped around his legs, looking straight ahead at the pool of water.

"There are things in me that are hard to explain," he said.

Judith listened silently. It had been a long time since he talked about his world, and she did not want to interrupt or say something that would inhibit him.

"I feel things, things about how the earth works," Malach said, his face serious and contemplative. "It's something that just happens, has always happened to me, since I was little, ever since I can remember. It moves inside of me, and all around me, even through me. I feel it when I walk, or swim, or even when I lie on the ground. When I close my eyes and concentrate, I see it. If I listen carefully, I can hear it too, distant and low, a sound that fills everything." Malach turned to look at his mother and could see the confusion in her eyes. "I know it doesn't make any sense to you."

"No, it doesn't, but I want to understand," Judith answered, putting her arm across his shoulder. Malach let her hold him. He looked ahead, remaining quiet again for a few minutes before continuing.

"When the forest cools and when it heats, when moisture moves through the ground or through plants and trees, I can feel those things. I can feel all that and much more.

"I know it's been with me a long time. It's not something that has words. It's just there, like breathing. You can think about it, make yourself aware, but there's no need to, it exists on its own. It's like that. All I know is that it's old, very, very old. I suppose ancient, from the beginning."

"From the beginning of what?" Judith asked.

Malach's gaze did not shift and he did not respond to the question. He sat silently for some time.

"Is there something wrong, or is that the way it's supposed to be?" Judith asked.

"Changes are happening, too fast," Malach said. "It means everything is going to be affected. Things can't change that fast. The tiny little water insects, the bugs, they're beginning to disappear. The frogs and turtles, the fish, birds, the land animals, those too. The plants and trees, everything is in danger. It's already started and it's happening everywhere." Malach turned and looked at her. "Life all around us is dying off, here and everywhere in the world."

Judith listened to his words and she grew silent. From the time

2

I t was Ginny's birthday and she and her two closest friends, Angie Clay and Julie Kozel, were excited for a dinner party at Mario's Italian Restaurant. The moms, who had become friends through the girls, sat at another table. Ginny was the last of the trio to turn twelve. Julie had her birthday three months earlier and Angie just weeks ago. Julie, imagining herself the mature elder, relished recounting every detail of her menstrual cycle, which started in the past year. Changes to her body, her more physically developed appearance and absolute preoccupation with boys dominated her conversations. Angie marked the entry to womanhood this spring, but she was moody and irritable with hormones flowing through her body. The dark drama of the classic films she loved resonated with her emotional state of mind. While Ginny was curious and knowledgeable about the physiology of the body, she rarely gave much thought as to when she might be next, though she knew it would be soon.

Three cheesy orders of eggplant parmigiana accompanied by garlic bread and tall sodas arrived at the table. The girls reminisced about their friendship, stretching back to kindergarten, though their memories were often stories recounted by their mothers and heard sufficient numbers of times to have become incorporated as their own. The one story that they all remembered occurred on the first day of school, during morning playtime, when they cautiously inched their way toward each other. Ginny made the first overture. She fished three tiny plastic toy animals from her pocket. The girls' eyes brightened with delight as Ginny showed them the tiger, deep orange with the black stripes partially worn away from frequent use, then offered to share the two others, the panda and the pony. Julie asked if she could play with the pony and Angie happily put her hand out for the panda. Pandas, Ginny said, were cuddly and liked to eat bamboo and sleep all day, and made great pets. Ponies loved kids and would take you on rides wherever you wanted to go. She told them the tiger was her favorite and she took it with her everywhere. Tigers, she said, were the strongest cats and dangerous, too. But she was not afraid of them and she was going to be a lion and tiger tamer when she grew up. She would make them eat out of her hand and be able to pet them. Her new acquaintances giggled. Together they sat in a circle of their own making while chattering and playing with the animals.

Birthday celebrations included this ritual tribute to their meeting before moving to more relevant matters. With twelve being the age of parental consent for a smartphone, they were now all communication compatible. Junior High School was what loomed on the horizon. The three elementary schools from neighboring towns would be merging together. They shared gossip about bullies, mean girls, cruel teachers, and indiscriminate detentions. It was time to renew their pact of friendship, loyalty, and protection. They would stand together in this dangerous new school.

Ginny joined the banter, but was thinking about the summer science program she would be attending at the Conservation Center. She did not mention this to her friends tonight, as she knew that it was of little interest to them. Ginny had been surprised to learn that the leader of the science camp was her mother's closest childhood friend when she was also twelve.

❦

Earlier that same day, Judith had dropped by the Conservation Center to visit Sky and take her to lunch. It had been almost two weeks since they had seen each other. She knew Sky was inclined to work long hours, sometimes skipping meals entirely. Despite days passing without a phone call, Sky never balked at an unexpected visit or impromptu invitation to lunch.

In the past year, Judith had started to leave Malach at home on his own sometimes, no longer dragging him along. She also grew more comfortable with Malach's relationship with his father. Mark took more interest in Malach's outdoor activities and bought him an array of nature books. Malach occasionally perused the material, but he seemed mostly interested in the names of animals, as the information and facts about habitat, life span, mating and reproduction, communication, and food preference did not draw great scrutiny. She felt that what he understood about the wild life surrounding them was something at an entirely deeper and more fundamental level than the facts and details common in these guides. Mark also thought it would be good for Malach to take on some responsibilities. So, in addition to his household chores, he had him paint the garage. Malach did not object, and was patient scraping the old peeling color, sanding where necessary, applying primer and two coats of paint. Mark also involved Malach in his annual book drive, sorting material by age and subject before boxing and distributing to underserved areas. Judith was pleased with the work and church collaboration as it gave Mark and Malach something to talk about. Malach often painted in the mornings and used the excuse of the hot weather to wander off into the woods by midday.

She and her husband had also been doing better as they reached an unspoken balance in their expectations of each other, though their relationship remained a conundrum for them both, neither truly understanding the other. Mark was a good provider, and that was something that she respected and grew to appreciate, not having known that security as a child. Judith felt she tried to open herself to Mark's unwavering belief, but came up unfulfilled too often. Mark's language of faith and purpose did not conform to any of the ragged foundations for relationship to which she was accustomed. They had been through cycles of hostility, as she found her voice and grew confident speaking her mind, but she recognized that she brought many personal faults to the marriage. She knew she was short tempered, suspicious, and secretive.

Judith parked her car and entered the nondescript one-story brick building that housed the Conservation Center's administrative and research offices. The Visitor Center was adjacent to the offices and was more welcoming with its large glass windows and high vaulted ceilings. Usually a volunteer worked the information desk, providing a map and brochure of the hiking paths and common local wildlife. When Malach had accompanied her when younger, he was drawn to the glass enclosed displays filled with taxidermy birds and small mammals. He often stared at them for long periods of time while she went to the offices to find Sky. Malach was well known by the many volunteers who were mostly local seniors and housewives. He showed interest when they welcomed him and tried to point out different animals in the vitrines, eager to share some noteworthy bit of information with him. While he took many walks on the trails with Judith and Sky, in the last year he preferred the wilderness near the house, often going deeper into the woods. When they did traverse the Conservation trails, it was clear that he did not like the elevated walkways over narrow streams, or the constructed bird blinds to observe waterfowl on the edge of the lake. The platforms perched on tall poles for osprey nests he found perplexing, as he did all birdhouses and feeders. He particularly disliked unleashed dogs that hikers brought with them and looked askance at domesticated animals of any kind. Judith was acutely aware that dogs became agitated and barked at her son or passively avoided him, some fearful of even crossing his path.

Malach and Sky had grown close over the years. He was inquisitive about her work, asked many questions, but made few comments. She enjoyed relating details of projects underway at the Center, some of them part of larger multicenter sites. Sky was pleased whenever he came along with Judith. On occasion she invited him to accompany her for a day trip to collect water samples, gather invasive plant species or insects from infestations, and to assess the general health of the land, air, and water. Mark approved of Malach's assistance with these studies and it seemed to improve Mark's view of Sky. He had become accustomed to her presence in the house and Judith's relationship with her.

Sky got up from her computer to greet Judith with a hug and sigh. "You couldn't have come at a better time. Everything is just awful today. I just want to scream. Please, just take me away from here, anywhere, please. I haven't eaten a thing all day. I'm jacked up on coffee, ready to come out of my skin. Three years of data on the water acidification study is missing. All morning dealing with a corrupted hard drive. You don't want to hear this."

Judith smiled, guided Sky by the arm and headed out the door. "Let's go before you change your mind." The heat was oppressive as they stepped out of the air-conditioned building. "It must be in the high nineties today. I thought it stayed cool in the mountains in the summer."

"Not this summer," Sky said. "Record breaking temperatures expected for the next few days. How about Peg's Diner? I could go for something from the all-day breakfast menu."

Judith drove to the diner, about a dozen miles away. Peg's was the meeting place in town, situated next to the post office and grocery store. It was crowded, but a table for two was available in the window. Neither required a menu and they each placed their order. They often escaped to Peg's for a meal or coffee, time to think, take a break and catch up with each other. After listening to Sky vent until the food arrived, Judith shared her conversation with Malach of the day before, wanting to see what Sky made of it. Her friend listened intently while eating her cheese and tomato omelet, buttering her toast, and sipping on another cup of coffee. Deliberate and slow with her meal, carefully considering Judith's concerns, long ago having recognized that accounts of Malach's actions were never easy to reconcile. She did not ask any questions but rather took in all the details.

"That's fascinating," Sky said. "He senses the changes happening in the environment, things that scientists are trying to study and understand, but at an entirely different level. It's amazing. He registers the nuances of everything around him, things we cannot even appreciate." Sky sat back, sipping at her coffee with both hands wrapped around the large ceramic mug. "I would love to talk to him about it."

"I don't want him to know I told you," Judith said. "We haven't talked like this in a while. I'm afraid to do anything that might upset that. I just don't like to see him like this."

"I understand," Sky said, letting the matter go. "Oh, I've been meaning to tell you, this summer we're offering a field science program, a kids camp but for more serious students. Why doesn't he come? I'll get his camp cost waived. He can be my assistant. I'd love to have him, and there will be other kids, maybe six or seven. It's only two weeks, eight to three, Monday through Friday. Maybe he'll make some new friends."

"Let me think about it," Judith said. "It might be good for him before school starts." She was always cautious of new undertakings and mindful of the unexpected.

҉

When camp began two weeks later, Sky greeted six of the youngsters who registered. All had arrived early and huddled together awkwardly. When she welcomed the group, Malach was not among them. She checked her watch and gathered the kids in the visitor center. Sky had each of them introduce themselves. It was a mix of boys and girls, ranging from a precocious nine-year-old boy, Benny, with binoculars dangling from his neck, to a quiet, awkward thirteen-year-old, Charlie, with hair falling over his averted eyes and oily skin and eruptions across his cheeks. Two other eleven-year-old boys, Brendan and William, who were friends, stood together. A skinny ten-year-old girl with a ponytail named Dara, sought out Ginny and stood silently at her side. Sky provided a brief overview of the study program with focus on the different habitats that they would be learning about, including the large pond and local streams, wetlands, open grasslands, and woodland areas. After checking her watch again, she began to worry, when to her relief Malach entered through the front door and mumbled an apology for being late. He stood next to the others who then redirected their attention back toward Sky.

Ginny recognized Malach immediately when he arrived, the two not having seen each other for many years. Ginny found it completely unexpected, and he, too, was startled to find her there. They exchanged smiles as Sky provided each of the kids with a Conservation Center shoulder bag filled with field study tools. Sky had each of the campers empty their bag so she could explain the various items, some of which included specimen containers, a telescoping insect net, a simple magnifying glass, a small ruler for measuring items, and a guide of common birds, insects, butterflies, and small mammals. They would have a chance to use the Center's microscopes to further examine specimens when water samples were collected next week. She handed each of the youngsters a water bottle stamped with the Conservation Center's logo and advised them to fill it from the cooler before they headed out the door. Sky emphasized that learning in the field was where science comes alive.

As they gathered their materials and followed Sky out the door, Malach and Ginny approached each other. "Hi, Malach, do you remember me?" Ginny asked nervously.

"Ginny. I thought you moved away."

"We did but not that far, just outside Ridgeland Falls." Ginny shifted restlessly from one foot to the other.

"I didn't know that."

"I was surprised to see you," she said.

"Same here."

Sky shouted back to the group, interrupting Malach and Ginny's conversation, and waved for all of them to gather around. "We're going to be exploring the large open field on the south side of the lake. It's a beautiful example of a meadow habitat with many native species of grasses and wildflowers, with a robust community of insects, butterflies, and pollinating bees. It's a wonderful location to collect plant and insect specimens. Even in this one meadow there are too many plants and insects to identify. We'll be entomologists, scientists that study insects, and botanists, scientists that study plants. We'll probably try to hone in on butterflies and dragonflies, maybe some good bird sightings as well. They're fascinating and easier to identify."

As Sky continued with her introductory talk to the campers, Ginny found herself distracted as she kept glancing over towards Malach. When he turned to see her looking at him, he smiled. She nervously nodded and then averted her gaze feeling embarrassed.

As the group headed out, Dara stayed close to Ginny. Malach took up the rear of the pack, the others ahead following Sky. Ginny turned to Malach to mention that Dara was only ten but loved science, hoping to make her young companion feel included but also to deflect the self-consciousness she felt with Malach. Dara sheepishly nodded as Malach signaled his approval.

"I've really been looking forward to these two weeks, how about you?" Ginny asked.

"Me, too," Malach answered with a nod.

"Do you know any of the kids here?" Ginny asked, feeling a little uneasy about what to say to Malach.

"Just you and Dara."

Dara sheepishly smiled. Ginny liked that he was considerate of her.

"How did you hear about the camp?" Ginny asked.

"My mom's friends with Sky. I've known her since I was little."

"That's funny. My mom knows her, too. They grew up together. She said she thought I'd like her."

"You will. She's great. She loves science and has a good sense of humor. Have you been out here before?"

"No, it's the first time. What about you?" Ginny asked.

"I come here often. I don't know how many times. There's a lot to see."

"I know it might sound weird or something," Ginny said, "but I kind of like bugs and plants. My friends tell me I should get a life, but they're not mean about it, we're really close so they feel they can say that."

"I don't think it's weird at all," Malach said.

"Thanks." Ginny felt a little more at ease. "I don't care what they say anyway. I do what I like."

"What are your friends into?" Malach asked.

"My friend Julie plays every sport," Ginny said. "She's really good. My other friend Angie has other interests, but not science. She's into art and movies and music. She has that creative gene. I think you have to be true to yourself or you wind up regretting it and feel you've been cheated. You've got to be who you are. I've never been good at sports, but everyone says, play soccer, play field hockey, join the basketball team. Honestly, I think it's a waste of time. Team spirit, camaraderie, after-game get-togethers, all that, it's fine for some people and I've got nothing against it, but it's not for me. Takes up your whole life, there's no time for anything but school and sports. Not like I don't want to be with people or have friends or anything, but I think you find your friends and if it's a real friendship, it sticks. Julie, Angie, and I, we found each other when we were little and have been close ever since. You don't need a team or a sport for that to happen. We each do what we like and we still do a lot together, that's what's great." Ginny stopped, realizing she was rambling and didn't even know if Malach was interested. She felt her face flush and a wave of self-conscious discomfort come over her.

"I know what you mean," Malach said. "I'm not a big sports person either. Not team sports anyway. I like hiking the woods, and love to swim. How about you?"

"I love to hike and swim," Ginny answered, feeling her heart beating quickly.

Sky turned to look for Malach and saw him at the back of the pack, walking alongside Ginny, both engrossed in conversation, animated and smiling. She was pleased that he was enjoying himself. Ginny was a pretty young girl, she thought, and liked that she did not fuss about her appearance. There was something honest and genuine about her. Her long brown hair was loosely pulled from her face and she had a generous warm smile and dark eyes that flashed with energy. Ginny so resembled her mother that it was difficult for Sky to take her eyes off of her. It awakened a dormant longing for her once best friend, Virginia, who was so much a part of her childhood. Until she met Judith, she had lost that sense of connection with a friend. Sky and Virginia had been inseparable and shared everything about their lives, but after the death of her mother, Sky had pushed Virginia away, much like she had everyone else. Virginia tried so hard to help, but she did not know what to do, and eventually stopped trying.

The year after her mother's passing, their lives began to move in different directions. Virginia started to connect with other girls and new friendships developed. Sky still remembered Virginia's closeness with Janet Hagan who replaced her. It had grieved her to see them laughing together in the school hallways. Her best friend gesturing in her familiar fashion, hands moving as fast as her mouth. She forgot what it was like to be free enough of her pain to have fun. Sadness, resentment, and isolation were her new companions. Watching Ginny interact with Malach, her hands expressive like her mother, a vibrant energy projected, opened a well of memories that brought tears to her eyes. With the kids so close, she quickly wiped them away and flipped her sunglasses down from their perch on her head.

Skylar. Virginia was the only friend who called her Skylar. She never gave it much thought other than Virginia's need to differentiate herself from everyone else, but the formality was actually more intimate, a personal bond and knowledge of one another, closeness that was like that of family.

When Virginia called a few weeks ago to enroll Ginny in the program, it was the first time they had a meaningful conversation since they were young girls. Before Virginia moved a number of years back, she had called Sky to inform her. It was out of respect for their once special friendship and perhaps a signal that Sky still held a place in her heart. Even though their contact and conversations since Sky's return had been brief and cursory, she would not disappear from Sky's life without a goodbye and a reminder that she was not far away. Sky was happy to hear from Virginia, her voice a warm remnant of earlier times. But seeing her daughter today surprised her, a mother and daughter so much alike, even in name.

The group found a comfortable place to sit at the edge of the meadow in the shade of a cluster of quaking aspen trees. "This is where we'll be working," Sky began. "It's home to a vast number of different species of native grasses and wildflowers. Meadows are more than beautiful; they sustain a complex ecosystem. So many lovely flowers make their home here. Bees thrive among them and are important pollinators for local agriculture. The meadow provides purification of run-off water from rainstorms and helps build healthy soil systems. It's home to countless insects, butterflies, and birds."

As she spoke, Sky noticed the darting looks going back and forth between Ginny and Malach. It was heartening to see Malach's spirits brighten and the weight of burdens that worried Judith, at least temporarily, lifted.

"Take a look around while we're gathering specimens," Sky continued. "You never know what you might see. There are large numbers of bird species living here, meadowlarks, bobolinks, a variety of sparrows. It's not uncommon to locate birds of prey, such as kestrels and hawks. There's lots of food for them in the field with many small mammals for prey. I hope we'll get to see some of them."

When everyone was ready, she suggested they form two groups. The field was enormous, an expanse of acres upon acres of rolling open meadowland. She reminded everyone to be sure to not stray too far. The four boys congregated together. Dara remained close to Ginny, anchoring herself to her, still uneasy about where she fit in. Malach joined the two of them. Sky recognized that this would be the arrangement for the next two weeks and watched as they moved out in different directions. She let Ginny, Malach, and Dara explore on their own while she followed the boys to make sure they behaved and were safe. She did not worry about the girls with Malach.

"Let's head towards one of those big patches of purple flowers," Ginny suggested. Dara followed in that direction as did Malach. Dara took out her guide and began to examine the flowers as she flipped through the pages. She was thoughtful and thorough, reading about the plant, and other similar ones.

Ginny reached for her guide but hesitated when she saw Malach lean over and smell the flowers. She then did the same. "It's so fragrant," she said. Malach pinched a stem off and offered it to Dara who was watching. She smiled and took the flower holding it to her nose, inhaling the scent. "I like it," she said. Several honeybees floated over the cluster of flowers along with other tiny insects, hovering and darting from flower to flower filling themselves with the sugar-filled nutrients at the base of the petals.

"Wild lupine," Dara announced. "The flowers, they're wild lupine."

Ginny checked her guide and agreed. "What do you think?" she asked Malach. He looked at her and nodded.

Dara pointed to another patch of the lupine right near them. "There's a butterfly over here, a black and yellow one. Should we try to catch it? We could just look at it. I don't want to kill it."

Malach could see her uneasiness with the idea of netting the butterfly. He approached it and slowly put out his hand as the butterfly floated next to his extended finger before it came to rest. Dara's eyes widened with delight. He brought it close for her to inspect. With its delicate wings extended, the near translucent dusty scales were luminous.

"It's beautiful, look at the blue markings near the tail. What kind is it?" Dara asked.

"It's an Eastern Tiger Swallowtail," answered Ginny. "They're pretty common, but always great to see, especially so close." Dara studied the butterfly until Malach raised his hand to release it. She wandered after it until it was out of sight.

"That was nice of you," Ginny said. "She really liked that."

"You know a lot about butterflies," Malach said.

"I like them. I did a project in school on butterfly migration. It's amazing what they can do. They follow the sun and the magnetic fields of the earth. Sorry, that's the geeky side of me talking."

"It's not geeky at all. It's important. No one knows much about those things."

"Thanks," Ginny said. "Most kids I know don't notice what's out-side. Sometimes I think that I should've been born two hundred years ago, when people paid attention to nature. I mean, we live in the moun-tains and it's so beautiful and there's so much to see."

Dara came running back a few minutes later, catching her breath and whispering excitedly about the bird the others were watching.

Malach and Ginny followed her as they headed toward the group. They all stood silently with eyes gazing at the large bird in the tree on the edge of the field. "Sky said it was not very common and we're lucky to see it," Dara said. The bird launched from its perch and took flight. Its long wings beating steady and strong as it circled wide across the field. Everyone's eyes were on it, holding their breath as it rapidly descended and flew low across the meadow coming surprisingly close to the group, the black tips on it wings and white on its long tail visible. It swooped away from them and flew into the distance still low to the ground before coming back their way and settling once again in a tall nearby tree. They watched the bird for several minutes before it flew off.

"That was amazing," Ginny gasped. "It came so close. I never saw a bird like that right near me. It's a Northern Harrier. It was definitely that bird. They call the male the 'gray ghost.'" Ginny held up the field guide with the picture for the others to see.

Sky looked to Malach who avoided eye contact with her. It made her a little uneasy. She shared some information with the kids about the bird, and then suggested they get back to finding wildflower specimens that they could share with each other later. Sky asked Malach if she could see him for a moment.

"Are we okay with the bird?" she asked.

"It's fine, no problem."

"Are you sure?" He looked at her and gave her a reassuring nod, one she was familiar with. "That's good. Everything else going okay?"

"Yeah. Everything's fine."

"Go ahead and catch up with your group." Sky was long past believing a sighting like that was coincidence. She had seen harriers before but never in that way.

Malach rejoined Ginny who had waited for him. "Have you taken any classes here before?" she asked.

"No," Malach said. "I think this is the first summer of the program, and we're the first campers, the guinea pigs."

"Maybe there should be an honorary plaque in the Visitor Center for us," Ginny said. "It could list the names of the founding campers of the first annual Conservation Center Nature and Wildlife Program. Dara Levos, field guide extraordinaire, Malach Walker, butterfly whisperer, and yours truly, Ginny Lucette, gray ghost buster."

"Good one," Malach said with a laugh. They traded smiles and their eyes met again, this time lingering longer. He made her nervous, but Ginny liked the way he looked at her.

"Can we go across the field and see if we can find more flowers?" Dara asked, interrupting Ginny and Malach's connection.

"I think I've had enough flower collecting," Ginny said. "How about we see what else is out here."

"Sky said not to go too far," Dara said.

"Don't worry. We're not going to get lost." She looked out at the land around them, the expanse of fields, the surrounding woods, and hills beyond that. It seemed to go on forever, a place where one could get lost, yet, being out here with Malach felt right.

"You're adventurous," Malach said.

"You seem surprised."

"No, well maybe, I didn't mean..."

"It's okay. Rules bother me. In school it can be soul-killing, the teachers laboring over their lessons, plodding along, as though we don't have a brain in our heads. Did they ever think that maybe, just maybe, the students might figure things out for themselves? There's a teacher I had this year, Mrs. Stebbens, she taught science. I think she's been at it since my grandmother was in school. Every lesson had to be a certain way, every project had to meet her approval, every notebook had to be kept in the same order. Science is supposed to be exploration, asking questions, not being afraid to make mistakes, discovering things. Nope, not for Mrs. Stebbens, if it's not in the textbook, you're getting off-topic. 'Don't want to do that, do we, Ginny, let's stay with the lesson for today.' She's like Novocain for the brain, very effective, keeps the neurons from working too hard, don't want to overload the system, it might explode." Ginny paused and looked over to Malach, trying to get a read again about his interest. With his nod and smile she felt she wasn't being tedious with one of her rants.

"Ginny, Malach, look!" Dara called back to them. Across the field was a herd of deer. They all stood their ground, not moving, a grouping of six females and four fawns along with three large bucks all oriented in their direction. "Are we too close?"

"We'll be fine here," Malach answered reassuringly. "They're just feeding and being protective of the young. Let's wait until they move on." The deer stood motionless for a minute or two and then the dominant buck turned and the herd simultaneously followed across the field and disappeared into the woods.

They continued to cross the meadow, searching for small animals, butterflies, birds, or any other surprise they could find. Dara stayed close to Ginny and Malach, excited to see the deer though startled by their proximity. She felt included with Ginny and Malach, and silently listened to their conversations, curious, intrigued, and feeling privileged to hear what older kids said to each other.

"Do you walk the woods?" Malach asked Ginny.

"I do some when I can. My mother thinks it's dangerous," Ginny said rolling her eyes. "What about you?"

"We live in the woods. There aren't any houses around so I can wander."

"Do your parents get all nervous?" Ginny asked.

"My mom used to, but she's better now."

"We live close to town," Ginny said. "Some idiot developer clear-cut the whole neighborhood before putting up the houses. I don't get cutting down acres of mature trees, to plant some nursery grown, flowering ornamental something or other in the front yard that's not even meant to grow in this area. Then fill in the space with weird shrubs that have to be watered all the time and grass that needs cutting every week. I wish I could go out in the woods when I want. My mother says, 'Be patient.' She says that for everything. I'm not a very patient person. What's the point, if something needs to get done and you have a sense of what's important; it's a pain to have to wait. I hate hearing, 'When you're older.' I think that's so condescending, and doesn't let you prove yourself."

"Age does not make one wise," Malach said, slowly enunciating his words for emphasis.

"Thank you," Ginny continued. "Some of the lamest people I know are older – dinosaurs, unable to change, unwilling to move beyond their narrow viewpoint. There's so much wrong with this world and no one does anything about it. 'Change takes time.' I hear that all the time and want to scream. Of course, it takes time because *you* make it that way. It doesn't have to be like that. I read something online last month that shook me up. It was a report about the melting ice sheets in Greenland and the glaciers in the Antarctic. They said the speed that it was happening at was unprecedented. It's going to cause the seas to rise and coasts around the world are going to be flooded. People are barely talking about it. Tell me why no one is talking about it. If that's happening why isn't it in the news every single day? Why don't we learn about it in school? Why have I never heard my parents say a word about it? What's wrong with everybody?"

Malach stopped, turned and faced Ginny. "You're one of the very few people I've met who really gets that."

Dara, unable to contain herself, blurted out, "My grandma lives near the ocean in New Jersey. When is this going to happen?" Malach and Ginny turned toward her.

"She'll be fine. It's going to take a lot of years," Ginny said.

They then heard their names called from a distance. Sky waved her arms and signaled for them to return to the group. They walked briskly together, Dara talking about the sightings and eager to share them with the others. When Sky saw them approach, she looked at Malach in the way she did when wondering if his world and the world of the two girls were safely coexisting. He gave the nod she was seeking. The group settled back under the shade of the trees where they left their packs and water bottles. They were all happy to have a drink, and unpacked their lunches and ate while listening to each of the others recount their morning.

Ginny was surprised by everything that was happening. She had expected to be busy collecting samples and identifying and classifying specimens, recording information like a young scientist learning first-hand in the field. Instead, she found herself excited to find someone who thought like her, who took her concerns seriously, who also paid attention to the world around him. She felt distracted, her heart beating quickly in her chest, and her mind racing. There were so many confusing feelings to try to understand about Malach, especially the way he looked at her.

Malach had changed so much since they were little and Ginny wondered if he thought the same about her. She remembered his thick hair and dark eyes and could see the same familiarity in his face, especially when he smiled. She liked the way he walked, his gait smooth, effortless, and flowing. Even the way he carried the Conservation Center bag swung over one shoulder, arm bent and fingers wrapped loosely around the straps. As she watched him, studied his movement, his features now more mature, she felt a sensation going through her that she had never experienced before. It was a warm feeling in her chest and tingling in her body, her head swimming. She had never imagined a boy would make her feel this way.

3

At the end of the first week of camp Sky drove Malach home as Judith was busy helping Mark with the annual book drive. She looked over to Malach who was staring off, lost in his thoughts. Sky cherished every opportunity to spend time alone with him, though she had been careful all week to not get in the way and allow him to have a chance to just be a kid. She wanted him to feel like the others, to experience the pleasures and joys of his youth. She understood what it meant to feel alone, disconnected from others, and was pleased when Malach was the one to start the conversation.

"You and Ginny's mom were friends when you were young?"

"We were," Sky said. "I guess you could say we were best friends at one time."

"Are you still friends?"

"Well, I suppose we are, but our lives have changed in different ways and we fell out of touch with each other for many years. Life's like that, unpredictable, and things happen."

"I know, but what happened to the two of you? Did you have a fight?" Malach asked.

"No, it wasn't anything like that. When we were young, we were together all the time. It was my life that changed more than hers. You know my mother died when I was about your age and it just caused many problems. It wasn't that we didn't want to be friends."

"Were you too sad to be with her?" Malach asked as he turned and faced her directly.

"I think I was, but I didn't know it at the time," Sky said, briefly taking her eyes off the road to look at him and acknowledge his concern. "Nothing made sense to me then."

"Do you hope to be friends with her again?"

"Well, I'm not sure what that would mean now. Time has passed, we have different lives from the ones we once led."

"If you were best friends, does that change?" Malach asked. "How do you stop being best friends? Isn't that always there?"

Sky was surprised by Malach's curiosity and candor about her friendship with Ginny's mother, but there was a heartfelt sincerity to his questions, which she respected and even appreciated. It was a deeper level of concern than she had received from her father, aunts and uncles, grandparents, or teachers at the time. A chance to talk, someone to listen and help her was something she had craved after her mother's death.

"Some of that remains," Sky answered. "But Virginia is married. She has children and a busy life with work and her family, and I suppose new friends."

"I mean, all those years when you didn't talk, did you miss her, did you think about her?"

"Sure, I did," Sky responded. "It was painful for me. There were many times that I wished that it could be like it was before. I'm not sure I knew if that was still possible or how to make that happen. Sometimes when we're struggling we don't always find the best solutions to our problems."

Malach listened and nodded his head. He sat silently for a few moments. "It would be sad," he said, "for a close friendship to die. I know it would be for me. Did you know Ginny and I were friends when we were little? I remember playing with her every Sunday at church. She was my best friend then. I used to look forward to seeing her each week. When I asked my mother where she moved to, she never told me that she it was just a couple towns over, not more than a forty-minute drive. I always thought it was far away."

"I didn't know that," Sky said, wondering if Judith had been deliberately evasive with Malach about Ginny after the incident at the church.

"I thought about her a lot," Malach said. "I never expected to see her again and then there she was on Monday, just standing there. I recognized her right away. It was awkward at first, but we were both happy to see each other. We'll be in the same school this fall."

"How nice. Is she like the way you remember her?"

"Actually," Malach said, "she's so much like the way I remember her. She has a way of just saying what's on her mind. I like that and other things, too."

"Like what?"

"She notices things around her, she sees and listens to the outside. I don't know any other kids who are like that."

They had pulled into the driveway of Malach's house and the conversation ended. Sky liked that he reconnected with Ginny. He needed to have someone his own age to talk to, to share his world and all that was important to him. Everyone needs a best friend and she wanted that for Malach as well. It had been so central to her own childhood even if she had pushed Virginia away in her grief. Malach understood this, like he understood so much about everything.

"Do you want me to stay until your parents get home?" Sky asked.

"You don't need to."

"I know, but I could make you something to eat. I could use a snack, myself." Malach smiled and nodded. They walked to the house, Malach a step ahead of her. He was becoming such a fine young man, she thought.

⁂

Judith was still at the church working with Mark. Together they carried boxes of books into the building from the back of an old rusted pickup truck that Mark had borrowed from a member of the church. Mark watched as she slid each box to the edge of the tailgate and hoisted it up, waving off his offer to help with some of the heavier ones. Judith stopped to take a moment to rest, wiping the perspiration from her forehead.

He leaned against the truck as Judith rested. She still looked young and vital to him, her face vibrant, her arms slim but strong. "Today reminds me of the day I first saw you. Do you remember?"

"Of course," Judith said. "I wasn't at my best."

"No, you weren't, but if it were not for that, we may never have met." He thought back about his decision to marry so quickly. His father believed it impulsive and he implored him to take his time, that he barely knew Judith. He also felt Mark was blinded by her beauty and was ignoring that she was troubled, an alcoholic, maybe even a drug addict. It was ironic because he never thought of himself as one to make rash decisions, rather he believed he was thoughtful, mindful of what was important, prayed and labored over important decisions. He had never felt more certain that she was meant for him, that their life would be whole and meaningful.

"I suppose that's true," Judith said.

"I've been thinking about the church and this place. We've been here almost thirteen years. That's a long time. I'm not certain if it's meant for us to spend all of our lives here or whether we should consider a change."

Judith looked at him, the expression on her face not revealing anything. "I'm not sure it would be best to move Malach."

"I know, but as his parents, it's up to us to make these decisions."

"I understand, but he's happy here," Judith said.

"Maybe that's true, but I don't know what you want."

Judith looked at Mark for some time before responding. "We've not always been partners in making decisions. Why do you ask me now? I've made my peace with our lives here."

"I hoped it could be more than that, but I can see that your happiness does not come from me. I know I have some responsibility for that. I used to believe that my choices would be best for our family. I would pray on it."

"Maybe talking to me more and to Jesus less might be a better way to work on our marriage. Couples make decisions together." Judith knew she was being deliberately hurtful as she raised her voice a level.

"I know that I may have been rigid, maybe controlling, too much like my father. It's not always easy to see those things in oneself," Mark said.

"Well, that helps, but you've never included me in the planning of our lives." Judith's words were very deliberate. She knew Mark had come to understand that she could no longer abide that behavior.

"I believed my decisions were best at the time," Mark said defensively. "When we met, you were, well… not exactly in a place to be making life decisions. I felt what I did was in both of our best interests."

"That was a long time ago. A lot has changed since then." Judith could feel her heart starting to pound and her face flush. "I've learned to make this work. We're civil. Why don't we just leave it at that?" She did not want to go down that road right now; she was too concerned about Malach, about his struggles, about changes ahead this year, about a new round of unknowns.

"There's a gulf between us, a big empty void. You push me away, your affections are infrequent."

"Is that what this is about?" Judith snapped. "Not getting your needs met?"

"That was not what I was implying. You're twisting my words. I only meant that we're not whole as a couple."

"I don't know what you want. I go to church on Sunday. I devote my time to this work. I carry boxes of books on sweltering summer days. I meet with the 'Ladies,' I organize bake sales and charity events. I do what is expected in this life. I've changed, and I can admit, in some ways for the better. I don't drink. I keep our home. I raise our son. Did I ever dream that I would marry a pastor, and do what I'm doing? No, never for one moment."

"I'm sorry you feel that way," Mark said, his voice dropping in defeat. Everything about the conversation was feeling wrong and not what he needed to address.

"It's not that I seek a different life," Judith said. "I can't even say what kind of life that would be." She recognized that Mark had asked less of her over the years, tolerated her absences from his world when needed, and tried harder than she did to maintain the façade of their so-called holy marriage.

"All I wished to do was to ease your pain," he said, "to help you find meaning in your life and in our lives." Judith felt he was not abiding by their unspoken rules of engagement and Mark found that his words were not leading to where he wanted to go. "There is solace to be found…"

"Please stop," Judith interrupted. "I'm not certain that any of this is helping. It's not that I presume to have the answers. In fact, I have very few. But please don't remind me that the answers are found in Scripture."

"You're being deliberately hostile," Mark said, then became silent. After a minute he continued. "I've been talking with my father. He asked if I was still open to coming back to the church. Malach likes Florida, you said it yourself when we visited last."

Judith let out a deep sigh. "I can't go back there. There's too much still to try to forget. Since my grandmother passed, there's nothing good for me there."

"There's a pull I feel," Mark continued, "to carry on the family work in the church. Perhaps Malach one day will follow that path as well."

"Malach? I'm not sure it's his calling." Judith resented him for even mentioning that.

"It wasn't mine at his age," Mark said. "It wasn't for my brothers, but it found me. One can never know. He's comfortable in the church."

"That's his nature, he's accepting and tolerant. I just don't see that for him."

"What if I do? Doesn't that matter?"

"I didn't know you felt that way." Judith tried to lend a compassionate tone to her remark sensing for the first time something vulnerable in Mark's efforts to talk today.

"Why wouldn't I? Living one's life serving the Lord, no matter what you say, has meaning and deserves respect. Bringing his Word to others does as well."

"I'm sorry, it's just that you've never mentioned it, that's all."

"He's my only child," Mark added. "I think about that."

"I know that bothers you," Judith responded.

"I had hoped and prayed for a large family, but it was not God's will and I've come to accept that. What about you, does it matter?"

"I didn't say that. Having Malach is more than I could have ever asked or dreamed for."

"You're a fine mother, but you and Malach live in your own world. I see it and have always recognized that need in you for him. But I do see that there's no room in that world for anyone else."

"No one prevents you from being a part of his life," Judith stated. "You have that choice. I don't prevent that from happening. It's up to you to make the effort, to let him know how you feel."

"The love for a child is a special love," Mark said. "All parents only want the best for their children. I'm no different. In fact, I have been thinking much about that. Only last week I spoke with Christopher Kingston. He and his wife Allison don't come to church often, but you might remember them."

"Of course. They have a lovely little boy."

"Yes, their little one just turned two. Chris wanted to thank me for my guidance when he struggled with the decision to adopt. His wife was so certain, but he wasn't sure he could raise a child that wasn't his own. He said his shame of being unable to have a child almost prevented him from the joy of bringing little Willy into their family. He wanted me to know his life is so much more complete and enriched now."

"That's lovely." Judith felt touched by the story.

"It was painful for him," Mark said, "to learn that it was him and not his wife who was unable to produce a child. It made him feel less of a man, and it almost led to the demise of their marriage. Acceptance and faith carried him through that." Mark paused and Judith was uncertain about what he was after. "Those talks had a powerful influence on me. It wasn't the first time I spoke to a couple about adoption, but it lingered with me."

"Is that what you want, to adopt a child and have more children in our home?" Judith asked.

"That would be a blessing, too, but that's not what I struggled with. After those talks I began to wonder myself about the reason for our not conceiving another child. One thing nagged at me, something I dismissed over and over when we married and I first learned about your pregnancy. Malach came a month early, but the doctor told me he was healthy and fine. In fact, he said that he was full term. I never said a word. I prayed and pushed the doubts from my mind. After my talks with Christopher, I saw a doctor. Not right away, but only this past spring. I explained the situation. He was quick to dispel my worries that having had one child meant that there was likelihood we could have more. But the tests revealed a different picture. He told me that I was unable to produce a child and had never been able to. Not now, not in the past, and not in the future. Malach is not my blood."

Judith was stunned, listened silently, her heart pounding. Mark paused and looked deeply into her eyes waiting for a response.

"Why didn't you tell me?" he asked. "Why?" She could hear in his voice not so much anger as pain, the pain of betrayal, a pain to which she was so familiar.

Judith felt numb. "I don't have an answer, but it's not for reasons you may suspect," she muttered. Tears welled in her eyes, and she began to cry. It came from deep within her; from a place she had not let herself near for so many years. It was a place of bottomless shame. She sobbed and her body shook.

Mark sat on the lowered rear tailgate of the pickup with Judith beside him. His head down, his body slumped. "I don't want our lives to be a lie," Mark said. "It's not the way we can continue to live."

Judith's struggled with what to say. This man had suspected the truth about her right from the start, and yet she was the one creating a veil of secrecy, living in the shadows, no different than she had all of her life.

"I suppose it's up to you," Judith uttered. "If you're done with me, I'll accept that."

"That's not why I'm speaking to you about this." Mark was anguished.

"What do you want?" she asked.

"My wife, my family."

Judith did not know what to say. She had never experienced this side of her husband, ever known him to be vulnerable, to hurt like she hurt. It was hard to find the words. "Even with all of my deceit?"

"I accepted you the way you are when I took your hand in marriage."

Judith nodded and started with her story. Mark knew so little about her past. She never offered and he did not ask. It was one part of their relationship she appreciated. She spoke and spoke while he sat at her side and listened. She filled in the gaping holes of her childhood, her family, her misery. Then, she tearfully recounted the events with her old boyfriend, Daniel, and their meeting before the marriage, her inability to face what she had done, and how she had deceived herself as much as she had him. She explained that Daniel was kind but he was not someone she loved. She informed Mark that sadly she had learned on their last visit to Florida that he had died in an accident during his time in the military. She did not know the details.

Mark was as drained as was she by the time she finished. He seemed oddly relieved to hear the truth, to have Judith open her heart to him. Uncertain how to respond, he took her hand in his and they sat silently. After some time, he asked, "And Malach, does he know any of this?"

"No," Judith softly answered. "I feel so ashamed, but I feel I've removed a weight from myself. I hope maybe even from us."

"I'm willing to try, I still love you," Mark said. He held Judith and she held him. It felt like the first true connection for both of them.

Judith took a deep breath and looked into Mark's eyes. "There's something else that I need to tell you. It's about Malach."

from? She could barely breathe and suddenly, out of nowhere Malach was there. He pulled the animal off of her and sent it away. It offered no resistance. Ginny stood right up, still shaking, when Malach took her hand and they ran together, leaving everyone behind, and as they fled her fear melted away. The feel of his hand entwined with hers was comforting and lovely. She looked at her shoulder and it was no longer bleeding. How did he do that? Then she remembered. He had that power. They laughed together. He hugged her and told her that she was brave. She looked into his eyes and kissed him quickly on the lips.

When she woke, Ginny could not get the dream out of her head. It turned over and over in her mind. In that mix of emotions were so many feelings she had never experienced before. She got out of bed and put the light on. The brightness in the room helped the dark thoughts recede. Her eyes searched her bedroom, her safe haven, and she began to feel grounded by the familiarity of the surrounding walls, the knowledge of her parents at the end of the hall, and even the reassurance of her two younger sisters in the adjacent room on the other side of the wall. On her dresser were some new clothes her mother had bought her for school, tags still attached, as she had yet to try them on. Her red and tan backpack leaned against the wall near the desk upon which sat her computer. She eyed her collection of books on the shelves over her desk, stories that enchanted or inspired her, biographies, and even some beloved picture books from when she was a little girl. Her eyes settled on three small plastic animals that resided for many years on the edge of the top shelf. The orange and black tiger had been her favorite. Next to it were the panda and the brown and white pony. Remembering how she had shared the animals with Julie and Angie on the first day of school was a comforting thought that further helped settle her nerves. She walked over to the desk and plucked the tiger off the shelf. Examining the small toy, she remembered how important it used to be to her. It was ironic that it was a tiger that disturbed her dream. She inspected it in her hand, noting how worn and dirty it was, then closed her fingers around it and held it tightly in her fist.

Quietly, she went down the stairs to the kitchen. She poured herself a glass of water from the sink and took a sip, which soothed her dry throat. She sat at the table with the glass in front of her as she collected herself. She could not remember the last time she'd had a nightmare. Her mother entered the kitchen only minutes later and could see in Ginny's face that something was not right.

"Are you not feeling well?" her mother asked. She felt Ginny's forehead to see if she had a fever. "We have a big day tomorrow."

"I'm fine," Ginny said. "I just woke up and couldn't fall back to sleep. Sorry, I woke you."

"Don't be silly. You know I don't sleep. Thought I might find some company when I heard the tiptoe in the hallway." Virginia always had a way of making Ginny feel that she was never a burden. "Did you have a long day? I've been so busy the past couple weeks we haven't had a chance to really talk about camp."

"I'm glad I went. It was worth it." Ginny knew she was the one who had avoided her mother's many questions the past two weeks, and did not want to start answering them now.

"What did you think of Skylar?"

"Sky? She's nice. Is that her name?"

"Yes. I think her mother and I were the only ones who called her that. Were the kids there nice?"

"Yeah, they were fine," said Ginny. "We just spent lots of time identifying plants and bugs, learning field procedures." The dream was still in her head and she found these questions hard to focus on.

"Were there any other girls?" Virginia asked tentatively, aware that Ginny could not have been more evasive about camp whenever she tried to talk with her.

"You know I don't care about being the only one," Ginny said with annoyance. "But if it makes you feel better there was a younger girl who signed up, too. She kind of clung on to me, but she was sweet. I know what that's like. She was out sick the last two days."

"I hope you're not coming down with whatever she has."

"No," Ginny said. "I'm feeling fine. I really am."

"What is it then?"

"I just had a bad dream, no big deal." Ginny sat with one elbow on the table and her head resting on her hand. Her mother waited and Ginny hesitated, but told her the dream. She could see a look of surprise in her mother's eyes. She filled in the details but did not include the part about Malach, just that someone chased the tiger away. In the past, telling her mother a bad dream or sharing something about a bad day quieted her fears and worries. This one was harder to shake.

Virginia stroked her daughter's hair, feeling an uneasy familiarity with the dream. "I don't know if you remember," Virginia said, "but you had a dream like that many times when you were a little girl." Ginny raised her head and looked quizzically at her mother.

"What do you mean?"

"It was the summer before we moved. Fortunately, it stopped almost as soon as we settled into the new house. But for most of the summer you'd wake crying from it most nights."

"When was that?" Ginny asked.

"You were just five and had a bad experience. We all did, but you were right there. It was at the old church we used to attend. I don't know if you remember it." Ginny remembered the church and some of the people there, but didn't remember anything bad.

"I'll never forget it," Virginia continued. "It was a Sunday and you were playing with the other children outside. A couple of the kids were near the woods by the side of the building. It's still upsetting to talk about it." Virginia sighed and continued. "There was a bobcat in the woods nearby. The animal almost attacked one of the kids. It was so frightening for everyone, absolutely terrifying. The old man, Roger Stine, you probably don't remember him; he was right there and chased it off. I never was sure if you saw it or were just upset by all the commotion and crying. You never would talk about it, but you started to have those dreams."

Ginny felt her thoughts racing. A near tsunami of memories flooded her mind. It was like a movie replaying in her head, sharp and clear. She had seen it herself, and now all of it rushed into her consciousness, filling her senses with the sounds and sights and even the smells of that day. She had stood right there and watched the entire thing. She had held her breath and could not take her eyes off the animal. It was so big. Her heart had pounded in her chest. She could feel it at this very instant. It all made sense now. She wondered how she ever forgot and whether anyone else witnessed what she did. Then she realized that her mother did not know what really happened. She looked down in her lap and opened her hand.

"Your tiger," Virginia said. "We went to the toy store when we moved into the house, some new things for your room. You only wanted the tiger. Do you remember any of this?"

Ginny looked at her mother, her eyes wide, and her mouth agape. "I do, I remember it now, I remember all of it."

"I hope it doesn't start to bother you again." Her mother looked worried and stayed with her for a while and then walked her back up to her room. She sat briefly on the edge of the bed, gave her daughter a hug, tucked her in, and rubbed her back, things she had not done in many years. Ginny could not shake the thoughts from her head, unable to sleep a wink for the rest of the night.

The dream and these memories were so unsettling, but they made sense, after all that she learned about Malach the past couple days at camp. It pushed the limits of her rational mind. The effect was profound, nothing felt the same, nothing felt normal. Being with Malach changed her and she knew it was only the beginning.

※

The next day Ginny and her family left for the final two weeks of summer to visit her grandparents in Ohio. It was an abrupt and disorienting transition, and she would not see Malach until school began when they entered the seventh grade.

School always grounded her, where she felt most content and fulfilled. Learning was what she most cherished and which gave her a sense of confidence, pride, and even an inner strength. The luster of academics now felt tarnished next to her newfound knowledge about Malach and a sense of urgency shifted to this unknown realm. Sometimes she wished that it could all be undone, everything put back the way it was. It felt too much and she could not find a way to make sense of it. Sometimes when thoughts of summer seemed to be fading, they would return with a force that collided with everything familiar and predictable. It would not go away, nor did she want it to.

The uneasy conversations with Julie and Angie about the lurking threats facing them in the new school – their fears of being exposed and vulnerable, now felt foolish and immature. No older peers were waiting to make their lives miserable, there were no confrontations or rejections from those arriving from the two other elementary schools, no boys determined to prey upon or humiliate them. It could not have been more uneventful. Ginny found her teachers all kind and serious-minded. She was tracked into the highest-level classes, and she even made some new acquaintances.

It was Malach that she could not reconcile in her mind or remove from her thoughts. She did not know how to talk about it with Julie or Angie, with her mother or anyone else for that matter. How could they even begin to believe or understand? She found herself quietly distant from them, their concerns and interests insignificant. She did not have a way to explain what she experienced. There had to be a scientific explanation, but she knew deep down that one was not possible. Once back at school with normal routines, schedule, work, the drama and gossip, the range of exchanges between the others all around began to feel meaningless. On the other hand, the summer began to take on the quality of a strange dream of its own and it was only Malach whom she wanted and needed to see and talk to.

It had started on the final two days of camp, with Dara out sick. The first of those mornings began much like the prior days, out in the field with a project to do. She filled another water sample tube from the lake, replaced the top and put it in the bag with others she'd collected earlier from the wetlands to the east, and from one of the two streams emptying into the lake. Sky had just checked on them and then headed off to be with the other group. Ginny kicked off her sneakers to work along the water's edge enjoying the coolness of the adjacent ground and the coldness of the water around her ankles as she waded in. It was so hot, the sun beating on her back. It was the warmest summer she could remember. She watched Malach kneeling and investigating something along the shore and had grown curious about his diversions and delays, moments to observe everything around him, even the smallest plants or insects. He never hesitated to pick up or let some little creature wander across his hand or arm. She thought he should be more careful, but to his credit, he was never stung or bitten. He seemed to have a knack for it.

She waded further into the water and continued to observe his examination of what looked like a grasshopper on his finger. She hollered to him and he looked up and saw her wave as she plunged into the water, wearing her shorts and tank top, coming to the surface with a loud wail.

"It's freezing, but it feels so good," Ginny yelled out. Malach smiled, slipped off his sandals and t-shirt, leaving them on the ground where he stood. Ginny had already dived back under and when she surfaced she turned back to see where he was. She swam further out and gestured for him to come and the two headed toward the point of the cove. Malach caught up and soon was swimming at her side. Neither bothered to check on the others, enjoying the chance to cool off from the heat. Sky and the boys had ventured off in the opposite direction around the bend of the lake to collect their samples.

"Let's just hang out in the water," Ginny said. "It's a perfect summer day." She was surprised with her own comment, as she would ordinarily be the one determined to complete every last experiment.

"No argument from me," Malach said. "No samples, no data collection, let the lake take us."

"Take us where?" Ginny asked.

"Not to a place, let's just listen to what it says and let it take us."

Ginny sometimes found Malach's words cryptic and confusing. She could not figure him out. He could be funny and even a little silly, but also serious and intense. Malach swam further out, Ginny at his side. A half dozen hooded mergansers flew low over the lake, right towards them. They skidded across the water as they landed on the surface only a couple dozen yards away. There were two adult males, a female, and three immature birds. The males were bold with their crests fully erect and the white hood patch well defined against their black heads. The female's crest was also fully exposed in its ruddy orange hue. The ducklings that followed were gray and indistinct.

"Oh my God, look at them," Ginny whispered, suppressing her excitement, afraid to startle the birds. "They're beautiful." They watched for a couple of minutes and then the birds began to run across the water, wings flapping as they took flight and ascended over the trees and were gone. "I can't believe how close they came." Ginny was elated with the sighting of the birds. "We've seen so many amazing things here."

"When you take a good look," Malach said, "there's so much that you can see. I do it by myself all the time, but I'm glad you're here." Ginny felt herself blush, and was happy they were in the water so he didn't notice.

"My father takes us camping every year," Ginny said, feeling the need to say something and not let Malach's comment linger between them. "We have a canoe that we lug along. We've been going for years. My father taught me to swim when I was two. He thinks it's never too young to learn. Mom wouldn't let us in the canoe even with a life jacket until we could swim. She's too cautious about everything. My father thinks everyone should be able to swim a mile, just to be safe in case you need to."

"He's probably right."

"Do you camp?" she asked.

"No. Florida is the only place we go when we are away. My grand-parents live there. If it were up to me, I'd live in the woods."

"I would do that," Ginny said. "One day I'm going to climb all these mountains." Malach watched Ginny as they continued to swim. She was very capable in the water and her breathing strong. "The water is so clear." Ginny took a deep breath, dove under and Malach followed. They were soon exploring the bottom in almost ten feet of water, up several times for air and each time back under. They moved into the shallower areas as well.

"Not many specimens," Ginny said as she took a breath. "The lake looks so beautiful. I couldn't believe it when Sky told us that it has been under restoration for years. Whoever thought about acidification and that a crystal-clear lake could be unhealthy."

"There's a lot fewer of everything in and around the lake," said Malach. "Fish, frogs, salamanders, all sorts of birds, especially ones that feed on fish, like osprey and kingfishers and loons. There used to be more of the mergansers we saw, too."

"It's so sad to think that this could happen and that it's taken decades to try to repair it," Ginny said as she paddled gently in the water, Malach floating next to her.

"There's barely anything left in the lake," Ginny said. "Sky said that they'd soon be restocking fish as the acidity drops further. That's a good thing. I wonder what the lake was once like, the way nature made it. You know, the plants, the fish, everything. It must have been something to see."

"It was so much more beautiful," Malach said.

They continued to swim as Malach led them across the lake. Together they crossed the narrow stretch in this long, thin curved lake. Just a few dozen yards off the far shore, Malach stopped.

"What are we looking for?" Ginny asked.

"You'll see."

The sun was bright overhead, the water clear right to the bottom, even in the deeper sections. Under they both went. Ginny found it no different than on the other side. They swam together and she wondered what he wanted to show her. They surfaced again.

"Take a deep breath this time," Malach said. Under they went, diving toward the bottom, she looked to him and he put his hand out, reaching for hers and held it as they floated suspended below the surface. She never held a boy's hand before but clasped his firmly. It was so serene and she couldn't have been happier.

Slowly, she noticed the water around them beginning to change. At first, it appeared that a cloud had crossed the sun, but it was not from the light. The water surrounding her was no longer a penetrating crystalline blue, it was visibly changing before her eyes as a green cast permeated the water, floating plant fragments and sediments coming from nowhere. Her eyes shifted and she began to register different plants. The aquatic flora was uniformly dense in some areas, some sections textured from the interspersed mix of vegetation; other expanses open with a gentle flowing current. She felt buoyant among the feather-like movement of aquatic plants clustered with delicate stems and spikey leaves growing in whorls; nearby were fragile long sinewy plants that grew to the surface, others bristle-like on wispy branches. They swam together, hands interlocked, watching as very small fish darted out of the camouflage of the flora and then as suddenly would disappear. They watched as dozens of larger fish moved through the water and came closer, a school of minnows off to her side. Soon there were largemouth bass, lake trout, pike, yellow perch, and fish she did not recognize.

Ginny watched in disbelief, as the almost barren water she had entered was now replete with a dizzying array of fish and plants. She suddenly became alarmed, as a huge snapping turtle approached them. The fish surrounding them retreated in the turtle's presence. Malach rested his free hand on the turtle's shell as it brushed up against him. As the snapping turtle moved off, he squeezed her hand to reassure her that everything was okay. He then signaled for them to ascend for air and as they swam closer to the surface he released Ginny's hand and she witnessed a change once again, the lake reverting to its clear, silent, emptier state. Gasping for air as they broke the surface Ginny blurted out, "What happened?" Her eyes locked with Malach. "What in the world just happened?"

It was the most unexplainable thing she had ever seen. Where did these fish and plants come from and where did they go? Why did they come to him? It was like the bugs and butterflies and maybe the mergansers but so much more. Malach looked into her eyes and gestured for them to head back to shore. They swam together and then sat in the shallow and spoke. Ginny felt her mind spinning, her body in a state of disequilibrium. She felt that she had been part of something supernatural. She also felt exhilarated, her mind racing and her heart pumping as though she was chosen and invited into a rarefied dimension.

She listened as Malach described his life. He explained to her that he had always been part of the world around him, that he could understand animals and that they have always been part of him and he a part of them. There was no separation. Since he was little, for as long as he could remember, it was in him. She remained silent as he talked, listening intently to his every word, his uncanny description of animals, his knowledge of plants and insects. In his voice she heard an enigmatic wisdom. Then he explained to her what she just experienced, the change in the lake. He told her it was hard to explain, but memories that were in him had begun to emerge. It did not make any sense to her, none of it. What she did know was that she had crossed a divide.

The following day when they had periods of time alone in the field, small birds landed on his hands, rodents scurried to his feet and let him pick them up, a ground hog, a porcupine, a family of skunk, all mysteriously appeared from out of nowhere. Each time it left her spellbound as she watched the exchange. She also felt her spirits soaring, her heart filled with exhilaration and joy. She did not want camp to end. All she wanted was more time with him, to know and to understand his world, this world.

After the end of the summer trip with her family, a long, painful two weeks of disconnection from Malach, she could not wait to start school. Then she learned that they were assigned to different teams and rarely saw each other and had no common classes together. In between classes when they had only minutes to go to their lockers and then on to the next class, she rarely saw him. She tried unsuccessfully to find ways to talk to him and was becoming more desperate. She did not want to make Malach feel uncomfortable, uncertain how he would respond. The notion of asking a boy to meet with her would have been out of the question before all of this, entirely unfathomable. She was not like Julie, who was bold when it came to talking to boys. With the start of the third week of school, Ginny decided that she would no longer wait. She chased him down in the hallway, knowing that she would be late for her next class.

"I have to talk to you," she said. "Can we meet after school today in the library?"

Malach nodded and smiled.

5

Malach entered the library with his backpack slung over one shoulder. Ginny waved to signal him that she was there and exhaled a sigh of relief. Though he seemed eager to meet, she still had a knot in her stomach, worried that he might change his mind. Malach walked to the back of the library where she was sitting. He took the seat across the table from her and dropped his bag on the empty chair next to him. It was quiet with only a few scattered students at tables on the other side of the room. She felt herself begin to relax, remembering the feelings that she had for him from the summer.

"How are you?" Malach asked.

"Fine. I'm glad you're here," Ginny said.

"Me, too. This was a good idea," Malach said before she could deliver an explanation for why she wanted to see him. "How's school going for you?"

"Besides the classes being ridiculously overcrowded with the teacher lay-offs, okay," Ginny said. "So much for education priorities for the future generation of our country. The youth of America can make due with less. What about you? Are your classes okay?"

"I guess so," Malach said.

"Do you see any of your friends from last year?" Ginny asked.

"Some of them," Malach said. "One kid who goes to our church. I've known him since we were little. We have a couple of classes together. I'll introduce you sometime. He's a good kid, very quiet and keeps to himself. He's smart and if you get to know him funny, too. You'd like him."

"Sure, I'd be happy to meet him."

"What about you, are your friends in your classes?" Malach asked.

"I don't get to see Julie except at lunch, but I see Angie. We have three classes together. We all see each other when we can. I'm sure it will work out. It's not school that's the problem, though I feel impatient being here all day. My mind is somewhere else."

"I know what you mean," Malach said. "By last period I can't wait to get out of here."

"I hope coming here was alright," Ginny said.

"No, seeing you isn't what I meant. I'm relieved to talk to you."

Ginny felt better when he said that. Malach had such an easy and unselfconscious way about him, but she had so many confusing feelings, so much she needed to say that she didn't know where to begin. She could feel the adrenalin pumping through her veins just thinking about it.

"I was hoping we could've talked sooner," Malach said. "I left you hanging at the end of the summer."

"You can say that again," Ginny said with a huge sigh. "You have no idea what it's been like. I was launched into space and came crashing back to Earth with no parachute, and then no one to talk to about it. It's been a crazy mental seesaw, one minute up and the next minute down. All these thoughts have been racing around inside me. I don't know if you ever experienced anything like that yourself. Well, obviously not. It's me, not you, who's going through this. I feel like I was in another world."

"No, just this world," said Malach. "A changing, unpredictable one, and getting more so all the time. It's what we're doing to it, and there may be no turning back. I can't get away from it either. It's on my mind all the time."

She was taken aback by Malach's remark, a bit confused. Since camp, she felt he was some kind of force of nature and never sensed anything bothered him.

"I'll help, if I can," she said. "I'm not sure how, but I'll try. I'm still trying to figure all of this out."

"I wanted you to know," Malach said. "I probably should have explained or prepared you. Sorry about that."

"No, no, there's no need to apologize," Ginny said. "I don't want anything to have been different. I'm just trying to make sense of it, that's all." Malach nodded, acknowledging his understanding of what she was experiencing. "Do other people know?"

"Barely anyone. My mom, and Sky, and a man from my church, Roger."

Ginny registered the name, remembering that her mother included him in the story about when she was little. She could not recall who he was, but he had been present, and must have seen what she had.

"My mom has always known," Malach continued. "She was right there from the time I was little. Constantly worried and stressed out. I don't like to be a burden to her. I know it scares her. She's so afraid something bad is going to happen to me. She's a wreck sometimes. Pumps caffeine into herself all day."

"What does your dad think?"

"He didn't know for a long time, but does now. We haven't talked about it yet. It's complicated. He also doesn't know that I know that he's not my real father. Probably best to not say anything about that."

"About that!" Ginny blurted out. "I don't mean to be insensitive but that's not the confusing or unusual part of this story."

Malach leaned back in his seat. A grin spread across his face and then laughed. She liked when he laughed. It made things feel normal.

Ginny asked. "Did your mom tell you to keep it a secret, about your dad?"

"No one told me, it's just something that I've known."

"Oh, another one of those things," Ginny said. Malach laughed again. She felt she could be candid and felt the same familiar comfort with him that she experienced this summer. "What about Sky? How long has she known?"

"A long time," Malach said. "I met her when she was hiking in the woods near my house when I was little. I could tell there was something in her that would understand. Same with Roger. I knew that when I met him. You're the only other person."

"Why me?" Ginny asked.

Malach paused and looked at her thoughtfully. "You're like that too, but more. And I think that you already knew. Do you remember, when we were little?"

"You mean the bobcat? I'd forgotten about it for a long time, but it all came back this summer. I remember it like it just happened."

"When we met again this summer," Malach said, "I knew that you'd understand."

Ginny felt enormous relief being able to have this conversation. On the one hand he was regular and easy to talk to, yet so much else about him was disorienting. It was as if his knowledge of the world separated him from everyone else. He knew what no one understood anymore. She envied that and felt a longing desire to know it, too.

They heard a commotion outside the library and looked up through the large wall of windows to the hallway. A tall boy was pushing and taunting another kid. To his side were his two friends, the shorter one stocky and restless, the other wiry and slouched. Ginny could see the scene register in Malach's face.

"That's Evan, my friend from church." He leapt from his seat and raced out into the hallway. Ginny followed. Malach shouted to the boy to stop. He and his two friends turned and laughed. Ginny could see in Evan's face the wrenching humiliation he experienced, his book bag emptied onto the floor, his hair messed up, and his shirt pulled and twisted. He was awkward and nervous as he picked up his eyeglasses that had been knocked to the floor in the scuffle.

"The hero to the rescue," the tall boy said, mocking Malach.

"Quit it, Brett," Ginny yelled. She had despised him from their elementary school days. She was not surprised to see that he was at it again.

"Sure, sure," Brett said with a smug look on his face. "Just fooling around." He half pretended to help Evan with his things and then bumped him with his shoulder knocking him against the wall. "I think we're okay now, aren't we, Evan? Just a misunderstanding. I hope you didn't wet your pants."

Ginny watched as Malach walked up to Brett and without hesitation shoved him so forcefully that he sent Brett flying back, feet leaving the floor, landing on his ass. Brett looked up startled, his eyes flashing contempt. "You messed with the wrong dude." He bounced up and charged Malach, who deflected him and sent him flailing, his face hitting the tile hard on the way down as he slid on his belly across the polished floor. His two friends passively watched without saying a word or coming to Brett's aid. As Brett scrambled to his feet, shaken, he raised his fists and slowly circled as he approached Malach. Malach did not flinch, his eyes locked on Brett. Brett abruptly lunged and took a swing directed at Malach's face. Malach pulled his head back as the force of the punch met air and left Brett off balance, his body now twisted to the side allowing Malach to step in and throw him to the floor for a third time, more forcefully than the last. Brett held his shoulder, his face red with rage, his eyes wide and wild, but now hesitating and looking for an escape.

The shouts and noise from the skirmish in the hallway created a small crowd. Some hoots and jeers came from the mix of boys who gathered for the fight, a couple of girls stood back. Within moments three teachers hurried out of the teachers' lounge just down the hall and provided the exit for Brett as they came pushing through the onlookers. One grabbed Brett by his arm, another Malach. Brett did not resist, was quick to blame Malach who was calm but unrepentant. Ginny helped Evan pick up his things and told him she was a friend of Malach's. He thanked her in a barely audible mutter of politeness, but only wanted to flee the glare of the crowd. The third teacher gently asked Evan to come to the office and escorted him quickly away from the scene. Ginny followed behind, wanting to be certain to provide her account of what she had witnessed. Her heart was pounding in her chest, shaken by the entire affair, but she felt a smug satisfaction that Brett finally got what he had coming to him. What surprised her, though, was Malach's reaction. There was something fiery in him that she had not seen before.

Judith tried to calm herself when she received the call from the school to pick up her son. After hearing that he was in a fight she was confused but relieved to hear that he was not hurt. That was not Malach. She left the house in a hurry and got in the car to head to the school. Tri-County Junior High was more than a half hour from the house. Judith had obsessed about Malach entering this large community of students. Endless worries filtered through her mind in these first weeks of school, but the prospect of Malach being in a fight had not been one of them. The school was an old brick two-story structure. It was quiet inside this late time of the day. The aging building was clean, with highly polished floors and recently painted green walls. She walked briskly along the locker-lined hallways to the main office, her heart beating faster with the anticipation of what she might find.

Malach sat in the anteroom to Principal Moody's office, Brett across from him, and Martha Olson, the Principal's administrative assistant, at the reception desk. Malach looked up when his mother arrived. Brett stared silently at the both of them.

"Mrs. Walker, thank you for coming. Mr. Moody wishes to speak to you before you take your son."

"Of course," Judith said before turning back toward Malach. "Are you alright?" He nodded affirmatively. "Is this the youngster who you had a fight with?"

"Yes," Malach answered.

"What's your name?" she asked the boy.

"Brett."

Judith could see the angry glare flashed at her son. She noticed the ice pack he held to his cheek and saw the swelling underneath when he adjusted it on the bruised side of his face. She looked to Malach, worried and perplexed.

The Principal's door opened before she had an opportunity to talk to her son. When Evan Doran and his parents, Caroline and Arthur, came out of Mr. Moody's office, the whole affair grew stranger. Judith exchanged greetings with the family she had known for many years. She could see in Evan's face that he was pained by what had happened and that his parents looked worried. His dad put his arm around Evan's shoulder and led him out of the office. Caroline told Judith she would speak to her soon. Judith only prayed that Malach was not responsible for any of it. She met alone with the Principal leaving Malach and the other boy in the outer office with Mrs. Olson. Principal Moody, with his carefully combed brown hair, tweed jacket and bowtie, carried himself with the presence of a concerned but no-nonsense school headmaster. He explained what he'd learned about the incident from Brett and Evan, as well as her son. He told her that some of the other kids present had been spoken to in order to corroborate the story.

The Principal described to Judith how the events had unfolded, Malach coming to the aid of a friend, that he showed courage and decency. Nevertheless, the school had a no-fighting policy that was strictly enforced, no exceptions, and Malach would be subject to a two-day suspension for a first offense. He hoped that it would be a valuable learning experience for Malach and that all involved would see the need to develop more effective ways to resolve conflict. He also believed that this would have no bearing on her son's ability to have a successful year.

After her brief meeting with Mr. Moody, Judith prepared to take Malach home. Having learned that he was helping Evan, whom Judith knew was a vulnerable boy, left her with a swell of pride in his actions. Mark would likely put a Christian, "turn-the-other-cheek" slant on the whole thing, but that did not worry her. She knew her husband was still mystified by her disclosures about Malach weeks ago and this would be easier to wrap his head around, maybe even something seen as normal. They had spoken several times about Malach, but Mark had yet to approach him, though she knew it was coming.

On the way out of the building, Ginny saw Malach and quickly came over to check on him. She was waiting for her mother to pick her up as she had missed the late bus. Ginny was furious to learn that he received a suspension, but Malach reassured her that he was fine. She didn't want this to be the way their meeting would end. She felt so angry with Brett. He was always so mean, never kind to anyone. Even when they were little, he pushed kids, deliberately tripped them, or ridiculed weak kids mercilessly. She still remembered him getting in trouble for making a small fire on the edge of the playground, and how upset she had been in the spring of third grade when Brett had thrown rocks at a nest of robins.

Judith had phoned Sky on the way to pick up Malach, as the Conservation Center was not far from the school. Sky had insisted on meeting her when she heard the shakiness in Judith's voice. When Sky arrived, Judith asked Malach to wait while she crossed the parking lot to talk to her. Almost simultaneously Virginia drove into the parking area to gather up her daughter. Sky now stood with her oldest and her newest friend. The three women remained in the parking lot and spoke for some time while Malach and Ginny sat on the school steps by themselves.

"Virginia, it's good to see you." Judith said. "I hope you and your family are well. We miss you at the church. It's been so many years."

"It's a mystery where the time goes. Is your son okay? Ginny called me and explained what happened."

"Thank you for asking. He's fine. Was Ginny present also?"

"Yes, she told me she saw the entire thing," Virginia said. Her words held an uneasy resonance for Judith.

"I must say it was a surprise to see her," Judith said. "I didn't realize that they would be in school together this year."

"They had a chance to reconnect this summer," Sky chimed in. "It was a pleasure to have them both at the camp."

"Oh, I didn't know Malach was there," Virginia said.

"Nor did I know about Ginny," Judith added.

The three women glanced together at the two budding adolescents sitting beside each other, deep in conversation. Judith looked quickly to Sky, unclear why she had not told her about Ginny.

"They seem to have gotten reacquainted," Virginia said.

"Yes, yes indeed," Judith added.

Virginia turned to Sky and Judith. "Maybe we could all get together for lunch sometime. I would love having a chance to catch up."

Sky nodded and Judith agreed.

"I should probably get Malach home. It's been a hard day," Judith said. She left Sky with Virginia and called to Malach. He exchanged goodbyes with Ginny and joined his mother.

Ginny picked up her bag and headed to her car while her mother continued to talk with Sky. She saw Brett at the other side of the parking lot with his father and observed a tense exchange between them, his father shaking a fist, Brett stoic and silent. Brett turned and saw Ginny. He glared at her, his eyes angry and cold. His father said something to him before Brett got in the car and slammed the door. They quickly drove off.

"You and Judith have become close friends," Virginia said. "She's a lovely woman. It would be nice for us all to meet but could we get together, just the two of us? It's been too long, Skylar. I mean it. We said we'd do it before, but it never worked out." Sky could see the sincerity in Virginia's plea, a desire to not let their interrupted relationship die. Sky thought about her conversation with Malach this past summer and smiled to herself about his wisdom about friendships.

"That would be nice," Sky said with a mix of apprehension and gratitude that Virginia was reaching out again. She recognized that she had only herself to blame for the evasiveness. It seemed silly now with so many years having passed.

When they met for coffee later in the week, their cars pulled up within moments of each other, like at the school last week and like so much of what they had done in the past, somehow always being synchronized with each other. Sky was initially apprehensive with thoughts of revisiting their past lives and was pleased that Virginia never raised the subject. Sky was surprised at how effortless it was to spend time with her old friend, the rhythm and flow of their conversation familiar. Virginia looked good, she thought. Her hair was still full and lustrous, her skin flawless, her fashion sense smart and elegant.

Sky found that she genuinely enjoyed learning about Virginia's life. Virginia did not talk to her with any reserve or filters. She shared stories of her three girls, her husband, Oliver, and her job at the local newspaper, doing layout and design. She was overextended with volunteer work at the elementary school for her two younger girls, coaching soccer, doing committee work at their church, while determined to preserve time for family dinners, and carving out time for yoga classes and planned date nights with her husband. In some respects, Virginia had not changed – organized, exacting, always doing too much and doing it all well.

Virginia was unceremoniously curious about Sky's work, interests, and social life. She knew Sky had a career, but was single and alone. She did not withhold the joys of her life out of fear that Sky might find it difficult to hear. That was not how they were as kids and she was not going to do that now.

"Ginny loved camp this summer," Virginia said. "She's all science, all the time. The books she brings home from the library surprise me – earth science, genetics, physics, marine biology, you name it. She takes it all in. She has a steel trap for a memory. I tried to get her to go to a horseback riding camp this summer, but she had no interest. I had long given up on team sports. She was the one who found the information about your summer program. I was delighted when I discovered that you were directing it."

"She was a pleasure to have," Sky said. "Very inquisitive and outspoken, doesn't hesitate to make her opinions known. Takes after her mom."

"Thank you. But she's well beyond me," said Virginia.

"I'm certain she'll be doing great things one day," said Sky. "You must be very proud of her."

"Very much so. Oliver and I both." Virginia said. "I'm so happy she got to know you. There's something else I'm curious about. Tell me about the boy. Malach."

"I think they hit it off," Sky said. "They worked together on field projects. I know that they were both surprised to see each other again."

"I had not heard a peep about him from Ginny until she called last week after the incident at school. That's unusual. She talks about everything. I always get an earful. I didn't think boys were on her radar yet, but she's at that age. It just rattles my mind to think about that. What's he like?"

"He has a big heart. A very kind boy," Sky said.

"You've known him for years. What else?"

"He's different, maybe like Ginny in that way. Smart, very… intuitive."

"And?" Virginia prompted and nudged.

"He's helped me out on projects at the Center over the years, a special kid. Understands things… in a big picture way. I have known him and Judith for many years now. They are like family to me. Honestly, I adore him."

"When I asked Ginny about him," Virginia said, "she told me the whole story about the fight, but she was evasive about him. She was keeping something from me."

"They're only twelve," Sky said.

"I know, but I have this sixth sense about this," Virginia said. "Oh, you're probably right, enough with this. You know how I can be. What about you, Skylar?"

"There's not much to know."

"You know what I mean. Is there someone in your life? Someone special."

"No, not currently," Sky said. "There was someone in college. It was serious, but it didn't work out."

"So…what happened?" Virginia asked, as she was not satisfied with the response.

"Alex Love. How's that for a name," Sky started. "He was a grad student and led the labs for my undergraduate Intro course in Environmental Science." Sky could see in Virginia's eyes that she was waiting, and though hesitant, she continued. "He was handsome. I'm embarrassed to say but I was unable to take my eyes off him. I flirted shamelessly with him. I didn't even know that I was capable of that." Sky remembered how she had been enamored with everything about him, though she feared he would not find her attractive, her nose too long, her hair too frizzy, her body not curvy enough.

"We started to talk after classes and then met regularly at a nearby café. He was smart, passionate about his work. I listened to his determination to prevent what he saw as a coming environmental catastrophe. The world as we know it is changing, he would tell me, and he was determined to do something about it."

"Did you love him?" Virginia asked.

"More than I thought possible. I was so attracted to everything about him, from his looks, his big personality, to how smart he was. I knew he would make a difference in the world, and I wanted to be part of that, too, to have a purpose. By the time the term was over we were sleeping together. He had a tiny apartment near campus and I more or less moved in with him, my dorm room mostly a place to store my belongings.

"For three years I believed that he was the one. I was certain he felt the same about me. He finished his program a year ahead of me and took a job during my senior year at Berkeley. I missed him so much. But soon, the calls came less frequently. The excuses were more common. He called me one night and told me that he met someone else. Just like that, it was over. He dumped me as though I never existed."

"I'm so sorry," said Virginia.

"It stung me in the same way my mother's death did," Sky said. "I retreated into my cocoon, put up the walls, moved back here, and just threw myself into my work." As much as Alex had been creeping back in her thoughts and dreams, she felt relieved to get it out and not have to dither around the edges with this. "Judith and Malach helped me find a way back into life again. Seeing you today, that helps, too."

"I'm always here, Skylar. I want to have you back in my life, too. We have too much history to let our friendship die."

"Thank you, and thank you for listening," Sky said.

Virginia reached out and took Sky's hand. "Life goes on," Virginia said, "and maybe I can help with that. There's someone I want you to meet."

There was no asking if she was interested, she just came out with it like she did when they were kids. "And who might that be?" Sky asked with a grin spreading across her face, realizing with the exception of a few bad dates, she had not been involved with anyone for many years.

"Calvin Trinker. Cal's the owner and editor of the paper where I work."

"Fixing me up with the boss." Sky laughed.

"He divorced last year. He and the ex-wife never had kids, she moved to Philadelphia, so it's not complicated. I never liked her. He could have done better. He's an impressive person, Skylar. He built our backwater of a newspaper into a real news outlet. More importantly, he's a terrific guy. I think the two of you would like each other."

Sky was momentarily speechless. She had not anticipated a blind date being arranged when she came here today. A flash of apprehension washed through her and she took a deep breath.

"There are things you can tell about people," Virginia continued, "and I see it in both of you. You both love what you do, and are genuine and real. And he's handsome. How can you go wrong?"

"How do you know he wants to go out with me?" Sky asked.

"I already told him about you. You know I get ahead of myself."

"Okay," Sky said.

"Okay? Is that okay, you got ahead of yourself, or okay, I'll meet him?" Virginia asked.

"I'll meet him," Sky said, surprised by the words slipping out of her mouth, but she felt something hopeful about it.

6

Roger sat with Malach during the church service. The Sunday ritual of climbing the stairs to the bell tower had been less consistent and predictable in the past year. Many Sundays Roger watched Malach scramble up the steps alone to ring out the bell for the start of the service. His health had not been good, and it was Judith who made sure he did not neglect himself. Having grown closer over the years, bonded by the shared knowledge of her son, Judith had come to feel like a daughter, doting and attentive. She took him to doctor's visits, asked the questions he never did, demanded all necessary tests, made sure nothing was left unattended, and insisted on the second medicine for treating his angina that was recently added to his cabinet of pharmaceuticals.

During the summer, Roger's spirits were also lifted by regular visits from Malach. He liked that Malach asked if he could help out once school was out. His mother thought it a splendid idea and would drop him off a few times a week. Not wanting to be a burden, Roger hesitated, but Malach was quick to reassure him that it was something he wanted to do and it would not interfere with his responsibilities at home, including his father's instructions for him to paint the garage. Judith concurred and provided careful directions for her son, with attention to helping in the house, doing any heavy lifting, and cleaning up around the property. The preacher was all for it as well. He took pride in seeing his son extending himself for others, especially a member of the congregation.

Yet when Malach came out for his visits, usually in the afternoon, Roger only permitted him to devote a little time to these chores before whisking him away to walk the low-lying areas on the property, ones that were mostly flat with a few gentle slopes. The new medicine was starting to help, but he had been weak for so long that it took time to rebuild his stamina. Malach knew when Roger needed to rest or waited for him to pop a nitro pill before they continued. When he took a nap later in the day, Roger would send Malach out to explore the mountain, as he would not hear of him doing chores while he slept. He knew the boy loved this new terrain and it was so rewarding to hear about his discoveries of the land that he had known so intimately for many decades. It gave him a sense of renewal, a belief in his own legacy being carried forward.

So much had changed in the boy's stories. He had grown up and long advanced beyond characterizing his adventures with animals. He would watch Malach move up the mountain when he sent him off before returning to the house in the afternoon when his own energy waned. Malach moved swiftly and agilely over the rough terrain. He glided up the steep elevations of the slopes, over the ruggedness of rocks and low brush, as though he floated on air. There was no pausing and plotting a path, no sizing up ways to bypass obstacles. It all happened intuitively and simultaneously with his movement. He was a creature of the wilderness. Roger could only compare it to the single occasion, when as a young man, twenty-six years old, on his birthday, he had sighted a mountain lion on his land.

It was a magnificent creature, dignified and self-possessed, its strength and power visceral and raw. It walked along the ridge overlooking the valley, above it a stubbornly exposed rocky face of the mountain located on the far edge of his property. Roger had gone out that day with his backpack and gear and plans for a few nights camping. He sighted the lion and silently watched from a cropping of low trees. It was believed that mountain lions no longer inhabited the region. To see it filled him with awe, and hope in the mountain regaining some of what had been lost. It felt as though the cat had come to take in the view, looking out across the valley, and then, when it was content, it turned and loped up the long, steep open expanse of the rocky face before disappearing from view. The speed and effortlessness of the boy's ascent reminded him of that rare and treasured sighting.

When Malach would return an hour or two later and Roger listened to him describe the places he'd been, it was difficult to grasp how it was even humanly possible to cover that much territory in so little time. It was something that even as a healthy and fit young man, he would never have been able to do.

Sitting next to Malach this Sunday morning in church filled Roger with satisfaction. The boy no longer regularly sat at his mother's side each week, or with the Jamisons. Over the past couple years Malach would join friends, but not infrequently took leave of them to sit with him. He had done so today after talking for a long time with one of those friends, the Doran boy who then took his place with his family. Roger could see in Malach's face that he was troubled by something and asked him about it.

"It's Evan," Malach said. "He had a bad week at school." Roger glanced over and saw Malach's friend across the sanctuary. "Some kids were picking on him, have been since the start of school. The other day I saw them bullying him, pushing him around, roughing him up, like it was a game."

"Damned awful what some boys will do," Roger said. "Never liked to see that. Your friend, he looks a mite frail and an easy one to go after. Those boys who were picking on him have about as much backbone and decency as a pack of hyenas trying to snatch a young stray from the herd."

"Evan's not a fighter. It's not his nature," Malach said. "There's one of them who's the leader of that pack. A kid named Brett. I know he's not going to let this go. He has to prove something and I'm sure he'll want to get even. He's that way."

"Those types always are. Don't ever turn your back to him."

"I won't, but I'm more worried about Evan. He doesn't have anyone else to look out for him."

"Maybe so, but it's important that you watch yourself, too."

"We already had a fight. He needed to know that Evan had someone on his side. I don't like anything about that kid. Evan already feels like he doesn't fit in at school and this kid taunts him, puts him down, does it so everyone sees, just to get a laugh."

"Sadistic little bastard," Roger muttered.

"I got suspended for two days. He had a bad bruise on his face. Honestly, I didn't care. It wasn't half as painful as what he put Evan through."

"Sometimes, it's what we have to do and we just have to take our lumps for it. You've done right by your friend."

Roger imagined Malach fighting this youngster. It was not something that he had considered before. Despite his power, his gifts, or whatever it was he possessed, he never had an image of Malach being aggressive. It was strangely incongruous with all the ideas he held about Malach, yet it should have been as obvious as the nose on his face. Why wouldn't he strike with the forces that lie within him if necessary? Roger couldn't get that thought out of his head. He was telling the boy to be careful, but this is the boy he had seen running with all kinds of wild animals, even a bear cub this summer, the mother, a ferocious black bear following behind. He had grown so accustomed to this that he had lost all sense of the danger these creatures posed. How could another twelve-year-old boy be a threat to him?

With the service soon to begin, Judith came down the aisle and nudged the two of them over. Roger had begun to feel like they were family and it warmed his heart to be sitting with both of them today.

"I saw Evan's mother," she said to Malach. "She thanked me for what you did. Evan told her you had his back." Judith turned to explain the situation to Roger, but Malach told her he had just filled him in. "She felt badly that you received a suspension and was going to talk to the Principal about it."

"I told her not to," Malach said. "It's not important."

"Evan said you threw Brett across the hall like he was an old sack of potatoes. He couldn't believe that you did that for him."

Roger listened carefully, imagining the boy heaving Brett with abandon, fascinated by that description, the power of it. Of course, of course, he thought.

Mark stood before the congregation, as everyone settled and silence filled the church. The service began and after prayers and some song, he took to the pulpit again for his weekly sermon. Judith imagined a lesson for Malach and his friend, but Mark spoke of something entirely unrelated. She and Malach along with Mark took time to linger with the congregants after the service, shaking every hand and offering well wishes to all. After everyone left, Mark told Judith that he wanted to spend some time at the church with Malach. She understood that they needed to talk and took the car to run errands. She turned back before driving away to see them standing together in front of the church.

Mark put his arm around Malach's shoulder and they reentered the building. The light filtered in through the windows giving the room a soft glow. It was still and serene. They walked to the front and Mark took a seat in the first pew.

"When I was in the garage this morning," Mark started, "before we left the house, I was looking for a screwdriver to tighten the hinges on the back door. I think for the first time since we moved in, everything was so organized, and the paint job made it look respectable. You did a fine job."

"Thanks," Malach said.

"I was also proud of how you extended yourself to Roger this summer. It made a big difference for him. He's very fond of you. The man has endured a great deal. It's a gesture of true compassion what you have done."

Malach nodded and listened. Mark looked about the chapel pausing in thought.

"We have created a life here for us. I have grown very fond of this place, the people in the community, the members of our congregation. I know this is the only home you have known, but do you like it here?"

"Why wouldn't I?" Malach said.

"I didn't mean to suggest that you didn't, but do you wonder about other places, imagine what it might be like."

"I think about it all the time," Malach said.

"You do? Any place special?"

"Not one place, every place."

Mark nodded quizzically and continued. "When I was your age," he said, "I imagined so many places I wanted to see, that I wanted to visit. I grew up in the church like you. I didn't always like it. It was too restrictive, too many rules, and I was going to get away from all of that."

"What made you change your mind?" Malach asked.

"I'm not sure I could say there was one thing, or even a moment of revelation. It was an unyielding attachment to my family and my community that I could not shake. It was not by any means perfect, but it was home. There was so much out in the world that called to me, but the hold of my family, my upbringing, the good works of the church made me look at things differently. I think I was able to shed the 'me' and began to think of the 'us.' That proved to be more powerful. In the long run, that was my calling for a meaningful life. I felt it in my heart. It was hard to leave home and come here with your mother, leaving all that behind. I still feel the pull sometimes to go back to where I was raised, wondering if being closer to all of our family would be best. But we have become a part of this community. Over these years I believe we have found that same thing right here.

We do not have to search for it, it's always right before us if we open our eyes and open our hearts."

Mark paused and looked at his son. Malach nodded as he often did when listening, letting his father know he heard what was said. His son was an enigma to him. He was a strong young man, carried himself with confidence, was smart and astute, and yet there was something worldly about him that was out of step with his small-town upbringing. It was funny, as he spoke to Malach about their lives, there was greater clarity in his own mind about what made it special here. He admired Malach even though he felt apart from him. It was sobering to think of the years flying by. Sitting alone with his son, he felt he had so little to do with whom he had become. His mother had done right by him and that was good. Mark felt uncertainty and sadness in his heart.

And what to make of what Judith told him about Malach, if it was, in fact, so. He was incredulous listening to her stories. What did they mean? Had he been completely blind to the child? He prayed more than usual in the past year. So many painful reminders about his own family, and the pull from back home. His father nudging him whenever they spoke, doing what he always would do, carefully laying the groundwork for what he would eventually expect, or perhaps require. He thought of what Judith wanted and even Malach. They were happy here. He had built the congregation from barely sixty families to almost two hundred. The church was full on Sundays. Why not grow old here? He and Judith were better, their talk cathartic and healing, or at least the start of change.

"Do you think about what you want to do when you grow up?" Mark asked.

Malach did not answer. Mark realized that he was jumping ahead and that it was important to get to the purpose of his talk.

"It's hard to know what the future will bring," Mark said. "But it's the present I want to know about. Your mother told me some things about you that I didn't know what to make of."

"I know," Malach said.

"She told you that we spoke of this?"

"No."

Mark ignored the remark and continued. "What can you tell me? Your mother says you have been blessed with a special bond with animals. I don't know what that means exactly."

Malach paused before answering. "It only means that I see, and hear, and understand the world around me."

"She tells me it is more than that. To be able to communicate with animals is an unusual ability." Mark raised an eyebrow and tried to sound genuinely curious.

"It's something we can all learn to be better at," Malach said.

"I am sure that's true," said Mark. "But how do you do that? Do you know?" The skepticism in Mark's voice was apparent; he had found it very difficult to believe what Judith had told him.

"That's hard to explain, but it's in all of us." Malach looked at his father then stood up and stepped into the center aisle of the church. His father leaned and looked down the aisle where Malach's attention was directed. Glancing up at his son he saw a smile on his face and then followed his gaze back down the aisle of the church. Malach knelt and waited as they both watched a tiny field mouse scurry toward him. He reached down as he gathered the small creature into his cupped hand. Mark startled and sat upright. Malach held his hand open but kept the mouse close to him.

"My, oh, my," Mark said with astonishment. "The Lord works in mysterious ways. How did you do that?"

"She's been in the building for a few weeks. The weather is getting colder at night. She found a place to spend the winter."

"Cute little thing. Have you taken her as a pet?" Mark said as he reached out to touch it. Malach gently drew his hand back.

"She's not a pet. She could bite."

"Oh," Mark said as his hand recoiled. "Best to be careful. I knew a boy when I was young who had a pet crow, he nursed it when he found it downed from the nest. The bird became very attached. Smart animal. He also had a knack for finding snakes, and he kept turtles, raised his own chickens, lots of cats and dogs. He fed wild birds. It was a veritable Noah's Ark at his home. Maybe you'd like a pet."

"No, thank you," Malach replied. "There are animals enough all around. We just have to respect and protect them. They're very precious."

"I agree. We do need to be good keepers of God's creatures."

"We're not doing a very good job of it," Malach said as he looked down at the small mouse in his hand.

"I wouldn't say that. I think things are quite fine."

Malach looked up at his father and after a long pause responded, "It's far more grim than you know."

"Nonsense," Mark said, waving his hand dismissively. "Don't believe all that talk you hear about doom and gloom. The truth is that there's nothing fundamentally wrong. It will get worked out, it always does." Mark began to feel a little restless and began to get up. "Come, let's see where your mother might be."

"This won't get better," Malach said firmly. "It's time for everyone to face that. You need to know that, too."

Mark looked at Malach and sat back down. "You don't need to worry about it," he said. "The Lord didn't create the world to fail."

"We don't know that," said Malach. "If people don't recognize what's happening right before them, it won't survive as we know it. The natural world doesn't work by our rules."

"No, it doesn't," Mark said impatiently, feeling Malach was overstepping his bounds with him. "It works through God's will and that's where I place my faith."

"Then your faith is misplaced," Malach said, challenging his father.

"I've not had anyone question my faith before," Mark said raising his eyebrows. He was startled by the boldness of Malach's remark and felt himself getting heated but tried to remain calm.

"If you want to talk to me about animals," said Malach, "if you want to know what this is about, then you need to open your mind to what's happening."

Mark looked disapprovingly into Malach's eyes, but his son did not blink. Mark thought of the response he would have received from his father if he had spoken to him in that tone – a sharp smack to the back of the head.

"Maybe there are some things we could be more conscientious about, but the world will be fine." Mark's words were slow and deliberate.

"We can't ignore the truth," Malach continued. "As much as we don't want to face it, we have no choice. All of life is beginning to die and it's our fault, what people are doing to the earth. What are we left with if we don't do something?"

"Yes, we must always speak the truth. God is truth," Mark said. He felt on the defensive and reduced to clumsy aphorisms. This conversation was harder for him than he had expected. He kept thinking of all Judith had shared recently. His mind kept shifting to the fact that Malach was not his biological child. It was one thing when he suspected it over the years, but after the tests he went through and then Judith's acknowledgement of this secret, it became even more painful. While he oddly had felt closer to his wife since then, he felt more unsure and self-doubting in his relationship with Malach.

"Truth needs to be spoken in families, too," Malach said, looking at Mark and waiting for a response.

Mark remained silent trying to balance his emotions, recognizing how little truth had been spoken in their home. Malach's words only confirmed the suspicion that his son knew the truth about this as well. He felt a momentary impulse to say something but was unable to find the right words. He then stood, took a deep breath and said, "Yes, but enough of this for now. Your mother is probably waiting for us outside."

Malach walked with his father back down the aisle toward the front of the church. Before they exited to the outdoors, Malach knelt in the corner of the entry and released the mouse that he still had in his hands.

"Are you leaving her inside?" Mark asked, to which Malach did not respond. Mark watched the mouse slip through a tiny opening in the woodwork into the wall.

"A church mouse," Mark said. "Everyone is welcome in the House of God." He thought about what just had transpired. Mark felt entirely unprepared for the turn in their exchange, feeling his son was lecturing him, and doing it in church. The whole matter shamed him.

Judith returned shortly after they stepped outdoors. They all drove home together, barely a word passing between them. Arriving at the house, Judith had Malach grab the two bags of groceries to take inside. She sat in the car with Mark.

"It's all a little confusing," Mark said and explained what happened with the mouse, but said nothing of Malach's confrontation with him.

"He gave you a glimpse," said Judith.

"If he can do what you say, he possesses a special gift." Mark paused, still distracted by what had just happened, still trying to find his words. He was angry with Malach's disrespect but even more so with himself, feeling inept as a parent. Also, if Malach had some special powers, he seemed reluctant to share them. Mark again felt slighted, as though his son did not see him as worthy of that respect, either. "Maybe the animals and what he can do are part of God's plan for us here," Mark wondered aloud, feeling the need to say something.

"Mark, please listen to me," Judith said slowly and firmly. "He's not going to be a church sideshow attraction. He's not a snake handler, not someone who speaks in tongues. He's our son and he's not here to help you make your mark in your ministry. Do you understand that? Do you?"

Mark was startled by her demand, not intending to suggest what

Judith had interpreted to his comment. "Of course. I'm sorry." He realized that he needed some time alone.

The following Sunday Judith left the service early with Malach to check on Roger. It was the first time he had ever missed. Malach was silent. She had the same sinking feeling. When they arrived, his truck was parked in the driveway. It was quiet when they entered the house. He did not respond to Judith's call. They found him lifeless in his bed, a serene look on his face. She took his hand which was still warm and realized he had passed only a little while ago. Malach stood at the edge of the bed and looked at his elderly friend. Judith admired their unusual bond and she cried. She could see Malach's pain, and the memory of his first loss flashed through her mind. She could still feel the moment of his anguish holding the small chipmunk that had sputtered its last breath in his small hand. She wrapped her arms around him and held him close.

After the ambulance arrived and the two paramedics removed Roger's body, Judith and Malach stood together outside the house.

"He told me he wanted to be buried here on his mountain," Malach said. "He showed me the spot this summer. He said no one knew that and wanted me to show the funeral people the place."

Judith followed Malach on a trail in the woods to the location he spoke about.

It was a large open field with a fine view of the valley below. There was a grand oak tree that stood alone in the center. Malach pointed to it and they approached it together.

"Right here," Malach said. "Right here."

"Are you sure? Not in the cemetery with his wife and son?"

"I'm certain. This is the spot. This was his favorite place. We came here often this summer. We sat right here on this rock and looked out and talked. This is the place he came to when Edie died and when Lee died. It was where he felt closest to them."

"Then, this is where he will take his final resting place," Judith said.

Judith looked up to a blue sky, felt the warmth of the sun on her face. It was a beautiful day, the final day of summer.

autumn

1

The air was heavy, storm clouds loomed above, threatening all day. Surrounded by early autumn foliage with tinges of ripening red, orange, and yellow hues, Malach and Ginny stood at Roger's grave, their hands clasped, fingers entwined. The wind swept across the field, a few fallen leaves tumbling across the small headstone of Roger Henry Stine. Below his name were the dates of his life, having passed just a week shy of his eighty-third birthday, and the inscription, "Nature's Strength Divine." It was a phrase Roger had used in the weeks before his death that had stuck in Malach's mind. When he shared that with his mother, it felt right to them to have it placed on the stone. Malach recalled Roger's dejected resignation when he spoke of the thoughtlessness and near absence of care he saw all around the world as though the land, the water, the air, did not matter. Roger had often expressed to Malach his belief that the whole earth was in danger, that people had lost their sense of presence in the world. It was pushed out of our very consciousness, replaced by selfishness and endless consumption. Day after day this went on in the name of progress with no respect or concern for the dignity, majesty, power, and beauty of what we had all around us.

Ginny wiped the tears that welled up in her eyes. She and Malach came to mark the fourth anniversary of Roger's death. She knew how much Roger meant to Malach. She leaned closer to him and he wrapped his arm around her shoulder. They looked at each other, the moment communicated and shared. After further reflection, the sadness slipped away for now, as all painful losses do over time. She gave him a kiss and they hugged each other.

"This was Roger's favorite time of year," Malach said. He had reminded her of that many times before, and Ginny knew that Malach was aware he repeated this when talking about Roger, but he always felt the need to say it. "It just lit him up, the chill, the color, the light of the autumn. He always told me that it gave him a sense of satisfaction when the year reached its peak before bedding down for the winter.

"I remember when I was little," Malach continued, "we'd talk about the changes all around – the colors, the smells, even how the sounds traveled differently. When I told him things that I noticed he listened. He wanted to understand what I saw and what I knew. He was the first person whom I felt really could see it."

"I wish I'd the chance to know him," Ginny said.

"You would've liked him, I'm sure of it. He had his own way of looking at things. He also could be the crankiest old guy, and I don't know why, but I liked that about him, too. I think it was because everything about him was so honest. He didn't care what anyone thought. He was a little like you."

"So, is that it? I'm like a cranky old man, that's what you think of me?" Ginny flashed her smile and grabbed Malach around the waist and spun around him and held him tightly from behind.

"No, no, that's not what I meant," he said as he twisted around, held her close and blew on her neck, which he knew tickled her. "Well, maybe just a little," Malach added. They both laughed aloud as she squeezed him. Even on a sad day of remembrance like today, being together with Malach felt right and good and even fun.

It was not long after the summer in camp together that Ginny spoke to Sky about a plan for her and Malach to help with projects at the Conservation Center. It would provide them a place to be together. Sky recognized this and allowed them to assist with data collection in the field, eventually sending them off without her oversight and without mention of doing so to either Judith or Virginia. Sky felt that they were old enough to decide for themselves what they wanted their parents to know or not know.

The Conservation Center was large and vast, and the two of them could comfortably get lost for hours before coming back. Ginny was baffled at first by Malach's spontaneous maneuverings and flawless orientation. She felt safe with him, but wanted to have that same confidence on her own, determined to figure it out for herself. Over time she became scout-like in her expertise. It started with maps and a compass, then land formations, streams, the movement of the sun across the sky, and then an unexplainable intuition that she experienced when Malach would just take her hand and tell her to listen and let herself feel the surroundings. It made no sense when she tried to do it on her own, but with her hand in his, an arcane and enigmatic knowledge flowed from him to her. It did not have words; it made her senses tingle, sounds and light were inexplicably palpable, the air alive and vibrant, smells beckoning. It defied logic and explanation. Doors briefly opened to her by Malach, awakening her to rumblings of the earth, enabling her to perceive and register ephemeral cosmic musings, glimpses of what once must have been visceral connections central to our very nature but lost long ago. These had become her alternate moments of reality. Malach was wholly of that other world, but he was not removed from this one. He inhabited both effortlessly and completely.

Ginny loved that he laughed all the time, found humor in the silliest of things, lifted her up, and filled everything he did with curiosity and fun. He was one of the standout students in all of his classes but never labored over studying or worried about grades. His physical prowess and athleticism were hard to even quantify, but he never had interest in playing a school sport. He lived in the moment, fulfilled and complete, and never followed anyone's rules.

Their relationship had matured over these past years from childhood to teenage friends and then into something different. She remembered it like it was yesterday. It was a cool damp day, almost two years ago, and they were hiking at the Conservation Center. The ground was hard with an early frost, a chill deep in her bones, her body cold. Malach gave her his jacket, wrapped it around her along with his arms and held her close until she stopped shivering. They looked into each other's eyes, their lips drawn to each other. His breath sweet, the texture of his lips soft against her mouth, his hair tangled, his skin warm even in the cool dampness, their bodies aligned and connected. It was their first kiss, and she knew she would never forget that moment. She had grown to love him in a way she did not know was possible, her feelings only becoming stronger over time. That love was entwined with everything they did together, especially in their exploration of the world all around them.

Roger's mountain had now become the place that she and Malach visited and explored. The land untrammeled and mysterious, grand sweeping vistas at the high elevations, streams of water surging through deep carved ravines, thick and impenetrable woods, lonely howls of wind ricocheting through the wilderness. Ginny treasured the forests that covered the region, the mix of deciduous hardwoods, oak, beech, and maple, with some areas dominated by one species more than another.

When Malach had her lie next to him on the forest floor under these trees, her head resting on his chest, she miraculously felt the otherwise imperceptible movement and energy between a mother tree and her saplings, an unspoken communication that put a smile on her face and nourished her own sense of hope that the world was strong and vital. She felt part of the generations of trees, being right there with old statuesque matriarchs, surrounded by their young, saplings many decades old, waiting, waiting, waiting for their time, still being nourished by a network of entangled roots, waiting for the grand dame looming above to succumb to age or to the elements and finally fall. Then the race would begin for those who were fortunate enough to secure a starting place, the handful of trees that established roots and life from the countless acorns shed over the one or two hundred years or more that a mother tree stood. And from them a sapling in waiting would succeed to take her place.

Virginia liked Malach and that made it easier for them to be alone together. She admired his intellect, respected his honesty and kindness, and trusted him. Even after their years of friendship and now as Ginny's boyfriend, Virginia still did not know about Malach's abilities. Ginny felt waves of guilt at the secret she kept from her mother, but believed it was not her secret to tell.

It was ironic that Malach became dependent on her when she learned to drive. She knew that he'd never bother to get his driver's permit, let alone his license. He had no interest, as it just didn't matter to him. It was another one of those things about him.

Driving allowed her much more freedom. Ginny felt liberated with her car and it was Malach's parents, or rather his father, who had trouble with the two of them being alone together. It was not proper in Mark's mind and he was very adamant about it. Malach listened to his father's lectures, but did not hesitate to let his anger flash and then go ahead and do what he wanted. Judith accepted this and even came to his defense, but his father never let it go. It made Ginny uncomfortable when she was around Malach's father, feeling he was judging her or frowning upon her moral character. The darting glances exchanged between Malach's parents never went unnoticed by her. When she picked Malach up on Saturday for the day and Sunday afternoon so as not to interfere with church, or other times after school, she arrived unannounced, as Malach had no interest in having or using a mobile phone. He liked her unexpected arrivals as much as ones they planned. She would try to hurry him along to avoid the discomfort she felt interacting with his father, yet in the past year she finally had accepted it for what it was and no longer obsessed about it.

Angie and Evan were the only others who knew about Malach, and it brought them all closer together as friends. Back when they entered eighth grade, Evan, still shy and awkward, had overheard Angie talking in their art class about a short movie she was making and the problems she was having with the editing software program. On the way out of class he surprisingly approached her and explained that he was familiar with the program and could help. Malach had always said that Evan was a computer genius. Angie discovered that he was the perfect technological collaborator, and there was nothing that she wanted to do that he could not help make happen.

The collaboration eventually grew into a friendship. It was not long after they started to work together, that Angie asked Ginny if she and Evan could tag along at the Conservation Center to make a video. Later that same day they witnessed Malach's encounter with a snowshoe hare as he snatched it up and held it. Its coat already turning winter white, as it was late in the season. They held their breath, busting with excitement, their minds spinning, while recording the entire encounter. For many more months they did not fully grasp the extent of what Malach was able to do and what he knew, but eventually they became part of the circle. Since that time, Angie and Evan had amassed hours and hours of recordings of Malach. They also understood that all of this would need to be safely guarded until… Until what, Angie was not sure, but she knew, like Ginny, and Roger, and Sky, and even Judith, that it was not yet time.

The four of them had started another unexpected project this past summer before the start of senior year. It had begun with a letter a number of months earlier from the Law Offices of Jensen, Simpson, and Lieberman. When Malach arrived home from school, it sat on the kitchen table, his mother hovering anxiously nearby. It was his birthday and the envelope was hand-delivered earlier in the day. He looked at it and then turned it over trying to search for a clue as to its purpose. After grabbing a large wedge of cheese and an apple from the refrigerator, he sat down at the table again, opened it and read the document. In the middle he got up for a glass of water and sat down again to finish it and then sat quietly, lost in thought.

Judith watched and waited for a response. "Is everything okay?" she finally asked, unable to contain herself any longer.

He looked up and handed her the letter. Judith carefully read it through and then reread it. Following a lengthy introduction by Robert Lieberman who sent the letter, he invited Malach, Mark, and her to a meeting at his office to review the estate of Roger Henry Stine. There was no explanation or elaboration, only that all the details would be provided in person. At the end of the week, Malach took the day off from school and he and his parents drove two hours to see Attorney Lieberman. They had not been away from home in months. Malach sat in the back, staring out the window, Judith nervously preoccupied, and Mark business-like in his focus to get them there. All three of them felt the anxious anticipation, and there was little conversation in the car. Once off the main highway they meandered through the side streets of the city until they approached the three-story brick town-house where the law office was located. The tree-lined street had only a few commercial stores, a coffee shop, children's bookstore, and a small gift shop. Walking to the office, Mark took Judith's hand. Malach followed a couple steps behind. They climbed the several steps of the old building and as they entered, admired the interior. There were detailed moldings and elegant wood finishing. William, the young office assistant, warmly received them and then escorted them upstairs to the conference room.

After a few moments Mr. Lieberman entered the room. He was a tall, lean man with a tightly trimmed beard beginning to gray and his salt-and-pepper hair cut closely to his scalp. He wore a dark suit with a crisp gray shirt and narrow dark striped tie. He had a beaming smile when greeting Malach and his parents, taking and holding each of their hands in a heartfelt welcome.

"Malach, Mr. and Mrs. Walker, it's a pleasure to finally meet all of you," Lieberman said. "How was your drive in today? I hope no problems with traffic."

"No, not at all. It was fine," Judith answered. Her nervousness about this meeting was apparent.

"The traffic was light and it was a lovely day for a ride," Mark added, trying to sound in command and assured.

"That's good," Lieberman said as his focus turned to Malach. "And you, Malach, how are you?"

"I'm fine," Malach said.

"Excellent. I've been looking forward to meeting you for some time. But first, I want to wish you a happy birthday. I know you turned sixteen this past week."

"Thank you," Malach said. "How did you know?"

"I'll explain all of that soon enough. So, what grade are you in now?"

"It's my junior year of high school."

Lieberman nodded but Judith felt he already knew this, too.

"I imagine you must be doing well with school," Lieberman remarked. "Mr. Stine spoke glowingly of you."

"He's a very strong student," Judith said, smiling uneasily when Lieberman praised her son. She found herself reminded about her reluctance to put him in school after the bobcat incident at the church. At the time, she even considered home schooling him. Mark insisted he be part of the community, so she acquiesced, and he was enrolled at the elementary school, even early for his grade.

"It must have come as quite a surprise to receive my letter so many years after Mr. Stine's passing," Lieberman said. "But that's what he stipulated and instructed in his final wishes. I've served as trustee of the estate since his death and that's the reason I've invited you all here today.

There are a number of things I would like to review as we read the trust that Mr. Stine established, and as you will learn, Malach, you are named the sole beneficiary."

"Beneficiary?" Judith questioned, surprised by that news. "Was there no family?"

"Mr. Stine's wife and only child predeceased him. I'm sure you are aware of that. He had only one very distant cousin, who was not named. When Mr. Stine lost his wife and son, not only was he grief-stricken, but he was uncertain to whom he would leave his estate, and it remained unresolved for a number of years. That is, until he met you, Malach."

Malach nodded at Lieberman's remark, not clear what that would mean. Mark and Judith looked at each other quizzically.

Mr. Lieberman directed his comments to Malach. "When Mr. Stine came in to review the new trust that I prepared, he told me you were an extraordinary individual, unlike anyone he had ever met. I was never clear what that meant and he never spelled it out for me, but I was very happy you came into his life. The loss of his family was so devastating for him. You brought him much joy."

"I was happy he was in my life, too," Malach said.

Mark interrupted. "Have you been the one responsible for the upkeep of the house and property these past years?"

"Yes. Yes, that was me. Well, not me directly. I would send someone up to check on the place, make sure the heat was on in the winter and the house maintained, took care of the taxes and the like. It was not much actually."

"Well, I must say," Mark continued, "we were surprised by the letter and the invitation to come here today. We all had a great deal of admiration for Roger. He was a model of strength and dignity in the face of so much personal tragedy. He was a man of simple tastes and needs. You may not know this but he was a regular member of our church and we knew him since we arrived in this area. He had a strong faith. I respected him, our whole family did."

"He was a special human being and certainly was a man of integrity," Lieberman said. "More concerned with doing the right thing than what may have been easier or more expedient. I know from my conversations with Mr. Stine over the years that he wanted to leave what he had to someone who appreciated and understood its importance. He loved the mountain that he lived on. He treasured it and it was a source of great comfort as well as inspiration for him. He wanted to be sure that the land would be entrusted to the right person."

"Malach and Roger were very close," Judith said. "For a young boy and an aging man, they had a remarkably similar sensibility. I guess you could say that they saw the world in the same ways."

"That's my understanding as well," Lieberman said. "Mr. Stine was very explicit in the way he wanted the trust established and the timing of notification. First, it was clearly stipulated, that Malach be notified at the age of sixteen, not a day sooner or a day later. He wanted you contacted on your birthday. That's how I knew it was your birthday this past week and why I had the letter delivered by courier on that day. I have to say, it was unusual for so young a person to be named without a guardian, but Mr. Stine insisted upon this and made it explicitly clear that I needed to make sure this happened. I informed him that the probate court would have a problem with it, as you are legally still a minor, and the judge would likely designate a property guardian unless he did. He assigned me that role to manage the estate until you reached your sixteenth birthday, and I gave him my personal promise to accommodate your wishes until you come of age. He wanted you to be the one making the decisions. He trusted that I would make that happen. He had much confidence in you and respected your ability to do what you felt would be best for his land and to do it responsibly."

"He never said anything about this to me," Malach said.

"He did not want to burden you with this until you reached the age of sixteen, but let me continue. As you certainly know, Mr. Stine lived alone the final years of his life in the family home. The house and all of its contents, including his pickup truck, all of it, will pass to you. Important waterways and a large lake are on the far west side of the property. The land he owns is beautiful and wild. Mr. Stine invited me to visit and hike with him there many years ago. What you may not be aware of is that Mr. Stine's property is the largest privately owned parcel of land in the region. It encompasses a little over seventy-three thousand acres."

"Oh, my God," Judith uttered.

"I see what you mean by responsibility," Mark said, as he sat back in his seat trying to take this in.

Malach listened silently.

"The original parcel has been in the family for well over one hundred and fifty years," Lieberman continued. "Mr. Stine's grandfather was a timber man and acquired more and more land over the years. He built a very sizable company that he operated with his only child, Mr. Stine's father. After the business and land passed to Mr. Stine's father, he chose to lease portions of it to a large corporate timber company. They harvested trees for many decades, hauling them out and sending them to their mill that still operates much further north. When the land passed to Mr. Stine, he limited the lumbering and then ceased all operations when their contract expired a few years later. That was over forty years ago. He felt it was enough. The land, he told me, needed time to repair and heal. There was never any further lumbering, though he usually received offers and incentives to do so every couple of years."

"I was unaware that his family was in the business," Mark said. "I knew his wife was a school teacher and that he had a small maple syrup operation at one time. Did it the old fashion way, with taps and buckets, no tubing running down the mountain."

"He enjoyed that," Lieberman said. "He sold most of it to local distributers, but gave some of it away. I looked forward to the gallon he sent me and my family every year, and we ate boatloads of pancakes drenched in Mr. Stine's maple syrup. While he did make a small income from his maple syrup business, the bulk of his income came from interest on his inheritance. At the time that Mr. Stine inherited the family estate, he was only in his late-thirties. His father passed at a young age from heart failure. Sadly, his mother died young as well though I am not certain of the cause. He had an older sister who died in childhood from polio. The family had amassed a significant amount of money from their lumber business and interests. Mr. Stine was the sole heir to a nearly three million-dollar fortune. Being a conservative man, not one for risky investment and disliking and distrusting the markets, he invested the money mostly in U.S. Treasuries. It is currently worth nine and a half million dollars."

There was silence in the room. Mark ran his hand straight back through his hair and Judith sighed, neither of them able to respond. Malach continued to listen quietly. Lieberman paused and looked to each of them, wanting to be sure they had time to digest this news.

"I know that's a large sum. The land, however, because of its size and absence of restrictions on its use, is a highly prized piece of potential commercial real estate. Since Mr. Stine passed, I've had several corporate offers for his land from two timber companies, one that leased it many years ago and a company newer to the region, and there are private real estate developers who are prepared to make offers with the aim of building luxury vacation homes on the property. The land itself is the larger of the assets in the trust. From the initial feelers that I have received, these investors estimate it in the vicinity of forty-five to fifty million dollars. I believe that is at the low end. If you add the value of the cash holdings along with the land, in my estimation the total value of the estate could reach sixty-five million dollars, perhaps more."

Judith looked to Mark and they both remained speechless. She turned to Malach who remained silent.

"What does this all mean and what do we do?" Judith asked.

"I know it's a lot to take in. For the time being, you don't need to do anything. I'll be drawing up the final papers to transfer these assets. There are tax consequences, but most have been minimized by careful estate planning over the years, but those that are due can be managed in several ways, and we can discuss that later on. It might be best to just think about all of this. My advice is, take all the time you need. I'm available for legal guidance as already stipulated in the trust and those fees have already been taken care of by Mr. Stine."

Judith was shocked, her hands trembled, panicked by the burden, responsibility, and attention that would fall upon her son. It was more money than she could ever have imagined and could not even begin to contemplate what a sixteen-year old would do with it. Mark looked a little wild-eyed by the news.

"Mr. Lieberman," Malach said. "Why did Roger want me to have all of this? Did he ever tell you?"

"We didn't talk or meet very often, but when we did, I always was taken with his directness and humanity. I've known him a long time. I was a young man when we first met. He had come down to meet with Albert Jensen who started this firm, and who passed away a decade or more ago. Mr. Stine's father had all his legal matters managed by Mr. Jensen. I was fresh out of law school and could not have been here for more than six months. I still remember it. Mr. Jensen came in to see Mr. Stine. He never worked on the weekends so I assumed it was for an important client. I was in the office doing research on a case. I let Mr. Stine in and informed him that Mr. Jensen had called and was running a little late but on his way.

"I admit that I was surprised when I met Mr. Stine. He was not the VIP client I imagined. But he was a straight shooter, no nonsense, and did not hesitate to speak his mind. I wasn't dressed for the office, just weekend clothes, hiking clothes actually, planning to meet with a friend in the afternoon and head up north for an overnight camping trip. I'm not from this area, but loved getting out of the city and being near the mountains. Everything was close enough. It was a beautiful late summer day.

"I think he liked that I was a lawyer and didn't act like one or dress like one. We spoke for well over an hour. My boss was running into all sorts of problems that morning. I forget the details about that, but I remember my morning with Mr. Stine like it was yesterday. When the boss phoned again, Mr. Stine took the receiver and told him to stop calling and just take his good ole time, that he was doing fine with the new lawyer in the office. At first, I was thrilled that he put in a good word for me, but by the end of the time spent together, I was just happy to know him. We spoke mostly about the outdoors, camping, being in the wilderness. He was a man of the land. He respected it and he was in awe of it. He had an attitude about nature that was different from anyone else I'd met. He also told me something that I never forgot. He said, that if we don't take care of the great outdoors, it would be lost forever. There's no second chance, no do-overs. This is it. It's all we've got and it's all we'll ever have. We hear those words a lot today, but back then, more than thirty-five years ago, there were few voices like that – very, very few, just lone calls in the wild.

"I know that's a long-winded and not very satisfying answer to your question, but he never directly explained to me why he wanted you to have all of this. I personally believe he saw something in you that made him feel you got it, that you understood what was important about the land."

Malach nodded and seemed to appreciate the thought.

When Judith, Mark, and Malach finally left the office, they stepped out into the fresh air. Judith's head was still spinning with what she had taken in, too much to sort out at that moment. She looked at Mark and Malach and felt that they all needed to ground themselves, starting with lunch. Mark agreed and thought the occasion required a fine restaurant. Judith was surprised by Mark's comment, as he was always frugal with money.

When they entered the "Sweet Dream Café," she noticed the crisp white tablecloths and fresh flowers on each table. Sunlight poured in through the large windows facing the street. They settled at a table and looked through the menu given to them by a young girl probably the same age as Malach. Judith noticed her flash a smile at him, which he returned. She knew he was a handsome young man, with a disarming smile and a physical presence as he just topped six feet. She focused her attention on the menu and noted the entrées priced at fifteen dollars or more. They did not eat out often, and their local restaurants often served large and inexpensive meals. Mark ordered the most expensive item on the menu, a salad with grilled salmon and she did the same. She knew that was not something either of them would have done before. Malach selected a large bowl of vegetable soup and a grilled three-cheese sandwich. There was a fleeting transformative moment when Judith placed her order, something inside of her that switched. Her thinking about money, the price of her meal, momentarily it no longer seemed even important. The dream, no the reality of wealth, was liberating, a breath of fresh air. All her life, money had been a concern, a preoccupation, at times a source of desperation. Mark eased some of that when she married. He was always a critic of our world of aimless consumption, yet he did not hesitate in ordering the nineteen-dollar lunch.

"It is a mysterious thing how the Lord works. What does one do with that immense sum of money?" Mark asked Malach. "Has anything gone through your mind about it, yet?"

"No, not really," Malach answered. "I'd never thought about something like that before. I guess I mostly want to figure out what Roger would have wanted."

"There is much good that can be done with a fortune like that," Mark said.

"What do you mean?" Judith interjected.

"Just that it can be used to do the good work of the Lord."

"It can help pay for a college education, too," she said.

"Of course. But that's just a tiny portion of what's there. There's so much need, there's so much good it can serve. It would even ease some of our own personal burden. A church salary only can take one so far."

"A new kitchen would be nice," Judith said.

"A car that we could rely on would be, too," Mark added with a smile.

"Maybe an exotic vacation and some new clothes," Judith added.

"I certainly could stand a new suit for work and I'd like to see you in a few new things." Mark smiled and winked at her.

"I had no idea that Roger had so much money and so much land," Malach said, not listening to their exchange. "He never mentioned anything about it."

"He also wanted it to be for you," Mark said. "For what you want, for what you see as fit. Each generation has to determine their needs and goals. Hopefully with an eye and heart guided by the Lord."

"The land was important to Roger," Malach said. "His life was about that. It's not really my money or my land."

"I know it is hard to imagine what you have been blessed with," Mark said, "but it is your money now and your land."

Judith listened to the conversation she and Mark were having in contrast to the words and concerns that came from Malach's mouth. They were of two very different realms. In only a couple hours, with the prospect of a fortune before them, she and Mark were leaping toward all the temptations and seductions that they ever could imagine, while Malach thought only about Roger and the land. It gave her pause and realized she needed to catch her breath and think about what this would mean for her son and for her and Mark.

On the drive home Judith was certain that they needed to keep this under wraps for now. It was nobody's business and she dreaded the thought of the gossip and talk that could lead from it. Mark agreed that no one needed to know. Malach did not respond.

Malach spent the following day with Ginny. She picked him up at home that Saturday morning and they drove to Roger's house. She listened wide-eyed as he recounted the day.

"That's so much money. It's ridiculous," Ginny said. "It's totally ridiculous."

"It sure is," Malach said. "I never, ever imagined that Roger had that much money. He never bought stuff. He fixed things that were broken instead of throwing them away. There was nothing pretentious about him. He never tried to impress anyone. He was probably the richest person around, and it didn't control his life."

"I think that's great," Ginny said. "It's just amazing that someone could be so grounded with that kind of wealth. I hate all the attention to consumption that we have in our face every day. It's all we hear about."

"That was Roger," Malach said. "He understood what was important."

"So true, but it's all yours now. What are you going to do?" Ginny said with a smirk. "Jet off to the French Riviera to sail on your new yacht, hobnob at cocktail parties with Beverly Hills celebs on Malibu Beach, plan luncheons with the venture capitalists on Wall Street all vying for your money…?"

Malach and Ginny burst out laughing. They were silly with laughter. She hopped up on the hood of her car, wrapped her legs around Malach who leaned back and she put her arms around him and rested her chin on his shoulder. They both looked at the house. The clapboards were faded and peeling, the walkway paving stones uneven and buckled. It was an old rambling house, probably more stately when it was built years ago by Roger's grandfather. The garage large enough for two cars, the shed looked to be built years later largely for storage.

"So, this is your new spread," Ginny said. "I suppose it will be fine with a proper make-over."

"Let's take a look," Malach said.

She slipped off the car and they walked around the house and entered through the back door that Malach knew did not have a lock on it. The house was unchanged from when he spent days with Roger during his last summer there. Malach picked up a frame on the fireplace mantel with a picture of Roger as a young man with his wife and young son. He had not noticed it before. Roger had a big smile on his face with his arm around Edie, holding Lee in his other arm. Malach placed it back on the mantel.

"They were really young there," Ginny said. There was another picture of Roger posed with his parents, all of them dressed for church or a wedding or something.

"Really young," Malach said.

"He looked a lot like his father," Ginny said.

Malach looked at the picture carefully and agreed. They poked around for a little while longer and then headed back outside. Malach opened the garage door where Roger's green pickup truck was parked. They stepped back out and he pulled the garage door shut. Malach suggested they take a short hike. He wanted to show her some of the property. They walked the mountain together that day for the first time. Instead of weekends at the Conservation Center, in the subsequent months, Ginny and Malach made the mountain their new destination.

2

ngie and Evan arrived at Roger's house uncertain about what to expect. Ginny had texted them earlier and asked if they could come to the mountain. Angie was always ready for being part of any project that Malach wished to undertake and she brought her new video camera in hopes of capturing something she could use. She purchased it just a few weeks ago. It was expensive, but her parents helped out, and she used birthday money that she had squirreled away along with savings from a part-time summer job last year working at the ice cream shop.

She hoped a new short film this summer could be added to her portfolio that she would submit with her applications to college. Yet, for the first time, she was feeling blocked, without even a clue as to what she would do. Angie was certain it was just nerves and the usual impossible expectations that she placed on herself. It just seemed that this film was more crucial and needed to be bigger, even momentous, a statement of purpose. She hated when she wallowed in the grip of indecision and fear. She did not want to become that kind of filmmaker – temperamental and brooding. Doubts were swirling this morning, but when she received Ginny's message, the timing felt fortuitous and she took a deep breath. Angie texted Evan and he told her he would pick her up in an hour. Evan had become her confidant, the one she bounced ideas off, shared insecurities with, someone she trusted completely. Besides Ginny, he had become her closest friend.

The material she had of Malach haunted her. She had viewed it so many times, trying to find the line and thread of meaning that would bring it all together. She and Evan were still mesmerized no matter how often they watched the recordings together. She had edited and reworked the material again and again, bouncing ideas off of Evan, ultimately compiling it into three one-hour films. Her mind raced with memories of those experiences. Malach with a young moose nestling its nose into his belly, Malach sitting on a log with an armful of young mink and laughing, Malach disappearing below the water surface into a beavers' den for a frightening duration of time, later surfacing surrounded by a half dozen of these endearing creatures. She did not know what would become of it all, but she did not dwell on that.

Neither Ginny nor Malach had viewed any of Angie's videos and she never mentioned that she had organized it into a documentary of sorts. Editing and reducing the work to only three hours was laborious as there was so much material and nothing seemed superfluous, redundant, or inessential. Yet it felt far from finished, not even a partially completed project but rather the start of something. She and Evan were in the films only peripherally, minor and inconsequential. It was Ginny who was collaborator and partner. Angie had watched the relationship between her friends develop for the past four years. It was evident to her from the beginning that its slow unfolding tempered the bond between them.

Malach and Ginny loved each other in a way that was complex and complicated, part passion, part a shared understanding of things that no one else fully got, and part preparation for something bigger. Their lives were distilled into this relationship and therefore too close for either one to step back and see the way she and Evan did. For now, all the recordings Angie had made were protected by encryption on her and Evan's computers along with a digital vault with two fail-safe back-ups that Evan devised.

When Evan arrived to pick her up, Angie's mother let him in and made breakfast. Evan ate a cheese omelet followed by a large slice of apple pie and tall glass of milk while waiting for Angie to get ready. He had become almost like family over the years, a regular presence in the house. When Angie finally came downstairs, they took off. She grabbed the breakfast bar that her mother held out recognizing that there was no chance of her sitting down for a meal. Angie liked that Evan seemed so comfortable with everyone in the family but was surprised when her mother asked recently about the two of them. Evan somehow had outgrown his geeky awkwardness and her mother pointed out that he was becoming quite handsome. He was tall, with very upright posture and a big warm smile. He was no longer thin and lanky but muscular. Angie looked at him differently after that conversation. He still seemed too much like a brother and she dismissed the matter.

On the drive, Angie looked at herself in the mirror on the windshield visor that was flipped down to block the morning sun. Her thick curly dark hair, sprinkling of freckles across her nose and cheeks, and round face would not relinquish her little-girl-like appearance. She stared intently at herself, wondering what kind of impression she made. She narrowed her deep blue eyes into a knowing gaze trying to create an intensity of presence, maybe the guise of a filmmaker others would be forced to take seriously. She looked over to Evan, his sandy brown hair long, his skin clear unlike when he was younger, and the stubble on his chin giving him a daring look. He felt her gaze, and glanced toward her.

"I've been thinking about making a new movie for my portfolio," Angie said, feeling a little uncomfortable with their eye contact.

"I think the two films you're planning to submit are strong," Evan responded.

He had told her that before. He had come to be a thoughtful critic, which she demanded, not liking his once positive take on everything she did. "Twelve Confessions," interviews with as many of last year's seniors during the final weeks of school and also the one done simultaneously, "Twelve Dreams," comprised of the apprehensions and ambitions of rising freshman, she also felt were her best work. They were smart and incisive and captured a vision. She still was not satisfied and was looking for another subject.

"Maybe a third film would help," Angie said.

Evan shrugged with a little smirk. She knew he was far more confident about the strength of her work than she was herself. She smiled to herself, recognizing the gentle acknowledgement he conveyed with a raised shoulder and half smile – his way of saying that he admired her.

When they arrived at the house, Ginny and Malach were already there. Angie and Evan both knew about Malach's inheritance but compared to all the secrets they kept about him, that one seemed relatively easy. They were familiar with the property from previous visits but never did more than briefly walk through the house. Malach laid out his plan. Angie and Evan listened, at first puzzled, then curious, and finally, with the laughter of conviction, agreed that they could pull this off. The whole premise was odd and intriguing, yet completely logical.

They started in the kitchen, which appeared to have been built over different periods by the look of work done to it. The appliances, Evan estimated, were at least thirty years old. He pulled out the refrigerator and looked for any information on the back, but there was only a model and serial number. He took a picture of it for later. There was a black gas stove that Angie thought was vintage and quite beautiful, something she recognized from old nineteen-forties movies. She tried to turn it on but it didn't work. Perhaps the gas had been turned off.

Ginny opened a couple of cabinet doors. There were mismatched glasses and three sets of dishes. She picked up a plate that had a dirty film over the delicate pattern of fruit with a gold trim border. "They look like grandma dishes," she said. She turned the plate over and inspected the back and read the inscription. "'*American Limoges*, 22-carat gold.' It's real china."

Malach took another plate and examined it. There was a chip on it.

"I wonder if these were Roger and Edie's wedding dishes?" He passed it to Angie and Evan to inspect before putting it back in the cabinet.

Angie opened the drawers in the kitchen finding a mix of unmatched utensils, before uncovering a silverware chest in the lower cabinet. She lifted it out and put it on the counter, opened the small chest and lifted a fork, carefully inspecting it. "Sterling," she said. The silverware was very tarnished and had not been used for a very long time. They each came to look before Angie closed the box and returned it to its location.

Evan examined the upper kitchen cabinets. One door had a loose handle, which he tried to tighten unsuccessfully by hand. After spending a few more minutes in the kitchen they moved into the living and dining area.

"These look like nice old wood floors," Ginny said. "We'll have to figure out how to remove them without damaging them."

"They're probably the original boards," Evan said. "I have an aunt who lives in an old house that has wide floor boards like these in the living room, and she told me that they were of higher quality years ago."

Angie pulled one of the dining table chairs out, and noticed the fabric on the seat, a green and yellow pattern with a mix of spots and worn corners with the stuffing poking through. The table had a dark walnut finish, the surface marred with random scratches. There were six chairs around the table with two extra ones at each end of the matching sideboard that was cluttered with framed photographs, porcelain figures, a coffee urn, and a pile of *National Geographic* magazines.

A bronze chandelier with a frosted glass bowl hung above the table. Cobwebs clung to the pendant from the crown to base. Angie turned on the light and only one of the three bulbs illuminated, the others burned out. In the bottom of the bowl the light revealed the accumulation of dead bugs. She stepped back and took in the arrangement of the dining room furniture, as though sizing up a set before filming. It felt frozen in time, decades old, a remnant of the past, the remains of a life. She heard the others who moved on to the living room, turned off the light, and joined them.

The smell of mildew was embedded in the fabric of the twin sofas and upholstered chairs having absorbed the dankness of a house unlived in for several years, and absent of a family for many more. The room was cluttered with extraneous seating along the walls.

"What do you think we should do with all this furniture?" Evan said. "Maybe it can be cleaned, some sold, and some given away."

"Excellent idea," Malach said. "Who does that kind of thing?"

"My Mom had the new sofa cleaned a few months ago when my little sister threw up on it." Ginny said. They all laughed. "I'll find out who did it. She also had some organization pick up the old stuff. It should be easy to take care of."

Off the living area was a small office with a desk and two well-worn brown leather chairs surrounded by over-stacked bookshelves and cabinets along the walls. It was a mess and looked as though it had become a storage area with several cardboard boxes stacked in the corners. Angie opened the curtains and lifted the shades to allow in more light. Even then the room remained dim.

Ginny and Evan were looking through the cabinets while Angie held up a framed wedding photo of Roger and his wife that was sitting on the end table next to the chairs. She watched as Malach sat at the desk and perused its contents. He gathered old mail and scattered papers and organized them into a few neat piles. There was a picture of Edie and their son, Lee, when he was a small boy. Malach opened one of the desk drawers and pulled out a box filled with letters. He took one out and read it silently then carefully folded it and put it back with the others. He looked up and saw Angie watching him.

"Letters that Roger and Edie sent each other when he was in the army," he said.

Angie nodded knowingly. Ginny looked up from the items she was going through and could see the sadness in Malach's face.

"Are you okay?" she asked.

Malach nodded.

"There's so much personal stuff here," Ginny said. "The cabinets are filled with journals his wife kept, patterns for her needlepoints, boxes of photos."

Evan had pulled some books from the shelves, which he looked through. Some of the old ones were gifts from Edie's parents and dated and inscribed. There were leather-bound volumes of Shakespeare sonnets and plays that Roger had given her for their first anniversary. "She must have been a big reader," Evan said.

"She taught high school English," Ginny answered. "Roger told Malach she read voraciously, French novels, Greek classics, the Canterbury Tales, English poets."

Angie thought of what they had begun to uncover in the dust and disarray. It was so intimate, the lives of two private people. It felt intrusive being in their home without them, going through their correspondence, the items that they began their lives with, the accumulation of articles that defined their spirit and passions, dreams and disappointments. Angie made mental notes about how she wanted to frame and document this process.

After going through the remainder of the house and basement, they all sat together at the small table in the kitchen and began their planning.

"There's a lot of stuff here," Evan said. "I hope I never let that happen to me."

"Roger was not even a materialistic person," Ginny said.

"What are you going to do with all of it?" Angie asked Malach.

"Roger talked all the time about the land and even though he owned it, he never felt it belonged to him. He was just the temporary steward, responsible for protecting it for the next generation. I'm sure he would have felt the same way about all these things. We should take care of what we have, and pass along what we can when we're done with it. Roger would always tell me that it's not about the stuff, but how we live our lives that's important."

"I think we should start next weekend," Ginny suggested. "We can do our research this week."

They looked at each other, smiles bouncing back and forth, but it felt more serious to all of them.

3

This was the first time Malach had seen the lake that was on the far edge of the vast property that was now his. Roger had talked about it, but never revealed that it belonged to him. It was many miles away from the house and it required hiking up and over a large stretch of mountainous terrain. When Malach explored the land during his summer visits with Roger before his death, he was always curious to follow each of the mountain streams from their source to their final destination. But his days were often short and he was there to be with Roger. Despite Roger sending him off, Malach was reluctant to leave him and wander for too long. His more distant treks were to the other side of the property, to some of the higher elevations. He was surprised to see the size of the lake, probably a mile wide and stretching two or three times as long. Two small islands, with outcroppings of rock and clusters of trees precariously balancing atop, stood side by side off to one end of the long lake. It provided perspective and scale to the surroundings and added to its picturesque beauty. Water emptied into the basin from two directions, feeding the lake. Surrounding it were hundreds and hundreds of acres of gently rolling woods. Along the north rim beyond the hills were steep elevations of mountains. It was the jewel of the property.

Malach took in the grandeur of the view, descended from the outlook point and hiked his way down the steep and rugged terrain, then continued through gradually sloping woods until he reached the water's edge. It had been a long walk from his vantage point to the water. On the farthest side of the lake there was a house nestled into the trees, a portion of the chimney and roof visible, and a dock on the water's edge. He was surprised to see it, not expecting a neighbor. The shore was rocky and his attention was drawn to two river otters that surfaced, propelling themselves out of the lake and sliding up and onto a large flat boulder. Malach stepped across some weathered branches and onto the rock with the otters. The animals nudged themselves toward him and settled at his feet. He knelt and stroked their thick and lustrous fur. He sat with them for some time and savored the moment.

During the past five days Malach had lived out on the mountain. It was early in the summer and there was ample food to forage and crystal-clear streams for water. A bed of pine needles sufficed for sleep, songbirds for company. He felt well-nourished from the various flowers, roots, seeds, and berries he found in abundance. Cleansing and invigorating swims were part of every day.

Lieberman had sent Malach a letter a few weeks ago, one of many that had been received in the past few months. This one was an offer from an out-of-state real estate company for this very part of the property. He wondered how they even knew about it, maybe from the owners of the house on the lake, maybe from an aerial sighting or map, or search on the Internet. Lieberman said that the developer was hoping to create a community of homes throughout the surrounding woods and along the shores of the lake. The entire valley was what he was interested in and he was prepared to pay whatever was necessary to make the offer attractive. The initial proposal was so much money, Malach thought, so much. There was no thought about the wilderness, the animals, the pristine mountain streams, the isolation that made the valley whole and complete. Rather, the vision was for luxury vacation homes for wealthy families to have the privilege of living in these beautiful surroundings. Many hundreds of homes would be built. It would include a small private ski area carved into one of the mountains, an eighteen-hole golf course, a small marina on the lake, a clubhouse to service the activities of the changing seasons. Malach was even offered a home on the property and a club membership as an enticement. He shook his head when he read that. It saddened him just to think that this spectacle of nature might be effectively bulldozed, trees cleared from vast swaths of land, roadway passages blasted, graded, and paved, docks constructed and projected along the shore, boats and jet skis screaming across the serenity of the lake.

Malach cringed whenever another letter came, though Lieberman never pressed him for a decision. He merely passed on the latest proposal. It would sometimes be days before Malach even opened the letters and he never answered any of them. It was always a developer, as though that title deserved special esteem or that what they did was elevating and improving upon what they touched, making it something more than it was. It made him so sad, so anguished to think of what could happen to Roger's land, and downright despondent to think of what was happening in the name of development everywhere. He knew that he would do everything in his power to make this stop, at whatever cost.

The house across the lake continued to distract Malach. He wondered who these neighbors were and how long they had been living there. He coaxed the otters back into the water, the two belching with their departure. Walking along the edge of the lake toward the house he could see the property up close. There was a pickup truck parked in the drive, two overturned rowboats on the side of the house. The white weathered two-story clapboard cottage looked like a smaller version of Roger's house, built long ago, and gracefully neglected. The gravel drive was rutted from the tire tracks of the truck, with the center filled with overgrown weeds and grass, the path to the front door a trail of unevenly placed flagstones, the window shutters awry and peeling green paint. He did not notice any activity, and despite the urge to knock on the door, he respected the privacy of the owners and headed back. Malach looked at the house, standing alone on the lake, quiet, contained, and serene, and then out at the view across the valley and imagined what it could become. Never here, he thought, ever.

❧

When Malach returned later that week, he was happy to see his friends. On the morning they would begin the project, he and Ginny arrived early with Evan and Angie pulling up minutes later. They exchanged hugs.

"How was the week on the mountain?" Angie asked Malach.

"There were some surprises, good ones. I was telling Ginny on the way over about it."

Angie unpacked her video camera. She checked the lens and battery and switched it on. "What did you find?"

[Record]

"A neighbor, on the far western part of the land. It's the only house on a beautiful lake. I don't think anyone was home when I was there, but I should be a good neighbor and pay them a visit."

"I'd love to see it," Angie said.

"You will, for sure."

"I can't wait, but today is the start of the project," she said. "So, what's the plan?" She was already well aware of what Malach had in mind but posed the inquiry as introduction and as a prompt for his explanation in his own words. Malach had grown accustomed over the years to her camera in his face and the questions. She liked his ease and presence in front of the camera, as it was now no different than when the camera was switched off. He was authentic and it made his other-worldly behavior feel believable. Malach was comfortable with sharing his thoughts of the world as he experienced it. His perceptions and understanding of its workings opened her eyes to that which she could never on her own have imagined, let alone understand. It moved her in a way that made her struggle to catch her breath, bearing witness time and again to something mind-bending.

There was no weird supernatural mystery or aura of subterfuge to the material she had been collecting, editing, and storing. As powerful as it was, she did not feel an urge to make it available as she would with her other work. On the contrary, she felt the gratification of being the sole chronicler of Malach's life.

Malach turned to look at the house as the plumber's truck arrived. She slowly scanned the scene and returned and rested the camera on Malach's profile. He turned and looked toward the camera. *Perfect*, she thought.

Angie knew that Malach was not inclined to make grand pronouncements, but rather responded within the immediacy of the moment. Reflections of the day and the summer ahead would be captured along the way.

She followed him and the crew to the house. A lot of packing still needed to be done. She watched as Ginny and Evan unloaded stacks of flattened cartons into the house. Meantime, Malach met with the contractors. He had such an easy way about him that most everyone was comfortable in his presence. She had watched that develop in him over the years. As much as he could be in his own head, preoccupied, burdened, and stressed by so much of what he would see and hear in the world around him, whenever anyone met him and spoke to him, he was present. Present, she thought, was the best way she could characterize him.

"Angie, did you meet Chuck Dowling?" Malach said, waving her over and then introducing her to the plumber. "I'm hoping we can remove the old boiler and oil tank today."

"Oh, I'm on camera," the plumber said. Angie shook his hand but managed to keep the camera rolling.

"I've known this young man since he was a baby. My wife drags me to church regularly. Nice house here, pretty spot. Need lots of work, best I can see. Who knew I'd be working for him so soon."

"What are you going to do with the old furnace and tank?" Angie asked.

"Usually it goes straight to the dump. Most folks don't bother, but the furnace and tank can be used for scrap. My brother will be here soon with the big truck. We'll empty and remove the tank, cut it up, and truck it all to the salvage yard. It will be gone in no time. Okay, are you done with me? How did I do? Was it a take?"

[Stop]

"Perfect. Thank you." Angie said.

Malach and Angie headed to the house where Evan and Ginny were getting organized. It would take them almost a week, but all of Roger and Edie's belongings were carefully boxed, the cartons labeled and then placed in the garage. Angie captured some clips from time to time, but mostly they all just talked and worked. There was a weight in the air as they packaged up the lives of a family. Malach had decided that all their intimate and private items would be taken to his house and stored. The second week the kitchen was taken apart. Household items, antiques, old clocks, silverware, china, particular pieces of furniture, were all scheduled for pick up by an auctioneer that Lieberman had recommended. The other furniture was sent for repair and reupholstering, clothes for cleaning, and then all were donated to the Salvation Army.

[Record]

"We had a good week," Malach said. "This was the hardest part, three lives put to rest. I'll remember them, you'll remember them, but after us and the others whose lives they were a part of are dead, they'll be another step removed, and in a blink of time they'll no longer be in anyone's memory. It's sad to think, but we all believe ourselves more important than we are."

Malach paused then looked up at Angie before continuing, "We don't think about life beyond ourselves, but changes we're causing to life all around us have already started, all because we can't figure out our place in this world. We never give it much thought beyond our own needs. We never consider what we're doing to the world, and even worse is that there's so very little time left to change."

Malach stopped, stared off again, and was done.

[Stop]

Angie put the camera down and thought about Malach's words. He had grown more pessimistic over the past year and that frightened her. They went to find Ginny and Evan who were inside. They all walked through the emptied house, stripped of furniture, curtains, rugs, fixtures, cabinets, appliances, and all the worldly possessions of Roger, Edie, and Lee. They had found so many of the items a new home. It now felt eerily hollow, cavernous, and empty. The water and electricity had been turned off, the pipes drained.

Step by step, over seven weeks, the work on the house and then the garage took place. The old slate shingles were carefully plied loose, planks of old boards released from the rafters of the roof, battens and joists dismantled, windows and their casings separated. Doors removed from their hinges, hinges removed from the frames, frames removed from the walls, plaster walls broken away, exposed copper pipes and wires cut and taken away. The roof came off, the ceiling next, the walls of the house stripped to the bone. Nails were extricated, the skeleton separated, floor boards lifted, tongue and groove joints pulled apart.

The building materials that formed to make this house were trucked to a reclamation center where it all would be reused.

It was slow and arduous in the beginning as the four of them struggled to use unfamiliar tools to safely deconstruct the house. Over time the work went more smoothly and soon only an old stone foundation and chimney stood adjacent to the exposed basement in the ground. The next day a large backhoe arrived, collapsed the chimney and foundation, filled the gaping wound in the ground with soil, and then the footprint of the property was graded. When the fall leaves came down weeks later there was no evidence that the house had ever existed.

4

Judith was relieved when Malach finally completed the project, worried throughout the summer about the community's response and the unwanted attention it could bring. While she understood Malach's intention, she struggled to reconcile it with the wish she harbored for him to live in that house one day, a longing for him to not go too far from home. She was already feeling that pang of loss inside her with college only a year away. She prayed that college was what he wanted, but that was not certain either. He routinely shrugged off her questions about it. She knew school was her hope for a more normal path for him, but deep down she knew that normal, ordinary, expected, predictable, were not conditions of Malach's life.

There was also more tension between Malach and his father. Mark was baffled by Malach's decision to take down Roger's house. He was preoccupied with Malach's fortune and had begun to sprinkle messages on prosperity into his sermons, hoping it might prompt reflection in his son. Mark did not see these as incompatible tenets, being affluent while also charitable and righteous. Malach dismissed these ideas, and sarcastically reminded his father what Jesus preached about the rich finding their way into heaven.

Judith knew Malach was preparing to fight for a world that he understood in a way no one else did, and one that he seemed determined to protect. Taking down Roger's house made sense in a certain way, permitting the land to return to its predetermined order, allowing the renewal of the earth, reclaiming the wild, preserving the web of all life that had begun to fray and tear. It was starting right here with the house given to him.

Judith looked at her watch and hurried herself along for her lunch date with Sky and Virginia. Sky had called earlier and said she had some important news. The thought of anything unexpected had begun to rattle her. She shook the worries from her head. If it was serious or about Malach, Sky would not surprise her in that way.

The three of them had begun to see each other more regularly. Virginia still did not know about Malach. Judith was uneasy about that, too. She knew that Ginny and her mother were close. She did not want her son to be the source of a gulf between them, but was also grateful that Ginny protected Malach.

When Judith crossed the street to approach the restaurant, Sky and Virginia were out front. Virginia threw her arms around Sky and hugged her. They looked to be celebrating something. Sky's face was radiant.

"Show her," Virginia said, her voice swelling with joy as Judith joined them.

Sky held up her hand, the engagement ring sparkling. "Calvin proposed last night."

Judith's eyes welled with tears for her dear friend and she held her close. "I'm so happy for you. He's a wonderful man," she said. Judith knew the pain that Sky had carried over the years, hoping that it finally would be eased. Calvin was a remarkable and kind man and Sky deserved someone like him.

"Thank you. Thank you so much," Sky said. "I wanted to share it with both of you, first. It's hard to wrap my head around. But it's good. I love him."

"Come, let's go inside and eat and celebrate," Virginia said. "I want to hear everything."

"Me too," said Judith. "Not one detail left out."

Sky smiled, kissed them both again. "Every detail," she whispered.

Judith found that the heartwarming news and lunch with friends was what she needed to shake off her gloomy ruminations. They spent two hours lingering over the stories about Calvin and his romantic proposal before Sky dashed out to get back to the office for a meeting. Judith and Virginia basked in Sky's happiness.

"I'm so happy for her," Virginia said. "No one deserves it more. It makes me want to cry. I hope her happiness has no bounds."

Judith nodded. "I couldn't be more delighted. I have to say, you have a knack for matchmaking. In the old days you might have made a career of it."

"It was just so obvious," Virginia said. "I'm sure you see it. They're just right together." Virginia had a twinkle in her eyes.

Judith nodded and smiled too. They each allowed the waitress to refill their coffee cups, both settling in for a talk.

"So…how are *our* young romantics doing?" Virginia asked. Judith expected the conversation to steer this way. "They've been spending quite a lot of time together. Ginny is always on the way out of the house. She's very independent and I can't keep track of her, but I hadn't anticipated a boyfriend in her life. First love has a power of its own."

"I can't say I see much of Malach either."

"They're very serious about each other," Virginia continued. "I like Malach very much. He's a wonderful young man. What worries me though is that most high school romances don't last, but there's something here. You know what I mean, and college is going to change that in some way. I just want to be sure they are prepared, and it doesn't interfere with their education right now. They're so young. What the future will bring, who knows. But heading off to different places, different directions, I wouldn't want to see either of them get hurt. I imagine lots of schooling ahead for Ginny. Science takes a long time. I don't know what Malach is thinking, but Ginny says he's so smart. That's the ultimate compliment coming from her because she generally doesn't think anyone is smart."

"The two of them are lovely together," Judith said. "I can't say I know what Malach's plans are or where he might end up, but I worry, too. But, they're both strong, both have firmly grounded convictions and a sense of what's important. I think they'll find their paths ahead."

"I hope so," Virginia said. "They're two determined young people. When they put their minds to something, no one's going to stop them. Look what they did this summer. My little girl tells me we have to change how we live. For her, this supersedes everything else. When we do have time to speak, I hear about climate change, shrinking habitats, acidification of our oceans, exploding human population growth, spread of infectious diseases, extinctions. When she decides to learn something, she's all in, an environmental expert. I guess all that work at the Conservation Center has stirred her new passion and probably did so for Malach, too."

Judith nodded and forced a smile as she nervously ran her fingers around the sides of her coffee cup.

"If I may be so rude to ask," Virginia continued, "and I know it's not any of my business, but taking down a perfectly good house, I just can't make sense of it. What was that about? Were you okay with it?"

"I didn't know quite what to make of it at first," Judith said, not sure how to have this conversation. "I mean, it was remarkably generous of Mr. Stine to leave his house to Malach, but I didn't really have any control over it. It was how Roger established the gift."

"He's very sure of himself, isn't he?" Virginia said. "Malach told me he felt it was important to return the land back to nature."

"Yes, he's confident about what he believes," Judith said, "and I think Roger's love and desire to protect the land was part of it."

"Most people would have sold the house and kept the money," Virginia said. "Might have been helpful for those college bills. An education costs a fortune today."

Judith listened and nodded again, not sure how to respond to that comment either.

"The two of them are cut from the same cloth," Virginia said. "It's not about the money, Ginny tells me. There are more important things than that. Maybe so, but try to pay the bills, take care of a family, and prepare for the expenses of higher education. Good luck doing that without money."

"I hear what you're saying," Judith said, knowing in her heart that what Malach was doing was far more important than money. She also found herself feeling a budding resentment that Virginia viewed Malach as an impediment to Ginny's future, or worse, an idealistic kid who did not appreciate what it takes to live in the world. For a moment she wanted to shout it out for all to hear, for Virginia to know that Malach had taken her daughter on a miraculous journey, opening her eyes to the world in a way no one any longer understands.

Judith listened to Virginia for some time. She took a deep breath and reminded herself that Virginia's concerns were normal and expected for a mother of a bright and talented teenage daughter.

Judith also found it ironic that, when the house was deconstructed and all the materials were sold or donated – the old lumber, hand hewn beams, wide plank floors, slate roof tiles, window frames, doors, brass handles, all the old fixtures, antique furniture, china and silver, volumes of vintage books, scrap metal – the return was almost thirty thousand dollars. The donated materials provided another twenty thousand in tax deductions. While not the amount the house would have commanded, it was not inconsequential and surprised her. Malach left the money with Lieberman in one of the accounts and never gave it a thought. More important than money she reminded herself; what he's doing is more important than money.

There would come a time when Virginia would learn about Malach. It made Judith uneasy to think about how she would react. No doubt she would be awestruck, but as Ginny's mother she would also be filled with apprehension. Ginny was closest to Malach, far beyond even her own connection as his mother. She felt fortunate that Malach had someone like Ginny, someone she knew he loved and who loved him, someone he trusted completely, someone who lifted him from the isolation of his world. Ginny was strong and compassionate, but Judith had begun to detect a strain surfacing in her face and felt for her, for her burden, the burden of knowing Malach like no other.

It was nearly the end of the first month of school, and there was a full day of events with an assembly and college fair for the seniors. Ginny and Malach met in the cafeteria when they arrived in the morning. They stood at the counter to order breakfast. Brett stepped ahead of them with his tray, bumping into Ginny, then ignoring her.

"Excuse me," Ginny said with annoyance. "You might want to watch where you're going."

"Sorry," Brett said with feigned sincerity. "Did I upset you? I hope you're not going to set your boyfriend loose on me." He locked eyes with Malach.

"There's no one in front of you, so why don't you keep moving," Malach said.

"Trying to get rid of me. I'm in no rush or are the two of you too good for me?" Brett glared at both of them.

Ginny stared right back at him and said, "I'm sure you've got something to do."

"Yeah, I've got plenty to do. Some of us work already. Too bad you and your friends couldn't find something constructive to do this summer, like a job, instead of tearing down a house someone could live in."

"Yeah, thanks for the advice," Ginny said.

"What the hell kind of thing was that to do anyway?" Brett blurted back. "Knock down a house for no reason. What the hell are you going to do," he said to Ginny, "live in a shoe box with your freaky boyfriend?"

Brett glowered at Ginny before turning toward Malach. "Were you the genius who thought up that whole plan? What's next, shut down the lumber mills and put people out of work?" He took a step toward Malach, puffing out his chest and raising his head. "Yeah, you two geniuses best get to the college fair this morning. They need people like you."

Malach stood his ground and did not flinch in Brett's presence, which only irritated Brett more. Brett had grown considerably during their high school years. He was taller than Malach and wide from hours spent lifting weights and bodybuilding. Brett and his friend often wore hunting clothes and often bragged about their plans for deer season. If they weren't talking about hunting, they spoke of their intention to get jobs at Northern Lumber Mills after high school. When his friend called him, Brett turned and walked away. Two younger students coming in his direction deliberately steered away from Brett and let him pass.

Ginny was reminded that when they were younger, so many kids tried to avoid Brett, not wanting to be noticed by him, afraid of any confrontation.

Malach's eyes followed Brett until he left the cafeteria. Ginny noted the serious look in Malach's face.

"He's just the same idiot he's always been," Ginny said nervously. "He thinks he's intimidating when he flexes those muscles or talks about his hunting rifle." Ginny felt uneasy about the entire exchange. "He still holds a grudge. You'd think he'd have gotten over that fight you had with him. How many years ago was that? I hate how he looks at you or makes some remark every time we see him. He gives me the creeps. Just please ignore him. Please," Ginny repeated. "He's not worth it."

"I understand," Malach said slowly nodding his head.

They found a table and sat down. Ginny bit into half of the toasted bagel she just ordered, offering Malach the other half. "I don't think I can stand a whole day of this," Ginny said. "College salespeople pitching their schools, telling you how special and important you are, how much they can enrich your life, helping you fulfill your dreams, and of course assisting you in taking out the loans to feed their machine."

Malach nodded. He had about as much interest as she did. "I'd like to take you to see the lake," he said. "Can we do that soon?"

'I'd love to see it," Ginny said. "Plus, you need to meet your neighbor."

Malach could see the signal in her eyes that was now so familiar to him. The slightly raised eyebrows that indicated that she was up to something.

"Let's go now," she said.

Malach laughed, not surprised to hear those words, and the two of them were out the back entrance to the parking lot, hopping into Ginny's car, and gone for the day.

Ginny was unusually quiet while she drove. Malach could see something was bothering her. "What's wrong?" he asked.

"I don't know. Senior year and college ahead, none of it means anything to me anymore. I've been thinking maybe a gap year would make sense."

She knew and so did Malach that this was getting harder for her. The time was approaching for him and college was not what was next. While he knew she was prepared to go with him, it created a great deal of conflict for her. Her parents would be angry and would blame Malach. She didn't care so much of what they thought about her, but didn't want them to hate him. Ginny began to cry. She quickly tried to wipe her tears with one hand while she was driving.

"I'm sorry. I don't know what's wrong with me. Everything is so confusing."

"What do you mean?" Malach said.

"You, what you do, what we do, what you've shown me. Sometimes it's so clear, and sometimes it makes no sense."

"I get it," Malach said. He took her hand in his. "I really do. It's understandable, it's normal."

"Understandable. Normal. I'm not sure I understand anything, and I'm certainly not normal anymore," Ginny said. "One day we're in the woods and a sweet little song bird comes close and I think how charming that is. And last week you held me tight before there's even a sign of a lightning storm and I feel energy sounds running through my body. How's that humanly possible? People are not supposed to feel those things. But you do and through you, I feel what you feel. Just try to imagine this from outside of you."

Malach squeezed Ginny's hand. "It's not going to get easier," he said. "You need to be part of this. I know that and so do you. We're close to the edge. There's so little time left. The die-off has started and I don't know where it's going to end. I need your help."

"I'm afraid that I won't be able to help or do what needs to be done," Ginny said. "I don't want to fail. It's so big and so important. I know there are a lot of people finally trying to make changes, marches and protests, but what they're doing isn't enough, not even close. Nothing is making a difference. It just keeps getting worse."

"You can do this," Malach said.

"Are you kidding? That's what terrifies me. How can I know the way to make people change, to get seven and a half billion people to try to live differently, to save this miraculous blue sphere spinning in the universe? I liked it better when you just whispered to little furry animals or summoned wild beasts. But I know it's so much more than that. But all of this knowledge, all of this wonder, all of these links to our past – how do I explain it? Who's going to believe it? Who's going to believe me? Who's going to listen?"

"We can't be afraid," Malach said.

She looked at the strain in his face and knew it was not a clear path ahead, even as his eyes expressed his understanding and empathy for what she felt. While she couldn't say it, she feared for him more than for herself.

"I'll be with you. I wouldn't be anywhere else," Ginny said. "You know that."

They sat quietly while she drove. Ginny's thoughts drifted. She remembered the day at the start of camp when Malach walked into the Conservation Center and back into her life. They were still kids and she was surprised to see him after so many years. She never could have dreamed at the time what that reunion would do to her, how it would reshape her life, and how it would change the way she looked at the world. Right from the beginning he made her so nervous, made her heart skip, and kindled feelings that she didn't know existed within her. These unfamiliar feelings, these secrets her body held in waiting, the feelings of loving someone grew and blossomed.

The feelings she had for Malach, the mysteries of the world he showed her, all of it was so confusing. Each time something was revealed it became as clear as day, something once unfamiliar now belonged to her. But the satisfaction and delight of the new might then collide once again into the black hole of the unknown, the clarity receding as quickly. The knowledge that she had absorbed over the past five years, the very intelligence of the world, was mixed with anguish and confusion when she searched alone without him beside her. Her place in the world, the world he introduced, was as emotionally confounding and intense as her feelings for him.

She loved Malach, longed for his kisses, the touch of his hands on her skin, the warmth of his body close to hers. He was her confidant, her guide, and her anchor. She needed him and she believed he needed her. Despite all of his mysteries, they exchanged a connection that bound them together, equal and balanced, giving and forgiving, hungry and sated. They shared a passion solely their own. Being with him made her see life so differently. She loved what she gleaned from how he lived his life. She understood that the world was moving along a path that was failing everyone. People wanted too much of the wrong things and ignored so much of what could be right. Despite all of that, she knew that when the time came she would not hesitate to do whatever needed to be done, and would be right at his side.

Malach held her hand as they drove. The fall foliage was at its peak. The sky was clear, and the day helped some to lift Ginny's spirits. They left the car on a wide shoulder along the county road about a half-mile from the driveway to the neighbor's house. She took a deep breath and shook off the doubts and uncertainty for now and they headed to the lake. A dark red weathered mailbox on the county road read Rothman. Malach was certain this was the road in. They continued down the dirt driveway and encountered an older man in the yard stacking firewood from a recently delivered pile. He was placing it in a wood rack when he noticed his two young visitors.

"How can I help you?" the man asked.

Malach approached with Ginny. "Sorry to be intruding. I hope it's okay that we walked in."

"No problem for me. Are you looking for someone?"

"I suppose you," Malach answered. "I wanted to introduce myself. I'm Malach and this is my friend, Ginny. We're neighbors."

"Is that right?" he said as he reached out and shook Malach's then Ginny's hand. "David Rothman. Pleased to make your acquaintance, but I don't have recollection of any neighbors. Not a house for miles around as far as I can remember. Only the beauty and solitude of mother nature."

"I'm at Roger Stine's old place," Malach said.

"Oh, I see. He was a very decent man. Knew him for many years, though had not seen him for some time before he passed on. Are you relatives or new owners of the place?"

"Malach and Roger were like family," Ginny said.

The man nodded and continued to lift some wood while they talked. He was tall and lean, spry in his step despite the gentle stoop in his posture. His hair was long and pulled back into a ponytail with a Yankees cap on his head. His face was etched with deep creases, but he had a welcoming and disarming smile, and his eyes brightened with a mischievous flash.

Malach and Ginny pitched in with the woodpile. "Thanks for the help, but you don't need to feel obligated to do that," Rothman said. "The old bones still operate, the body has not exhausted its utility, and on most days the mind is clear. But thank you for your generous offer."

"It's a big pile," Malach said.

"I don't think I've seen a more beautiful view and surroundings," Ginny said.

"We've been fortunate to have spent our lives here, me and my wife. She's in town doing some errands."

"Is it just the two of you here?" Ginny asked.

"It is now. Raised our two children here, my son Jack, and daughter Lilith. Both are married with families of their own. We've added a wonderful daughter-in-law and a wonderful son-in-law to the family. Jack has two girls and Lilith two boys. Even the grandchildren are starting to grow up."

"Do you get to see them often?" Ginny asked. Thoughts of leaving home were still going through her head.

"Both kids moved on from here after college," said David. "It had become too remote for them, both eager to explore the world, ready for a change. I understand that, but it doesn't make me miss them any less. While they're too far for my liking, at least they are close to each other down in North Carolina. Their families get together often. It also makes it easy for us when we visit."

"Are you thinking about moving closer?" Ginny said.

"Actually, we've been entertaining it. We first talked about it a few years ago, but there was no real interest in the house and we only started reconsidering it again a few weeks ago and wouldn't you know it an unsolicited letter arrived from someone interested in the house and property."

"A developer?" Malach asked.

"Yes." David laughed. "In fact, it was a developer. Wants to build houses. I suppose that's what they do everywhere. Build more and more houses. We have about thirty acres and some of it has beautiful views of the lake. The lake isn't ours. We just have access and a small piece from this side with the shoreline. I don't like to think about what they may do, disturbing the beauty. It's hard to blame them. It is alluring. It was for us once upon a time. I worry we're not likely to get another taker if we let this one slip by. Denial is a powerful thing, allows one to clear the conscience and sleep better at night."

Louise drove her Jeep down the drive and waved as she saw David and the visitors. She got out of the vehicle, called out a greeting and then opened the back hatch, which was filled with grocery bags. Louise was tall and refined, with her gray hair pulled up behind her head, dressed in a wool sweater and matching hat.

"We have ourselves a couple of young guests," David said and then introduced everyone.

"What a pleasure," Louise said. "We don't often get surprise visitors. Please come in for a drink or snack."

"Thank you, but that's not necessary," Malach said. "We don't want to impose, just stopped by to say hello."

"They're our new neighbors or such," David interjected. "They live at Roger Stine's old place."

"How interesting," Louise said. "Please, I insist that you come in for a snack."

"Thank you," Ginny said.

"We'll grab those bags for you," Malach added.

The house was warm and welcoming. Lots of pictures on the walls, an old wooden table in the kitchen in front of a big picture window looking out over the lake, a wood burning stove in the corner.

Louise noticed Ginny's attention to the view. "It's a pleasure to look out at that every morning," she said. "We've been able to do it for forty-nine years. When we found this old house, I don't think I hesitated for even a moment. That was some time ago, back in nineteen-sixty-nine. We had both finished college a number of years earlier and met doing political work. The sixties, those were turbulent times."

"Were you involved in it?" Ginny asked.

"Right in the middle, civil rights marches, protesting the Viet Nam war, trying to make this country more fair and honest. I guess we were two idealists. We thought we would change the world. Eventually, we decided to see if we could do something better out here. It was a big leap for a girl who grew up in Manhattan."

"I was only in New York once," Ginny said. "A world apart from here. Did you ever regret it?"

"No, no regrets," said Louise. "We're both writers, so the solitude and reflection it affords suits us. Though sometimes I wonder if we could have made a bigger impact elsewhere. We certainly get away from time to time. Back to the city or travel. It was a safe and sensible place to raise children. But everything has a time and a place."

David served tea and put a plate of cookies on the table. "I made them last night," he said. "Let me know if you have ever had a better chocolate chip cookie."

"What do you both write?" Malach asked.

"Louise is a wonderful creator of children's literature," David said. "Quite good at it, mostly for middle school readers. And I muddle about and labor over my poems."

"Oh, don't let him make you believe that his work is insignificant," said Louise. "Writing good poetry is a daunting task. He's had several collections of his poems published."

"That's true, and they've been purchased and read by a good fifty or sixty people," David said with a loud laugh.

"Stop that now," Louise said. "One doesn't write for that reason. You write because you have to, you have something that has to find its way out. It's a way to speak about the human condition. We forget what's important, what values we stand for, sometimes get pulled into the atrocious cycle of... Sorry, I don't want to be so negative. I hope the two of you reach for the stars, for dreams that are important and redeeming."

"I'm a firm believer in that," Ginny said.

"That's wonderful. Enough about us now, what about the two of you? What are you doing? School? Travel? Work?" Louise asked.

"High school," Ginny answered.

"Oh, I thought the two of you older," said Louise, finding herself puzzled by these two youngsters.

"We are. Seniors," Ginny said with a grin.

"Plans yet for next year?" Louise asked.

"I don't know," Ginny said. "I'm thinking of a gap year."

"She's the top student in the school," Malach added.

"Good for you," Louise said.

"Nothing more important than an education," David said. He popped up and poured everyone more tea.

"I worry that there are some things that don't allow for the luxury of a long and formal education," Ginny said. "There's so much wrong in the world and not a lot of time to repair it."

"We understand the sense of urgency," David said. "When we were young, everything felt imperative and required immediate responses. You don't want to lose that. It happens when you get older, and all sorts of other callings fall upon you. Back in the day, we felt it couldn't get worse. Then you get complacent, minimize the problems, rationalize the inconveniences, become distracted by the everyday. Time has a way of slipping by. I pick up the newspaper each morning and shake my head. We live in an irrational world. Go for it I say. Just go for it. If I were younger I would, too."

"You still can," Ginny said, and David smiled.

"It warms my heart and gives me hope for humankind," Louise said, "to hear you talk like that and to see two young people ready to make a difference. We haven't given up yet, quite on the contrary, we'll fight to the very end."

After their talk Ginny asked if they could look around. She had never seen the lake before. David and Louise were more than happy to take them on a hike to some of the prettier views.

"Do your children and grandchildren come here often?" Ginny asked as they took in a sweeping vista of the lake and valley.

"They come for Thanksgiving every year," Louise answered. "We visit them otherwise. They have busy lives."

"What do they do?" Ginny asked.

"Our son is a financial consultant," Louise answered. "Lilith and her husband are both lawyers. They are very successful. They have lovely homes and they travel everywhere. Coming out here is not their thing. We'd thought that the house would stay in the family, but they have no strong attachment to the area any longer."

"We hate to leave this place," David said, "but the children and grandkids are more important than the house. It's beautiful down there and the winters more forgiving. Next week the buyer is coming to look around. He's already made an offer and sent us a deposit. The check is still sitting on my desk. I'm reluctant to deposit it. Ambivalence, nostalgia, uncertainty of what will happen when we leave, I don't fully know. He's bringing his lawyer to sign a purchase and sale agreement."

The four of them walked down toward the water's edge. There was a clearing with a log that had been placed across two flat stones creating a bench. It had the initials of their children carved into it, its bark long gone, the wood weathered from many seasons exposed to the weather. Louise sat on it next to David, as they both needed a chance to rest their feet.

"There's ancient mystery in these surroundings," Malach said. "There are few places as beautiful in the area."

"David has written a moving collection of poems inspired by the land here," Louise said.

"We've seen the changes to it, firsthand," David said, "ones that are not so obvious, and it's heartbreaking. Right here in these North Woods during the nearly fifty years we've been on this lake, we are witnesses to what's changing. It shouldn't be happening so quickly. Winters are the most noticeable. Only decades ago we would always have bitterly cold stretches, snow falls and drifts that blanketed the valley. We still get intense storms but there is a shift in patterns and frequency. The lake was routinely iced over until well into the spring. Not anymore, longer stretches without ice cover are common now in winter.

"David has been documenting this since shortly after we arrived," said Louise. "He has several notebooks, or I should say oversized leather-bound folios overflowing with tabs, inserts, tables, along with detailed descriptions of everything around us."

"Since we moved here, I've been recording my observations," David interjected. "It was for my writing initially and a homage to Thoreau. You know he kept detailed journals at Walden that scientists use today to measure and track changes. Over the years I became somewhat expert on the wildlife and plants of this valley. I record storms, temperature readings on designated dates, spring arrival of migrating birds, first buds on the trees, first flowering of the local wildflowers, shifts in the wetlands downstream from the lake, and countless other data. At first, it was part of my personal diary, later research for my writing, and the last couple decades it has become my siren song. Just take the bird count for instance. We used to observe a host of species, boreal birds at the southern stretch of their range. Are you following what I'm talking about?"

"Yes," Ginny said. "I'm with you."

"Good. The birds that we cherished as our neighbors – gray jays, black-backed woodpeckers, yellow-bellied flycatchers – they're disappearing from this range. Maybe moving north, maybe the populations are in decline, but they're not the numbers I once observed."

"It's all of those things and more," Ginny said. "They're losing wetlands to development, the patchwork of habitats that link them are interrupted, many are shifting north, and all their numbers are declining. The rusty blackbird is suffering the biggest toll."

"You've been doing your homework. Good. Good. And the loons, tragic, the haunting calls undulating across the lake, the eerie primordial shrill. Not so much anymore."

"There's a lot going wrong in the world," Ginny said. "But this is the one thing we can't ignore any longer. We're killing the world around us and we have to change the way we live."

"Ginny, I wish I had an answer for this," David said. "I've read, I've observed, I've even mourned the losses, but I don't see that we have the will to change."

"You can join," Ginny said. "We're going to stop this."

"I love your optimism," David said.

Malach flashed a smile and a nod to Ginny. "She's going to make this happen."

"I hope that you do," Louise said.

"We have to," Ginny said. "I'm terrified about what's happening around us, in our own back yard, and it's so much worse in other places around the world."

"You've both grown up here?" Louise asked.

"Yes," Ginny said.

"So how is it that you're at Roger Stine's place?"

"Well, we're not exactly," Ginny said. "Malach was given the house by Roger after he died. He's was the closest Roger had to family."

"Oh, I see," said Louise. "But I heard that the house was knocked down. Are you putting up a new home there?"

"What do you mean?" David asked. "I hadn't heard."

"When the plumber was here last week," Louise said, "cleaning the oil burner, he told me."

"Chuck Dowling?" David asked.

"Yes."

"It did come down," Malach said. "We didn't knock it down. Ginny and I and two close friends carefully took it apart one piece at a time and sent all of it off for salvage, or reuse, or just gave it away."

"You kids did that!" David said joyously. "Took apart a house. How fabulous. The whole thing is strangely beguiling. Dismantling an entire house. Pray tell, speak to us."

Ginny smiled, glanced to Malach and they exchanged a knowing look. Malach described at length the machinations and workings that went into the project. Louise and David were riveted with their attention, finding the whole enterprise refreshingly captivating.

"There's no plan to build another house," Malach said. "Just the opposite, the plan is for no house at all, perhaps forever. Just leave the wild, wild."

"Bravo!" David bellowed. "The impact may be small, but the symbolism is grand and potent."

They spoke for some time about the house, David and Louise gratified to hear of a well-executed mission.

Malach walked closer to the water, and knelt down. "It would be a shame for all this to get lost," he said. "Sadly, like you have noticed, the changes are taking hold. Changes that would happen over thousands of years are now happening in just decades. It seems imperceptible to some, but when you pay close attention over time, like you have, even over the course of one lifetime it starts to become clear. It's going to be catastrophic."

"There's hope, there's always time for change," Louise said.

"I wish that were true," Malach said. "It can't be stopped. It's only a question of how willing we are to try to limit it."

David and Louise listened, trying to make sense of their visitors.

"Let me show you something," Malach said. He splashed his hand in the water and moments later one of the river otters that he had encountered a few months ago surfaced and waddled to his side. Louise startled and David's eyes widened. Malach rubbed the otter's head.

"I've never seen anything like that," David said.

"The animals here live in relative safety from people," Malach said. "That's always a good thing. The buyer for this place will build houses all across your land. He ultimately wants the whole valley and what he will do to the land will change and affect everything that lives here. It will no longer be wild." Malach stood up, the otter craning his neck up toward him. Malach stroked its head one more time and then waved it back into the lake.

"How did that happen? How did you do that?" David asked, while Louise sat spellbound while watching Malach and the animal.

"I'll try to explain that in a moment, but first, I have a request. I'd like you to sell your house and land to me. I'll pay you whatever the developer offered you or whatever you think is fair."

1

t was Tuesday before Thanksgiving when Mark received the call. It was very early morning, the hour when a ringing telephone delivers bad news. Judith was startled awake, her heart pounding. Mark picked up the call after the first ring, also jolted from sleep. His voice was still as he listened. Judith looked for a signal or cue but his face was blank. Stoically, he fought back tears while comforting his mother who was on the other end of the line. Judith nudged him and he turned and grimaced as he told her his father had died. She reached out and put her arm around him as he continued to talk. She began to make out the broken details communicated from the half conversation that she could hear. His mother recounted how she woke to find her husband sitting on the edge of the bed having trouble breathing, heaviness on his chest. The ambulance arrived quickly and Mark's father was rushed to the hospital. At the emergency room tests confirmed that he had an unstable cardiac condition and arrangements were being made to transport him to the large medical center an hour away for evaluation by the cardiac surgical team. In the short window before he was moved, he suffered a massive and fatal heart attack. Several times during the conversation Mark reassured his mother that they were coming as soon as possible and that he would make the calls to his brothers. He was comforted knowing that Eileen, his mother's longtime friend and neighbor, had been at her side almost immediately after she heard the ambulance and police commotion outside.

After the call Mark and Judith sat silently together before getting up. Judith looked at the clock. It was just after four in the morning. She put on her robe and went downstairs to the kitchen.

When Mark entered the kitchen, he slumped into his chair. "I never expected this," he said. He took a sip of coffee and placed the cup back on the table. Mark did not touch the toast and honey Judith had prepared. He stared ahead, his face ashen, tightness in his lips. "He always seemed so strong, never had health problems. He lived a good, clean, and righteous life."

Judith let him sit with his thoughts and feelings. Soon he began to sob. She let him cry, as she understood well the healing power of tears. Judith had such mixed feelings about Mark's father. There were not many adults in her early years that showed her kindness. Even when he had barely known her he had welcomed her into the family though she was never certain that he was pleased with their hurried courtship and marriage.

Judith's attention shifted to all the preparations that would need to be made both here and for travel to Florida. She had invited Sky and Calvin and the usual three lone members of the church for Thanksgiving dinner. Sky and Calvin would be able to fend for themselves, but arrangements for the others would require sensitive planning. Plane reservations to Florida for the family during this busy holiday season would take some doing. She did not want Mark to have to worry about any of these matters.

After a while Mark rose from the table and said he was going to make the calls to his brothers. She listened as he used the phone in the kitchen. Judith had never felt close to either Thaddeus or Simon. Both were married, had children and lived relatively close to her in-laws, yet it was Mark who was the one his parents reached out to, be it for his guidance, prayer, or just an opportunity to talk.

Mark spoke first with his oldest brother, Thaddeus. It was not an exchange of shared grief, but rather a contentious and irritated argument. The call was brief, followed by a heartfelt talk with Simon. She knew Thad and Mark did not see eye-to-eye on very much and this was certainly the case when it came to their father. Thad and the

Reverend bristled in each other's company – resentments by the son, disappointments by the father. As the eldest, Thad had suffered the most. He despised the control, the questioning, and the obvious discontent with his choices and direction of his life. His twice-divorced wife was frowned upon, his incomplete education considered irresponsible, and his rejection of a faith-based life indefensible. In his early years, the Reverend believed he could tame his oldest son by fire, but Thad's similar temperament only made their standoff more volatile and destructive for each of them. If it were not for Mark's mother, there may have been no visits at all. Simon was often spared, as he was passive and accommodating. His reserve and inhibition, the Reverend had felt, made him weak and unsuited to follow in his path.

"You knew what my father was like," Mark said as he and Judith sat back down at the table. "Just a blistering presence, unyielding and abrasive. It's difficult imagining him sitting on the edge of the bed, shaken, fragile, gasping for air, barely a whisper of himself, alone in the dark. It was not his nature. I never even considered him vulnerable. It is a painful reminder how it can all be over in the blink of an eye." Mark shook his head. "Only seventy-one. It sounds trite, but life is so short."

"The Lord works in mysterious ways," Judith said, the words slipping from her mouth surprised her, but were received by Mark with a nod of approval.

"Yes, He does," Mark said. "Often we don't have the answers and have to let ourselves accept God's will. That is true with so many of the difficulties we encounter in our lives and relationships."

"I've gotten better with that," Judith said trying to be supportive. She felt the fear of death that used to inundate her as a child, always too close. Belief in God never provided a buffer or security then, and as much as she tried now, it still eluded her, and didn't provide the comfort she needed.

"We have gotten better," Mark said. "That is a good thing and I'm thankful for that, especially when we face a day like today. It's hard not to reflect on the meaning of our lives when we straddle the worlds of life and death."

"I understand," Judith said. "We've made a life. For me that's an achievement. I don't say it enough, but I want you to know that I don't for one moment feel unappreciative of the efforts you've made and of the life you've provided. I know it hasn't been easy with me. I'm still trying even after all these years."

"It's comforting to hear you say that," said Mark. "I know now that I have not always been the kind of husband you needed or the kind of father you would have wanted me to be for Malach. Too often, I have been blinded by narrow thinking, but have come to see where that originates in me. I think about the life I had lived with my father and realize I have often repeated it in our home. It has taken me a long time to find my way, maybe too long now to make a difference."

Mark and Judith looked at each other and he took her hand. "I hope we can continue to make our marriage strong, for us, but also for what lies ahead for Malach. He stretches the bounds of all explanation. I've not even an inkling of where his life is headed. While we look at it differently, it remains a mystery. Even in faith there is not the comfort of certainty as to what he will face. We have to live with that."

"His time under our roof is coming to an end," Judith said. "What does life even look like for someone like him?"

"I don't have that answer, either," Mark said, his voice full of sincerity.

Her relationship with Mark had taken so many turns over the years that she sometimes did not fully recognize herself in this marriage. Time had softened her hard edges, Mark's eventual willingness to meet her where she was, more than halfway, lowered the friction between them. But more than anything else, they were willing to face each other, to utter the words "I'm sorry" when necessary, and to start over and try again. Mark was able to accept her damaged nature, but never her willingness to go her own way.

Malach, of course, remained a conundrum. He led them, and that was harder for Mark to accept than for Judith. She discovered early on that all she could provide her son were protection and love. Mark had never been able to accept those limitations and constraints, and always believed his role was to raise a decent, honest, and God-fearing human being. He had come to envision Malach as working through the hand of God. She could never wrap her mind around that. He was her child but also part of this world in its entirely complex and little understood form. It had been a framework that gave her some comfort, something less mystical to hold onto.

It was a little after six when Malach wandered into the kitchen. He could see the sadness in his parent's faces.

"What's going on?" he asked.

"Your grandfather had a heart attack last night," Mark said. "He's no longer with us. We received a call from your grandmother early this morning."

Mark approached and wrapped his arms around Malach, holding him close. It was an unusual show of affection, though Malach reciprocated the embrace, feeling the loss as well. Mark then stepped back, straightening himself, and looked to Judith and to Malach.

"I would like for the three of us to go to church this morning to pray." Looking to Malach, he added, "After, if you want, you can go to school or take the day off."

A few hours later the three of them pulled up in front of the church. Mark opened the front door and they entered together. Malach noticed a field mouse in the same opening in the wall as when he first spoke with his father years ago about his understanding of the animal world. They entered the chapel and sat together in the front pew. Firmly upright, Mark held his hands clasped in his lap. Malach and Judith sat in contemplation beside him. Mark's eyes were closed in silent prayer for several minutes before he spoke.

"My father devoted his life to the church and service of others. He had a very strong faith. He was firm that the teachings of Christ are immutable, the very word of God. He was an old-time preacher, just like his father before him. But he also believed that there were mysteries that no man and no woman could fully understand, and it was through the teachings of scripture that we hope to find comfort and solace." He directed his words to Malach.

"Your grandfather was a complex man. He was righteous and devout but not easy. I always believed that his wrestling with faith as a young man fostered that in him. When he was eighteen he joined the Navy during the Vietnam War. He was in and out of ports across the Asian Pacific for three years. He saw places and things he could never have imagined. It was so foreign to him, never having been away from home. It was a hard path in the service. He was hotheaded, quick to temper, sometimes a doubter, and sometimes the guy who preached too much, but he believed that his military service was instrumental in preparing for the ministry, a test for what he would face ahead. It opened his eyes, being in worlds so different from his own. It made him a more complete person, able to bring compassion and empathy to others.

"Malach, your grandfather once told me that he thought you had 'the calling.' For him that meant you had the ability to lead and bring the Word to others. I believe, like he did, that in your own special and unique way, you will bring an important message to others."

Judith was surprised to hear these comments. She knew Mark had changed in the long time they had been together, but it moved her to see him reach out to his son, as he floundered with his own painful history and relationship with his father. After some further prayer they left the church and returned home.

When Judith and Mark flew out later that day, she tried to reassure herself that a flight would be found in the next day or two for Malach. It made her anxious thinking about leaving him behind.

Returning to Florida was always difficult, but she did not allow herself to think about that yet. It would inundate her in due time as it always did. Soaring above the blue and luminous sky, Judith was wistful looking out at the billowing cumulus clouds, admiring the splendor of the openness around her. She wished there were a heaven, a place of peace and compassion.

Ginny came to the house to see Malach after his parents had departed for Florida. She found him in the kitchen with a big bowl of cut fruit in front of him. He got up to greet her and she comforted him with a hug.

"How are you doing?" she asked.

"Not so great, but I'm glad you're here," he said. "Do you want some fruit?"

"Sure," she said.

Malach spooned some sliced apples, pears, and bananas from the bowl onto a plate and she sat down at the table with him.

"It was a shock for everyone, especially for my father," Malach said. "He's having a tough time. He and my grandfather didn't have an easy relationship. My grandfather wasn't warm and fuzzy, always preachy, and got under everyone's skin. He drove my cousins crazy. He didn't care. It was for everyone's good."

"And I thought your father was tough," Ginny said. "Maybe it comes to him honestly."

"The apple doesn't fall far..." Malach said.

"No, it doesn't, but it better in your case, as far away from the tree as possible," Ginny said as they smiled at each other.

"Getting old isn't something I look forward to," Ginny continued. "My grandmother was sick for so long before she died. The last months of her life she was in a nursing home. It was so sad, everyone there was waiting for her to die. The doctors gave her so much medicine she was barely conscious. I knew it was killing my father to see her like that. As hard as it was, I think he felt some relief when she passed away, not for himself, but for her. I think I'd like to die like your grandfather, just fast when the time comes. No suffering."

Ginny filled her plate with more fruit. "These bananas are perfect, just the way I like them, not too ripe." She placed the bowl in front of Malach who also had another portion.

"There's no escaping suffering," Malach said. "It's like that everywhere in nature, but we don't see it, we've become too removed, but it's no different for people." Malach had taken a mouthful of fruit and paused to chew and swallow. "My father has given a million sermons about Heaven, but even with the promise of eternal life, everyone in the church is basically afraid to die. Everyone everywhere is afraid to die. You'd think it would be just the opposite, the part of life we'd all look forward to if we truly believed."

"I never thought about it like that," Ginny said. "My grandmother was going to die no matter what the doctors did, they told us that themselves, but it didn't stop them from trying everything to give her another day or week, even if she didn't know what was going on."

Malach nodded while eating. "It's hard to let the people we love go. I wish we did the same to save the world around us."

"I guess learning how to die isn't that different from learning how to live," Ginny said. "Another one of those things people haven't figured out yet."

Ginny got up and took the container of milk from the refrigerator and poured herself and Malach each a glass and brought them to the table. "So how are you getting to Florida?"

"No word on a flight yet, probably tomorrow. I'm on standby," Malach said. "Sky is going to take me to the airport early in the morning and I'll wait for a seat."

"I'll drive you," said Ginny.

"Thanks, but it's a long ride," Malach said.

"I wasn't thinking about the airport," Ginny said. "We'll just go direct."

"That's an even longer ride," Malach said with a smile.

"I know, but I want to, if that's okay with you?"

He leaned over and gave her a kiss. "I'm not sure Virginia and Oliver will be too hot on it."

"I've already cleared it with them," Ginny said.

He knew she had not. She was never good at deceit. It was not her nature. "So, when are we going?" he asked.

Ginny had that twinkle in her eyes. "Soon, after we get your things together and pack you up. Maybe have a little time for us. It's going to be a lot of hours sitting in the car." She took him by the hand and led him up the stairs to his room. She closed the door behind them though no one else was home. After lingering over a long kiss, she pulled her shirt over her head and then unsnapped her jeans and stepped out of them. She held him close running her hands along his body. After unwrapping her arms from around him, she unclasped her bra dropping it to the floor and then slipped off her panties. Standing naked before him she looked into Malach's eyes and then undressed him. Together they slid under the covers and into a bed for the first time.

Ginny thought of the many times they found each other, bodies wrapped together on a bed of ferns, or pine needles, or leaves, the sounds and smells of the mountain surrounding them. Laying with him on a soft mattress, facing each other, a pillow under her head and his, with a blanket over their bodies felt delicious, and in the Minister's house, a forbidden pleasure.

She kissed him and then rolled onto her back and pulled Malach on top of her. Her mouth met his again as her eyelids gently shut. Warmth emanated between their tightly pressed bodies as she held him close, her legs wrapped snugly around his. From deep inside of her escaped a soft moan.

Afterwards, lying in each other's arms, the comfort and contentment she felt slowly began to recede. The urgency of time and all that they were preparing for felt imminent. Ginny held firmly to Malach but was determined to not let fear take hold of her. The apprehension had been creeping up on her more and more frequently. She told herself it was just the anticipation of that next step. Yet, never had she imagined taking on something of this magnitude and consequence. So many people were finally trying to force changes, but she knew it was Malach who could make the difference.

"We have to get on with this," Ginny said.

"We already have," Malach said.

"What do you mean?"

"The Rothmans, you won them over."

Ginny rolled her eyes. "I think the otter didn't hurt, not to mention the fact that you could actually buy their property."

"No, it was the message," he said.

"They were already converts."

"Maybe so," Malach said. "But my grandfather used to tell me, you change hearts one at a time."

"Well," said Ginny, "two down then, and only seven billion, four hundred and ninety-nine million, nine hundred and ninety-nine thousand, nine hundred and ninety-eight to go."

"We're off to a good start," Malach said.

"Maybe we are," Ginny said. She looked into his eyes and thought how she found everything about him wondrous. "I know I've told you this so many times, but I'm ready. It's too important for half measures, compromises, and baby steps. It's a battle for survival."

"I believe in you," Malach said, "and so will others. You happen to be very impressive for only seventeen."

"Never too young, I say, and the boy wonder I sleep with makes an even bigger and better impression."

"I'm not so sure of that, but either way, we're a good team," he said.

"I suppose we are."

After they showered, something else they had never done together before, she sat on the edge of the bed with a towel wrapped around her body and watched Malach while he gathered his clothes and packed a bag. They were a team, but she wondered if she could do any of this without him. When Malach was finished she dressed, stopped in the kitchen and filled a grocery bag with the rest of the uncut fruit in the kitchen, made a pile of peanut butter and jelly sandwiches, grabbed the remaining granola bars in the basket on the counter, and filled two water bottles from the tap. They loaded the car and smiled at each other.

"By the way, we're going to pick up Angie and Evan," said Ginny. "They decided they're coming, too. It'll make the driving easier. Before you ask about their parents, they're on board, too." Then she began to laugh. Ginny stopped at the small convenience store a short distance from Angie's house, the launching spot for their get-away.

"So, we're all going to Florida," Malach said once his friends loaded their bags, offered their condolences, and got in the car. "Are any of you thinking about telling anyone that we've taken off on a fifteen-hundred-mile road trip or are we going to have the police in a dozen states chasing us?"

They all looked at each and laughed.

"We'll text them when we have a couple hundred miles behind us," Ginny said.

"That sounds about right," added Evan.

Angie nodded in agreement, her head down as she was fiddling with her video camera.

2

When they arrived in Florida, it was late afternoon on Thanksgiving Day. The weather was balmy and clear with many cars parked in front of the house that was filled with relatives and close friends ahead of the service and interment the next day. Malach's oldest cousin, Tater, was the first to greet them when they pulled into the driveway. He was leaning against his car not ready to go inside. He was in his early twenties, his hair unruly and dangling in his face, a week's growth of stubble on his face, cargo shorts hanging loosely from his hips, wearing a Mötley Crüe t-shirt, fitting too tightly to his body.

"Hey, Mal, how goes it? You made it. I hear you drove all the way down. Hope it was a good trip." He hugged Malach and slapped him on the back. "I see you came with the entourage. So, who do we have here?"

Malach introduced his friends to Tater who shook everyone's hand and patted each of them on the back as though they were old friends.

"Are you Malach's girlfriend?" he asked Ginny.

"Yeah, that would be me."

"Well, hope that's working for you. He's a bit of an oddball."

"Oh, yeah, I know that." Ginny said. Malach erupted in laughter, as did Angie and Evan.

"Hell of a long trip to make," Tater said. "You all must really like funerals."

"Not especially," Ginny said. "But the ride with this motley crew was worth it."

"Good one," Tater said, nodding his approval.

"So Mal, did you ever imagine the old man would go like that? I thought he'd live forever, my punishment for not being a believer. Didn't see it coming. Seemed tough as nails. Always on my case to get back in the fold."

"I was surprised as anyone," Malach said. "Tough guy. Determined to save souls."

"So, Ginny," Tater said, "you'll get a taste for the nut job family your boyfriend belongs to. My Daddy, he's inside but I think he would have skipped all this if he could have. The old Reverend fucked up my old man. It's a wonder I turned out the way I did."

"A downright miracle," she retorted. Now all of them began to laugh out loud.

"Damn, you don't miss a beat," said Tater. "I like you, Miss Ginny. You're hot shit. Mal, you found yourself a good one. Does she got a sister?"

Malach put his arm around his cousin's shoulder. "Too young for you. Maybe we should go inside and let them know we made it."

"I'm glad I'm not the only one this late for Thanksgiving dinner," Tater said.

The Walker brood was a fractious and contentious lot. They did not comport themselves like a family coming together to support each other in grief and to ease their loss. Tater's younger brother, Charlie, came over as they walked in. So different from his older brother, his hair buzz cut, dressed in a Gators jersey, sports pants, and high-top sneakers. Only twelve, he was happy to see Malach, gave him a fist bump and a warm welcome. He was less effusive with Ginny, Angie, and Evan, seemingly awkward with strangers.

Several other relatives approached Malach to welcome him and his friends, everyone aware of his journey. Tater's father, Thaddeus, could be heard across the room, loud and oblivious to the volume of his voice. Ginny turned to see him making a point with his wife. It didn't interrupt the gathering as everyone kept talking as though it was normal.

"My parents," Tater said to Ginny when he saw her looking in their direction. "It doesn't take long to get a glimpse of it. I told you he was fucked up. Never a moment of peace with him no matter where you go. You'd think by now he would have learned that the old lady isn't going to be pushed around. Got to give her that."

Ginny gave him a more compassionate look of understanding. It was no longer funny. She was less prepared for the greeting from Malach's father. There was barely a welcome from him.

"So, you have arrived," Mark said to Malach, his eyes briefly darting toward Ginny. "Your mother will be happy that this trip has finally concluded. It was not what anyone needed right now. I would have hoped that you had the judgment to know this." He turned and stared at Ginny, again. She stood firm, as she had grown accustomed to the Reverend's judgmental remarks.

"My friends just spent two days on the road to help me get here and to show their support and pay their respects. I would think you might see that as an act of kindness. The Christian thing to do."

"I do not need a lecture," Mark responded. "Arrangements were being made for you."

"I guess they were unnecessary."

Judith observed the friction between Malach and his father, and immediately hurried across the room to intervene.

"Enough of this," she interrupted. "I don't even want to know what this is about, but it just has to stop. If there's a problem, we'll deal with it later. Mark, your cousin, Stevie, and his wife want to see you." Mark turned to look at Malach and Ginny before he went off to talk with his family. He left without further comment, and Judith could see that he was annoyed with himself for his eruption.

She gave Malach a hug, offered an apology to Ginny, and welcomed

Angie and Evan. After checking in about the trip she reminded each of them to be sure to call their parents to let them know that they had arrived. Her phone exchanges the past two days with their mothers had been stressful. There was a lot of food on the table, though everyone else had already eaten, and she encouraged them to help themselves. Judith pulled Malach aside as his friends went to fill their plates.

"I'm happy you're all here safely," she said.

"We're fine. It wasn't a hard trip," said Malach.

"Try not to get upset with your father. He's been edgy since we arrived. You know how the family can be when they're all together. I didn't realize how much your grandfather kept things calm and civil. He was a strong presence in the family."

"You mean how the Good Shepherd tended his flock by cowing everyone in fear."

"You know he loved you," Judith said.

"You mean as much as he could love anyone," Malach said.

"Maybe so."

"You don't pick and choose in a family," Malach added.

"Your father would like you to do a reading at the service tomorrow," Judith said, trying to move on with the conversation. "Each of your cousins will be. Do you want to look at it?"

"I can read just fine."

"I know he was angry, but he'll get over it," Judith said.

"He needs to treat my friends better," Malach said. "If he has a problem, he can take it up with me."

"I understand. I'll talk to him," Judith said. "You're fortunate to have such caring friends in your life. I wish I'd been so lucky when I was your age. I love you. Go have something to eat with them."

Judith had been frantic the past couple days with the kids on the road. But it was also a period of reflection that helped her begin to accept that Malach was a young man now, and she could no longer manage and control what he did. While her head told her she had to let him go, her heart struggled to relinquish him.

Judith found Mark, pulled him aside and asked him what had happened. He impatiently dismissed her, but despite the family gathering and the somber occasion she pressed him. She was annoyed that so soon after his moment of genuine desire to be a different father, he quickly fell backwards.

"It was disrespectful, that's all," Mark said. "We're here to pay our final respects to his grandfather and the past two days we have to be distracted by this trip. He may understand things that we don't, but this is not one of them."

"They only had good intentions," Judith said.

"He does whatever he wants and you make excuses for him," Mark said. "It has been that way his entire life. Responsibility, consideration, especially at this moment in time, would have been appreciated. You can see for yourself what a mess we have here. The family cannot be civil for a few days until we put my father in his grave."

"Maybe there's something to learn in that," Judith said. "Instead of acting like your brother Thad, fighting with his wife, angry and impatient with his kids, maybe you could find a more understanding and caring path with your son."

Mark's eyes widened and he clenched his jaw, indignant with Judith's remark. "Enough. This is neither the time nor the place."

Judith realized it would be best to let this go for now. It didn't even seem related to Malach. Mark was being pulled into the fray of old family conflicts that he found demoralizing. She knew he had little tolerance for the messy parts of family life. Like his father, he operated on another plain that bore little resemblance to the gritty reality of the lives of the people around him. During their early visits home years ago, Mark would often be critical of her, while excuses were made for his family. It took time for her to see that she was the expedient scapegoat for the frustration, disappointments, and shame that his family's behavior created for him. Listening to him talk the past few days opened her eyes to how much he silently endured, how much he forced himself to rationalize, and how constricted his perceptions were about his father.

Judith left Mark with an aunt while she made her way to the kitchen where she poured herself a cup of coffee. Her sister-in-law, Kathy, Thaddeus' wife, joined her. She was complaining about Thad, going on and on about him, oblivious to Judith's absence of interest.

Judith looked around Mark's home. It was so different from the one she grew up in. The kitchen was warm and cheerful, with yellow wallpaper and sheer white curtains. It was not ostentatious but it was neatly furnished and immaculately clean. Very clear lines of division marked the traditional roles in the family. It was a recipe that Mark carried into their marriage. Mark did provide. She raised Malach, or watched him raise himself, yet the house was never well tended to and her cooking not even a close approximation to that of her grandmother. It was one of many sources of conflict in the marriage. In the beginning she did not have a clue about how to make a family operate, and Mark came with a manual.

The funeral the following day was attended by hundreds of people, congregants, community leaders, neighbors, friends, and family. There was a genuine outpouring of grief at his unexpected passing. When the pews were filled, the overflow left many standing in the rear. Mark stood in front of the congregation, and began by asking everyone to rise as he led with a prayer.

"I am moved by the support and love shown by each and every one of you who has taken time from your day to be here with our family to pay your final respects to the spiritual leader of this church. While I have been away for many years now, I feel the long shadow of this community, which since my youth helped shape who I have become. All of you have been part of my life, both right here in this house of worship, and in our schools, shops, and in every corner of our community. So many of you have remained, others returned from near and far. My mother, my brothers, their wives and children, my wife and son, we all thank you."

Mark spoke about his father, his good works, his legacy as a man of God and leader in the community, and also his role as husband, father, and grandfather. He shared some old stories, family remembrances, had each of the grandchildren come forward to read a biblical passage, and then finally introduced Malach, who spoke last.

Angie knew it would probably be frowned upon, but she quietly and as unobtrusively as possible began to record. She and Evan had found seats towards the rear. Ginny was seated with Malach and the family. The church was very different from what she was accustomed to. It had an old time Southern flavor that fit with what she imagined it might be like. God and church felt more central to the lives of the people here and she saw that in their words and overtures of comfort with each other.

[Record]

Malach stood at the pulpit and placed the unopened Bible he held in his hand down instead of reading the passage his father had selected and then shared his own thoughts.

"My grandfather was a difficult and stubborn man, very difficult and very stubborn."

Angie liked his opening line, finding his expression and the emphasis placed in his words immediately capturing the attention of those in the audience. It put a smile on her face.

"He was hardest on those closest to him, especially his own children and grandchildren. For him there was no equivocating when it came to faith. He was determined to instill in each one of us a strong belief and for all of us to lead righteous lives. He didn't just nudge us in that direction, he pushed, and he demanded, and sometimes even hurled us head first along that path."

Angie had never given a lot of thought to Malach's religious upbringing. He never talked about it. She knew both Ginny's family and Evan's were churchgoers, but it was not part of her upbringing. She could probably count on one hand the number of times she attended a service. It struck her now as odd that she had never considered Malach's own thinking about religion and how he understood his own unique circumstance in the world. How could she have been documenting him for so many years and not have tried to understand that part of his life?

"Some of us took to it better than others," Malach continued. "Some followed in his path, some of us rebelled. You all know our family and understand what I'm talking about."

There were lots of nodding heads, some laughter, and a few voices calling out acknowledgement. Angie held the camera steady and focused on Malach. He seemed so comfortable in front of the crowd. He always had an easy way about him, but it was different seeing him like this.

"Living up north, I saw him the least of all the grandchildren. When my parents and I visited, he would try to take time to spend just with me. Often we went on long walks, to the beach, sometimes to a park, or to the nearby wildlife refuge. He knew I liked the refuge best.

"On our walks, I always got a sermon. I didn't mind his stories but I wanted to know if he liked what we were seeing, all that was around us. It always seemed to me he was more interested in the message he was sharing than sharing in what I was experiencing. I just wanted to know if he liked nature. He told me he often had little time for that, but reminded me that, in his view, the world we lived in was perfect.

"I asked him why, if he thought it was so perfect, he didn't go out and see it, and enjoy it, and want to take care of it. He didn't say anything until one day when we were out on a hike, his eyes were opened for a moment. At the refuge, on one of the trails near the water, was a pair of spectacular birds, two rare and endangered whooping cranes. Their necks were outstretched, their eyes on us, as we stood silently still. I could see the look of joy in his face.

"I told my grandfather that those birds were in serious trouble, that only a few remained and that they may one day be lost forever. He was surprised to hear that, but believed it was out of our hands, that it was God's will if the birds were to live or to perish. He said that the animals were important, but that they do not have souls and that I should not forget that it is man who takes precedence.

"It bothered me that he felt that way. I told him that I didn't think God was going to save them, that it was up to us. He grew impatient, and then skeptically asked me, if this was so important, what was I going to do to save them."

Angie looked to Evan and they both liked where this was going. "He's a natural," Angie whispered.

"I told him I was going to open our eyes to what we are doing, and allow us to see what miracles of nature are being lost.

"He patted me on the head in a way that made me feel dismissed, that I didn't know what I was talking about. I can be stubborn, too, and told him not to do that. He looked surprised, not used to being challenged, but stopped and thought about what I had said. After a long pause and reflection he told me that if I believe very strongly in something and it's right and just, then I have to fight for it because most people don't want to hear these things. He said, 'Preach hard, preach strong, preach everywhere, even at a funeral if it's important enough.' So, here I am at my grandfather's funeral to tell you the world around us is in terrible danger. It is changing because of what we all do, because of how we live, and because of how little attention we pay to what exists around us. We have grown indifferent and so removed from the natural world that we no longer understand how important it is to our very own lives. My grandfather did not understand this either. But if we let the animals and the plants die, we will have lost more than we realize. For if we let God's Creation begin to die, a part of our soul will die along with it."

Evan nudged Angie and they exchanged a look.

"I believe it's going to take sacrifice," Malach continued, "personal sacrifice and even more than that, it's going to take a fight. What are we willing to give up to make sure there's enough room on this Earth for everything that lives here, and to protect it and sustain it? It's going to mean changing the way we all live. If we are to be stewards of the earth, we're failing and we have not learned one of the important lessons of life, that our spiritual life cannot be sustained when we are removed from the natural world. It's our path back to the Garden of Eden itself, and the hope for closeness to God."

Malach suggested a silent prayer for his grandfather, asking everyone to take the hand of the person to the right and to the left of them and those sitting at the end of the row to reach to the person in front of them allowing all in attendance to be connected. Angie hooked her arm with the young woman at her left while Evan held her by the waist. With her free hand she focused the camera on Malach, while waiting for some sign, some moment of revelation. Malach walked over and took Ginny's hand to link himself to the congregation.

Make something happen, Angie thought. Please, make a mark, but nothing occurred. She was not sure what she had expected, but felt a pang of disappointment. She hoped to capture the first occasion of Malach's presence on others. His words would have to suffice for now. Too many people, she wondered. At least he tried and there would be other occasions. She glanced quickly at Evan and could see his grimace as he shared her sentiments. She kept the camera steady, zooming back to include more of those in the church. Angie then focused in on Malach's parents and could see a mix of pride but perhaps apprehension in their faces. Ginny remained still, eyes closed, hands held with Malach and his mother.

Then Angie saw a flickering flash of light and could smell a change in the air, a briny odor, heavy with the humidity and the presence of the Gulf waters. Evan squeezed her shoulder. An urgent hush and then gasps came simultaneously from the mouths of the several hundred people assembled. Murmurs, breathlessness, and sighs filled the room. A realization swept the chapel as all present recognized that they were witness to something extraordinary, a vision and not a flight of their own imaginations. She slowly scanned the camera, pausing for close ups of wide-eyed looks, opened mouths, turning heads, whispers and nudges, bewildered faces. Standing amidst the coastal waters and open skies, all those present were surrounded by a spectacular scene, though not one that could be captured on film. There were not two, but dozens and dozens of the magnificent white cranes, perhaps a hundred or more, their large wings with black tips rapidly beating, long legs and outstretched necks extended as they propelled themselves forward and aloft in flight. The soaring birds were so close, the sounds of their wings audible as the steady beat lifted them higher and higher into the sky until they disappeared into the distance.

Then, it was over, not more than a few minutes had passed. Angie turned to Evan and could see the same wave of exhilaration that she felt deep in her body, a giddy excitement of endless possibilities. She guided her camera for a while longer until she felt that the occasion was captured.

[Stop]

The following morning Malach, Ginny, Angie, and Evan loaded the car and began their trip back home. It had been a long and emotional day at the church after Malach's eye-opening revelation. For Ginny, Angie, and Evan there was an understanding that a threshold had been crossed.

3

The first of many waves of spoonbills flew overhead, wings beating in deliberate, unhurried, and measured rhythms, then gliding with blushing pink wings spread, white necks outstretched, heads and long flat bills prominently displayed. The large birds moved across the vast estuaries toward the marsh waters. They descended with their green heads and beaks projecting forward, cherry colored legs extended, wings holding firm as they splashed down one after another after another. Hundreds upon hundreds of these beguiling exotic creatures congregated in the shallow waters.

The tangled mangroves and surrounding ponds and waterways stretched endlessly in every direction. Mixed with the spoonbills were other wading species – herons, egrets, and ibis. Foraging for small fish, shrimp, crustaceans, feeling for prey with the tactile senses of their gray shovel-shaped bills, the birds found ample nourishment. They busily attended to the business of feeding as the water in the marshes ebbed with the shifting tide, the fish and other small animals now more tightly clustered as the spoonbills stirred the water while snapping up a meal.

It was warm and humid, the sky clear but for a few billowy clouds. There was a stunning remoteness to these coastland waters, a maze of meandering waterways, ponds, thickets of tangled plants and trees, islets and islands – an aquatic plain of beauty. The birds arrived and departed, some taking briefly to perches in the dense tendrils of the mangroves. Morning feeding slowly unwound as the birds finally took flight as the water level began to rise with the reversal of the tide. It then grew tranquil and still in the heat of the mid-afternoon sun. Deeper into the mangroves there was a racket of sound. Thousands of nesting spoonbills clustered in a tight and dense rookery in the canopy of the trees.

Angie, Evan, Ginny, and Malach huddled closely together knee-deep in the water among the nesting birds. Ginny stood beside Malach, her arm wrapped around his waist. Angie at his other side, her hand holding tightly to Malach's upper arm, and Evan next to her, their hands locked together. Silently, they took in the avian spectacle. The young chicks, only weeks old, often two or three to a nest, were hungrily taking food from the gaping bills of a parent, small heads reaching deeply into an open gullet as they greedily consumed the meals brought to the nest. Wide-eyed, feathers white and ruffled with a tinge of pink, a hint of the color they would eventually boldly wear, were the small and vulnerable chicks, not yet ready to fledge.

Well off to the east a swell of waterfowl lifted from the coastal waters close to the open gulf. They were distant, but there were many thousands, tens of thousands of these varied ducks, geese, and gulls. They approached and passed overhead. Their presence penetrated the space above. The power of flight stirred within Malach and his friends a deep reverence for these creatures. For Malach, Ginny, Angie, and Evan, it opened their imaginations and let their spirits soar. In this expansive estuary on the boundary between the mouth of the great river and the open waters, at the base of the continental tidal basin, birds ruled the air and land. Wind-swept and expansive, there was an all-encompassing presence of the undisturbed and untouched natural world. Nothing man-made as far as one could see, nothing man-made at all.

They watched as massive flocks of birds gave way to empty skies and then were filled with avian abundance once again. Pitch-black darkness in a sky brimming with the sparkling display of millions of visible stars alternated with the blinding brightness of the midday sun, blistering and oppressive heat and winds. Thunderous claps of lightening, torrential rains, chilling winds, and then silent stillness, moody mists of fog. Shifting shapes of the waterways and land were transformed before their very eyes. The cycles repeating, changing, evolving. Untethered, time flowed directionless. Night and day flickered in alternating sequences, the seasons changing, rushing forward and backward. Standing in the subtropical wild, before settlers, before the first indigenous tribes, before the human migration into the Americas, memories of the great delta plain rushed through Malach's mind, the depository of its natural history.

The flow of the seasons, the years, the millennia, the transformation of the land and water, the movement of the birds, all of it grew in intensity and pace, moving faster, quicker, as their minds swelled, bodies vibrated with energy, a beating, pulsing, driving force, until Malach expelled a gasp of air from his lungs, releasing his hands and arms from his friends, finally breaking the connection to this ancient reservoir of life. Abruptly jarred, then slowly, ever so slowly, Ginny, Angie, and Evan readjusted the contours of their minds to the material elements of the present moment. The four of them were displaced back on the shoreline of the state park, dry sand underfoot, looking out on the gentle breaking waves of the Gulf of Mexico, a container ship far off on the horizon, a sailboat a few hundred yards out into the water, some plastic debris washed up at the water's edge, the place from where they started, the spot from which they never moved. Angie turned and looked at grasses, shrubs, and palms on the high ground, a path opened through the brush leading to the parking lot several hundred yards back.

Ginny knew that this was different, as did Angie and Evan. There had been other occasions since her first introduction to Malach's "memories." Even Angie and Evan had their experiences. Two days ago at the funeral they all had another glimpse, but today they tumbled head over heels through time and space, transported to and from an increasingly forgotten world.

With her mind reeling Angie caught her breath and switched on her camera, holding it in her hand, directing it toward Malach. It was one of those occasions when she did not want the recording to intrude into the moment.

[Record]

"What just happened?" Ginny asked Malach. Visible in her face was the bewilderment that they were all experiencing.

"Everything began to accelerate," Malach said. For the first time, he appeared shaken by what was happening to him, and what he was revealing to them.

"Are you alright?" she asked.

"I think so. Everything that's locked into these surroundings is flying out faster and faster, right into me. It's so much stronger than I realized, the power from the river, its energy, everything that it contains, everything that built the delta and supplies its life, everything."

Ginny understood what he was saying. They were at the mouth of one of the natural wonders of the world, the end point of a river basin stretching from the Rockies to the Appalachians, and as far north as Minnesota and Canada, countless small streams, rivers, tributaries, larger rivers, drainage for forty percent of the country, funneling into the Mississippi and into this delta. Despite its size and grandeur, it had been under siege for more than a century – dams, levees, channels, dredging, a constant battle to control it, to restrict its movement, to impose by whatever means necessary containment so as not to let it interfere with progress and development.

"I know that was a whirlwind," Malach said, "but it just happened." Malach could see the shocked expressions in the faces of his friends and difficulty they were having even finding words to respond to what they had just experienced. Malach was aware that he, too, was still spinning. "What we're doing to the river is pushing at me like a freight train. It's a fight for survival."

Ginny took a deep breath as she looked out at the water. What they had witnessed minutes ago was not what was before her now. In less than a century the land lost to the delta was enormous, a couple thousand square miles, the size of a small state. How could that even be possible, she wondered. The delta was slowly and inexorably being lost, no longer being replenished sufficiently by the flow of sediment, too many diversions, interruptions, restrictions. The ocean levels were slowly creeping higher, too. The systems and environments dependent upon a healthy river were in jeopardy. But it was not just this great river; it was happening all over the world – the aquatic arteries of the planet were sick and suffering and it made her feel the same way.

Angie looked to Evan and then raised the camera and held it to his face, framed tight and close. "Tell me what you experienced today." After he spoke, she did the same with Ginny, posing the same question, listening to her friends trying to give shape and meaning to what they witnessed. She gave the camera to Evan and he recorded her as she described her experience.

[Stop]

Malach listened to his friends before his attention was drawn to the water where hundreds of gulls and terns bobbed. They were hearty and strong, survivors for countless thousands of years. Left alone, they would be fine. But he knew and could see, and even feel, their decline. Ginny came over and put her arms around his waist. He did not seem himself on this trip. She first attributed it to the loss in his family, but it was apparent that it was more than that.

The movement through time had first shocked and upended her thinking, then exhilarated her. It was not a slice of time but the accelerated flow of millennia. All that she had been teaching herself about the world began to take shape in a new and powerful way as she actually experienced the magnitude of the changes. They were so potent and suddenly visible for her. It steeled her frayed nerves.

Ginny watched Angie and Evan take a breather together as they walked along the shore. They just needed some time to take it all in, she thought. They would be fine.

Her mind returned to the river, what Malach had shown them. A million years in the making, thousands since the last ice age. Throughout time it had been wild and alive, moving, changing course, the sediment flowing through it and building the delta, home to vast wildlife and tens of millions, maybe hundreds of millions of migrating birds. Now in only a handful of generations it no longer resembled what it once was.

"We haven't learned very much about what we're doing to the river," Ginny said.

"No, we haven't," Malach said. "You can't domesticate a river or you begin to suffocate and kill it. I don't know that anyone will listen."

"Now you're the one going all negative on me," Ginny said. "Once more people begin to know you, things will happen. What you did at the funeral and now this. It's on us. We've got to do this. Our generation has to be the one to make this stop. We don't have a choice. The next generation won't arrive in time. Hell, we've got nothing to lose, do we?"

"No, nothing at all," Malach said. He loved Ginny's determination. She hugged him and kissed him on the nose. Malach forced a smile.

"Let's get on with it," Ginny said. "Where are we going next?"

"Good question. How about something to eat," Malach said. "I hear New Orleans has great food."

Ginny knew they all needed some time to regroup. "I think that's a great idea, exactly what we need. I'm starving," Ginny said. "I can't wait to try some local pecan pie."

They looked over toward Angie and Evan who had walked down the beach and were holding hands. "What do you think?" Ginny said.

"I noticed, too," Malach said.

"See, good things are already starting to happen. You blew our minds today, no one can think straight. Everything is upside down. People fall in love. Yeah, food will help."

Ginny was happy to see a real smile on Malach's face, but his melancholic mood and uncertainty stayed with her. She had never seen that in him. He was looking out toward the horizon and she could see he was eyeing a group of large birds soaring high in the distance riding the thermals. Vultures. Their presence a reminder that death is always near and present. Everything was accelerating in unnatural ways. The birds, like almost every living creature on the planet – except people – were declining in number. The science was clear about that and it was another thing that she could not let go of. More than a billion birds alone died every year by what people were doing to the world around them, and even more frightening was the decline of most vertebrate animal populations by more than half in the past fifty years. The extinction of species was already progressing in unnatural and unprecedented ways.

Ginny watched the vultures as she and Malach walked back toward the car. She thought about the funeral again, the hundreds of people who came to pay their final respects to Malach's grandfather, an overflow crowd. One lost human life and the world mourns. Why have we lost that reverence for all the life around us? Have we removed ourselves so far from it that there is no longer any equivalence between our lives and the living world that sustains us?

Yes, Ginny thought, I need something to eat.

4

I t was Sunday morning, several days following her return from Florida, that Judith first spoke with Evan's parents. She had known Caroline and Arthur for many years. She cared more deeply and felt closer to them than any of the other members of the congregation. She liked that Caroline saw the trip that Malach, Ginny, and Angie had taken with her son as adventurous, and comfortable that the four of them were still not back. Judith was still mindful of how cautious, quiet, and even fearful Evan had once been. She remembered that as a young boy he was always at his mother's side, frightened looking, and so skinny that it looked as though a strong wind might blow him over.

"How else is he going to learn to fly if he never spreads his wings?" Caroline remarked. "Besides, they're not kids anymore, but four smart and capable young adults, all sensible with good judgment. The spontaneity and brashness that it takes to do this is something that I wish I had more of in me when I was their age."

Judith held Caroline's words in her mind and tried to balance them with the events at the funeral. Even though Caroline did not yet understand or know about the lives of the kids, it was comforting to hear her frame their trip in a positive way. But during those few minutes, barely a week ago, so much had changed, and since then she believed she was changing, too. Mark was outright awestruck, convinced that the Lord was working through Malach. Why else, he told her, had this happened in a church?

"I feel so fortunate that Evan has a friend like Malach," Caroline continued. "You know how much I respect him. Don't worry so much, they'll all be fine." Caroline kept talking, but Judith had trouble fixing her attention on her compliments.

After the "Revelation," as Mark kept calling it, there was so much buzz at the church and an overwhelming certainty among those present that they had been witness to something deeply spiritual, perhaps the very workings of the Holy Spirit. Judith stayed back and watched as Malach was surrounded and literally swarmed by the attendees. It was Mark who suddenly rushed to be at his son's side. That was when she noticed Angie, camera held high and recording, Evan nodding his head in recognition of something familiar, and Ginny with a look of satisfaction on her face. What else had they experienced, she wondered? Where were these four young people headed? Yes, Judith thought, fly they must, taking to the wind and letting themselves soar, but what if it draws them too high, too close to the sun? She shook that thought from her mind and refocused her attention, calmed herself, and responded to Caroline's remarks.

"The four of them will fly and go on to make the world a better place," Judith said.

"Of course they will," Caroline added with certainty.

Days of rumination consumed her, not knowing where Malach and his friends were traveling, but she was less driven by fear. When she received the call from Calvin two weeks later, shortly before the kids returned, it did not surprise her. It was inevitable, and she had been preparing for whatever may lie ahead. She had already noticed that in her conversation with Caroline and understood that wherever her son was headed, it was now out of her hands. The next steps had begun. It was also time for Calvin, and especially Virginia, to be included. Then it would need to be Caroline and Arthur, and Angie's parents, Martha and Donald.

She put on her coat, wrapped her scarf around her neck, grabbed her purse and walked along the path from the house to the car. The air was crisp and clear, the leaves long off the trees. She paused, inhaled the late autumn smells and looked around. It was quiet, the animals distant when Malach was away. She looked at the stream of missed messages from Sky, then got into the car, started the engine, adjusted the mirror, and drove to meet Calvin.

Calvin greeted her and together they sat at the table in his office while he began to share the news reports that he pulled from the wire service.

"I noticed the first of these more than a week ago," Calvin said. "I thought it was just oddball and tabloid. Late last night, I don't know why, or what reminded me of it, but I happened to mention it to Sky. She was very curious, peppering me with questions. I couldn't for the life of me understand her fascination with it. She came with me to the office at the crack of dawn this morning before going to work to see if anything else was reported. We poured through the wire services. That's when I discovered the other stories. She was flabbergasted, slumped into her seat, and told me to put on my seat belt and get prepared for the news story of my life."

"Of course," Judith said surprised by her own calm. "Everything Sky told you is true."

"Okay," Calvin said, his expression betrayed his still hidden doubts. "Virginia doesn't know about any of this, but Sky felt that she needs to hear it from you."

❧

Malach, Ginny, Angie, and Evan drove along the road adjacent to the complex taking them through an abutting neighborhood of small, working class homes. Some were tidy while others weathered and neglected. Ginny turned and headed toward the refinery to get a closer look. They sat in the car and took in this vast array of structures along the eastern bank of the Mississippi.

The oil refinery was a massive labyrinth of tanks, pipes, compressors, pumps, and smoke stacks. Its sprawling and eerie presence was gritty and unnatural. Menacing in size, dominating its surroundings, foreign and aberrant, a tentacled creeping industrial beast, puffing foul breaths of combustible smoke. In its heart lay the remnants of the earth's living past, millions and millions of years of organic decayed material, reservoirs of latent energy that had rested undisturbed until dredged up at this brief moment in time. Sucked from the land and sea floors, and fed to the fiery creature, this complex nurtured a larger and more powerful living beast.

"It's astounding how big this is," Evan said. "It just goes on and on and on. We studied the processing of crude oil in Mr. Shelly's class last year, but I never gave much thought to what one of these plants looked like."

"We love our fossil fuels," Ginny said. "The bigger the better and at any cost."

"Mr. Shelly said this is something we should know about," Evan continued. "Because we live our lives completely dependent on it."

"So, enlighten us," Angie said.

"The abbreviated version or the full step-by-step process?" Evan asked with a smirk.

"Short and simple will do," Angie said laughing. They exchanged a look and then both laughed at some inside joke.

"Are we going to be let in on this?" Ginny asked.

"It's nothing," Angie said and burst out laughing. Then Malach began to laugh too.

"Oh, so this one's on me," Ginny said, and then realized they were tweaking her for her long-winded rants and scientific explanations. Her grimace soon turned to a smile and then she began to laugh, too. "Just wait. I don't forget." The four of them laughed even harder.

"Do you really want to know?" Evan asked Ginny.

"I do," Malach interrupted.

"Okay," Evan said. "First, despite what all this looks like, what goes on inside this place is not that complicated. After the crude oil is extracted from the ground, or wherever they find it, and is delivered here, it goes through a process to separate it into its parts. Crude is basically made up of all the decomposing and decayed plants and animals that have accumulated over millions of years mostly at the bottom of old sea beds. With grains of sediment also accumulating on top of this material over eons of time, the weight, pressure, and heat converts it to crude. The crude oil is made up of various hydrocarbons and these different hydrocarbons are used for making different products, everything from gasoline, to oil, to tar, to the components needed to make plastics, and tons of other things, too."

Evan looked at his friends to see if they were following. After nods by all he continued.

"In the refinery, the different hydrocarbons in the crude are separated by heat. Those different compounds turn to a vapor at different temperatures, and a distilling process then captures those different vapors. With the components separated, they can also be combined in different ways to make even more products. The problem is that the crude is mostly made up of carbon and when it is processed and used, the carbon is released into the atmosphere along with hundreds of nasty chemicals, many of which are toxic. We poison the water, we poison the land, and we heat up the planet. There you have it."

"Thank you, professor," Ginny said.

"You're welcome," Evan said and bowed.

"So this is the dark source of our changing planet," said Ginny. "The place where the potions are brewed to power the world and simultaneously and sinisterly destroy it. How in the world do we make this stop?"

Malach looked slowly around, took a deep breath, and gave a big sigh.

Ginny, Angie, and Evan stared at him. The looks flashed back and forth between them. They all knew what they faced was dire.

Malach's words were simple but fiery. "We all have to want much, much less of this," he said. "It's the only choice we have. There is no option here. People are going to have to demand it and make this stop."

Evan felt the seriousness of his tone. Sometimes he felt Malach might bring the whole world crashing down – the world as they knew it, everything that they believed, the predictability they expected, the formulas they used to live their lives, all of it would become uprooted. He did not know what that would mean, or what might happen as result, but it was long overdue, and perhaps their only hope.

As Evan looked at the refinery – the size of a small city – he thought about his science teacher and how he explained how people transformed the natural world. Since the very first labors to tame the wild, beginning ten thousand years ago – growing plants and domesticating animals for food – the path of human manipulation of nature had known no bounds. It had begun as survival for the family, for the group, for the tribe, the march of civilization. Back then, no other considerations had mattered; no thought had been given to what the consequences might be or what could be lost in the process. At some point, industry had changed everything again. The behemoth of mechanical engineering that stood before them, the means of converting natural resources into power provided the mechanism of transformation in new and breathlessly rapid ways. With it progressed the advances in every part of life. Invention and endless possibility were unleashed. Yet, it was not accompanied by a vision, a plan, or a consensus on how to protect the world. While understandable for most of our history, everything now is shouting at humanity to change. We once did not know better, but that no longer holds true.

Evan wondered, how is it possible that as a civilization we cannot see that the more we take, the closer it brings us to undermining our very own survival? Being so removed from the natural world, we cannot see that our actions threaten our very existence. We are of two worlds when we must find a way to be one. The paradox twisted and turned over and over in his mind, as did Malach's ultimately simple dictum, "We have to want much, much less of this."

"Hey, are you okay?" Angie asked. "You look like you're somewhere else."

His eyes found Angie, a concerned look on her face.

"Yeah, I was just thinking," Evan said.

He put his arm around her. As they stood and looked out at the oil refinery, a pickup truck approached. It slowed and the passenger rolled down his window, noticing the out-of-state license plate and asking if they needed some help.

"The car is fine," said Angie. "But I do have a problem. This is the scariest looking place I've ever seen."

"Sure as hell is," said the young man, laughing and nodding his head in agreement. "It's a monster. But it's our monster. We're headed into the belly of the beast to feed it."

"You both work here?" Angie asked.

"Sure do," the driver answered. "Lots of folks work here, thousands actually. It's sort of the family business for some, one generation after another. Just a big mom and pop shop."

"So, if it's the family business you can take some visitors in to look around."

"Maybe you should think about a trip over to Orlando," the passenger said. "I know it looks like fun and games here, but this ain't Disney." The two chuckled.

"I'm serious," said Angie. "We'd like to see how this works."

"Like I said, visitors can't wander in. The foreman would have our heads if we tried that."

"We'll be discreet," said Angie.

"I'm sure you will, but the four of you might just stand out a bit."

"I'm trying to make a film about the refining of crude oil." Angie held up her camera. "Does that help?"

"Sorry," said the driver.

"How about an interview then?" Angie asked.

"Are you undercover investigators or something?" the driver said with a grin.

"Why, is there something we shouldn't see?"

"Whoa, I didn't say that. Are you looking to stir up some trouble?"

"No, not at all. It's just for my high school film project."

"Came all the way down here for that?" the front passenger asked skeptically.

"No, we drove down for a funeral. My friend's grandfather died." She pointed toward Malach.

"Oh, sorry about that," the driver said, "mighty sorry."

"Thank you," Malach said.

"What kind of interview were you thinking about?" asked the passenger.

"Some information about your work, how the plant operates," Angie said.

"That's it?" the driver asked.

"Yeah, that would do it."

"Hell, why not. It may be our only chance to be film stars," said the driver. He pulled the truck up ahead of their car along the shoulder. The two hopped out and they introduced themselves. Ginny flashed Angie a look of approval.

"So how does this work?" the driver asked as he ran his fingers through his hair and then straightened his shirt.

"I'm going to ask you some questions, then you answer them. That's all. The same for you."

"No, I'll let my buddy do the screen test. I think he's cut out for this. Maybe it'll be his big break." The two of them laughed.

"That's fine," Angie said. "One interview will work for me. Are you ready to start?"

"Sure, let's do it."

[Record]

"Can you tell us your name and something about yourself," Angie said.

"I'm Tyler Landry. I've been working here at this oil refinery facility in Louisiana, one of the biggest in the world. I started five years ago when I was eighteen. After high school, I came right down to apply for a job. I don't mean the next week or next month, I mean the next day. I had my mind set on it."

"What made you want to do this job?" Angie asked.

"Well, my mother wasn't keen on it. She thought I should try the local college, but I didn't have any money saved and she needed me to help out. She didn't want to ask but I understood. The starting pay is good here and you can work your way up."

"What sort of work do you do?" Angie asked.

"I'm in the receiving department, responsible for loading and unloading of tank trucks and rail cars. You know, those big oil tanks on the back of eighteen-wheelers or on freight trains. Making sure product is safely transferred, going through the declaration of inspection for each transfer, making sure there are no leaks or mess. Weighing the vehicles so they don't exceed DOT regulations."

"Sounds like hard work," Angie said. Tyler was tall and strong and had a physical presence in his navy-blue industrial coveralls with the company logo on his chest, and heavy work boots. She had asked him to put on his work uniform before the interview along with his white hard hat. He was happy to oblige.

"Twelve hour-shifts, we can get overtime, too. Helps the paycheck. Especially now that I have a family."

"Can you tell me some about your family?" Angie asked.

"I've got a wife and a little girl. My wife, Erin, and I met right after high school. Never thought I was the marrying type, but I knew right off she was for me. She's smart, has a good job, dental assistant. We're paying off her student loans and saving for a house. Want to get out of this neighborhood – for Dolly, she'll be four soon." He gestured toward the area they had just driven through. Angie decided she would get some footage of that later.

"What worries you about this area?" Angie asked.

"I don't care so much for me, but I want my wife and little one to have a nicer place, clean air. It smells from the plant. Not all the time, but some days are worse than others. Last month the sulfur was strong. They say it's safe. Dolly has asthma, the doctor says it's mild, but it can't be good for her. We do get good health insurance, so that helps."

Angie could tell he wanted to get some things off his chest, so she just let him talk. She was always surprised how people would open up when there was a camera in their face and say things they would not otherwise disclose.

"A lot of us in the area work at the plant. It's hard to fight them and work for them at the same time. It's not like they threaten to fire us, but you worry it might just come back to bite you in the ass. Besides, there are no other decent jobs where I can make the money I do here. Maybe I should have listened to my mother and gone to college. She always told me that if I had a better attitude about school I could have done real well."

"What did you want to be?"

"A marine biologist," he said without hesitation. He perked up when he talked about it. "I love those shows with the scientists and divers. Studying the oceans and the reefs. Seems like a hell of job. I don't know if I'll ever get that kind of job, but I want to scuba dive in the reefs one day. The colors, the fish, everything is exotic and a little magical there. Might do it with Dolly when she gets older. She can't get enough of that movie, you know, the one about Nemo."

It saddened Angie to think that he was trapped here, in the clutches of the monster. Perhaps we all are, she thought. She could detect a slight chemical smell in the air as the wind shifted, fumes drifting towards them. It was mild but unpleasant. She had not noticed it before.

"What do most of the workers think about it here?" Angie asked.

"Most of us love it and hate it. A lot of guys like me started after high school. There are the engineers, computer guys, the business guys. They all have college degrees and high paying jobs. It's different for them. The rest of us just put in an honest day's work. Sometimes our dream jobs are not realistic, but you can dream. No one can take that from you."

"Do you ever wonder what it was like here before the refinery?"

"It's been here long before I came into the world. My father worked here and his father before him."

"What does your father do now?"

"He died when I was twelve. Cancer, smoked too much."

"I'm sorry," Angie said, finding it ironic that Tyler just offered his condolences to Malach a few minutes ago. His caring words to Malach were genuine and clearly came from an honest place.

"I remember when he used to go to work when I was little," Tyler continued. "I wanted to do his job. Back then, I think I liked the coveralls and hard hat. I knew it took a lot out of him. He told me that I could do better, but I never thought there was anything wrong with what he did. A lot of kids I knew, their dads worked here too. It seemed normal. He told me the oil industry made our country strong and that was a good thing. But now, I'm not so sure. When you're around this place, you know it's not all good."

After a few more questions, Angie thanked him for the interview.

[Stop]

✦

"The first story came in from Baton Rouge, Louisiana," Calvin said. "Two young oil workers reported it. The thing is that the story was so farfetched that no one believed them, but the two workers are straight arrows, and a local reporter found them very convincing. It just seemed more than what they could make up." A few days later a report came in from Columbus, Nebraska and in another week, there was one more from Grand Forks, North Dakota. The final one was yesterday from Westchester County, New York.

✦

The drive north from the Mississippi delta to the headwaters in Lake Itasca, Minnesota, took Malach, Ginny, Angie, and Evan through the center of the country. The path was not direct, mostly off the interstate highways, with detours into the farm belt. It was astonishing, driving across flat, endless farmland. The open expanse of the Great Plains, stretching in every direction, was so different from the landscapes Angie had ever seen. Her parents had taken the family to the Grand Canyon a few years back but they had flown over this part of the country seeing only the patchwork of planted fields from above. It was so flat, she thought, the horizon line perfectly straight, the land gradually receding into the distance. The fields had been long harvested and turned for the winter, leaving large clumps of rich dark soil in wide corduroy stripes across countless miles of land. Occasional farmhouses were tucked back off the road, usually a cluster of buildings, a house, one or more barns, sometimes several steel silos, large tractors parked for the season. They followed the Mississippi north through Louisiana, Arkansas, and Missouri, before heading west into Nebraska and then up through Kansas and the Dakotas.

"It's been so long since I've been through here," Ginny said. "Summer vacation in fourth grade. We took a trip to St. Louis for a family wedding, with a stop in Wichita to visit my father's college roommate and his family, then north to South Dakota and Mt. Rushmore. Wheat, corn, sunflowers, soybeans filled these fields. I remember it so well. It impressed me more than the Presidents. My father said, 'We feed the world.'"

Angie intermittently recorded the open fields while they drove. Hours and hours they had been on the road and the fields kept coming. It never seemed to end. It was so austere, but its minimal and expansive scope was hypnotic. Long after the harvest it was now devoid of anything but dark empty land. Some sections were pocked with the low stubble of severed husks of dry corn stalks extending to the horizon in gentle wavy lines.

"Can we pull over for a minute?" Angie asked.

"Sure, I could use a rest," Evan said as he slowed and stopped along the road. The roads like the fields were empty, not another car in sight. The four of them stepped out of the car and stretched their limbs.

"Your father was right," Evan told Ginny. "We feed the world. It's nothing but farmland everywhere. We've been driving forever and it never changes."

Angie had walked to the edge of the field. She turned on the camera and looked back toward Malach.

[Record]

"What used to be here, before the farms? Angie asked.

"An endless prairie of grasslands," said Malach. "So many different plants and animals were all a part of it. Tens of millions of bison roamed these plains, all sorts of birds, insects, and small animals. Almost all of it has changed, probably more so than most areas in the world. Everything has been plowed under and a single crop planted." Malach looked sadly out at the landscape. He bent down and picked up a clump of dark soil, it crumbled in his hand.

"The amount of food grown is staggering," Ginny said.

"How else can we feed everyone?" Angie asked.

"I read that forty percent of all the habitable land in the world is used for farming," Ginny said. "And by 2050 there will be another two billion people to feed, by the end of the century four billion more. Is the whole world going to be a farm? What happens to everything else? Is it going to be just people and farms?"

"There are too many of us," Malach said looking out over the great expanse of land. He then turned to his friends. "We have to be fewer, far, far fewer. We have grown beyond reason and now it's time to make our numbers smaller and be just one part of the rest of the world. It's our responsibility."

Angie recorded Malach's comment. How, she wondered, does one even begin to get the world to think about fewer human beings? It's antithetical to people's beliefs, to ask them to stop having so many kids, to shrink the number of people in the world. That would take another leap of faith.

[Stop]

5

Alex Love's plane sat on the tarmac of Los Angeles International Airport for two hours waiting for an unusually virulent lightning and thunderstorm to pass. All aircraft were grounded until the worst of the weather had moved through. He had his laptop opened but had been unable to concentrate on his grant proposal. In fact, in the past three days he was unable to focus on anything but an overriding fixation to get on this plane. He had taken the redeye to New York many times before, often to conferences, but this would be the first leg of a different journey. Alex had a two-hour layover at Kennedy, and hoped that despite the delay he would be able to make his scheduled flight for the second leg of his trip. In Albany, he had reserved a rental car and would then drive north. It was eight days before Christmas and it was nonsensical to be doing this. He had work and family responsibilities. His ex-wife and son would undoubtedly find this to be another one of his selfish disruptions to their lives. He had promised Will that he would take him on a ski trip to Colorado when school recessed for vacation, and he was determined that this year nothing would interfere with those plans. The only plausible excuse would be the poor snow conditions in the Rockies, which continued to deteriorate due to warm weather. Alex knew he would not be forgiven and no excuses would suffice unless there was literally no skiing, which was not likely, and then he better have made alternative arrangements.

Madeleine and he had started to have civil exchanges in the past year, and he knew that was potentially in jeopardy if he disappointed Will again. There were even moments when he imagined a possible reconciliation, but he knew that would never be. He had been a lousy husband and an equally bad father. As much as he wanted to think that he was doing relationships better, Alex knew he was no different during his marriage to Madeleine than he had been throughout his first marriage to Roslyn. That, too, ended poorly after only four and a half years. Fortunately, there were no children from that doomed attempt at commitment. He rationalized that dismal first relationship with the fact that the both of them were one-issue people – their research. When their mutual sexual attraction began to subside there was not much left. Ironically, even in that marriage, Roslyn had felt he was the one too self-absorbed and initiated the divorce. The end seemed to come abruptly for him, but she saw his surprise as just another example of his obliviousness to the state of their lives.

Alex thought about the drive ahead through the Adirondacks on his way to some remote destination. He was not entirely sure where that would be, but three nights ago it was clear as day in his dream and on the following two nights it was virtually shouting at him. He was not one to even remember his dreams, but these consecutive evenings of lucid and beckoning images were unshakable. He could see it all in vivid detail – the destination, the route so clear that he did not even bother to check a map or GPS for the trip. He felt convinced that he had actually been there and would recognize the way once he got in the car and started to drive.

The southern part of the eastern forest-boreal transition, that encompassed most of the Adirondacks, was well known to him though he had never visited this biome in the United States. Alex spent much of his professional life studying forests, beginning with the temperate rainforests of the northwest when a graduate student in Oregon. His fieldwork then helped to document the next two decades of the destruction of those old growth forests. Those particular forests in Oregon were now almost all irretrievably lost to development, roads, and clear-cut logging. It was not just the tropical rainforests of the Amazon that were being devoured, but it was happening right here at home in temperate climate regions. Protected areas in Northern California, and further north in Washington state and Canada precariously survived. When he first hiked the woods, it was magical. The dense trees covered in rich coats of moss and lichens, vast beds of ferns, narrow rushing streams winding through canopied forests, lush green vegetation along the banks, surprises of precipitous drops and waterfalls, were enchanted primordial wonders.

The plane was finally moving and they were in the queue for takeoff. Once up in the air Alex opened his laptop and scrolled through the lecture he was scheduled to deliver next month. He was invited to share his insights and vision for facing the global challenge of stemming relentless deforestation. The data was clear about the dangers and threats posed by the growing destruction to these pristine areas, from reduction in biodiversity, to effects on the purification of water, to the diminishing of an invaluable sink for the storage of carbon. The protection of the great forests of the world would require commitment for which he was not sure there was sufficient resolve. There was a small window for action – the next decade or two would be critical. There was no longer the luxury of kicking the can down the road.

The images of his dreams floated though his head. The forests of the eastern forest-boreal transition, he was certain. The beautiful conifer and deciduous trees, some old growth areas and the boreal forests at the high elevations unmistakably placed his destination there. It was an odd unfolding of events for him, being a man of science, committed to facts, data confirmation through replication, peer review, and the scientific method. He was now veering off on an intuitive, cosmic journey that baffled him and held him tightly in its grip.

This destination would take him to the same area where an old girlfriend had grown up. Memory of this first serious relationship, evoked in the debris of his failed marriages, made all that was happening even the more confusing. The ending of that earlier relationship was the epitome of selfishness and narcissism, those attributes he had honed well over the years as Roslyn and then Madeleine had constantly reminded him before each told him to leave.

Like his two ex-wives, Alex knew this girlfriend had deserved better from him. He had a hard time shaking her from his thoughts. It was twenty years ago since he had last seen her. He wondered if she was still doing science. He had always felt she was not cut out for the rigor of high-level research, not likely to make an impact. There was something very kind about her, and selfless, of which he knew he had taken advantage.

⚜

The Advocate
Baton Rouge, Louisiana

Oil Refinery Workers' Tale of Mystery

Tyler Landry, 25, and John Bergeron, 26, on their way to work, encountered four out-of-state high school students. What started as a friendly stop to check on the teens, ended with an experience that they believe has changed their lives. After sharing with these visitors information about the refinery for a high school class project, they were the ones taken on a trip that they can't explain, but which opened their eyes to the world. These two hard-nosed realists reported entering a journey through time and bearing witness to the Mississippi River before European settlers, before industrialization, and before oil refineries.

"Don't ask me how it was possible, but it happened," stated John. "It was real as day," Tyler reported. "The river never looked so beautiful, the wildlife never as plentiful, the air never as clean. After it was over, the birds came, real birds. Thousands of them, mourning doves, white winged doves, ringed turtle-doves, birds that I would ordinarily be out hunting this season. The young man, he summoned them, just like he showed us the river."

While the story is eerily supernatural, hundreds of workers at the refinery were witness to the thousands and thousands of birds that descended upon them. There is no explanation, but Landry and Bergeron and their co-workers are not changing their story.

◈

When Malach, Ginny, Angie, and Evan finally arrived home, three weeks from when they first left to travel to the funeral, their absence had already taken on entirely different meaning for their families. The news reports and Judith's best effort to explain the unexplainable left Ginny, Angie, and Evan's parents incredulous. The sheer enormity of it all overpowered the unspoken resentment of having been kept in the dark for so many years. It was as though Malach's gifts, or power, or message conformed their minds to the logic of its long-held need for secrecy.

At school there was persistent gossip about their prolonged absence. The curiosity was raised many decibels when a student with a brother stationed at the Strategic Air Command Base outside Grand Forks, North Dakota, began to spread a crazy story his brother read in the local paper. A copy of the online version was soon circulating the school.

Ginny found herself terribly uncertain upon her return home. First, there were the long conversations with her parents and then the flood of questions and frenzy of attention by classmates and teachers, all requiring a shift in her thinking and mind set. She was riding on adrenaline since the funeral and struggled to bring herself back down to earth. Every question was both a distraction and an urgent plea in need of a meaningful response. Everyone was important in an entirely different way. Change happens one heart at a time, she kept reminding herself.

There were not many days of classes left before Christmas break. She had little motivation to return to school, but her mother insisted as though resuming a normal schedule would translate into a return to a normal life. When the morning bell rang, Ginny found herself in the hallway after everyone had entered their classrooms and could not coax herself into English class.

"Ginny, wait, please. I've been looking for you all morning. Can we talk?" Her old friend Julie was coming in the opposite direction. Ginny had not had a meaningful conversation with Julie in years. Their lives had diverged down different paths some time ago. Not by intention, just by dissimilar needs and interests. Julie, along with Angie and herself were, at one time, inseparable.

"Sure," Ginny said. "I'd be happy to."

Julie took her by the hand, looking around to be certain there were no teachers nearby and headed to the stairwell on the far side of the school away from the administrative offices. They sat down together on the steps.

"How are you?" Julie asked. "There's so much drama in these halls. It's not just the senior class, it's the whole school and into the Junior High. You've been out so long that the gossip mills were running on overdrive. Yesterday, the place nearly imploded. The newspaper story was crazy. What is this all about?"

"We're all fine," said Ginny. She could sense Julie's anxious anticipation and belief that their history together still bound them and would allow her to get to the bottom of what was going on. Julie was holding her phone in one hand, resisting the urge to tweet out the first disclosure of anything Ginny might say.

"Do you ever think much about how we live our lives?" Ginny asked.

"I don't know what that means," Julie answered.

"Just that as a person, a human being living on this Earth, have you ever wondered? We have lots of things, go to a good school, have families who care about us. But do you ever have a desire to know what it takes to make our lives so comfortable? What we do to the land and the water, to the air, all the plants and animals to get to live these lives?"

"I guess. But what does that have to do with what's going on?"

"Everything." Ginny said. She tried to explain some of what Julie had read. Julie looked perplexed and skeptical and also a little giddy with getting some of the story directly from Ginny. A teacher came through the hallway and interrupted them and hurried them off to class.

Ginny lingered in the hallway. She felt wholly ineffective with her explanation to Julie, thinking that only Malach's presence, his magic, created the power and urgency needed for delivering the message. She walked to her locker and placed her notebooks inside, pulled out the jacket that she put there fifteen minutes earlier, and went out the back door. She walked across the parking lot, started her car and drove to the lake where she knew Malach would be this morning. He would not be coming back to school this week, not ever. The lake was his place for solitude and reflection. She needed to see him and talk. She also knew that his plan for this week would accelerate everything.

Ginny's conversation with her parents had been complicated. Her father spent much of the time trying to normalize her life and find a framework that was logical and acceptable, and most importantly, to find a way to reassure himself that this was okay. She did not offer him a comforting or simple way to wrap his mind around her life, which was not what was needed. It was different with her mother when she came to Ginny's room as she was preparing for bed her first night home.

"I believe everything you've told me," Virginia said. "I can make sense out of none of it. I only wish that I had known sooner, to just be there for you. At least I think that's what I would've done."

Tears filled her mother's eyes as Ginny could see her struggle. "It's so much," her mother continued. "It breaks my heart that you did this all alone."

Ginny was well aware of the changes in their once tight relationship. She knew that what Malach shared, what he opened her eyes to, changed everything between the two of them. Maybe she should have told her mother sooner, but she always feared that she would have intervened, distanced her from Malach, and Ginny knew she could not risk that.

"Mom, you didn't fail me. I knew you were always there."

"But I wasn't. I should have sensed the change."

"There's no way you could have," said Ginny firmly as she tried to reassure her mother.

"You were so young, you still are. And this is so big," Virginia sighed.

"You always told me to think big, to do important things."

"I know, I know," Virginia said through her tears. "But this…"

"Scares you?"

"I don't know what to make of it," Virginia said as she wiped her tears. "It terrifies me."

"You've made a perfect life for us, but you know I've never been good at following the path. I found something, or it found me, and I can't walk away from it. I have to do this. Bad things are happening and I have to do something about it. I've seen things that have changed me and I can never undo that. It's part of me. Everyone needs to know what I know."

☙

Grand Forks Herald
Grand Forks, North Dakota

Four Out-of-State Teens Cast Magic over the Plains

Erik Johansen, his wife, Lorna, and their three children, Gary 18, Dirk 13, and Melinda 12, encountered four teenagers passing by their ranch and experienced something unexplainable. The Johansens have been raising American bison for more than a decade and have a small herd of 100. The animals are not like domesticated cattle and can be dangerous. A full-size male bison can weigh close to a ton and stand six feet tall. Even those raised as livestock maintain their wild natures.

When a young man was noticed on their grazing land among the animals, the family was alarmed, fearing for his safety. His three friends watched from a distance. Gary, their oldest son, arrived first, calling to the young man to move away from the animals. Soon, the rest of the family arrived and together they witnessed something extraordinary. The young man, named Malach, was standing by the dominant male who seemed to behave submissively in his presence, gently nudging his head against him. After a few minutes the young man left the herd and joined the family and his friends.

It was what happened next that left the Johansen family utterly speechless. After a pleasant talk with Malach and his friends, Ginny, Angie, and Evan, the family reported that they experienced an unexplainable vision. They looked over the prairie and before them was a vast herd of bison. The house and barn, the power lines, the corralled area, were all gone. It was as if they were back in time when these great animals roamed and ruled the Great Plains. "There were thousands and thousands of them, maybe tens of thousands," Gary reported. "When they began to run it was like thunder. There were no nearby farms, just prairie grass in every direction. It was so amazing."

Mrs. Johansen described it all as "very emotional. I can't explain what happened but I can tell you this, there was something about that young man and what he showed me that opened my eyes. It made me think long and hard about what we've done to the land and whether we have lost more than we have gained."

❧

Darnell Johnson walked to Central Park from his apartment on 136th Street straight down Malcolm X Boulevard. It was the most direct path. His binoculars were in his jacket pocket and his field guide in the other, one hand resting on each. When he wasn't in school, at his part time job at the grocery store, or taking care of his younger sister, Darnell was in Central Park. Regardless of the season there was more than enough to discover, being surrounded by the reservoir, lakes, and ponds, the woodlands, and Ramble, the open fields, all of which attracted their own particular birds. He had been coming to the park since he was twelve, and over the past five years he came more and more frequently. He couldn't get his mind off the sighting he had three days ago, a boreal owl. It was far off its northern range, a very rare visitor but not unheard of in the park. He was convinced it was not a saw-whet or screech owl. He had a remarkably clear sighting, close, ample light at dusk, but hoped for another chance to observe it. It was not a bird he ever imagined he would see in his life. It was like it came to him. When it visited his dreams two nights ago, he believed it was talking to him, not in words but through its presence and was sent to take him somewhere. It was clear, too, where he was to go. The dream was stronger and more powerful the next night. His mother believed dreams held messages, and when he explained everything to her and then told her that he was leaving the next morning, she nodded her approval. He was planning to go, regardless, but was happy it did not create a problem.

༄

Harita Bhatt had packed her car the evening before, set her alarm for four-thirty, and left her apartment in Chicago well before sunrise. She relished the stillness of the city so early in the morning, barely a vehicle on the road, only an occasional pedestrian, quietness hanging over the buildings, high-rises, bridges, corridors, and even parks that most persons rarely experienced. It was her preferred part of the day and the time she regularly arose. As a little girl in India she loved the coast. Before the sun broke the horizon, she went to the sea, to be present for the stirring activity that a new day brought. During family vacations to the beach in the summer her parents and brother sunned themselves, cooled off in the water, read books, and took long strolls along the shore. She was always knee deep in the tidal pools, uncovering crustaceans and when a little older, diving in the reefs, studying the spectacle of the coral and countless exotic fish and other mysterious creatures. There never was a doubt in her mind that she would pursue her education in marine science. Her entire life she had been enamored by the sea.

She was headed to the Woods Hole Oceanographic Institute in Massachusetts for the next three months to follow up on her long-term research project. She was feeling appreciative that her old childhood friend Emelia and her husband David had offered their beautiful vacation cottage for her to use during her stay, freeing her from the dingy apartment she ordinarily would rent. She and Emelia had been close friends since high school when Harita first moved to America. At a time when Harita felt isolated and alone, her new friend was there for her. Her work never felt more urgent, but the recurrent dream of the past three nights, which made no sense, summoned her elsewhere and would not relinquish its hold.

Warren Blithe took his car and left before the sun rose. He had not asked for the car, but the new BMW arrived after his early acceptance to college. His father was proud, another son heading to the family alma mater. Certainly, Warren had good grades, but he never sweated the outcome, with all that his family donated to the school for what was now three generations. His family had more money than any family needed or deserved, and to have to join the family business to make even more money, to acquire more real estate, to invest in more companies, disheartened him. The gap year that he was considering felt equally empty. In fact, nothing felt meaningful with the exception of the swirling thoughts going through his head since the incident last week. If it were not for the story in the local newspaper, everyone living nearby would have been happy and relieved to just forget what happened. If he had not been at the party and seen it himself, he wouldn't have believed it possible and would have dismissed it, too. But it didn't let go of him, and then came the dreams the past three nights, which only magnified the urgency to take this trip. All he knew for certain was he could not ignore any of this.

Harrison Patch
Westchester County, New York

A Dark Cloud Descends on Grand Estate: "Is it a Message?"

In one of the most exclusive enclaves in the country an unusual natural event was reported. It occurred at the Vance estate on Sunday afternoon. Robert Vance, his wife, Rita, and one of their two teenaged children had returned from a preholiday vacation at their home in Bermuda, one of three vacation homes that they own. The Vance compound, renowned for its lavish main house and two guest cottages, rests on twenty elegantly manicured acres of gardens with stables, a pool, and tennis court. The Vances are known for their oversized life style. When they arrived at the gate of their home they took notice of four teenagers walking along the road near their property.

An afternoon holiday party was scheduled for later that day. It was when guests had arrived that things began to grow strange. With the unseasonably warm weather, guests were being served cocktails on the patio. The bare trees began to fill with crows, at first a small flock then hundreds and then thousands surrounded the house. The forty guests fled to the indoors as birds kept coming. One guest, who asked not to be named, said it felt "Hitchcockian." After half an hour the birds took to the air, and headed in the direction of the four adolescents who had been seen earlier by the house, seemingly following them down the road until they entered their car; and when the teens drove off, the birds scattered to the wind. A security guard had spoken with the teenagers. He indicated that they were polite and did not seem to be causing any trouble and readily gave their names when asked. One of the teenagers, named Malach, made a comment he found confusing, "That living like the Vances was no longer an option." When asked what he meant, he said, "That what is torn from the earth for them to live this lifestyle is not theirs for the taking. He told the guard to let the Vances know the earth is sending them a message."

A local ornithologist believed the birds were likely reacting to weather changes, though reports by the national weather service showed no patterns of weather fluctuations expected in the forecast for the coming week with the current warm front enveloping the northeast. Make of it what you may, it was not a common occurrence; and who knows, with the concerns of late with the state of the environment, maybe it was a message.

When Ginny found Malach at the lake he was sitting near the water's edge on the bench the Rothmans had built. They were still living in the house, though Malach had now acquired the property. He had Attorney Lieberman arrange for them to stay until they resettled in North Carolina. Ginny could see the deep reflection in Malach's face.

"I knew I'd find you here," Ginny said. She sat herself down beside Malach. "I can't be in school either. Angie and Evan are feeling as restless as me. They asked if we could meet up with them later in town, when they get out. Both are without a car. Their parents are tightening the reins. Not grounding them, but finding excuses to make it difficult."

"I get it," Malach said. "Sure, we can pick them up."

There was a flock of redpolls perched in a nearby tree that Ginny noticed. They wintered here, migrating south from the Canadian Arctic. They were delightful little birds and she adored their red crowns, though the red coloring on the breasts of the males was gone in the winter. She thought of how Malach used birds to send messages. There was power and symbolism in their presence and he knew that.

Malach looked up and saw the birds. It was a large group and they took flight before settling in a tree closer to them.

"Tomorrow everyone will come together at the field," Malach stated.

"I think that's the best place," Ginny said. "It's special with the mountains surrounding it." She was more nervous than she had been in some time. It was so important. How he would make it happen was something she had not asked. She sensed the burden he was feeling and she did not want to add to it. "I believe in you."

Malach looked at her and nodded. She put her head on his shoulder and he wrapped his arm around her. "I'm just the warm-up act. It's going to be your stage."

She knew it was not about her, but Malach never wanted her to feel her part was any less important. "Make sure you have your material worked out. I want the crowd ready for me," she said.

"I'm working on it," he said. She forced a smile.

"The Rothmans are still away visiting their kids until after the New Year," Ginny said. "They'll be disappointed to miss out."

"They'll be here," Malach said.

"Oh… I'm glad. I really like them. It would be nice to get old like them. They have a spark that doesn't go out."

A small redpoll flew and perched on the bench next to Malach. They both immediately noticed an unusual red mark on its wing, blood. Malach reached for the bird and inspected the wound. "Not sure what this is from. Not a good thing before winter." He lifted his hand and the bird darted away.

"I hope he makes it," she said.

"Not sure he will."

Ginny found it sad, but had grown to accept the cruel workings of nature. They sat silently for some time. She had not had a lot of sleep these past weeks. It was hard to quiet her mind.

"Let's take a walk," she said. They got up and spent time in the low elevations, smelling the late autumn scents with the air still surprisingly mild and sky partially overcast. She took Malach's hand as they slowly walked quietly together.

When they met up with Angie and Evan in town later in the day, there were many students from the school walking about, taking in the nice weather. Ginny had not thought about this and within moments they were circled by dozens of classmates. Their friends and peers were tentative at first, not sure what to say. But soon the questions started to fly. Awkward joking gave way to more pointed questions and more serious inquiry about what was going on.

Brett and his two friends soon approached the group. Brett had his Rottweiler on a leash close to his side and several students stepped back with the guttural rumblings of the dog. Brett eyed Malach and then looked at the large group of kids from the high school surrounding him.

"This your fucking fan club?" Brett said sarcastically to Malach and then glared at Ginny, Evan, and Angie. "You four are the talk of the school. What kind of freaking shit are you up to? You don't think anyone really takes the stunts you're pulling seriously?" Brett held his dog close to his side and stepped closer to Malach.

Malach stood his ground, Ginny beside him. Evan moved closer to his friends. "It's serious for all of us," Malach said.

Brett fixed his eyes on Malach, his jaw tightly clenched. Brett loosened his grip and released some of the leash letting the dog lurch forward. Everyone instinctively leapt back while Malach immediately stepped between the dog and Ginny. Brett pulled back slightly on the leash, but his dog was only more unsettled in Malach's presence.

"Just back your dog up," Malach said, his voice still calm. "No one appreciates how poorly trained he is."

"You've got that wrong. He does just as I tell him to," Brett snapped back.

"Then back him off," warned Malach.

"Oh, you're not a dog whisperer, too?"

"Get him under control," Malach said more forcefully.

"I don't know what you're up to," Brett responded, "but all this nature boy talk is bullshit. There's nothing wrong with the way things are."

Brett's dog was barking wildly as Malach stepped closer and loomed over the animal. Soon the bared teeth and growls gave way to whining and a whimper as it retreated, its body shaking. It then squatted and urinated on Brett's pants and boot. There was an awkward silence, then snickers and laughter from those watching. Brett's face flashed red and he smacked his dog on the head and abruptly tugged the leash.

"Fuck you, you'll regret this," Brett shouted at Malach and then he slinked off.

There was momentary silence between everyone present, and then many rumblings about Brett. So many found Brett threatening and even scary. Ginny did not like anything about what transpired. Brett grew only creepier in her mind, and his unpredictability scared her, too. She was happy to see him leave and exchanged a look with Malach, who gave her a reassuring nod. After a few minutes the crowd gathered back around and the questions continued.

6

When Sky and Judith drove into town for breakfast the following morning, cars were parked everywhere. Peg's Diner had a line snaking out the door and halfway down the block. Without exchanging a word, they watched the crowds for a few minutes before stepping out of the vehicle.

"It's happening here," Judith said. Her voice was emphatic and there was neither a trace of alarm nor the past threads of fear that used to overwhelm her.

Sky took a deep breath as they walked toward the diner. Sky approached a young woman, her long dark hair pulled back in a ponytail, freshness of youth in her face. She wore a red and gray wool plaid jacket with a dark scarf wrapped around her neck, skinny jeans and well-worn hiking boots. Sky wanted to get a read on what she knew and how it was that all these people came to be here.

"What's going on?" Sky asked the young woman after she introduced herself and learned the woman's name.

"Oh… I'm not sure," Beth responded hesitantly. "I'm not from around here. I was just trying to get something to eat. Is it not usually this crowded?"

"No, it's not," Sky answered.

"Do you know what's going on?" Beth asked.

"It's hard to explain," said Sky. "If I may ask? What did you come to town for?" The flustered look and struggle for an explanation convinced Sky that it was Malach's doing.

"Where are you coming from?" Sky asked.

"I live in Denver."

"How did you get here?" Sky asked.

"I drove. I know this might sound crazy, but I've been having… well, a strong feeling that I needed to come here."

"Is there a hotel or motel nearby?" interrupted an older woman standing behind Beth. She had a thick head of gray hair, a deeply creased face, and carried a walking stick. "I don't know how long I'll be here," the woman added, "but I'm not leaving until I understand what's happening."

Sky nodded.

"We're all here for the same reason," the woman said to Beth. "You couldn't ignore the call either."

"No, I couldn't," Beth answered with relief, realizing that she was not alone in what was happening to her. Coming here at first frightened her even though she was a confident traveler, having spent the last two years crossing the globe. Despite a mountain of college debt and only a tiny amount of money from a summer job, she set out to see the world and write along the way. Moving unhurriedly from one locale to the next, she took jobs when she needed to replenish her funds, lived in hostels, and sometimes befriended others who put her up for short periods. There were so many beautiful places to experience, but what she also encountered along the way was unexpectedly dark and disturbing. There were rainforests cleared and burned for industrial farms, mountains and forests decimated to excavate coal, wetlands filled to build retirement communities, coastal waters choked by dumping and pollution, constant expansion of development into wild places. Soon her destinations were no longer random, but guided by a systematic need to see the destruction inflicted on the planet firsthand. Her travel here was entirely different from all of that. She was prodded, first by her dreams, and then a mysterious pull to cross the country to this very place.

"It's a good thing you followed your instincts," said the older woman to Beth. "I'm Mary, Mary Lopez." She shook both Sky and Beth's hands. She carried herself with unflinching determination about the circumstances that drew her here. "It was a dream, the same one for three nights. It knocked and knocked and knocked and it wouldn't relent, getting louder and louder, until I let it in and then followed it here."

Sky could see the knowing look in the young woman's eyes.

"I came all the way from Galisteo, New Mexico. It was a long trip, but I'd have come from China. I don't mince words, not at my age. I say what's on my mind. Something important is going to happen here. It might as well be Judgment Day. I have two children and three grandchildren and I'm here for them."

Sky thought about this woman's words. Maybe she was right and Judgment Day was coming.

While she spoke with Mary and Beth she looked up and saw Judith wandering among the visitors, greeting and having brief conversations with one and then moving on to another. Judith suddenly waved Sky toward her with some urgency. At the same moment, Sky's phone rang and she picked up and spoke to Calvin. Before Sky could share the message, Judith was at her side and said, "It's time. We have to go."

Sky nodded knowingly. "Calvin said the people were starting to gather at the field near Woodland Creek." It was also the place she had been preoccupied with all morning.

They hurried back to the car and headed out, the destination about twenty minutes away. It was congested as they got closer and cars were left on the shoulders of the narrow road as people walked in the direction of the field. Sky and Judith parked and followed the others. It was eleven in the morning. Sky turned to a woman walking alongside her and asked what made her come.

Harita felt pleased having someone to talk to. Despite the crowds and the knowledge that they all were here for the same unexplained reason, she had not yet spoken to anyone. It was though she could not puncture the cocoon that had enveloped her the past three days. "I know this sounds rather odd but I had a dream and then, I don't know how else to explain it, I was pulled here." Walking with the others, saying it aloud to the stranger, momentarily allowed her wild journey to somehow make sense, and helped ground her. These people must have experienced something similar to her. But why was she in the mountains? The overpowering dreams this past week and her entire life were about the sea but as she drove east she was pulled to the mountains, these very ones. Everything about her work had grown more urgent in recent years. After decades of work on the study of the oceans, the threats and dangers were increasingly alarming as was the aching fear that grew inside of her as she became more convinced that life in the oceans could collapse if change was not taken.

"Do you know what this is about?" Harita asked.

"I do, but not fully. It's hard to explain," Sky answered.

"Do the others know?"

"I don't believe they know any more than you."

The travelers began to congregate in the field. Sky could see the uneasy shuffling and mulling about. Many of them began to talk with each other and looks of relief framed some of their faces as they began to share their stories, though the anticipation weighed heavily. Sky could see that Judith was unusually serene with a look of satisfaction in her face knowing that the years of secrets, hiding, protecting, were no longer necessary and that the time had come.

The beautiful field where they assembled in the valley was once part of Roger's land. It was about a mile from where the house was once located. The grasses and plants in the field were already flattened from early frosts and sleet before the warming again late this season. From the road the field stretched back into a valley with a sharp elevation of wooded and rocky cliffs on the northern side. It was scenic, particularly from the cliffs. From there one could look down on the gathering with a beautiful view of the land.

Warren left his car unevenly parked in a tight space along the road with the hundreds of others. He worried that he was late and the crowds had already moved through. There were a few stragglers. A crow was perched on an overhanging branch above as he walked along the road. Thoughts of the birds at the party stirred in his mind once again and he knew in his heart that those birds and this event were not unrelated. The people all around offered no clues and they seemed as mystified by the experiences that brought them here as he was.

Alex had parked his rental car and walked to the sight. This place, though he had never before visited, was uncanny in its familiarity, the very scene that played over in his dream on consecutive nights, each time exactly the same. The winding turns and the stream running along the road were precisely as he remembered them. What surprised him were all the others following to this same destination. His mind was spinning. There was nothing cohesive or unifying about the people he was among.

Darnell hitched a ride from the bus terminal where he made his last stop on the way here. It was more than an hour south, as close as he could get by public transportation, but he found a ride when he stopped in the nearby convenience store to get a soda. The man was a middle-aged minister from Kentucky. While he ordinarily would never have spoken to this person, they oddly struck up a conversation as they stood together in line. When Darnell explained that he was headed north the man generously offered him a lift, telling him that sometimes, unplanned travel takes us down new roads that God has in store for us. He seemed harmless enough and Darnell desperately needed a ride so he accepted the invitation. During the trip the man talked nonstop. He said he was from coal mining country and spoke about the hard life of the miners. He knew that life from the inside out. His father was a miner once but died young, as was often the fate of so many others. He, too, spent two years in the mines before deciding to become a minister.

He wanted more for all of those risking their lives in the mines, right now, in this life, and not just in the hereafter.

Only when he and Darnell approached the area did they realize that they were headed to the same destination. Once they parked, they exchanged a warm handshake. The minister blessed him and wished him well as they separated and each proceeded down the road to the field. Darnell was near awestruck by the beauty of the mountains. He had never been out of New York City. He had looked through books and pictures of such places, but this was the real thing and he felt very emotional. For a moment he wished he had brought his binoculars, but then realized he did not need them to discover something new, not here; everything around him was novel and inspiring. He wanted to take it all in, a full broad panoramic view. He saw an older man and woman walking ahead of him. As he got closer they smiled and welcomed him as though they knew why all these people were here. They asked his name and then introduced themselves, David and Louise. They were warm and friendly, but he moved on. It was the young people who captured his attention, as almost everyone was young. There were so many more of them.

Malach, Ginny, Angie, and Evan drove down the dirt road and parked on the property that once was the location of Roger's house. They looked around the site, detecting barely a trace of what once stood right in their presence. There was something gratifying in seeing how the earth healed itself. Together they began to walk toward the field. When Warren stepped out of his car he saw the four of them coming down the road. He walked ahead of them with a few others, looking back several times before slowing, and then stopped to wait, as he felt drawn to them.

"Are you all going, too?" he asked, trying to make conversation, knowing full well they were.

"Yes, we are. What's your name?" Evan asked as they all introduced themselves.

"We're glad you're here." Angie said.

"So am I. But it's so confusing."

"It gets worse before it gets better," she said.

As they strolled along the country road, some of those nearby started walking quickly to join them, finding comfort being with the group.

Sky and Judith stood among the crowd. Mark was already present and joined them. Calvin arrived minutes later with a photographer from the newspaper. Evan's parents spotted Judith and approached, and soon Angie's parents arrived. Virginia and Oliver walked hand in hand as they entered the field. Judith felt a deep swell of satisfaction seeing Ginny, Angie, and Evan's parents here, being able to experience first-hand what their children had been part of for the past five years.

When Malach and the others approached and entered the field there was a clear sense by those present that he was the one they were waiting for. Darnell watched them move right through the middle of the crowd. The four of them stopped and spoke to many of those present thanking them for making the trip. Darnell looked on awkwardly from the side. They began to move in his direction and Malach's eyes met his as he walked toward him and then reached out to take his hand.

"I hoped you'd be here," Malach said to him. Malach introduced himself and Ginny. Evan and Angie had already walked ahead and were talking to others.

"Boreal owls regularly winter here. On a rare occasion they have been sighted in Central Park. I've always had a special affection for those birds. I believed you might, too."

Darnell smiled, beginning to put the pieces together. "I'm not sure how to explain it," he said. "But it was important for me to see one. I never thought I'd ever have the chance." Darnell oddly felt as though he and Malach already had had this conversation. Malach's words to him about the owl felt familiar much like when he saw the owl in the Park, a connection with that bird and with something bigger. He knew it had come from so far away. Venturing into Central Park had once felt like that for him. Being here today did as well.

"We'll talk more later," Malach said. "You understand things that few others do."

Darnell nodded and felt for the first time in his life acknowledged by someone who spoke to the peculiar connections he sometimes experienced with the world around him. Malach and Ginny moved on.

Darnell was the first to notice the small number of redpolls nearby. He had never seen those wonderful little birds before but in a book. Soon there was a large flock of them perched in the leafless oak trees at the edge of the field. It was exhilarating seeing so many. The birds were fluttering in and out of the trees and making noise that drew the attention of some of the others. He could hear Malach saying something and everyone's attention shifted toward him. Darnell looked back at Malach as he stood near Ginny and watched as he took her hand in his. The other two, Evan and Angie, were standing nearby. He listened as best he could to Malach as he spoke to the crowd.

The chatter of the small songbirds grew louder, rising notes and trills that resonated as hundreds and hundreds, thousands of them continued to converge in the trees. Soon attention was drawn in their direction, as Malach was now silent. The birds took to the air, lifting from their perches. Everyone was riveted to them. A wave of the birds along with their rhythmic sounds echoed all around. The redpolls swooped down and then flew off, but were still in sight. They turned and careened back in the direction of the crowd. They were high above and began to circle in wide aerial swaths; building momentum each time they passed. The crowd watched the birds for some time before the massive flock suddenly swooped down, just feet above the heads of the people. As everyone instinctively ducked, Darnell leaned into the direction of their flight and then felt a swell of energy inside of himself, a surge both foreign and sublimely familiar. A powerful draft caught and pulled him, near whisked him up into the air. Turns and twists were spontaneous, reflexive, synchronized automatically with the redpolls. Darnell's mind opened, the light more exquisitely refined, the beating of wings audible and rapid, frenzied speed and wide arcing turns conformed to his body, down and then up and around. He was exhilarated, the little birds with the red marking on their foreheads carried him alongside them, and then he was just part of them, one pulsing beating organism.

Each time they circled, more and more of those present felt the movement take them aloft, soaring in flight as the birds rose higher and farther in a path of widening revolutions over the valley until everyone was included.

Ginny felt the stirring in her body from the moment the birds took to the air, every nuance of flight that Malach experienced was hers, and then shortly after she felt Darnell, the first of those present being pulled along with them. The lift and rapid elevation, the hurried, accelerated movement up, the wind in her face, the fall air in her lungs, her senses acutely attuned to the light and air, her mind filled and expanded. She felt stretched, unwound, racing, driving speed, outside of herself, no self, moving in synchrony with the redpolls.

The birds moved higher into the sky, and, when reaching the apex of ascent, suspended motionless, before reversing in a rapid plunge back to earth, precipitously falling, gravity drawing them down, down, down. Ginny clutched Malach's hand feeling the splits, the separations taking hold for everyone present, each on their own conducted path. Malach was simultaneously with each of them, and with her hand in his, she was part of every journey, too.

Harita felt her stomach sink as she plummeted from above, weightless in free fall, heart pounding, racing down toward the earth, breathless, an adrenaline surge rushing through her body, and then crashing into the sea, into the clear blue waters of a vast reef system. Her mind was spinning, but as she moved through the warm waters, calmness washed over her like a healing salve. She was home but felt neither the physical sensations of buoyancy nor the awareness of wellbeing that usually enveloped her when in the ocean. Rather, it was the absence of all that, as though the water was not a magical place she was visiting, but no different than breathing air, the place where she belonged. Vibrant and alive, exquisite coral, luminously colored fish and sea creatures cascaded through this underwater paradise. Dense with seductive hues and amorphous shapes of the hundreds of coral species in an underwater garden of captivating polyps, domes, caps, mounds, and skeletal forms. She had never seen so rich a panorama of coral quilt work, exotic fish, and sea life. It was how she believed it once was, but it exceeded her grandest imagination.

The movement began again, as an enormous school of emperor angelfish approached. The yellow and blue stripes tracing the length of their bodies, a dark blue mask across their eyes, the fish were exotic and mysterious. Sensations flowed through her body as they pulled her along, riding with the school, flashing movement, darting turns, all in synchrony, an underwater equivalent of the furious flight she had just been on, actions instinctive and instantaneous. As part of the network of the reef, she felt bonded to the intricate web of plants and creatures. Her mind aligned with the sentience of the sea, complete with its own symphony of sounds, light, and intelligence.

Warren soon felt the illuminating elements of the sky and air, his body surging in flight, moving in a rapid succession with the birds, expansive and unified, then all thought evaporated from his mind, his body soaring, consciousness tingling until the plunging free fall, and an abrupt veering as he entered the endless space of rugged rock formations, twisting canyons, and sweeping desert sands. The walls of the canyon with eroded white, gold, and rose-colored sandstone formations drew him into the inhospitable landscape, earth-baked, eroded, and wind blasted. A solitary raven soared above the austere and mysterious outpost of the lonesome wild. In the heart of this far ranging landscape, Warren felt connected, linked to and part of something rooted deep in the fabric of the natural world. Whole and complete, unexplained meaning filled the void that had once pervaded his life.

Beth took a deep breath as her heart skipped in her chest. She was petrified of heights but into the sky she was carried. The speed and crafted turns of the redpolls, one way and then the other, were exhilarating and near heart stopping, until the racing speed escalated and created a vortex of movement and space. She was propelled through a vacuum of stillness that expelled her into the humidity-drenched lowland forests of the Amazon basin. Moving with a small group of plum-throated cotingas, she darted through the lush density of pristine forest growth. The beautiful turquoise birds carried her on their wings as she weaved through the extraordinarily dense foliage of soaring trees and layer upon layer of luxuriant undergrowth. Onto a perch she settled, verdant beauty surrounding her, a rushing narrow river below, a tangle of vines, shrubs, and impenetrable growth in every direction. Streams of emerging sunlight filtered through the canopy, above it a cloud of evaporating moisture from an earlier downpour while below spread a mist filled haze. A discordant symphony of forest sounds was impossible to discriminate, buzzing and clicking of insects, trills, whistles, and chirps. Sounds came from every direction, yet the creatures were fleeting or remained hidden or camouflaged by the thickness of the rainforest. Above was the bustling presence of noisy foraging capuchin monkeys, beside them scarlet macaws in a large flock. The immense assortments of plants and animals were everywhere as she was once again in flight through the endless forest, untouched by human presence.

Careening back into the sky, flying faster, no longer with the tiny birds, but rather in flight with a lone boreal owl, Darnell crossed the northern coniferous forest, the air icy cold, the ground snow-covered, the moon full in the cloudless sky above, his body acutely attuned to every visual movement, nuance, and shade of light. Through and above the trees, he felt its presence, an isolative bird, surviving on its own in a vast wilderness of wintery stillness. The owl flew, and Darnell felt Malach's presence along with that of the bird as he glided across the vast landscape and expanse of the mountains and frozen terrain. Never had he felt such solitude around him. Calm and peace spread wide across the wilderness. He watched from above and witnessed the order of the natural world below – the long cold season and the scarcity of prey pushing the limits of survival.

Ginny's mind was overextended as she simultaneously entered the rich verdant foliage of the Amazonian rainforest, the barren frozen landscape of the boreal forests, the wind-swept, rippled sands of the great deserts, the kaleidoscope of colors and shapes of the tropical and subtropical coral reefs – so many images, so many places, all at dizzying and overwhelming pace, hundreds of them. Then entering a zone of fluidity, the competing environments smoothed as she was catapulted across the globe, from the depths of the seas, to the peaks of great mountain ranges, across the tundra, grasslands, and plains. Her hand remained firmly in Malach's grip as she followed him on this miraculous journey, the memories of the untrammeled world, untouched by man.

Judith swayed with blissful glee, attached to Malach again for the first time in years, gliding on his wings, her spirit lifted, her heart full. Mark held himself close to her side, his mind reeling, before surrendering to the forces carrying him through the heavens. Soon she was lost in the skies and through the valleys of these mountains. As Judith looked from her elevated flight she eyed a wounded young buck staggering below. As she swooped down she saw the blood coming from its throat, its body jerking before being brought to the ground by a lone wolf. It sent chills through her. Soon it was behind her and she lifted high and beyond this exposed area across the density of the forest. The scene flickered disturbingly in her thoughts and then disappeared.

Crouched behind a cluster of rocks and forest undergrowth along the ridge overlooking the field on the north elevation, Brett peered over the gathering. Watching from his lookout, he strained to make sense of the hundreds of people who had come today. They all stood in the same direction, arms slightly apart from their bodies, heads moving, and shoulders straining in unison, while thousands of birds circled above them. What the fuck, what the fuck was going on, he thought. Images of Malach spun in his head. He felt a deep hatred for him. Malach made him look a fool too many times. No one gets away with that.

He pointed his hand at Malach, lining up his aim as if he were going to shoot him. *Bam, bam*, he muttered and then laughed. That would feel good, he thought. He watched for some time. This isn't normal. He's going to ruin everything, the lumber mills, his job, he felt certain of this. He waited and watched.

The redpolls circled overhead, and several minutes later, nearly an hour from when the journey had begun everyone was pulled back, each from their own all-encompassing pathway and retracted into the flock, and as the birds descended so did each of those present, back to the valley that surrounded them.

7

itting with the Rothmans in their kitchen, Ginny and Malach drank tea and ate sandwiches that Louise had prepared. David and Louise had returned home only the night before last. "Beckoned home," David said, and "not for a single moment hesitated." Ginny and Malach had come to the lake after the gathering to think and plan. The few hundred who had been present at the gathering had slowly dispersed, though no one left the region, each person prepared to remain for whatever might come next.

"I've been writing all my life," David said. "I choose my words like special friends, constructing sounds and cadences with those very words, developing stanzas infused with layers of meaning, yet I have not one word, let alone a single idea to explain what happened today."

"Maybe it's not an explanation that we need." Ginny said. "Imagining the journey and memories that you had today, recreating that for others, that would be a valuable contribution. It'll be hard for those not here to find a place in their minds for this. It's going to be a daunting task to overcome the obstacles we face and to then change the path we've all been on. It will take a revolution in how we live and that will require the inspiration of poets."

"It will no doubt take a great deal," Louise said. "You are two remarkable young people. How fortunate we've been to have you come into our lives and to be part of this. While we once thought retirement in North Carolina was next, I think we've found the work for the final chapter of our lives."

"You know you can stay in the house for as long as you want," Malach said.

"David and I have realized that preserving the lake and valley is paramount, and removing this domicile when you feel it's time is not something we will lament. Returning as much land back to the wild is far more critical, starting right here. Finding a way to build a new world is what's important. So much needs to change."

"We're going to meet in the field again," said Malach. "The day after tomorrow. It will be important, a next step."

"Of that I have no doubt," said David. "No doubt at all."

"It's been a long day. Would it be okay if we stayed the night?" Malach asked. "I don't think anyone knows where we are. Some time to rest and get a good night's sleep."

"Of course," Louise said. "The guest room is made up. It's very cozy."

Later that evening Malach and Ginny lay in bed under the warmth of a fluffy down comforter. It felt so perfect in each other's arms and Ginny imagined the simple pleasures of a quiet and uncomplicated life. That was not in her immediate future, and maybe it never would be. While it was becoming harder for her to settle most nights, Malach was already sound asleep. She knew the day had taken a lot out of him. Her mind was still racing, barely having had time to decompress despite Malach's efforts to help her through what she experienced. She was not prepared for the hundreds of memories that Malach uncovered for those present. He no longer needed to be physically in contact with others to transfer the experiences. It opened many possibilities and more than that, no one was any longer a passive observer but pulled into the world directly. She felt the strain Malach endured as she joined with him and simultaneously followed the divergent pathways created for each person in the field, and like the soaring flock of thousands of redpolls, none of the split paths collided with one other.

She knew he was pleased with how the day had unfolded. He

felt the call was heard and that each person who came would have an important role to play as they moved forward. Of all these people, it was Darnell with whom he seemed most intrigued. He saw in him a special awareness. Malach had asked Angie and Evan to take him home with them tonight. Darnell needed a place to sleep, but Malach also wanted his friends to share more of what they had experienced and learned.

Ginny knew that Malach envisioned a very different world. Not a throwback in time, not a world without all the advances of science and medicine and rational governments. It was not a Walden of the twenty-first century. It was the world that could be. It was a much smaller, more civilized and advanced world of people living alongside the paradise that was our birthright. The natural world had to be protected at all costs – what was already lost restored, what was threatened protected, and what was still wild left untouched.

David and Louise sat at the table late into the evening. The wood-burning stove warmed the kitchen area. Their minds were still in overdrive. They shared their experience with the similar careening paths they had flown on across Manhattan Island. The Hudson River and the Palisades defined the region for them both.

"Manhattan, before any settlement," David said. "A beautifully complex environment with rich flora and fauna from the region. It was not that long ago, and now, a concrete city with only a tiny manmade oasis of a park in the center. What do you think he's telling us?"

"Oddly, I don't think he wants us to turn it back to nature," Louise said. "Even if we could miraculously do so, I think just the opposite. Maybe we need to dream of the cities of the future, more compact, and a place where we can all live, while the rest of the world remains pre-served as wild and untamed."

"I can't explain it, but I felt that, too," said David.

In the morning, David walked down the long drive to pick up the morning newspaper. He had slept little during the night. He left the house quietly to avoid waking Louise. It was crisp but still unseasonably mild for the time of year. The sun was barely poking above the hills. He unfolded the paper and was startled with the bold headline. He was so consumed with what he had experienced that he had not given thought to the news impact it would have. The editor of the local paper, Calvin Trinker, had prepared the story. *Malach Walker, A Messenger for Our Time*. The report filled the entire cover with a full two-page spread inside. A picture of Malach and another with him and Ginny were included with the story.

Calvin and Sky had spent the late afternoon and early evening on the finishing touches of the story. Calvin had been preparing the broad strokes from the moment he and Sky began to uncover the news reports of Malach, Ginny, Angie, and Evan's travel over the past weeks. Since then he had spent every waking hour with Sky, listening to her account of Malach's life. He did not want to interfere with Malach's orchestrated plan, but he also knew that the first story needed to be reliable, undistorted, and unvarnished. The truth of Malach's life had to be told by those who know him. What was happening was so important that Calvin did not want the gristmill of garbage news to have the first hand at this, turning it into a circus. Interest in Malach would become a tsunami of fascination.

Sky and Calvin had been up most of last night, managing to get only a few hours of sleep before heading back to the paper. Sky understood that it would be a momentous day. She sat with Calvin in his office through the morning. He read some of his emails aloud while she listened to requests from reporters and editors looking for personal comments on this groundbreaking event.

"I've watched Malach grow up," Sky said. "From that very first day when I witnessed that red tailed hawk hover in flight just feet above him, that little boy giddy with delight, a mysterious bond of connection between them, I was overwhelmed and confused and so filled with emotion. Now the world will have a chance to know him, too. What you wrote is honest and compassionate. I don't think his introduction to the world could have been done any better. I'm proud of you." Sky wiped tears from her eyes, the well of feelings she was having was hard to control. She got up from her seat and gave Calvin a hug.

"Yesterday changed everything," said Calvin. "It isn't that I ever doubted you or him, but seeing and experiencing what we did... well, it brings it to another level."

"It's going to get crazy around here, isn't it?" Sky said.

"This will be in every media outlet by the end of the day," Calvin said. "We'll be inundated by tomorrow, if not sooner, with satellite vans, camera crews, reporters, coming from near and far. Do you think he's ready for this? Ginny and Evan and Angie, too, they're just kids and the glare of it – the eyes of the world will be on them, scrutinizing everything about their lives. Yesterday will seem like a sleepy day at the park compared to what's coming next."

"I honestly don't know how they'll handle this," said Sky. "Malach probably better than the others, but I just don't know."

"Where is he now?" asked Calvin.

"When I spoke to Judith last night she said he didn't come home, nor did Ginny. I suspect they tried to find a quiet place away from all of this."

"I hope so. It may be the last time he'll have that luxury," Calvin said with a sigh.

"That's a sad thought."

"His life is going to be forever changed," said Calvin.

"Yes, but it was never normal," said Sky. "There's never been anyone like him."

"I suppose you're right," said Calvin. "What do you think is next?"

"All I can say," said Sky, "is that he wanted everyone present to know something deep and fundamental about the world. In that one moment in time, I felt a connection that was lucid and clear and impossible to have known otherwise. It was as if I had rediscovered a lost experience, lost to me, lost to people everywhere. We no longer have those connections. I think that's what he was telling us. We must understand that our very existence is still tied to it."

The phone rang and Calvin answered it. She realized the floodgates were opening but prayed that Calvin's breaking story would provide a floor of reason and rational inquiry to what will invariably veer in wild directions. Sky got up and went into the next room to check on the coffee she had made and prepared a cup for each of them. When she returned she saw an alarmed look in his face.

"Who was that?" she asked.

"Someone from the Department of Homeland Security. An Undersecretary of something."

"Homeland Security," Sky said with confusion.

"He wanted to know what was going on up here. He sounded like a bureaucratic troubleshooter trying to head off a crisis. He asked me if I knew that a story like mine would incite people. He told me he heard that I was a reputable journalist, but this was crazy."

"What did you say?"

"I invited him to come on up and see for himself. He told me he had already sent a team and wanted me to meet with them this afternoon. He wants to get out ahead of this."

"That's disturbing," said Sky. "I never thought of Malach as a threat to our national security."

"Yeah, it's hard to figure that one out. I know some journalists in D.C. I'll reach out to them later to see what I can learn about this guy. I have his name. Meantime, let's get breakfast and see what's happening in town."

Judith was surprised with how soundly she slept overnight. She felt elevated by all that had happened the day before and a deep sense of contentment filled her. Malach was ready, and what he planned to bring to the world had begun. Mark did not sleep a wink. He was preparing a sermon, trying to find a way to explain his son's life, to give credence to the miraculous workings that he'd witnessed.

Mark was at the kitchen table with his pad and pencil, organizing his thoughts. He barely looked up when she came in.

"Good morning," she said. There was a long pause before he responded, lost in his sermon.

"It's extraordinary," Mark responded. "All I can say is that it was more than I could have ever dreamed."

"What did it mean to you?" Judith asked with no trace of irony or distain.

Mark did not hesitate. "It's the hand of the Almighty working through our son. He is truly a Messenger or maybe even a Prophet, showing us a path for our lives. Nature cannot be subordinate to our needs. It's God's own handiwork and we need to respect it like the word of Christ himself. The warnings are as clear as day. The earth is burning. It is hellfire that has started. How much more do we need to see?"

Judith was taken back with the sureness and certainty of Mark's reaction, but who was she to dismiss that any longer.

"And to you?" he asked.

Her attention was drawn to the newspaper that was on the table. Judith lifted the paper and looked at the oversized headline above the picture taken of her son yesterday. It was a partial profile of him looking over the crowds, his gaze penetrating. His dark hair was wind-blown with thick locks tucked behind his ear, stubble on his chin and the sides of his face.

Alex drove his car into town. He had slept in it last night, as there was not a room to be had in the area. It was mild for the season, so he made do with a wool blanket he had purchased at The Mountain Store nearby. He was still having trouble assimilating the events of yesterday, but was utterly overcome with awe and a renewed sense of purpose. Yet, he also realized that, as amazing as this was, he was not going to be able to make this right with his son. He already cancelled his flight back for tomorrow despite knowing that Will and Roslyn would be unforgiving even under the circumstances. He wished Will was present and a part of this. It was, after all, about his future. Most of those assembled were not much older than him. It was now their battle to fight.

It was very early but there were many cars in town with crowds of people on the streets. He headed toward the local diner but as he began to cross the street he stopped in his tracks when he saw her. Sky had been in his thoughts since this journey began. He watched her walking hand in hand with a man as they approached Peg's Diner. Alex knew that he no longer had any place in her life. He veered off and went to the convenience store instead of the diner and ordered a cinnamon roll and a large coffee. He picked up the local newspaper and saw the headline. He headed back to his car and read the story through before he even took a bite of his food or a sip of his coffee. To his astonishment, it was Sky who provided the background story of Malach's life. She had known about him for years.

He desperately wanted to speak to her but hesitated, certain she would be put off by his presence and see his overture as self-serving. He knew from his dream last night that tomorrow there would be another gathering. Maybe he would be able to talk with her there. In the meantime, he'd try to find a place to sleep for tonight. His back was hurting and he needed a bed. Regardless, he was not going anywhere.

Warren read a series of texts and checked several missed calls from his mother. His parents were in L.A. but were heading to the house in Aspen for the holidays as planned, and they wanted to know if he'd arranged his flight. His brother was already there with his girlfriend for their college break. Warren responded to the messages and told his mother that he was fine but needed to delay travel for a day or two. He had no intention of going skiing or even heading home, but did not want to deal with all that right now. Suddenly, everything from his life seemed pale and insipid in the shadow of what he had experienced. The people he had met since he arrived were so different from his insular world, and he felt fortunate to be among them.

He stuffed his sleeping bag into its sack and walked toward his car. Wrapped snuggly in it, last night he had slept under a clear star-filled sky and felt he had experienced the heavens for the very first time. The insignificance he felt within the vast cosmos was unburdening and strangely reassuring. The world, the Universe itself, was so clearly not about him. At the same time, it never felt more meaningful.

Sitting in the warmth of his car he fumbled through his backpack and found his toothbrush. He looked into the rearview mirror and ran his hands through his thick dirty blond hair fluffing up his matted head. After brushing and rinsing his mouth, he found a clean tee shirt, underwear, and pair of socks. Quickly, he undressed and put on the fresh underlayer of clothes. He felt refreshed and immensely satisfied as though he had just completed a long physical journey. The dream last night would keep him here until tomorrow and longer if necessary.

He drove to the small town that he had come through yesterday, parked his car, and then headed to the diner where he waited in line. He was asked to share a table, due to the overflow of people and took a seat across from an older woman.

"Good morning, welcome. I could use the company," said Harita as she stood, shook his hand, and introduced herself. "I imagine you've been a part of this, too."

"Oh, yes," he said.

"My head is still spinning," said Harita. "What about you?"

"I know exactly how you feel," said Warren. "For me, there was life before what happened to me yesterday and life after."

"So true," said Harita. "I thought I wasn't in my right mind when I was pulled here. But now, I'm thankful for it. If I hadn't come, I would have regretted it for the rest of my life."

Warren nodded in agreement. "I don't want to sound trite, but it has changed my life."

"I don't think that's trite at all. I've been around a long time and experienced a lot of things, but nothing that will ever compare to this. It's been transformative. In a way we've crossed a divide and became the recipients of something very special. It's astonishing, really."

Harita found her conversation with this young man a welcome release from the pent-up emotions of the past several days. He was inquisitive about her work and she liked his intensity, but also sensed a burden with which he was struggling. "Enough about me," she said. "Tell me about, you."

Warren liked that she was direct, her handshake firm, and her deep dark eyes bold and inquisitive, even though she was so tiny and delicate. He found her so different from his mother, the antithesis really. He liked that she was a scientist and spent her career studying the oceans, doing serious and important work. His mother was a lawyer but she had never practiced. In fact, she never did anything but buy clothes, houses, luxurious furnishings, and ridiculously expensive artwork. When she wasn't consumed with all that, she was busy collecting stories from her exotic trips to share with a coterie of like-minded friends. That was the life she provided for him. He had never felt more removed from it.

"There's not that much to tell," he said. "I haven't done a whole lot in my life that's important. And the way I was raised, I no longer want any part of."

"Not to worry, you're young," Harita said. "Your life is just beginning."

"I suppose, but the world I've lived in is alien to the way life should be lived."

"That's probably true for all of us," said Harita.

"You don't understand. My family lives in a way that is distorted and grotesque. It has no real substance or meaning. My parents don't even try. Let me give you an example. We have a house that twenty people can live in comfortably. But it is just for my parents, my brother, and me. Their idea of nature is a luxury cabana at the beach with attentive staff close by and their very large boat anchored off shore to admire."

"I think I get it," said Harita.

"I don't want that anymore," Warren said. "I've felt it for a long time. At first, I was just embarrassed, but didn't really understand what was truly wrong with it. What happened yesterday made it so clear to me that we're losing our world and we may never get it back. We have to change and fast. We have to aspire to different heights."

"There were a lot of young people present yesterday," Harita said. "I don't think that was by accident. There's a war that has to be fought to save the world. Like all wars, the old and privileged start them, and the young have to do the fighting to make things right."

Harita's comment resonated in him. In the wake of the vast expanse of space he had entered yesterday and the deep sense of peace he had experienced, a bond was forming that pulled him now with inexplicable determination. If he had to literally fight for the preservation of the world, he would.

"Wars have been fought over far less important things," Warren said.

"They certainly have. My generation has neither the courage nor determination to get it done. I hope and pray yours can. There's a life of importance and meaning in that."

Warren and Harita finished their breakfast and left the diner together. She encouraged him to get to know the others, the young people here. They had work to do. She handed him her card and told him to call her for anything.

Warren gave Harita a hug and said good-bye.

*

Louise had prepared a hot breakfast for everyone. She had not had the pleasure of doing that for her own children in some time, and her grandchildren had the most peculiar eating habits, ones that she could never make sense of but which their parents readily indulged. A stack of hot buttermilk pancakes with warm maple syrup and a hot pot of tea she hoped would be comforting in these dizzying days.

Ginny felt more rested, following several hours of uninterrupted sleep. It was early as neither she nor Malach were late sleepers though there were days recently when she did not want to get out of bed. Malach was sensitive to her moods, knowing the stress she was experiencing.

A fire was flickering in the wood-burning stove when they entered the kitchen and looked out at the lake. It boosted Ginny's spirits. She found the Rothmans so welcoming.

"Thank you for this beautiful breakfast," said Ginny. "It's so kind of you."

"It's nothing, my dear," said Louise. "Besides, it's our pleasure to have you as house guests."

"Or rather, we should be thanking you for this breakfast," David said to Malach and Ginny, "for having us as house guests."

They all laughed as they helped themselves to the pancakes Louise had placed on the table. David poured the tea.

"It will always be your house in my mind," said Malach.

"There's an extensive story in the paper about you this morning," David said. Louise looked surprised, as he had not mentioned it to her. "You too, Ginny. It includes a long segment about you and also mentions your friends."

"Who wrote it?" Ginny asked.

"Calvin Trinker."

"That's good," she said.

"The paper is in the other room on my desk if you care to read it."

Malach continued with his breakfast. Ginny sat more contemplatively, considering the implications. "There will be more stories coming, I suppose," she said.

"I can only imagine that there will be a great deal more," said Louise.

Ginny nodded her acknowledgment and looked to Malach who offered a reassuring look.

After they had finished their meal, Malach started the conversation.

"I want you both to know that I'm happy that you want to be part of this. You both understand so much." Malach looked to David. "And you know it will take nothing short of a total transformation of our lives to stop it. The damage to the world is approaching much faster than once imagined."

"It aggrieves us both," said Louise.

"It will not strike us like a giant meteor but it will be no less cataclysmic," Malach continued. "Not everything we've already done and continue to do can be reversed. We can lessen the blow, but the window is quickly closing to achieve even that. Sadly, every day, dozens and dozens of plants and animals vanish from the face of the earth. Each dying leaves an empty place in our world. The loss of a species should happen only a handful of times in a whole year. Instead, it's now thousands and thousands of times. There are no villains out there doing this to us. It's not evil oil companies or coal mining operations. It's not the auto industry, or huge factories. They are not the primary problem. It is us. We demand what they have and they gladly hand it over."

"It's very sad," said Louise. "All I do know is that however many years we have left to contribute, we will."

"None of us have very many years left to change this," said Malach. "Whether it is one day or a month, a year, or a decade, it's no longer something for the next generation or the next century. It must be now."

Ginny listened to Malach's words and knew that what he had started in the past few weeks would move people, maybe move the world to change. It had to. It was the only hope.

After breakfast Ginny and Malach sat by the lake. Ginny had not looked at her phone all morning and did not read the newspaper story. When they went inside, she saw there were dozens of texts from Angie. Ginny phoned her and listened to Angie's recount of the chaos in town, the flood of reporters and waves of people arriving. Ginny listened quietly, then told her that she and Malach were going to stay put at the Rothmans until tomorrow and thought it best for them to do the same at her house.

Through the remainder of the day and into the evening Ginny grew more pensive. She stayed at Malach's side, and tried to draw on whatever inner strength she could muster. She wanted to be steady and strong, but as much as she tried, it was difficult. The Rothmans, too, felt the enormity of what was at hand and tried to be as supportive as they could before the next gathering.

Ginny and Malach wandered off to their room later that evening and just flopped down on top of the covers, still dressed, and stretched out beside each other, heads resting on puffy down pillows. Her breathing was heavy, exhaling each time with a sigh. Ginny snuggled close to Malach's side, his arm wrapped around her. Many thoughts floated through her mind. Malach had exposed her to so much, to nature in all its beauty, unpredictability, and contradictions. She had come to appreciate that the natural world is driven by its own forces, and no plan or ambition is beyond the scope of its laws.

"Are you ready for tomorrow?" she asked, knowing what his answer would be and that it was she who was not.

"We'll be fine," he said. "We have a message and we're prepared. But no matter how hard we fight, we're as likely to fail as succeed. People are outlier creatures in this world. We no longer fit in, but believe the world can be made to conform to us. That's our greatest failing. Finding a way to live alongside, while also protecting the natural world, that is the only hope. If we fail, what will be left will be a very different world than the one that people have ever known. It may one day even be a world without people and one devoid of so many of its treasures, but nature finds a way to go on, to grow again and to thrive, to create new life. As long as a spark of life survives, so will the natural world."

"Then we're just going to have to make certain we don't fail," she said.

That reassuring look crossed his face and he closed his eyes. She closed her eyes, too, and tried to clear her mind. Sleep came quickly and her night was filled with dreams.

Standing knee deep in the lake with Malach, both of them much younger, cold water dripped from their bodies having surfaced from deep below. The reflection of the sun shimmered across the water and she squinted her eyes for a moment.

How do you do that? she asked him.

Do what?

You know, communicate with the animals.

I don't so much talk as listen to them.

But how's that possible? she asked.

You can do it, too, he said. *Listen, they'll tell you their secrets.*

I don't think I can.

It's less mysterious than you think. It's in all of us. We've just forgotten how to do it.

That's silly, how do I know that this is even real? Maybe it's just a dream.

Don't doubt yourself or you'll never be able to do it.

It's too hard, she said.

Not as hard as you think. You just have to believe what's right in front of you.

I don't know if I can do that by myself, she said.

We all need to learn how, and then when we do, everything around us can be heard and seen in a new way. That's when the animals and the world all around are in us.

No one will believe that, she said. She dove back into the water and watched the passing of a school of small fish and then eyed and swam toward a huge turtle. As she approached, it descended and was out of sight. She then came back up for air.

Keep at it, he yelled to her.

She tried over and over, and then the turtle passed by her again. She followed it and the turtle turned and looked right into her eyes. They saw each other and she felt it, being part of its world and part of the world all around. Then she reached out and grabbed onto its shell and kicked her feet as it pulled her along. When she came up again, she looked to Malach who laughed and nodded his approval. A wave of exhilaration swept through her and she yelled out.

Yes, the animals, the world, are in me!

Ginny did not wake until the sun started to filter into the room. A crocheted blanket that had rested at the foot of the bed now covered her. Malach must have placed it over her during the night. She slept right where she had collapsed, never undressing or slipping under the down comforter. Ginny found Malach sitting in a well-worn uphol-stered chair across the room. He sat with his chin in his hand as he looked out the window, deep in thought. When he felt her eyes on him, he turned toward her.

"Good morning," he said.

Ginny smiled and pulled the blanket closer to her. "Have you been up long?" she asked.

"For a while. I hope I didn't wake you."

"What time is it?" she asked.

Malach looked at the clock on the nightstand. "It's 6:30."

"We should get ready."

Malach stood up and walked over to the bed and sat beside her. He leaned over and gave her a soft kiss on her lips. "You had another good sleep," he said. "You needed that."

"It felt good." Ginny had thoughts of the dream tumbling over in her head, but didn't say a word.

"There's so little time for what has to be done," Malach said. "I suppose we should try to make it a good one today."

"You usually do," said Ginny with a smirk. "I feel so nervous though."

"You're doing a great job," said Malach. "You know what has to be done. That's everything. As much as all of these people are moved by what they have experienced, they are just learning. And then there will be the others closed to it, completely. I can't change that with what I do. It's going to require more."

"I know," Ginny said.

The numbers of arrivals continued to grow throughout the morning. Sky and Calvin estimated at least three or four thousand people had already gathered and many were still finding their way to the field. It was approaching noon and they were anticipating Malach soon. There was more planning on everyone's part today. The sheriff brought his three deputies to help with traffic. An emergency vehicle was parked nearby in case someone was ill. He did not want to be caught unprepared.

Malach and Ginny arrived on foot with Angie and Evan. Darnell and a large group of young followers walked beside them. There was a lot more excitement, and the crowd was loud and enthusiastic. A cheer erupted when Malach was sighted and the air was charged with energy. He talked to each and every person near him, shook hands, waved and flashed his infectious smile. Ginny walked next to him, greeting people as they passed through the crowd. Evan and Angie, too, welcomed all who made the trip. News crews shouted out questions and even the skeptics among them seemed excited to be present.

Brett dwelled on the past days and could not shake the anger he felt. It grew inside him like a living thing. He followed the crowds and read the stories, and all of it funneled into a well of hatred he harbored inside. He was more prepared and silently found his place again on the rocky and wooded overlook above the much larger crowds today. Why were these people fooled? Why did they see Malach as some savior of the world? There was nothing that needed to be saved and certainly nothing that needed to be saved by him.

Brett carried his rifle with him, the weight and balance of the gun comforting in his grip. He watched from his perch as Malach and his friends were welcomed and fussed over. He lifted his .30-06 hunting rifle to his face and looked through the scope. The crosshairs found Ginny. He adjusted his aim elevating the barrel slowly and gently, moving from her waist to the center of her chest. He was most comfortable shooting from the kneeling position where he found his aim most accurate. Shooting standing or prone was not his thing. The new scope with the etched reticles provided a near lock on long distant targets. He pulled the trigger. *Click, click*. Hit, hit, he thought. Even the sound of the empty chamber in his unloaded rifle sounded right. Then he slowly trained the rifle on Malach. I can take them both down. *Click, Click*. Again, the hollow sounds of action sent an exhilarating wave of righteous revenge through him. I can do this. It will only take two shots each. He placed the rifle back across his lap. He loved this gun, but knew he would have to dump it in the lake, out deep. He had other rifles. No one would know that this one was missing. By the time the commotion settled he would be long gone. Just scramble right back up the rocky terrain behind him, in a minute he could be over the shoulder of these lower hills and back through the woods to the gravel road off the county road. No one saw him park there and with all the traffic no one would notice even if they had. He would drive south to the hunting grounds he frequented. The lake there was deep and there was a ledge from where he could dispose of the gun. He had another rifle in the truck. He'd fire a few rounds. Of course, he'd have gunpowder residue on him. The ballistics would not match and maybe he'd have a buck to bring home. It would be neat and clean.

Brett took his rifle and loaded six rounds. Everything involved in using the rifle pleased him. Malach and Ginny were in an even better location than the other day, oriented in his direction, on slightly elevated ground, easy targets. He looked down on them and believed that this was justified. He could do this. It was payback time. All this is craziness. Someone had to bring it to an end and it might as well be him. He took a few deep breaths – him and then her. He had to be sure to take Malach out first. Ginny would be easy and if he couldn't get her, nothing was lost as long as he got him. The other day, his dog whimpering and pissing on his pants and boot, he couldn't get it out of his head. His face burned red with the thought, and the feelings swelled in him again. Don't be distracted, he told himself. He blinked several times and brought the rifle up and took aim. Staring down the barrel of the rifle he found Malach in the crosshairs, took several deep breaths and slowly exhaled after each one. Steady and calm, he thought.

The first shot rang out across the valley. Malach's hand moved to his chest as his body jerked back. Brett watched him stagger. Then he noticed Ginny was lying on the ground. Holy shit, he thought, the bullet went through him and hit her, too. Only one bullet. Malach fell to the ground. Ginny's hand reached out and found his and then Brett could not see anything else as the crowd swarmed around them.

The force of the next strike sent a bone-crushing shudder through Brett. His head hit the ground with ferocious speed, so quickly he could not even utter a sound. Jaws locked tightly around his head, weight heavy on his body, the cracking sound through Brett's head and neck was audible to him until the quick twisting jerk left him in a lifeless heap, his face contorted, the flesh of his neck and cheek torn, his head wrenched unnaturally backwards, his body mauled. The majestic mountain lion raised its head, looked out over the valley below, paused momentarily and then retreated back up the rugged lookout into the brush and disappeared toward the high elevations of the mountains and into the distance.

8

Ginny and Malach were rushed to the hospital in the ambulance already present at the field. Sharp blasts sounded from the ambulance's siren and also from one of the sheriff's cars as it cleared a path to rapidly exit from the area. A wave of panic and confusion swept through the crowd. Shaken and tearful, numbed and disoriented, a pall of despair settled over those at the site.

Upon arrival at the emergency room a team of medical personnel were waiting and moved into action. The EMTs shouted out details of the shooting and the status of their patients as care was transferred. Ginny was circled by the attending physician and nurses who checked vital signs, started a transfusion, assessed the wound site, directed her for x-ray films, and moved her to the care of the surgical team that was assembled. During the trip to the hospital the EMTs had been able to stanch Ginny's bleeding, start an intravenous line, and deliver her with slightly weakened but stable vital signs from the bullet wound in her upper chest area.

Virginia and Oliver were in a panic as they arrived. The unthinkable terror of their daughter's life in grave danger nearly drained all life from them. Oliver was pale and wide-eyed, Virginia frozen in fear. A nurse sat with them, trying to provide support but not unrealistic expectations. She explained that Dr. Finny was a highly experienced trauma surgeon, and their daughter was in good hands. For two and a half hours they waited in an interminable limbo. When Dr. Finny finally came to report on the operation, Virginia and Oliver were barely able to speak.

The surgeon pulled a chair up in front of them and took Virginia's hand. Step by step, he explained the nature of the injury and the surgical procedures involved. Ginny had been struck by a single bullet from a high-powered hunting rifle. It created an entry wound in her upper thoracic cavity just below her clavicle. While such injuries can be extraordinarily dangerous, she was remarkably fortunate. The bullet did not strike any major blood vessels or organs. It tore through soft tissue causing trauma and bleeding, and fragmented the side of her scapula. There was no excessive internal bleeding. It was as if the bullet found the lone path that was least likely to inflict serious damage. Her shoulder blade required a plate and screws that would remain permanently in place. The work of the medics on the scene was done well and had prevented dangerous blood loss. He found the surgery to have gone smoothly and without complication. Ginny was heavily sedated and started on IV antibiotics to prevent infection. With the exception of any unforeseen problems during the next twenty-four hours, Dr. Finny was hopeful she would make a full recovery. They would be able to see her, but she remained unconscious in post-operative care. Virginia and Oliver held each other as the tears erupted, the release now providing relief and hope.

Oliver remained with his daughter while Virginia tried to compose herself and check on Judith and Mark. She found them in the emergency room along with Sky and Calvin. Judith stood in one of the examination rooms off in the corner of the unit where Malach had been taken. She remained immobile at the side of his bed, her face drawn and pale. Mark sat hunched over in a chair beside them with his face in his hands. Sky was at Calvin's side, her eyes swollen from crying. When Virginia approached, Judith asked in a barely audible whisper about Ginny. Virginia hugged her, but Judith was rigid and her expression frozen and unyielding. Virginia could barely look at Malach, his lifeless body covered to his shoulders with a sheet. He had died almost instantly, the bullet penetrating his heart before exiting his body and striking Ginny. Judith had been unable to move from his bedside. Virginia could not withhold the wave of grief that erupted. Sky approached and held her, and they sobbed together.

A few hours after the surgery Ginny awoke and found her mother sitting quietly near her bed. Virginia's face brightened and a warm smile spread across her face. Inside, she choked back the pain of having come too close to the tragedy that Judith and Mark were now enduring, but could not suppress the thoughts of what the pain of that loss would do to her daughter. She was not sure how to tell her about Malach, or whether it was even the right time. She wanted her to rest, to heal, to be whole again.

Ginny tried to talk but her throat was dry and irritated from being intubated during her surgery. The attending nurse came to the bedside and checked the various monitors. She told Ginny that the surgeon would be up shortly to check on her and asked her to rest for now. Ginny dozed off and Virginia waited for the doctor.

Dr. Finny greeted Virginia and Oliver while he received the latest report from the nurse. Ginny opened her eyes again and the surgeon spoke to her. He had the nurse adjust her position to make her more comfortable and she took a sip of water for her throat. Dr. Finney was pleased and informed Ginny that she came through the surgery splendidly, and was confident that she was going to be fine but needed to give herself time to heal and recover. After he left, the nurse told them that a bed was being prepared on the medical floor where she would be taken soon. For now, she suggested she not talk and try to rest. Once she was moved, they would get her up for a short while. Ginny dozed again and didn't wake until she was out of post-operative care. Virginia and Oliver were present in her hospital room when she woke again. Ginny focused and then in a whisper spoke to her mother.

"Malach…" she started and paused.

"Yes, honey," Virginia answered. She looked into her daughter's eyes, already feeling the pain she was enduring, but before she could speak Ginny continued.

"Where is he?"

Virginia hesitated, and while Ginny could see in her mother's face what she already knew, she asked again.

"Downstairs. He was shot like you were," Virginia said, the words almost too unbearable to utter.

"I know, but where did they take him?

"He's gone, Ginny. He didn't make it."

"But, where is he? I want to see him."

Virginia looked to her husband, not knowing whether Ginny understood.

"He died from the gun shot," Oliver said.

"I know he's dead. I felt him leave me." Ginny turned away and tears fell from her face.

"We'll talk to the nurse," Oliver said to his daughter.

"Who, who would have done it?" Ginny asked, her voice faltering.

"We don't know yet," said Virginia.

Virginia could see Ginny's entire body trembling. She held her hand. "I'm so sorry." Virginia had few words to offer, only her presence and love. She stayed at Ginny's side throughout the remainder of the day and slept in the recliner chair in the room through the night.

Calvin's story in the newspaper the following morning confronted the tragedy of Malach's death, the loss to the world, and the personal anguish he felt. The news accounts of the strange but compelling story of this young man spread rapidly. Fascination, skepticism, and incredulousness sparked the imagination of those attending to the reports of Malach's unusual, elusive, and inexplicable life.

There were many news stories collected from those who had been present at the first gathering. They shared their remarkable experiences and seemed determined to keep alive what they witnessed and learned. When Ginny left the hospital four days later, it was Christmas. She was met by a large group of reporters eager for an interview, but her parents shielded her and whisked her to the safety of their home.

After Malach's funeral and in the following days and weeks, the sounds, the words, the moods of the shooting and its aftermath echoed over and over in Ginny's mind and consumed her thoughts and dreams. The boundary between wakefulness and sleep blurred and the unremitting repetition of events beat on incessantly. The faces of the others, so many others who came to pay their respects, loomed frighteningly around her. Words of condolence were hollow to her ears, the depth of her sorrow bottomless. The horror of her loss was only matched by the brief but terrifying last seconds of Malach's life. As her hand had held tightly to his, she could feel the life draining from his body. In those moments she was one with his final thoughts, his last testament and warning of the world that we may face. Rapid images flashed through her mind. Exotic coral reefs barren and lifeless, verdant rainforests silent wastelands, old growth forests burned and charred, pristine coastlines flooded, lush deltas absent of growth, once dynamic skies of soaring birds silent and empty, monumental glaciers evaporated. The eradication of so much life and the emptiness left by Malach's death reached down and pulled at the core of her torn and broken self. With every breath she took, she descended deeper into her despair. Late into the night the aching loss choked all hope before sleep would finally overtake her, and her dreams took hold.

She looked everywhere but Malach was nowhere to be found. She called his name and searched for him. Where was he? Why were there so many people? A swell of dread flowed through her and then the sound of the firing of a gun rang out. Reaching and touching the burning pain in her chest with her fingers, it felt wet and she realized it was blood. Then she remembered that Malach was lying right beside her, both of them on the ground. His eyes were closed and body still. She reached for his hand and then together they flew high, racing into the sky. It was then that they saw the mountain lion moving quickly across the more exposed higher elevations. Its movements were swift and powerful. Then, abruptly, she was back on the cold ground and, seconds after that, no longer with Malach. She got up and ran to see the crowd surrounding something. Pushing through the people she saw him, his body being lowered into the earth. She felt woozy in her head and screamed but nothing came from her mouth, her legs and body leaden, unable to move. No breaths would come. No air. She was suffocating.

Ginny bolted awake, her heart pounding in her chest. She took a series of deep breaths and each time she inhaled she felt the pain high in her chest. It was the same dream, again and again. Ginny sat up and got out of bed. She could not endure it one more time tonight. Sleep had become so elusive and when it did take hold, it only punished her. The remnant pain of her wound was her sole comfort, anchoring her to her body and pulling her out of her head with all its tormented memories, briefly separating her from the terror that engulfed her. The light from the clock glowed in the darkness. It was only a little after three in the morning, still too many hours before the sun would come up. She switched on the lamp on the nightstand and a harsh glare filled the room, slowly easing as her eyes adjusted to the light. Silence filled the house.

A vase of flowers rested on her dresser. Angie had brought them a few days ago. She told Ginny about "Malach's People," as she had come to call them, those who were at the original gathering. A few were still in the area, the others had returned to their lives. They had organized into a group and recently had reached out to Angie.

Ginny could not think about this or what to do next, her head and her heart were too broken to work in that way. It all felt so pointless and hopeless. She was moving through the world in a vacuum, everything looked distant and sounded garbled. All that Malach would have brought to the world would now come to an end and there was nothing she could do. As much as she had shared the journey, his connection to the world around him and his ability to bring others along, were his gift alone.

She opened the top drawer of the dresser and took out a small, unwrapped box, the Christmas gift she had purchased for Malach this year. He did not care much about gifts for himself, but she always got him something, and he never forgot her. She opened the box and lifted out the brass antique pocket compass, held it in her hand and admired the aged quality of the patina. She pressed the stem to open the case, let it rest in her palm and oriented it to the north. Engraved on the inside of the cover was a poem by Robert Frost. She thought it fitting and ironic, a present for the boyfriend who had always traveled his own road and never got lost. She watched the gentle quiver of the hand on the dial. Her sadness was so heavy, but what was worse, and something she was reluctant to tell anyone, was that she was gripped with fear.

She felt so shaken and vulnerable. Leaving the house to attend the funeral panicked her and that terror remained silently under the surface. Since that day she had rarely been outdoors with the exception of a visit to Malach's parents and two follow-up consultations with the surgeon. Though school had resumed many weeks ago, she had yet to return. Her mother was increasingly worried about her. It was visible in her face despite her smiles and encouragement.

Sky came to visit often, patient with whatever amount of time Ginny could tolerate. Mostly, Sky spent time with Virginia. It was during these visits that Ginny would learn about Malach's parents. She could tell by Sky's evasiveness that their marriage was suffering and their lives splintered. Mark managed his grief by immersing himself with his mission to spread Malach's message, desperately trying to not let it die. Judith was barely able to get through her days. Ginny recognized this when Judith came to the house to visit. While being with Ginny or in the company of Malach's friends provided brief solace, it could not conceal how utterly devastated and broken Judith was. Ginny knew because she felt what Judith felt.

During their last visit she learned that Malach's attorney, Robert Lieberman, had visited with the Conservation Center Director, Board of Overseers, and Sky. At the meeting they were notified that the Center would be the recipient of Malach's estate. Malach had wanted Roger's land to be protected and the money to be used to further that purpose and to support the work of the Center. Sky wanted to know Ginny's thoughts about renaming the Conservation Center in honor of Malach. Ginny listened and understood their intentions, but did not hesitate a moment before telling Sky that she knew it would be the last thing Malach would have wanted. He believed the land did not belong to him or to anyone else. Sky understood that, but was unsure what the outcome would be.

After Sky had departed, Ginny thought much about Malach's gift to the Center. It was so like him to do what he had done. It left her with a good feeling inside, something she felt she had lost the ability to experience.

In subsequent weeks, Ginny worked with a tutor on completing the missed and outstanding work for graduation. Sporadically, assignments were finished and returned. Before the trip to Florida, Virginia had pushed Ginny to complete and submit three college applications, and now she was trying to provide a path forward for her daughter.

Angie and Evan came to the house every day, unfailingly. They, too, grew increasingly worried about her. They arrived after dinner with a different agenda.

Angie gave Ginny a big hug. "We have to talk."

"Sure," Ginny said, sensing a change in Angie's tone. When they had visited in the past several months, they brought snacks, tried to talk about movies, or shared new music, to Ginny's halfhearted attention. She refused their efforts to take her out, even for a drive or some food. They had abandoned conversations about school or even reminiscences about Malach, as that usually left Ginny more sullen.

"We want you to see something that we've been working on," Angie said.

She shut the door to Ginny's bedroom and Evan slipped the laptop out of his backpack, flipped it open and turned it on. Within a few moments, he clicked on a video.

"What is it?" Ginny asked.

"It's a documentary," Angie said. "This is the first part. It's about an hour long."

"Angie's been working on this for the past three years," said Evan.

"It was not a solo project," said Angie. "Evan was my collaborator every step of the way."

Ginny looked quizzically at them both. "I'm sure it's good."

"It's not just our movie. It's also yours," said Angie.

"Okay," Ginny said a bit confused. "What's it about?"

"Let's watch and you'll see. Make yourself comfortable." Evan placed the laptop on the bed in front of them so they could all view it clearly. Ginny sat up against her pillows, Angie beside her and Evan squeezed in, too. Evan started the video. The camera panned slowly across the landscape. It was autumn and the leaves were off the trees. It was a beautiful day. Ginny recognized the location at the Conservation Center. The video cut to a close up of Malach. He had a curious look on his face as he glanced down at something that seemed to delight him. As the camera panned back, it was then visible; a snowshoe hare sat in his lap, its coat almost fully white late in the season. It poked its nose into Malach's and a warm and contagious smile spread across his face. Ginny remembered the day like it was only yesterday, the first time Evan and Angie came with them. Then the frame widened and it now included

Ginny who stood several steps back laughing together with Malach. They were so young. A look was exchanged between them, a connection that was already forming. Ginny was flooded with emotions seeing the two of them together like that as she wiped away tears. She was riveted to the screen.

Malach nudged the hare off his lap and he got up and began to run, Ginny followed on one side and the white furry creature on the other. Finally, he shooed it away and the camera followed it across the field until it disappeared into the brush. Then he and Ginny ran in the opposite direction and the snowshoe hare came tearing out of nowhere and leaped into his arms. This time Malach placed it gently on the ground and it scooted off again. The scene cut back to Ginny and Malach, all smiles, finding the entire exchange ridiculously fun. They both turned to the camera, their faces challenging the viewer to decipher the magic. By the end of the movie the developing bond between them could be felt. Two very young adolescents whose smiles, darting eyes, knowing looks, and innocent flirtations, all seeped to the surface.

Since Malach's death, Angie had revisited the endless hours of video she had captured of him. Each encounter was breathtaking and inexplicable, as if she entered an enigmatic and dreamlike landscape that seemed to teeter on the edge of fantasy and reality. She and Evan began to register something they had not fully recognized before. Ginny was part of Malach's world in a way they were not. She had begun to sense the world in its many mysterious layers, linked to its resonating energy, to the spectrum of animal signals and communications, to the very intelligence of the currents of the natural world. While she may not have been able to conjure those connections herself, she had known them like no one else. That was evident in the video recordings. Angie reedited the footage and it was no longer just Malach at the center, but Ginny, too.

Ginny let out a sigh when the video ended. She looked to her friends with warmth and heartfelt appreciation. "That was wonderful. It must have taken a lot of work."

"It's just the first of five, one-hour videos," Angie said. "It has grown in the past year and it was hard to edit down to just five hours."

"Five," Ginny said with surprise. "I had no idea. Why didn't I pay attention to that? You were always recording."

"Probably for the same reason Malach never did. I was documenting your lives, and we were all consumed with being on the journey. Everything paled next to that. It was just not important."

Ginny nodded. "Can I see another?"

Evan and Angie exchanged a look and then started part two as they sat back and watched for another hour. While there was not a great deal of talking or dialogue in the first movie, this one had much more. Not big pronouncements, but casual, unpretentious comments by Malach of his unique world of knowing, seeing, and feeling. It was Ginny who was the narrator, reflecting on the extraordinary linkage between Malach and his surroundings. Even as a thirteen-year old, she had poise and presence that was already evident and only became clearer over the years.

After they completed the second video they watched the remaining ones with barely a break or interruption. The three of them laughed and cried, yet were constantly mesmerized with the reminders of the extraordinary path they had been on. At two o'clock in the morning they finished the five-hour saga. Physically exhausted and mentally drained they slept huddled together on Ginny's bed, until they awoke the next morning.

❧

"Thank you," Ginny said. "It was amazing to see that all again. It's so sad to think it's gone."

"It's not over," added Angie.

"I wish that were true," said Ginny. "But without him it has lost its power."

"You saw what we saw. You're the link," Angie said emphatically. "You were always joined in a way no one else was. He didn't just take you on this journey, you were in each other's minds, linked and interconnected."

"It's not what you think. I could only be part of that when he was with me. But that's gone now, for good."

"It doesn't have to be. You have to find it, share it, and spread it. It's only you."

Ginny grew quiet and tears filled her eyes. "I wish I could."

"Of course, you can," Angie said firmly.

"I just can't."

Angie looked squarely into Ginny's eyes. "We know who you are. You never give up."

Ginny looked at both of them. They each knew her better than anyone and at one time they were right, but now she couldn't even get out the front door. "I'm sorry. I can't do that anymore."

"There's no alternative," Angie said. "There's not a 'no' option. You understand that. You have to do this."

Ginny was silent. "I'm getting tired. I think it was too much seeing all of this."

"Damn it, Ginny. Don't play that 'I'm tired' thing again with us. I'm not going to accept that, and you know damn well Malach wouldn't have either. Is that how you're going to remember him, honor what he gave us, what he was beginning to give to the world."

"That's not fair," Ginny said with tears welling in her eyes.

"There is no 'fair,' in any of this. Do you understand?"

Ginny avoided her eyes.

"Listen to me. For the past three months Evan and I have been here every day, every single day, for you. We lived it, too. We get it."

"No, you don't!" Ginny shouted back. "You have no idea."

"There's no time for anymore self-pity. We have work to do. There's not a day that goes by that we don't feel Malach's loss. And yes, it was more complicated for you, but it's not just about you or me or Evan, it's bigger than that."

Ginny turned away.

"Don't blow me off, Ginny. Look at me. We need you. Evan and I can't do what you can do. You have to get out of this bedroom and get your ass in gear. Do you hear me?"

Ginny began to cry, her face in her hands, deep sobs convulsing from her body.

"I'm paralyzed, and I don't know what to do. I can't get the pictures of Malach out of my head. They're with me every second whether I'm awake or asleep. Lying next to him, feeling life drain from his body, watching him lowered into his grave. It's etched in my brain."

Angie looked to Evan, both of them shaken by her unrelenting nightmare, but determined to help her move forward.

"When I found out it was Brett," she continued. "That he shot Malach. I haven't been able to think straight." Ginny's voice rose, her face reddened, her body trembled. "I knew Brett was dangerous. I felt it. His hatred of Malach was so intense. So why didn't I do something? I could have stopped it. Malach didn't have to die. If anyone had to, it should have been me, not him. His life was so much more important, yet he's dead and I just get stitched up. How's that fair? What sense does that make?"

Angie sat beside Ginny and hugged her tightly. Ginny collapsed in her arms and erupted in anguished tears. She cried and cried, and the tears did not seem as though they would ever stop. Finally, gasping, Ginny caught her breath and slowly calmed herself.

"No one could have stopped what happened," Angie said. "You can't do that to yourself. It's not fair to you and it's not fair to Malach."

Ginny listened, looking into her friend's face, into her heart.

"Healing takes time," Angie continued. "I understand that. But this wound is going to be raw for a long time. It's just the way it is. We'll help you. You're not alone."

"I love you both," Ginny said. "I hear you. I want to do more, but I'm too afraid."

"Afraid," Angie said. "I'm sorry. Everything that happened is as horrible as it can be, but we don't have time for fear either."

"I can't control it. My body trembles, my heart pounds out of my chest, I can't breathe, I can't even think. Dying would be easier. I meant it when I said I couldn't leave the house."

"Okay, then we will figure that out, too. We'll be right at your side until your strength is back."

Angie got up and went to Ginny's closet. She pulled out a pair of jeans, a shirt and sweater, socks and boots. We're going to start today. Right now."

Ginny had a look of alarm in her face.

"We're not going to let anything happen to you," Angie said. "I promise. Come on. Get dressed."

Evan awkwardly turned his back and Ginny pulled the flannel top over her head and stepped out of the flannel bottoms. Angie handed her the clothes as she slowly put them on.

"Where are we going?"

"Today is the final day of winter," said Angie. "It has been a long, dark, painful season. We need to heal and to rebuild. We'll start with getting some food."

"And then?" Ginny asked.

"Tomorrow morning," Evan said, "I'm going to release the entire five hours online. We'll see where that goes."

A look flashed between the three of them. Angie recognized a fleeting moment of Ginny's former determination that she had not seen these past three months.

As Ginny took her first steps out of the house, her heart raced, but she took a deep breath and then another. Angie looped her arm through hers and they walked to Evan's car.

Virginia watched from the window as her daughter and friends drove away. Oliver had kept her clear of Ginny's room earlier when the shouting began and kept her from checking on her as they went out the door. Tears of hope now filled her eyes as the car pulled away. Oliver took her hand and she squeezed tightly. She knew that her daughter was destined for something important. She just never imagined that it would be trying to save the world.

Every day for the next five weeks Angie and Evan came to the house and Ginny left with them. At first, it was for short periods, then for the entire day. Some nights she did not come home at all. Virginia did not ask or question them, but watched as her daughter began her recovery from the depths of her terror and despair. Her body continued to heal and her spirit was rekindled. She marveled at her daughter's courage and strength.

Ginny stood in her room and looked in the mirror over her dresser, the weight and strain of her ordeal reflected in her face. The journey she had found herself on over the past five years was sometimes difficult to even fathom. So many thoughts turned in her head. As the months had passed since Malach's death she struggled with holding onto every memory of him. Time was both healer and enemy. She did not want even one moment with him to be lost, and when she could not recall something that had once been fresh in her mind, it sent a wave of panic and then sadness through her.

Ironically, it was through her dreams that she began to find peace. Once an unremitting source of her torment, her dreams now kept her connected to Malach. It was not just that she was able to look into his eyes, hear his voice, feel his body, and even hold him again, she was also carried back to the places that she had feared had been lost forever. Memories of all that Malach shared with her about the world remained alive in her dreams.

Ginny looked around her room. It contained the articles, remnants, and even silly reminders of her childhood, each one holding a little piece of the story of her life. Her attention was drawn to the small plastic tiger sitting on edge of the top shelf of her bookcase. It felt like her whole life was defined by that object.

Soon, it was time to go and she was uncertain when she would be back. Ginny reached into the drawer and found the gift that she had once planned to give to Malach. Removing the compass from the box, she opened and held it flat in her hand. Ginny thought about what lay ahead knowing there was no clear path or direction, then snapped the compass closed and slipped it into her pocket.

She placed her car keys on the dresser and picked up the bus ticket purchased the day before. Her backpack was full and rested against the wall near the door. With Angie and Evan, she would be traveling in just a few hours to New York City, the first stop of many events scheduled. Every single person from the original gathering with Malach would be present. All of them had worked tirelessly to organize this event and the ones to follow. It was where the next part of the journey would begin.

Earlier this morning a text arrived from Evan to let her know that the number of people who had viewed the videos online continued to swell. He also informed her that a short fifteen-minute preview to introduce her was compiled from the videos and would be shown on a large screen at the event in Central Park.

It would be Ginny's first time in front of the cameras. The crowds expected were going to be immense and media attention would be focused on her. She took a deep breath and tried to calm her nerves. She did not know where this would lead. Like the fate of the whole world, she was heading into the unknown.

Ginny felt a twinge in her chest and rubbed it. She pressed her hand to the location where the bullet had penetrated her body, carrying with it a part of Malach's heart. It was how she had come to think of the shooting. With her hand resting on the wound site, thoughts about the dream she had on the last night spent with Malach were in her head. She smiled to herself in the mirror.

Yes, the animals, the world, are in me.

acknowledgements

To my wife, Roberta Paul, my first and best reader, unhesitatingly my most honest critic, and unfailingly my greatest supporter. She always speaks from the heart. I love you and could not have done this without you.

Thank you to my long-time friend, David Pollack, whose incisive reading and critical insight are deeply valued and respected. I would like to express my gratitude to my dear friends, Beth Kantrowitz and Ben Scheindlin, for their patient and helpful reading and rereading of the many drafts of this novel. To my neighbor and friend, Lisa McElaney, for her early edits and discerning input. Thanks to my dear sister, Lisa Sucoff, who brought thoughtful reflection to her reading of this book. To my parents, Max and Thelma Cohen, who have always been my biggest fans – this book is also for you. To my readers, Victoria O'Keefe, Rebecca Cohen, Maxine Paul, Vadim Mejerson, and Victoria Hall, thank you.

I would like to thank David Provolo for the beautiful design of this book. To Abe Morell for the flattering photograph. Thank you to Ineke Ceder for helping to prepare the manuscript for publication. I wish to thank Tim Huggins for his expert guidance to the workings of the book world. A special thank you to Katie Eelman for bringing her knowledge and skills to the publishing and promotion of this book.

Finally, I would like to extend my heartfelt appreciation to my editor, Mary Sullivan Walsh, for her wisdom and judgment in helping to make this a better novel.